Priscilla

Priscilla & Aquila

A NOVEL

Lois T. Henderson
and Harold Ivan Smith

1817

Harper & Row, Publishers, San Francisco

New York, Grand Rapids, Philadelphia, St. Louis
London, Singapore, Sydney, Tokyo, Toronto

FIRST HARPER & ROW PAPERBACK EDITION PUBLISHED IN 1986.

Designed by Jim Mennick

Library of Congress Cataloging in Publication Data

Henderson, Lois T.
  Priscilla and Aquila.

  1. Priscilla, Saint, 1st cent.—Fiction.
2. Aquila, Saint, 1st cent.—Fiction.
3. Church history—Primitive and early church,
ca. 30–600—Fiction. I. Towner, Jason.
II. Title.
PS3558.E486P7   1985   831'.54   83–48429
ISBN 0-06-063868-0 (pbk.)

90 MPC 10 9 8 7 6 5

Editor's Note

Lois T. Henderson's death in July of 1983 was a great tragedy and a great loss to the Christian publishing and reading community. But at that time she had completed twenty-seven preliminary chapters of her new novel on Priscilla and Aquila and had discussed with me the dramatic ending of the story. Neither one of us knew how divinely appointed that conversation would become in retrospect. But it allowed me to go ahead with completing the novel confident that it could be done in the spirit and in the manner Lois herself would have chosen.

Harold Ivan Smith valiantly took up the challenge of anticipating the details of Lois's plot and wrote eleven chapters to end the story. My thanks go to him for completing an arduous task under difficult circumstances. Readers can look forward to the publication of Harold's own novels.

Also deserving thanks are Al, Lois's husband, for all his cooperation and work and Ray, Lois's brother, for his enthusiasm and advise throughout the project.

This story about a New Testament marriage excited Lois as much or more than any of her other books and it is to her and her memory that we dedicate this final grand novel.

R.M.C.

Harper & Row San Francisco

=1=

In the women's quarters of a public bath in ancient Rome, a door between the tepidarium and the caldarium was pushed open by a slave to enable her young mistress to leave the warm anteroom and enter the area that contained the hot bath. Priscilla, sitting on a wooden bench in the anteroom, frowned as the steamy air pushed through the opening. That heat might seem delightful on a cold winter day, she reflected, but in late summer the hot pool was just something to be endured before one could plunge gratefully into the cold, refreshing water of the frigidarium.

Priscilla pushed back a strand of red-gold hair that had fallen across her flushed face and glanced over at her mother on the opposite bench. She had bathed daily with her mother since she was a tiny child, and knew every move of the routine. Now she watched Flavia's careful use of the strigilis, the narrow, flexible leather strap that scraped perspiration and yesterday's oils from the skin. She felt as much admiration for her mother's strong, sure hands as she felt for her mother's wide mouth, arched brows, and round cheeks. She had always felt that her own blue eyes with golden lashes, and her own delicate features, were pale and insipid next to her mother's dark beauty.

"I don't suppose we could omit the hot bath today?" Priscilla suggested.

Flavia Justinius shuddered delicately. Although she was no longer as slender as she had been when she was young, she still moved with a feminine grace that Priscilla was sure she would never be able to duplicate. "The shock of the cold water would be too great if our bodies weren't properly heated," she answered her daughter. "You know that. I've told you often enough."

Priscilla shrugged her narrow shoulders and concentrated for a few minutes on using her own strigilis to cleanse her skin. When she spoke, her low, husky voice, an odd contrast to her slight, slender body, was stubborn. "I would rather just jump into the cold pool in the frigidarium and then get dressed and go to Grandfather's library."

Flavia's smile was sympathetic. "You would spend every waking hour in his library if we let you. Your grandfather has made you more like a scholar—a male scholar, at that —than a young woman. I sometimes think your father and I are wrong to let you spend so much time at his villa."

Priscilla didn't answer for a few seconds. She and her mother had gone over this time and again, but even when Flavia was protesting most about her father-in-law's bad influence, Priscilla suspected that she harbored a secret pride in her daughter's scholastic ability.

"You don't have to worry," Priscilla murmured. "You know I don't go around flaunting what Grandfather has taught me. I act as demure and stupid as I can."

Flavia's eyes flashed. "No one has ever suggested that you should act stupid. But if you want a husband, you have to act like a woman. You have to be a little shy, a little helpless. Men don't appreciate women who are too clever."

"Grandfather does," Priscilla argued and knew immediately that she had said the wrong thing.

"Precisely why I object to his constant tutoring," Flavia retorted. "Now come in and bathe yourself. Maybe the hot water will cleanse you of an insolent tongue as well as a day's accumulation of soil!"

Priscilla draped her towel around herself and stood up. "I'm sorry," she said simply and sincerely. To offend her mother was the worst thing she could do, and she always hated herself when she did it. "Forgive me."

Flavia also stood and pulled a towel around herself. "My highest goal in life is to prepare you for a good marriage. You know that."

Priscilla slipped her hand into the crook of her mother's arm, finding a familiar comfort in the soft warmth of her mother's skin. "I know, Mother," she said in her most docile voice. "And you don't have to worry. Not really. When some man asks to marry me (if one ever does, because where almost all women have dark hair, who would want me?), then I'll be everything you've taught me. Honestly, I will."

Flavia touched the silky red-gold hair that was knotted loosely on top of Priscilla's head. "Don't be critical of your hair. It is one thing that will probably attract men," she said. "It makes you different."

Priscilla looked with open envy at her mother's glossy black hair. "I don't mind being different," she confided. "I just wish it weren't because of something like the color of my hair. I'd rather it be because of what I'm like inside."

"Well, don't worry about it," Flavia said. "What will be, will be. Now, come, we'll go into the caldarium."

There were several other women in the pool sitting on the ledge that led into the shallower end. Priscilla glanced at them, saw none of her own friends or acquaintances among them, and so she concentrated on the business of bathing as quickly as possible. She dropped her towel on the heated floor and stepped reluctantly into the water. She thought again of the appeal that this part of the daily ritual had in the winter months when it was often cold and damp and miserable outside, so that stepping into the caldarium was like a warm embrace.

It's odd, Priscilla reflected, *that our opinions and attitudes can be altered by things we can't even control.* She glanced at her mother, wondering if she should express the idea to Flavia, but decided against it. Her mother would only chide her for thinking of unanswerable things instead of considering the obvious, like a new hair style or a new way of draping a stola. *I'll talk to Grandfather,* Priscilla decided. *He'll understand what I mean.*

She felt perspiration form on her forehead and roll down her temples. Although the strigilis had removed all of yesterday's oil and the perspiration of the past twenty-four hours, Priscilla knew that she would never feel clean sitting in this hot water with the din of the calling and laughing of the other women and the children pounding in her ears.

"Enough?" she asked her mother and was delighted to see Flavia nod her head in agreement. They stepped out of the water, wrapped themselves in the large linen towels that they had dropped, and made their way into the frigidarium. The floor was not heated as the other floors had been, and the heavy roof and walls kept out the weight of the sun. Just at that moment there were no other women in the round marble pool of cold water, and, impulsively, Priscilla dropped her towel, took a flying leap, and plunged over her head into the cold, clear depths of the pool. Giggling and gasping, she shot to the surface, and paddled and pushed her way to the edge.

"Look at the water you've splashed all over!" Flavia said. "That was probably the most childish thing you have done in a year!"

"I *feel* like a child," Priscilla said. The water was so cold that she was shivering, but she felt refreshed and clean for the first time since they had entered the warm anteroom. "Come on, Mother. This is marvelous!"

"It may seem marvelous for you," Flavia grumbled. "I've reached the age where it takes more courage every day to get into this pool. By the time I'm forty—and that's only one more year—I may omit this part of the bath and just go directly from the caldarium to the unctorium. Especially in the winter."

"Coward," Priscilla scoffed, laughing. "And besides, you'll never be old. Never, never." She flicked a few drops of the chilly water off her fingers toward her mother, and Flavia jumped back with a girlish squeal.

"See!" Priscilla observed with satisfaction. "Come on, jump."

"No," Flavia retorted. "I don't want to get my hair wet. I'll just step in. And carefully."

Priscilla grinned and then flipped over and thrust her face deep into the water. She wouldn't have dared behave so, had there been other women in the frigidarium. But for this one moment she could submerge herself in the tingling coolness and feel the shock of it surging through her whole body.

Flavia stepped resolutely into the cold water. She gasped and shivered, but forced herself to stay submerged for several minutes. Then, with a look of relief, she climbed out and reached for her towel.

"Priscilla!" she called. "Come, stop acting like a ten-year-old and get out of the water. What are you going to do about your hair now? It's soaked."

Priscilla obediently left the pool. She was shivering violently from the chill of cold water on flesh that had been deliberately heated, but at the same time she felt vigorous and alive.

"I'll just let it hang until it's dry," she answered. "Grandfather won't mind. He doesn't pay any attention to my hair."

Flavia shot a quick look at her daughter. "Did you ask permission to go to your grandfather's villa?"

Priscilla dropped her eyes. "I'm sorry, Mother. I meant to ask, and I forgot. May I go to his villa?"

Flavia sighed. "He'll spend the whole time teaching you and you have already spent an hour or more in the library this morning. Isn't that enough reading for one day? You'll make your eyes weak if you spend all your time with a scroll in your hands."

"We won't read all the time." Priscilla's voice was eager.

"We'll talk mostly. We might study a little Greek, but most of the time we'll just talk."

Flavia turned to walk into the unctorium, the room where the bathers applied oils and perfumes before they got dressed, and Priscilla followed her meekly. Once in the unctorium, Flavia concentrated on applying a light, fragrant oil to her dark, smooth skin. Following her mother's example, Priscilla dipped her fingers in the flask and rubbed the oil lightly, quickly into her own arms, legs, and across her shoulders. Without speaking, she and her mother applied oil to each other's backs; then they pulled their stolas over their heads and began the complicated matter of pleating and draping the loose garments until they hung in sculptured folds.

Her head bent so that she could watch her fingers shaping the pleats, Priscilla finally spoke into the silence. "Is it all right, Mother? May I go to Grandfather's? I won't stay long. I'll be home in plenty of time for dinner."

Flavia hesitated. "Does your grandfather speak to you only about learning? About religion? Does he ever talk to you about—well, about getting married?"

Priscilla looked at her mother in amazement. "That's not for him to talk about, is it? I thought that was only for mothers and daughters to discuss."

"Mothers only prepare their daughters for marriage. They don't make the arrangements. Fathers do that, or grandfathers. Or any male member of the family."

Priscilla grinned. "My father is too busy with his shop to think about getting me married. He still thinks of me as a child."

"Your father is more observant than you think," Flavia returned tartly. "But he may depend on your grandfather to make the arrangements because your grandfather knows more important people and has more contacts, so he is in a position to do something about it. We are all agreed that you must marry someone who is a Jehovite."

Priscilla felt a sharp constriction in her chest. They had been talking about marriage for her, she realized, and probably recently. Maybe seriously. She had thought, ever since she had passed her twelfth birthday three years before, that she would be ready for marriage when her parents decided the time was right. But she wasn't ready.

She tried to make her voice sound normal. "Well, of course, a Jehovite. I would be miserable with a pagan, or a worshipper of Jupiter or Diana. Now that we know of the Lord God Jehovah . . . "

"And not only a Jehovite, perhaps also a Hebrew," Flavia interrupted. "Some Hebrew Romans have successful positions or shops or crafts. Some of them even have small villas like ours. Not all of them live in the apartment houses where families are crowded in close to each other. Some of them . . ."

"Some of them or *one* of them?" Priscilla asked shrewdly.

Flavia refused to meet her daughter's eyes. "It's not for me to say," she answered stiffly. "Wait until your father or your grandfather is ready to talk to you."

Priscilla felt a quick rush of relief. Apparently no decisions had been made yet. She still had time to be with her grandfather, still time to learn and grow.

"You never answered my question," Priscilla reminded her mother. "May I go to Grandfather's?"

"For no more than an hour," Flavia said. "I'll walk with you to the corner of his street, and I'll send your brother after you before dinner is ready. And when he comes, you're to leave with him at once. No more of the coaxing you did last time, so that you were both late for dinner."

Priscilla flushed, remembering. Junius was not at all like his sister. He hated studying and cared for nothing but the Roman games. He was tall and muscular, dark with his mother's Roman good looks, and he considered Priscilla's desire to study every day with her grandfather a waste of time. He said so over and over. Yet, because he was gentle and easy to persuade, Priscilla could coax him to linger long enough to get them both in trouble.

"I'll remember," she promised her mother. "I'll come the minute Junius arrives." Her quick docility was as sincere as her occasional rebellion. "Are you ready to start out?"

Flavia's dark hair was twisted into a smooth, shining knot on the back of her head, and the drape of her stola looked as though carved out of marble. Priscilla glanced down at the damp, clinging strands of light hair that fell over her own shoulders and at the folds of her stola, which never achieved the perfection of her mother's. "I'll never look as nice as you do," she said to Flavia in a tone of despair.

"Catch your hair back with this bit of blue ribbon," Flavia said consolingly, taking it from the bag in which they carried the cosmetics, strigilis, and towels. "And here, pull the front of your stola so." Her square dark hands lifted the bright mass of Priscilla's hair and twisted it into a respectable neatness. She twitched at the front of Priscilla's stola and it was as though she had performed a bit of magic. The careless, awkward look was gone, and Priscilla looked nearly as neat, nearly as proper as her mother.

"You never know who might see you," Flavia said pointedly, as they walked together out of the women's door of the public bath.

It was an odd thing for her mother to say, and the oddity of it caused Priscilla to be aware of the people who stood outside the baths talking. She was usually so deep in her own thoughts that she hardly noticed who was on the steps or in the exercise yards. But today she darted glances from under her golden lashes. There was no one of importance, she decided, only a group of Hebrew Jehovites standing on the steps. She recognized them as being members of the synagogue her family attended, but she had never spoken to any of them. She had seen them many times before, but today her awareness had been heightened by her mother's odd remark.

Her glance ran over the arguing men and rested briefly on the young man who stood slightly apart from them. *I've seen him at the synagogue, too,* Priscilla thought with a tiny shock of recognition. *He's the one who read from Torah three Sabbaths ago.*

In the one quick glimpse she allowed herself, she saw the boy's curly black hair, his heavy-lidded dark eyes, the soft dark beard that covered his cheeks and chin, and the gentle curve of his mouth that seemed to be a direct contradiction to his haughty eyebrows. He wasn't looking at her, not really, and yet Priscilla knew that he had been looking at her, that he was as aware of her as she was of him.

She felt her mother's hand tugging on her arm. "Don't dawdle," Flavia whispered. "Come on."

She was suddenly aware that her mother was speaking to her, had been speaking for some time. "Listen to him," Flavia was saying. "It's why I'm letting you go over today. I think he might mention it to you."

"Mention what?" Priscilla asked.

Flavia made an exasperated sound. "Haven't you been listening at all? I said your grandfather agrees with me that it's time for you to marry. He has someone in mind, I think. Today might be the day he talks to you."

Priscilla stumbled on the rough pavement and was grateful for her mother's hand that still held her arm.

"You will listen?" Flavia shook Priscilla's arm with impatience. "You will pay attention to what he says?"

Priscilla nodded. Hadn't she always paid attention to her grandfather? But her heart was lurching strangely as she walked down the Street of Poplars where her grandparents lived, and she realized that for the first time in her life she was reluctant to enter her grandfather's house. In the late sunshine, the golden-green leaves of the tall poplars trembled all around her in the breeze, as if sympathetic to her own inner trembling.

⹀2⹀

The Hebrew men who stood on the steps of the public bath paid no attention to Priscilla and Flavia. Their argument, swift, articulate, intense, absorbed them entirely. But Aquila, the young man who stood alone, saw every movement the girl made. Her quick glance, blue and gold in the sun, shimmered in his blood. For weeks he had been obsessed with thoughts of her. Oh, certainly he had seen skin with a darker, richer sheen, bodies that were fuller and rounder, and dark eyes that were bolder and franker. But there was something about her. Her red-gold hair was like a light in this city of dark-haired women, and her face had a distant preoccupied look that tantalized and excited him. He didn't find it difficult to make most girls aware of him, but this girl was different.

He was brought out of his meditation by a sharp jab of an elbow.

"Don't stand there looking like a fish. Your mouth is open. Close it!"

Aquila blushed. Uncle Joshua had not been as absorbed in the argument as he had appeared to be. The boy closed his mouth and grinned at the older man.

"I am simply listening in astonishment to the wisdom of my elders," Aquila retorted. "So my mouth hangs open in amazement."

"Your mouth hangs open because that girl just walked by, the one with red hair. I'm not a fool, my boy. Hasn't your father pointed out to you that it would be simpler if you married a Hebrew girl and preferably one from Pontus, so that you and she would share both your faith and your place of birth? Why do you make things hard for yourself? And your father?"

"My father knows the girl's grandfather," Aquila informed his uncle. "And she and all her family are Jehovites. They've accepted our faith completely. So—" His hands moved out with an eloquence that suggested he had explained everything.

Joshua shrugged. "It would be easier for your mother if you would bring home one of our own."

"My mother understands," Aquila insisted. Why was he standing here arguing with his uncle?

Joshua's glance at his nephew was shrewd. "It happens that I know her grandfather, too. He's a prosperous and clever man. He may not want to give his favorite granddaughter to a foreigner."

"He himself knows what it is to be a foreigner," Aquila said, no longer wondering why he was taking the time to argue. If Joshua also knew old Marcus Justinius, then it was important to gain Joshua's support. "Not only a foreigner, but a slave. You surely know that he was captured in Gaul when he was very young. He should know better than anyone else that a foreigner—even a foreign slave—can become prosperous."

"Not everyone is as fortunate as Marcus Justinius," Joshua responded. "He had a doting owner who had no sons. So Marcus was given his freedom, his owner's name, and the villa that had belonged to his owner's father-in-law. He was lucky."

"Shrewd, too," Aquila insisted. "He would understand the problems of being a foreigner."

Joshua shrugged again. "Maybe, but sometimes these converts to Romanism, as it were, are prouder than native Romans who were born here, in the shadow of the Circus Maximus."

Aquila and Joshua had pulled away from the others, and their discussion was low voiced.

"All of us are 'converts to Romanism,' as you say," Aquila persisted. "Or at least to some degree. My father gave me a Roman name. We bathe in the Roman baths. We sell merchandise on Roman streets for Roman money. I hope that Marcus Justinius will understand this and not consider me unsuitable."

There. It was out. He had admitted to someone other than his father that he wanted that girl. He wanted to run his hands through that mass of bright hair until her eyes warmed with an awareness that would dispel forever the distant, cool look he had seen so often on her face.

Joshua's eyes twinkled. "It may be necessary to sustain you with raisin cakes," he said.

Aquila laughed but he felt his face flush again. His uncle's allusion to the Song of Solomon was appropriate, but a bit malicious. Aquila was indeed sick with love. He no longer slept well and food did not taste as it used to. But he would not confess this to the man who stood laughing at him in the sunshine. He had, in fact, not even confessed it to his father. He had merely said that the girl was pleasant to look at, that her family was admirable, that their attendance at the synagogue was faithful. Now his uncle had probed beneath the logic and the common sense. His uncle had seen the hunger in his eyes.

Joshua's smile faded and his eyes were serious. "Listen, my boy, a wife is more than just a pretty face."

"I know that. I've been taught all the important things."

"Has your father pointed out to you that Roman women are given freedom and an authority that our women don't have?"

"Yes, of course. He wasn't any more enthusiastic in the beginning than you are. But now he's willing to ask. Now he says he will go to Marcus Justinius and ask him to talk to his son, to the girl's father."

" 'The girl,' you say. What's her name?"

"Prisca Justinius. But they call her Priscilla, 'Little Prisca.' Her family calls her Priscilla."

Joshua turned away from the boy and then turned back. "My own son, your cousin, died before he was old enough to marry. Because my own marriage is a good one, I have always grieved that he never knew that particular pleasure. Perhaps I, too, can speak to Marcus Justinius. He owes me a favor." Joshua had said, "I, too," Aquila realized, and his voice shook as he asked, "Has my father already spoken to him? Have you and my father discussed this together?"

Joshua patted the boy's arm. "If fathers informed their sons of every step in the process of arranging a marriage, the young men would be in a constant turmoil. Better by far that you just go about your daily business of preparing skins and making tents. Let your father worry about marriage."

"As you say," Aquila agreed, but he wondered if his uncle could remember the agony of desire and the fear of rejection that tortured young men.

"Back to work," Joshua said. "The time of rest is over. But listen," he added as Aquila turned to leave, "I'll do my best for you."

Aquila grinned at his uncle as hope spurted up in him. "Thank you, Uncle," he sang out, and turned to run along the street that led west toward the Porta Capena. Beyond the Capena Gate lay the area where the open air shops were built, where Aquila's father followed his trade as a maker of tents. It was too hot to run, Aquila knew, and all the good of the baths would be lost if he ran in the late afternoon heat. But if he walked sedately, the hope and excitement would burst inside of him. Sweating, he decided, was preferable to shattering into a thousand pieces.

At the gate of her grandfather's villa, Priscilla stopped and looked around. In spite of her apprehension, she could not suppress the familiar feeling of pleasure that filled her. The villa was not elegant, just a small house built of native stone, with only enough land to provide room for a few fruit and olive trees, their dusty leaves wilted in the summer heat. But it was located on a hill, and from the gate, there was a clear view to the west, unimpeded by either trees or the large, expensive houses that lay in the distance between the Justinius home and the Capitoline Hill.

The hill was too far away, of course, for Priscilla to see the milestone at the base of it that indicated the distances to all cities in the Roman Empire. But although she could not see the milestone, she could see this most famous of the Roman hills against the hot, hazy sky and she never ceased to be impressed by the grandeur, the richness, and the color of the panorama. Her grandfather had once said he thought his view was a gift from God and then he had laughed and said he had become more Hebrew than he realized. Certainly it was not customary for a Roman mind to attribute the good things in life to a deity.

"Come in out of the sun." Linia Justinius's voice was still sweet and clear in spite of her age. *If my grandfather feeds my mind,* Priscilla thought with sudden delight, *Grandmother feeds my heart.* Linia was small, faded, and worn, but still beautiful in the same way that an old piece of valuable tapestry retains its beauty. She was standing on the small portico beckoning to her granddaughter. "You'll get sunstroke," she added firmly.

Priscilla ran to her grandmother and hugged her. They were about the same size, and they looked at each other smiling.

"Your grandfather is in the peristyle," Linia announced. "Go out and join him and I'll have Dena bring you some cool apricot juice. He needs to stop worrying about his accounts and relax for a little. Now that you're here, he'll do it."

"I'd love some apricot juice," Priscilla admitted, dropping a kiss on her grandmother's cheek before she let her go. "And a small cake to go with it would be wonderful."

Linia shook her head. "How anyone can be hungry on

such a hot day!" she marveled, but she was smiling as she walked toward the kitchen.

Priscilla was smiling, too, as she stepped into the atrium. A delicious breeze drifted through the open doors and through the aperture in the roof that allowed rain water to fall into the small pool in the middle of the atrium floor. The cushions on the furniture and the hangings on the walls were all in shades of blue and green, so that the entire room had a cool, fresh look. It was only in the winter that Linia brought out her little store of crimson cushions and shawls and piled them on the wedding couch so that they appeared to give out as much heat during the cold months as the small brazier in the corner.

Priscilla crossed the atrium, made her way through the inner room where her grandfather worked in cooler weather, and came at last to the peristyle, which was entirely open to the sky. Carefully pruned trees threw a canopy of shade over the stone benches and the grass. The room was more garden than house, but in hot weather it served as the heart of the home.

Marcus Justinius looked up and watched Priscilla approach him. She could see the pleasure that warmed his eyes, but neither of them spoke until she was standing in front of him.

"Good afternoon," he said formally. "Are you well?"

She spoke as formally as he, saying the words she had been taught to say when she was very small. "Good afternoon, Grandfather. I'm very well. And you?"

He nodded. "I, too. Will you sit here?" He indicated the other bench, and she seated herself primly. She might leap childishly into a pool with her mother watching, but she would never act like that around her grandfather, who demanded much more of her than anyone else did. He would expect her to act as she had been trained.

"Has your day been pleasant? Did anything interesting happen at the bath?"

For a second she was tempted to say, "I saw one of the young men from the synagogue." But she swallowed the words. "A pleasant day," she murmured. "And the baths were as usual. In this weather I hate the hot bath. If I had my way, I'd never go into the caldarium until fall comes."

"If you had your way, you would go completely undisciplined," Marcus said, but there was no censure in his voice.

"One thing, at the bath," Priscilla said suddenly. "I had this thought. About how differently we react to something that does not change. I mean, the caldarium is always the same temperature, but it can be either the most wonderful or the worst part of the bath. It depends on how we feel about it, and how we feel is affected by conditions in life. Ordinary things like weather."

Her grandfather nodded and his eyes warmed. "So many people take things for granted," he said. "One must have a sense of wonder, a sense of awe. I was reading only this morning some words of David, the great King of Israel. Here, let me read them to you."

He picked up one of the scrolls that lay on a small table and searched through it until he found the words he wanted. "Listen," he said. He read the words in Greek, and although she had to concentrate to understand, she was able to follow the meaning. " 'When I consider the heavens, the work of Thy fingers, the moon and the stars, which Thou hast ordained; What is man that Thou dost take thought of him? And the son of man, that Thou dost care for him? Yet Thou hast made him a little lower than God, And dost crown him with glory and majesty!' "

The old man looked up at her. "Do you understand?"

"Not every word," she admitted. "But enough to get the thought. He's saying that no one can really understand why or how God does certain things. Isn't he?"

"Well, perhaps not entirely. But he is able to marvel at wonders he does not hope to understand. That's what I want you to do. I want you always to see life with the eyes of a child."

"And Mother wants me to grow up," Priscilla could not resist saying.

"Growing up has nothing whatever to do with it," Marcus argued. "I am an old man but I can still wonder and marvel, still stand in awe."

Dena, stooped and frail, came into the peristyle with a tray in her hands. Linia followed and Priscilla saw that her grandmother carried a heavy jug while Dena carried only the light tray. *Neither she nor my grandfather have forgotten how it was to be a slave,* Priscilla thought. She jumped up to take the heavy jug from her grandmother's hands. Putting it on the table, she turned to take the tray from Dena.

"Umm," Priscilla said with appreciation. "Honey cakes. And I'm starved."

Dena smiled, putting up her old hand to hide her toothless gums. "When you're married, I hope you still live close enough to come every day. Otherwise we won't have honey cakes."

It was the sort of remark Dena had been making for years, but this time Priscilla caught the quick look that flew between her grandparents.

"I hope so, too," Priscilla said lightly. "I would soon die of starvation if I didn't have your honey cakes, Dena."

Dena laughed and went back toward the kitchen. Marcus spoke to his wife. "Will you sit with us? It's too hot for you to do anything but rest. Did you bring three cups?"

Linia smiled and sat down. "Yes, I brought three cups. I'm not interrupting a lesson?"

The juice was cold enough that the jug was sweating in Priscilla's hands as she poured the golden liquid. She handed a cup to each of her grandparents, offered them the cakes, and when they refused, put two of the little cakes on the mat beside her. "No lesson," she assured her grandmother. "We have only begun to talk. Later a lesson."

"Perhaps, perhaps not," Marcus said. "I have something to discuss with you that has nothing to do with lessons. This might very well be the time to do it."

Priscilla deliberately lifted her cup and took a swallow of the juice even though she was suddenly filled with uneasiness.

"Anything you wish," she murmured to her grandfather, picking up a honey cake. She was acutely aware of the tart taste of the apricot juice in her mouth, and the sticky feel of the cake in her fingers. Instinctively she knew that this was going to be one of the most important moments in her life and she felt a sharpening of all her senses. Whether the moment brought joy or pain, she wanted to miss nothing.

"It's about your marriage," Marcus said abruptly. "You're old enough, you know. You have been for more than a year. It's time."

Priscilla laid down the small cake and licked the honey from her fingers. "Have you chosen someone?" she asked carefully. If she did not speak with care, she might disgrace herself by crying.

"We have a possibility in mind. You will not be forced if the young man is odious to you or if you feel you simply could not marry a Hebrew."

At his last word, Priscilla saw again, as clearly as though he were before her, the young man who had stood with the arguing men on the steps of the bath.

"A Hebrew? Would his parents agree to his marrying a Roman?"

Marcus made a rueful sound. "A polyglot Roman at best. Oh, your mother is pure Roman, it's true, and your father has certainly absorbed Roman ways. But me—I'm a Gaul, and your grandmother, too. No, Aquila's father recognizes that in today's world, things are not what they used to be. He wouldn't consider you, of course, if you were not a believing Jehovite."

"They are Jehovite Hebrews, then?" Her mind stored the name *Aquila,* but her question was asked in the same careful voice.

"Very. They're of the tribe of Levi, the priestly tribe.

What's more, the boy has a good trade—he's a tent maker —and his father's villa is as large as ours. You would be well cared for."

But would he talk to me? she wanted to cry out. *Would he understand what I'm really like?*

She did not say these things. No one knew the answer. No one could. She picked up her honey cake and took a bite. "Tell me more about him," she said at last, brushing a few crumbs from her stola, and saw her grandparents relax. "I'm willing to listen at least."

= 3 =

"You see," Priscilla said at last after her grandfather had told her everything he knew about Aquila and his family. "You see, I haven't given much thought to getting married. I know girls do. I know they should. My mother has talked of little else since I was twelve. But I've been thinking of other things."

"It's my fault," Marcus confessed. "Your grandmother has told me often enough that I have filled your mind with unsuitable ideas for a girl."

"I don't think they have been unsuitable." Priscilla's husky voice was even deeper with stubbornness. "If God has given me a mind, shouldn't I use it? If I have been blessed with an intelligent grandfather who is willing to teach me, shouldn't I learn? Just because I'm a girl—"

"It's no disgrace for a girl to be intelligent," Marcus interrupted. "Not in Rome. And when you seemed eager to listen and to study, well, I—I taught you."

Priscilla tried to smile. "It would have been better, of course, if it had been Junius who wanted to study."

"It would have been good," her grandfather agreed. "But it wouldn't necessarily have meant that you would have been overlooked."

Priscilla knew her grandfather said that more to convince himself than to reassure her. She knew, because she had been told, that Marcus had tried to make a scholar out of his sons and then out of his grandsons. But only Priscilla had responded to his teaching with an eagerness that had delighted him. But she didn't contradict the old man. What difference did it make?

"What do my parents think?" Priscilla asked abruptly. "Do they approve of this—this Aquila?"

"They agree with me that it would be a good match. The question is, how do you feel? Would you consider the young man?"

"How can I know?" she cried. "How does anyone know before the marriage takes place?"

Linia spoke up, "You can't know. Not really. But if he comes from a good family, if the men have a reputation for being kind to their wives, if the boy has seen his mother treated with respect, then likely he would be good to you. That's the important thing—that he be good to you."

"Is he—is he intelligent?" Priscilla asked so hesitantly that her grandfather leaned closer in order to hear.

His face warmed with instant comprehension. "Hebrew boys are well educated," he said with reassurance. "He reads Greek, he is well acquainted with the Scripture, he has scrolls in his house. Does that answer your question?"

She nodded, but she knew it was not a complete answer. Did Aquila think about the sort of thing she and her grandfather had been talking about, the sort of thing King David had written about? Was he curious about the world? Would he be curious about her?

"When will you decide?" she asked slowly.

"When can *you* decide?" Marcus responded gently.

She shook her head. The appearance of Dena at the door saved her fom the need of saying anything.

"A man at the door wishes to see you, sir," Dena announced. "He says his name is Joshua and that he's a maker of tents."

Her face said as clearly as words that since her master had no need of tents, she would be happy to send the caller away if that were Marcus's desire.

But Marcus smiled. "Ah, yes. Joshua. An uncle, I believe, of the young man we've been talking about, Priscilla. Invite him in, Dena."

Priscilla felt a wild and ridiculous rush of fear. She

wanted to run and hide, to be anywhere but here on this bench. Her hair was not properly dressed, and her hands felt sticky from the honey.

"You can stay and meet him," Marcus announced. "It might be well for you to see a member of Aquila's family."

"But I'm not properly dressed," Priscilla protested, her voice trembling. "He'll think me untidy."

"He'll think you charming," Marcus insisted, for once insensitive to his granddaughter's panic.

Linia spoke in a surprisingly firm voice. "She may stay only long enough to meet him. Then she can come with me into another room. It will be better that way."

Priscilla cast a grateful look at her grandmother as Dena returned, ushering in a small, dark man dressed in the flowing robe worn by most Hebrews.

Marcus rose courteously and the two men clasped each other's arms.

"I am honored," Marcus said.

"You are sure I don't intrude? Is this a bad hour to come?" Joshua's Latin was heavily accented but correct.

"You do me honor. Here, this is my wife, Linia. And my granddaughter, Priscilla. My friend Joshua, from Pontus, one of the Roman provinces near the Black Sea."

Joshua inclined his head to Linia with a smile and his expression did not change when he turned to Priscilla. But the girl was sure he missed nothing—not the disarray of her hair or the stickiness of her hands or the way her lips trembled.

"This is the second time I've seen you today, Mistress Priscilla," Joshua said courteously. "My nephew and I were on the steps of the bath as you walked by."

"My nephew and I," he said. The only young man in the group had been the handsome boy with the arrogant eyebrows and the curly hair. So now *I know what he looks like —the man they have chosen to be my husband.* Priscilla's heart pounded, but she managed a polite greeting to Joshua be-

fore she heard her grandmother say, "If you will excuse us, we will leave you to your talk. Come, Priscilla. Your brother should be here any minute to take you home."

Gratefully, Priscilla followed her grandmother from the peristyle, aware that her throat was dry and her knees wobbly. *It is really worse,* she thought in confusion, *to know who Aquila is. When he was only a name, he was less frightening somehow.*

Aquila's eyes were shining. "Did he sound as though he approved? Did he indicate that the girl would say yes?"

Joshua's voice held a blend of amusement and irritation. "I wish you'd stop referring to her as 'the girl.' She has a name."

"Priscilla, then." But he said the word awkwardly, as though his tongue found the syllables strange. "What did he say about her?"

"He said he had discussed the subject with her. She has said neither yes nor no at the moment. They had only begun to talk about it when I arrived. She looked frightened to me."

Aquila's voice was hurt. "Frightened? I'm no monster, to harm her."

Joshua shrugged. "How is she to know that? She's only fifteen, her grandfather said. Old enough for marriage certainly, but young enough to be afraid of it. Give her time to think about it and make some sort of decision. The thing doesn't have to be decided today. Or tomorrow."

"And what heavy subject so absorbs my brother and son that they never even hear me when I come into the room?" The speaker was Reuben, Aquila's father. Like his son, he was dark with strong, craggy features. But unlike his son and his brother, his face was not lightened with the quirk of humor that softened and curved their lips.

Aquila spoke quickly: "I'm coming, Father. I only stopped to speak to my uncle for a minute."

Reuben frowned. "I sent you to search for the awl I had brought home to sharpen last night. You didn't return, so I left your mother in charge and came myself. And I find the two of you gossiping like old women."

Joshua grinned. "Now, my brother, don't be angry. The boy came racing in, more eager to find that awl than he would be to find a sack of jewels. And I waylaid him. I told him I had been to speak with Marcus Justinius."

Reuben's look of irritation deepened. "I'm not sure that it was right for you to go to see him. I had already spoken to him. I don't want him to think we're groveling."

Joshua dismissed the idea with a flip of his hand. "I know Marcus well. We have discussed many things many times. Particularly our faith. When he started to attend our synagogue, he and I agreed to study together. I merely told him that my brother was too modest, that he would never reveal the true worth of his business—or his son."

"And what did he say?" Reuben's voice was almost casual.

They talk as though it were not even important, Aquila thought, clenching his fists to help calm himself. *Who would know, hearing my father and uncle talk, that my life is being decided?*

Joshua smiled. "They give girls a lot of freedom, these Romans. It's up to her, Marcus said. If she wants Aquila, the family will agree."

"How can she know?" Aquila cried out. "She's never even spoken to me. How can she decide?"

"Her family knows your family," Reuben said sternly. "That's enough for any girl. You have a good trade, a good background. What more can she want?"

"I saw her," Joshua said to Reuben. "She was with her grandfather when I arrived." He turned to Aquila. "I have a feeling that when she walked past us this morning at the bath she noticed you, even though she seemed to be looking at nothing."

A small shock ran through Aquila. *What did she think of me? Am I only ordinary looking to her? Would she prefer a smooth-shaven young Roman? Will she find my beard offensive?*

"Looks are nothing," Reuben grumbled. "She should care only about his background, about his work, about his faith. And she's only a child. They should tell her what to do."

Joshua put his hand on his brother's arm. "As I was just saying to Aquila, give her time. Let her think about it. Let her see Aquila again on the steps of the bath. He will be surrounded by the men she sees every Sabbath in the synagogue. She will understand, then, that he is worthy of consideration."

"And if she decides I'm not?" Aquila's voice was hoarse.

"Then she is a foolish child," Joshua said. "But I tell you, my boy, she did not look like a foolish child. Frightened, but not foolish. Have faith."

"And if she turns you down, there are other girls," Reuben declared. "Good Hebrew girls from Pontus or even from Israel. I have said that you will be married by the time cool weather comes. And I am a man of my word!"

"Thank you, Father," Aquila muttered.

"Now, then, are you two coming back to the shop?" Reuben went on. "We have another hour of work before we come home for dinner. There's my awl, there on the bench. Come then."

"Just what we intended, of course," Joshua murmured. "Come, my boy."

Aquila followed the older men obediently. But his thoughts were churning in hot rebellion. He didn't want just any girl. He wanted Priscilla. *For the first time,* he thought with a twist of wry humor, *I can understand why the patriarch Jacob was willing to work an extra seven years for Rachel. He must have felt about Rachel the way I feel about Priscilla!* Aquila glanced around guiltily, wondering if his thoughts had been presumptuous.

The other two men had dismissed the thoughts of marriage from their mind. They were deep in a conversation about some new residents of the Hebrew community, and their voices were filled with disapproval. Aquila edged closer.

"Phaw!" Reuben said. "Unbalanced or misinformed people have been claiming the arrival of the Messiah for centuries. With our people dispersed and the homeland under Roman rule—" he lowered his voice and looked carefully around, "this can hardly be considered a good time for a Messiah to arrive."

"I don't know," Joshua said. "They speak with a real power. You ought to listen to them at least."

"I have enough problems at the moment," Reuben said, casting a look at Aquila. "I don't need to get myself involved in some big fight in the synagogue, with part of my friends taking one side and part of them taking another. I don't want to get mixed up in it."

Aquila entered the conversation. "This Messiah," he said. "Is he a king, an emperor, or what? Is he in Israel?"

Joshua shook his head. "I don't know anything really. But I think the talk is that this Messiah has already come and lived and died."

"See!" Reuben sneered. "What kind of Messiah could he be if we never even heard of him while he was alive?" He turned to Aquila. "Don't get involved. You've always been too curious about religion. You know how disgusting the worship of Mithras was in Pontus, and yet you insisted on asking questions, pushing your nose in where you didn't belong. Have you forgotten what a relief it was to come here and find a good solid synagogue with men who loved the Law? What's the matter with you?"

Aquila looked abashed. His father was right. He still had nightmares about the bloody baptismal ritual he had heard about from an unfaithful initiate of Mithras. The Jewish community in Rome had once seemed safe harbor after a long voyage on an unhealthy, stagnant sea. And yet there was still a thread of unrest running through his mind, a continuing sense of search for something. He didn't even know for what.

"For most of us," Joshua put in smoothly, "a glance at other religions only convinces us of the perfection of our own. You needn't fret, my brother. If Aquila listens to these men who claim the Messiah has come, he will soon see through them if they are false. Don't be afraid. The boy is grounded in the faith."

Reuben shook his head. But Aquila felt a strange sense of reassurance. It was true. He was indeed grounded in the faith. Nothing could change the fact that he was of the tribe of Levi and that he had been taught since earliest childhood the truth about God and the way to worship Him. Nothing could change that.

He dropped back behind his father and uncle and allowed his mind to drift away from the discussion that still absorbed the older men. *Maybe Priscilla will make up her mind in a day or so,* Aquila dreamed, *and then the engagement could be announced and I could have a chance to speak to her, to look into her face without embarrassment. Maybe by October, the wedding could take place. October is a good month—cool at night and pleasant during the day. And besides, in spite of the fact that she is a Jehovite, she is Roman enough that she probably has all the usual Roman superstitions about unlucky days. There are very few unlucky days in October. We could plan the wedding for about the middle of the month and—*

"Aquila!" His father's voice cut into his dreams. "Are you blind? Here's the shop and you're walking right past it."

"I'm sorry," Aquila mumbled, feeling even his ears getting hot with embarrassment. He had always prided himself on being in control of his emotions, and here he was acting like a lovesick fool!

Fortunately his father only made a sound of disgust before turning to his work. But Joshua's grin was frank, and his eyes were warm with understanding. Without saying a word, he made it clear that he understood exactly what was happening to Aquila and furthermore, that he did not feel any ridicule. *It is normal and right,* his smile seemed to say, *to dream when you are young.* Aquila grinned back at his uncle, feeling suddenly confident that everything was going to turn out well.

= 4 =

Although many of the shops near the Capena Gate stayed open seven days a week, Priscilla liked the fact that her father had formed the habit of keeping his shop closed on the Jehovite Sabbath. True, he lost a little business, but she knew that he believed his new faith demanded that much of him at least. Furthermore, her grandfather supported his son in this, and Marcus Justinius was a man to be respected and imitated.

Lucius Justinius had admitted to Priscilla once that he often wondered if just closing the shops on the Sabbath was a sufficient statement of his faith. She remembered the time that he had confessed that there had been moments in his first fervor of conversion when he had seriously contemplated submitting to circumcision, learning and following every letter of the Jehovite Law, and even going to Jerusalem to make sacrifice in the temple there. But common sense had rescued him before he had gone too far, he had admitted with a look of obvious relief.

Priscilla had pretended to agree with her father's statement that surely the Most High God did not demand as much from Jehovite converts as from those born into the faith. And yet something in her nature craved total commitment, and she had felt a sense of disappointment that her father had not followed his first impulses.

She found some comfort in Lucius's decree that every member of his family attend services each Sabbath at the synagogue. She had absorbed the teaching like a sponge, and nothing pleased her more than to be allowed to spend the long Sabbath afternoons with a scroll in her hands. She knew that Junius, who hated studying, was restless and unhappy every Sabbath, and that her mother, too, found the enforced inactivity difficult. Flavia missed the bath most of all, Priscilla suspected, and found any day too long that did not allow her to follow her normal routine. But Priscilla was her father's most ardent follower as each Sabbath came.

But for a month following Joshua's visit to Marcus's home, Priscilla begged to be excused from the usual routine. Finally, however, her father put his foot down.

"Of course you'll go to the synagogue," Lucius declared, on the last day of August. "No more staying home with the slaves to keep you company. I won't consider it. What's the matter with you?"

"I just want to stay home." Her husky voice was stubborn, and her eyes failed to meet his. "I'll study the Law all the time you're gone. I'll—"

"You'll do nothing of the sort," Lucius said. He turned to Flavia, who had come into the room. "What's the matter with her? It's your responsibility to see that she's obedient."

Flavia's glance at Priscilla held a mixture of compassion and irritation. "She's afraid she'll see that young man. Aquila. Now that she knows who he is, she's afraid to be near him."

"Well, she's not going to be allowed to speak to him. And the women are kept well apart from the men. She's being foolish." He was talking to his wife, but his eyes were fixed on Priscilla.

"Yes," Flavia agreed, her voice soft, "she's being very foolish. Unless she sees this young man a time or two, unless she allows herself to make up her mind about him, she's going to be miserable. I've told her so over and over."

You're talking about me as if I weren't even in the room! Priscilla thought miserably, but she recognized that it was her own fault. She was the one who was being uncooperative and stubborn. Everyone had been kind and understanding and generous. No one had demanded that she make a quick decision. Her parents, her grandparents had all tried to be patient, but she was aware that they were getting more and more upset.

"If you won't have him, say so," her mother had said several times.

"What do you have against him?" Lucius asked reasonably.

"His family is a fine one," Marcus had insisted.

"I know his mother," Linia had whispered once. "She's a happy woman. I can tell."

They were all justified in their growing concern, but Priscilla's uncertainty only seemed to grow. It was her duty to get married, and she knew that she really had no choice about that. The question was simply: would Aquila do?

But if not Aquila, then who? She agreed with her parents that it would have to be someone who shared their faith, and would a Roman who had come late to a belief in Jehovah be as comforting as a Hebrew Jehovite whose faith had been established all his life?

"Well, enough of this," Flavia said abruptly. "The time of meeting is nearly here, and I will hear no more of this foolish argument. Prisca, get your pallas so we can leave at once."

Her mother's formal use of her name did not escape Priscilla, and she hurried to her room to get the sheer shawl she wore over her head. She had gone too far with her stubborn indecision, she realized. Before this day was over, she had to have an answer for her family. But what should her answer be?

Spontaneous prayer surfaced in Priscilla's mind. Although she always joined silently in the chanted prayers of the Jehovite congregation, personal prayers were not common with her. But now she knew she needed help. "Please, God," she whispered. "Show me what to do. Please show me."

It was a childish prayer, she thought, remembering the cadenced, beautiful prayers of the rabbi, but it was sincere. God would simply have to help her.

At the synagogue, Lucius and Junius joined the men in the center of the room. There were a few benches for the older and more respected men of the community, and the younger men and boys sat on the floor. The synagogue was simply a small house that had been willed to the congregation when one of their wealthier members died. Only a simple altar, a highly polished box to hold the sacred scrolls, and brass oil lamps winking in the dark little room contributed a semblance to a house of worship.

The room contained no ornate carvings, none of the rich hangings or gold-covered statues that filled the Roman temples. The small synagogue had seemed very plain to the Justinius family when they had first seen it. But, like the faith it represented, it had acquired an aura of loveliness as Sabbath followed Sabbath.

Priscilla and Flavia joined the women at the far edge of the room and found a seat on one of the benches there. Priscilla glanced among the women quickly, caught her grandmother's eye and smiled at her, and then saw Marta, her closest friend. Marta's family, like Priscilla's, were Romans who had become Jehovites, and although Marta had little patience with Priscilla's obsession with studying, the girls were good friends. *Maybe Marta could tell me what to do,* Priscilla thought, and immediately dismissed the idea. She had asked God for guidance, and certainly the opinion of another fifteen-year-old girl could never be considered the word of God.

A hush fell over the gathered people, and then an acclamation rose in a soft wave of sound. The words were perhaps the earliest words taught to any Jehovite child, and they had been the first ones committed to memory by the new converts who made up nearly half of the group: "Hear, O Israel, the Lord our God is one Lord."

Priscilla pulled her attention away from her grand-mother, away from her friend, and concentrated on the familiar words. There was such comfort in them, such certainty. It might be true that her grandfather and her father had been the first to embrace this faith in the Israelite God, but Priscilla had come to believe in Him because she herself was convinced He was real. She said the words in a whisper, inside herself, as was proper for a woman, but no man in that room said them with greater conviction.

I was foolish not to want to come, Priscilla thought, feeling the words swell and burst and spill over in her heart. *Just because I might see Aquila across the room. Just because he might see me. I was foolish. This is the place for me to be.*

It was time for the reading of the Law. There was a stir among the men, and Priscilla was aware that one of them stood and walked to the table in front. He faced the congregation, unrolled the scroll in front of him, and started to read.

Priscilla had seldom paid much attention to the readers at the synagogue. It was always one of the young men, but she had been too absorbed in the words to think about the person reading them. When Marta had commented on one or another of the boys, Priscilla had felt only scorn.

But today everything was different. Priscilla knew, without looking, that the reader was Aquila. He had read before, many times—she knew his voice—but when he had, she had not known or cared who it was. Now she heard the words, and her heart squeezed like a suddenly clenched fist.

Aquila's voice shook a little, as though he were nervous, and Priscilla closed her eyes, wishing she could close her ears. She had thought, only a minute before, that the synagogue was a place of security and comfort and now she was faced with the reality of Aquila that could not be overlooked.

As he continued to read, his voice smoothed out and

became steady and strong. Slowly, Priscilla opened her eyes and timidly glanced up. Aquila read,

> A voice is calling, "Clear the way for the Lord in the wilderness;
> Make smooth in the desert a highway for our God.
> Let every valley be lifted up,
> And every mountain and hill be made low;
> And let the rough ground become a plain,
> And the rugged terrain a broad valley.
> Then the glory of the Lord will be revealed,
> And all flesh will see it together;
> For the mouth of the Lord has spoken.

Aquila looked up from the scroll, his reading finished, and at that moment, a shaft of sun came through the open door at such an angle that it struck Aquila's face with light.

Priscilla's heart clenched again. Before she could lower her eyes, Aquila looked at her. It was not an obvious thing, he did not deliberately seek her out. As a matter of fact, he looked a little dazed from the reading, dazzled by the incredible beauty of the words he had spoken and by the sunlight that struck his face. Nevertheless, their eyes met for one fraction of a second, and then he looked away and Priscilla bent her head.

But she knew that God had shown her what to do. Why else would Aquila have been chosen to be the reader on this particular morning? Why else would he have chosen the words that always shook her heart with delight? Why else had the sun touched him with brightness? And why had their eyes met?

God had told her as clearly as though he had used words that she would do well to choose Aquila.

Nothing like this had ever happened to her before. Her faith had been growing into something good and strong.

But she had not been one to think much of miracles or of God's direct presence in her life. She had thought that the patriarchs were the ones to whom such incidents happened. Not the ordinary people of this time. But she had been wrong. She felt some joy, but mostly a strong sense of duty.

I'll be a good wife, she promised herself, unaware of anything or anyone around her. *I'll put my studying aside, I'll think only of the things that are proper for a woman. I'll do everything my mother says to do, and I won't show off my learning to my husband. I'll be sweet and pliable and as womanly as he wants me to be. I'll learn to fix my hair properly, and drape my stola, and be like Mother and Grandmother.*

Her fervor of commitment sustained her throughout most of the worship service. It was not until the last prayer that she felt a sudden sense of loss. *Maybe,* she thought in desolation, *there will still be times when I can read and study and learn, if I never let my husband know. And I never will. Never.*

The childish promise seemed wholly right to her. For years her mother had counseled her how a woman should act if she wanted a man to love her. And Flavia, with her dark beauty and her winning ways, had made Lucius a happy man. Even their daughter had to be aware of that. It seemed to Priscilla, stirred as she was by the events of the morning, that she was almost taking a holy vow as she made her solemn, inner promise. In that moment, in the dim little synagogue, Priscilla felt that she had taken the pledge of marriage as surely as she would take it on her wedding day.

She waited until sundown to make her announcement. Somehow it did not seem fitting to declare her intentions while it was still the Sabbath. So all during the hot afternoon, she sat quietly in the peristyle and read one of the scrolls. To her astonishment, she discovered that she had part of the Book of Proverbs in her hands. The final portion of the book had always seemed to her to be a description of her mother and her grandmother. Today, for the first

time, she wondered if the words would ever be applicable
to her.

An excellent wife, who can find?
For her worth is far above jewels,
The heart of her husband trusts in her,
And he will have no lack of gain.

Priscilla sat dreaming in the hot, drowsy afternoon. Once
she lifted a hand to push back her hair, and was suddenly
sharply aware of its silky weight. Maybe Aquila would find
it beautiful. Her face felt hot, and she bent her head.
Against her closed lids she saw Aquila's face as it had looked
when the sun touched it—the dazzled brightness of his eyes,
the curve of his mouth under his beard, the tumble of his
curly hair.

Does he think about me? she wondered. *Does he try to imagine
how it would be to unpin my hair and watch it fall over my
shoulders?*

She had never thought of anything like that before, and
it made her feel very strange, but perhaps this was the way
a girl ought to feel about marriage—frightened, of course,
but curious about the man she would marry.

Another spontaneous prayer surfaced in Priscilla's
thoughts. *Oh, please,* she prayed, *make him—make him—* But
she stopped in confusion. Aquila was already what he was,
and she had decided to marry him. She had no right to ask
God to change him. She could only ask God to change her,
to make her as she should be. *Make me a good wife,* she
finished her prayer.

Her head had been bent for so long in her meditation
that she was surprised to discover when she looked up that
the sun had set and the Sabbath was over.

She heard her mother's voice and the other sounds that
indicated the household had resumed its habitual flow. She

stood up, feeling her knees tremble as she walked into the atrium.

"Father," she called, "Mother, where are you? I want to talk to you both."

Her mother came instantly to the door. "Is something wrong?" she demanded.

Lucius came up behind his wife, his eyes still sleepy-looking from his nap. Priscilla felt her heart melt as she looked at them.

"I've made up my mind," she said breathlessly. "I am willing to marry Aquila. I'm sorry I took so long to decide."

Flavia's face glowed. "You're sure? It's what we want, of course, but I want you to be sure."

Priscilla nodded. "I'm sure." She could never tell anyone that God had seemed to speak to her during the meeting.

Lucius grinned. "If we hurry, we can get to your grandfather's villa and back before dark. They, too, should know of this good news."

"Yes," Priscilla said, "let's hurry. But first—" She ran across the atrium and threw herself in her mother's arms and then turned to her father. "If my marriage can only be like yours!" she whispered.

"It will be." Lucius was very hearty. "Only use your mother for an example and you will be a perfect wife."

Clear color flushed Flavia's cheeks at her husband's praise, and seeing it, Priscilla knew that she would do everything in her power to be what her family wanted her to be.

= 5 =

The air coming through the narrow window that opened into Priscilla's tiny bedroom brought the fresh, cool scent of autumn. She awoke to the taste and touch of the cool air, and she smiled sleepily. Then the smile faded as she suddenly became aware of what this day held in store for her. It was her wedding day.

She lay perfectly still for a few minutes, but her mind darted back to the time when Aquila and his father and uncle had come to her home, and the betrothal had been solemnly declared. How frightened she had been until the minute she had dared to look into Aquila's face and had seen that he was as frightened as she. She remembered vividly how the tightness of her face had relaxed and a smile had curved her lips. He had smiled in response, and for a second he had looked like a little boy. In that instant, she had known she need not be afraid. There were surely gentleness and humor in this young man who stood beside her, and her heart had found comfort in that knowledge.

How formal Aquila's father had sounded saying the prescribed words—slightly altered so that they were acceptable to a Jehovite.

"Do you promise to give my son, Aquila, your daughter, Priscilla, as wife?"

At the use of the diminutive of her name, Priscilla had again glanced swiftly at Aquila and had seen the flush on his face. Had he wanted it said that way, or had they not known her real name was Prisca?

And her father's answer, also modified from the traditional Roman custom. "May the Most High God grant his blessing. I promise."

Reuben's and Joshua's voices had come out in unison. "May the Most High God grant his blessing."

Priscilla had wondered fleetingly if her Roman friends would smile at the invoking of blessing from just one god. But the thought evaporated when Aquila had taken her left hand a little awkwardly and had pushed a heavy silver ring on her third finger.

Everyone had relaxed then and started to talk, and wine had been poured into cups as pledges had been laughingly made. There had been no opportunity for Priscilla and Aquila to talk together, nor had there been since, but even now, several months later, Priscilla could remember the touch of his hand putting a ring on her finger.

I may never be able to share my thoughts with him, Priscilla thought, still lying quietly in bed, *but I know I can be content, because there's nothing about him that is offensive to me. In time, when I'm used to marriage, I'm sure I'll find as much pleasure in his touch as all the love poems say I will. Surely that's important, too.*

Her mother came swiftly through the door. "Are you awake?" she asked.

"Yes, wide awake. I've just been lying here thinking."

"Happy thoughts, I hope." Flavia's voice was light, but there was a tremor in it.

"I was remembering the day of my betrothal."

"With regret?"

Priscilla sat up and smiled at her mother. "If I told you that I was remembering it with joy, would you think me shameless?"

Flavia's face brightened. "I would think you a very normal and loving girl. You have been taught what is expected of a wife. If I thought that you would come to find your wifely duties a joy rather than an obligation, I would be very happy."

Flavia's face was crimson, but she did not lower her eyes.

Priscilla searched for the right words. "Mother, I've seen how you feel about Father. So how could I believe that married love was anything but beautiful? I don't know what kind of husband Aquila will be, but he appears to be kind. If God gives us children, I'll be content. But if God also lets me love my husband, I will—" Her voice faltered.

"You'll be most wonderfully blessed," Flavia said. "As I have been. Now, get up. There's much to be done, and the sun will soon be up. The witnesses will be arriving as soon as it's light, and then the groom's family will be here. So hurry."

Priscilla swung her legs over the edge of the couch and stood up. Impulsively, she threw her arms around her mother. Flavia was not usually demonstrative, but she returned Priscilla's embrace warmly.

"Thank you for being such a good mother," Priscilla whispered. "I know sometimes I've been a great worry to you."

"But I won't worry any more," Flavia promised, her voice breaking. "I have dreamed and prayed for a good marriage for you. After today, I will be content."

"I'll miss you," Priscilla said, still holding her mother in her arms.

Flavia's voice became matter of fact, and she gently pushed Priscilla away. "Nonsense! I'll see you every day at the baths and every Sabbath at the synagogue. We'll have dinner together occasionally. It isn't as though you were moving clear into the city or into a home with rigid rules about the daughter-in-law never going out."

Priscilla pulled her tunic up over her head, and when she spoke her voice was muffled by its folds. "If we lived in Israel in the old days, I'd have been almost a prisoner in my husband's home. I'm glad things are different now."

She had been at the public bath the afternoon before, but she had bathed again at bedtime, using basins of water her mother had heated for her. Now she had only to step into the *tunica recta,* which was to serve as her wedding dress. Woven in one piece, the straight white tunic fell from her shoulders to her feet. She had tried it on for the first time the night before, and she had found its folds of thin wool soft and comfortable.

Flavia took up a woolen sash and wound it about Priscilla's slim waist. Her deft fingers tied the unfamiliar Knot of Hercules, which only the young husband would be allowed to untie.

"There!" Flavia said and patted the sash.

Priscilla's hand stole up and fingered the knot. How would Aquila act when he untied it? *Oh, please,* she prayed silently, knowing she had no right to name God's name in such a prayer, *let him not act silly and laugh.*

"Now," Flavia said, her voice brisk. "Sit on the couch and I'll do your hair."

Priscilla obediently sat down and Flavia stood behind her. Using the traditional spear-shaped comb kept only for brides, Flavia began to work on the silky red-gold hair that fell halfway down Priscilla's back. The front hair was divided into two sections and drawn back from Priscilla's face and then fastened at the back of her head with crimson ribbons. The back hair was divided into four more sections, each caught with a ribbon.

"How do you know how to do it?" Priscilla asked. "You haven't had that many brides to practice on."

Flavia laughed. "Oh, I don't know. I guess Roman girls are born knowing how to fix a bride's hair. I don't even know what it means—the six sections and the ribbons. I only know that's the way it must be done."

"I hope it doesn't have anything to do with appeasing the gods," Priscilla said. "It's harder for a Jehovite, isn't it? I mean, we like the old traditions, but we don't want to do the silly things like dedicating my old locket to the household gods. And yet I'd have felt foolish wearing a child's locket on my wedding day, and I couldn't just take it off without any ceremony."

"We did it just right," Flavia said comfortingly. "When you took it off last night and said, 'With the help of the Most High God, I now become a woman!' I think it was just right."

Priscilla smiled gratefully. "It's hard," she confided, "to fit traditions to new beliefs."

"Hard," Flavia agreed. "But when the traditions are obviously pagan, we have to either discard them or change them to fit our new beliefs."

Flavia was rarely articulate about her faith, and Priscilla had often wondered if she went to the synagogue simply because her husband demanded that she go. But this simple statement seemed to indicate that Flavia had some convictions of her own.

"You're absolutely right," Priscilla said. "Now, does my hair look all right?"

"It looks beautiful. Here's the veil." Flavia picked up the sheer, bright material from the wall shelf. "You better put it on before we go out of this room. You don't want anyone to see your face on your wedding day."

"Don't I get anything to eat?" Priscilla asked wistfully.

Flavia laughed. "I was so concerned about your hair and your dress that I completely forgot the food. Of course you must have something. We won't get to your husband's house for the feast until noon probably. You'd surely starve. Just wait here and I'll get some fruit and bread. You'll have to be careful though," she added anxiously, "that you don't get fruit juice on your dress."

"Bring grapes," Priscilla suggested. "Or dates. Something not drippy."

"I'll be right back," Flavia said.

Priscilla sat stiffly, careful not to muss her tunic or her hair. The sheer, flame-colored veil that would cover her hair and face lay beside her, and she fingered it lightly. *It will make my hair look like I'm on fire,* she thought and giggled.

"You sound happy." Linia Justinius's voice came lightly from the doorway.

"Grandmother!" Priscilla jumped up and drew Linia into the room. "Do I look all right? It's all right for you to see me without my veil, isn't it?"

"You look beautiful!" Linia turned Priscilla around, examining her carefully. "Your mother has done a perfect job of fixing your hair, and your tunic is lovely. Wait till your young man sees you. He'll swoon."

She laughed, sounding like a girl, and Priscilla hugged her quickly. Just at that moment, Flavia came into the room with a small tray of grapes and bread and a cup of milk. Priscilla looked from her mother to her grandmother. *These two women,* she thought gratefully, *have done as much as my grandfather to make me what I am. They have made the part of me that my husband will know.*

"You know," she confided, reaching out to her mother, "when Aquila pretends to tear me from your arms, it will be more real than he realizes. Leaving you both *will* be sad."

They did not contradict her. Sadness, as well as joy, was on their faces as the three of them clung together.

"Are you ready to leave?" Reuben's voice was unexpected, and Aquila jumped a little. He was standing in the room that was to be his and Priscilla's, staring at the wedding couch that had been given to him by Marcus Justinius.

"It's a very Roman thing to be in a Hebrew house," Reuben grumbled, glancing at the couch that had held his son's attention. "Are we going to be expected to put it in the atrium after tonight?"

"If we're Roman enough to have an atrium, I guess we're Roman enough to have a wedding couch in it," Aquila said lightly. He wanted to keep everything as light as he could. It might help him control the trembling of his hands and voice.

"As long as we keep clear of the Romans' temples and

gods, I suppose a piece of furniture won't hurt us," Reuben agreed with reluctance. "But stop looking at it and answer my question. Are you ready to go?"

Aquila glanced down at his toga. For all his father's complaints about things Roman, both men were dressed in the plain white toga of the Roman citizen. As an indication that he was the groom, Aquila wore a wreath of flowers around his head. The scarlet blossoms had been gathered by Priscilla and sent over the night before. Neither the color nor the fragrance of the flowers had moved Aquila as had the thought that Priscilla's hands had picked the blossoms and had woven them into a crown.

"I'm ready," Aquila said. "Is the family all gathered together?"

"The family, our friends, the clients. There's really quite a crowd out there. I hope we have enough food."

"My mother and my aunts have been cooking for weeks," Aquila reminded him. "We have enough food to feed half of Rome."

"Well, we'll see," Reuben conceded. "Come on, then. It's time to go."

The time had finally come, Aquila exulted. All the long waiting was ended at last and soon, in an hour or less, Priscilla would be his wife. No wonder his hands trembled and his heart kept skipping beats so that it stumbled in his breast.

Aquila walked behind his father to the outer room where at least fifty men were gathered. There were members of the synagogue, relatives, business associates, and a few clients who depended on the beneficence of Reuben and his brothers for their daily provisions. As soon as they all caught sight of Aquila, there was a loud cry of greeting and good wishes. Some of the remarks were warm and generous, a few were coarse and earthy, but Aquila responded smilingly to all of them. Nothing that anyone would say to him could offend him today.

Joshua pushed his way through the crowd, and his grin was warm as he clasped his nephew in his arms.

"The day is here at last," he cried heartily. "Now we won't have to see you mooning over your work any longer. Now you can settle down and do your job properly."

Everyone laughed as Aquila returned his uncle's grin.

"Then let's waste no more time," Joshua went on. "The bride is surely getting impatient."

With much merriment, the men crowded out into the street, taking Aquila with them in such a rush that he felt as though he had been picked up and carried along. A leather bag of dried raisins and nuts was thrust into his hands, and he began to scatter them about in the prescribed manner. Children scrambled for the treat, calling their thanks and adding still another festive note to the noisy procession.

"You've just beaten me by a few weeks," a young man called out to Aquila. "I'm to marry the best friend of your bride. Marta. Had you heard?"

Aquila looked into the face of his best friend, one of the young men from their synagogue. "Cordelius!" he exclaimed. "No, I'd heard nothing. We can plan to see each other often, then. Our wives will like that."

"And I'll expect you at my wedding," Cordelius responded. "With as much pleasure as I'm attending yours."

"A bargain," Aquila responded. "There's nothing I'd like better."

His attention was pulled away by the claims of other friends, and when he glanced back a bit later, he saw Cordelius and Joshua deep in conversation. That the subject of their talk was serious was obvious from the intent, sober look on their faces. A surge of the happy crowd pushed Aquila closer to his friend and his uncle, and he was in time to hear Cordelius say, "Ah, but if you'd only listen to all I have to say, you, too, would know that Jesus of Nazareth is indeed the promised Messiah!"

"Come," Aquila chided. "No ponderous religious discussions on my wedding day. This is a time for joy. Not for long faces."

Cordelius laughed. "Some day, my friend, you'll understand what real joy is when I've told you what I know to be true."

"Perhaps." Aquila's tone was casual. "But for now I have other things to think about. And you, too, both of you. You have to help me celebrate my marriage."

"Who better than I?" Joshua responded. "A man of age and wisdom, who knows the joy of a submissive and obedient wife!"

Everyone close to them shouted with laughter. It was common knowledge that Joshua's wife was salty-tongued and quick-tempered—as well as warm and generous. But it was also common knowledge that Joshua was perfectly contented.

In the midst of the laughter and shouting, Aquila was suddenly aware that they had reached Lucius Justinius's villa, and that Lucius and his father, Marcus, stood at the doorway with hands stretched out in welcome. Aquila felt himself being shoved forward, but before he could feel awkward, both Lucius and Marcus had moved forward to embrace him.

"My son," Lucius said politely.

"My grandson," Marcus murmured and then added, "We give you the most precious thing we own. Care for the gift tenderly."

The words were spoken so softly that no one else heard, but Aquila nodded soberly. "I will," he promised and knew that in that instant he had taken a vow.

The older men clustered around Aquila and steered him into the doorway of the atrium. There was room for only five or six of them, but Aquila was aware that he had his father and his favorite uncle, as well as Lucius, Marcus, and Cordelius at his back when he entered the room. *Enough support for any man,* he thought wryly.

The curtains that covered the door opposite the entrance to the atrium were pulled aside, and Priscilla stood in the opening facing her groom. The flame-colored veil, held in place by a ring of flowers on her hair, floated around her. Aquila recognized the similarity to the crown he was wearing and for an instant he wondered what she had been thinking when she gathered and wove the flowers. *What is she thinking now?* he wondered.

"Your bride," Lucius said.

Aquila stepped forward and reached out to take Priscilla's hand. There would be no ceremony but this: the clasping of hands in front of witnesses. Would her hand be cold, resistant, and stiff, with the fear his uncle had noticed the day he had called on Marcus Justinius?

To his intense joy, Aquila realized that her hand was lifting toward his even as he reached out. Her fingers, warm and soft, curved around his as naturally as though they had held his hand a hundred times.

The young couple moved together to stand before a small table on which an oil lamp burned.

"You will be my wife?" Aquila asked the ritual question so softly that only Priscilla heard him.

Her answer came in a clear, honest voice. The old Roman words were so ancient that no one knew their exact meaning, but they were part of every Roman wedding. "When and where you are Gaius," Priscilla said, "I then and there am Gaia."

Old names. It might have been more Jehovite if she had said *Adam* and *Eve,* Aquila thought. Or more modern if she had said *husband* and *wife.* But it all meant the same, and the promise had been made.

Flavia stepped over to them, and her arms came around Priscilla. Aquila pretended to wrest his bride from her mother's embrace, but for a second Flavia held tight. Then abruptly she released her hold and Priscilla came lightly, freely, into Aquila's arms. Briefly, before the cries of congratulations broke out, he held her, aware of the sweet fragility of her, wondering if under the bright veil her lips were trembling or smiling.

6

The wedding procession, as it wound away from Lucius's villa, was a merry one. Torch-bearers and flute players headed the column of laughing, shouting guests, and after them came Aquila and his father, uncle, and personal friends. Priscilla walked between two young boys, each holding her hand, and behind her walked a third boy carrying a distaff and spindle, emblems of domestic life.

Even in all the merriment, Priscilla eyed the distaff and spindle with some distaste. She knew how to spin, of course, and do all the other things that Roman matrons did, and she supposed in time she would even come to enjoy them. But the flowers and torches were certainly more attractive than the tools of domesticity.

Tucked in her sash were three coins. At her mother's wedding, two coins had been used as offering to the household gods and to the gods in general. Obviously, this was an impossible gesture for Priscilla to make, and yet she knew Flavia wanted the tradition of the coins. So Priscilla had suggested that one coin be tossed to a beggar child as a symbol of charity and that one be given to the rabbi as an offering to the Lord. Of course, there was no problem with the third coin as it was to be given to Aquila at the door of his father's villa as a token of a dowry.

At a corner, Priscilla freed one hand to toss a coin to a small ragged child, and when she saw the rabbi walking with the men, she sent one of her escorts running with the coin and an explanation.

At the door of Reuben's villa, the procession stopped long enough for Priscilla to wind bands of wool about the doorposts and to anoint the threshold with oil, as an emblem of prosperity.

Finally, she turned to Aquila and put her third coin into his outstretched hand. "Everything I have," she said quietly, "I bring to you."

Aquila seemed totally unaware of the guests crowding behind them. He took the coin and dropped it into the pocket formed by the belt.

There were no ritual words for him to give in answer, and she expected him to turn without speech and carry her into his father's door. Instead, he leaned toward her and whispered, "And everything I *am,* I bring to you."

Deeply moved, Priscilla gazed up at him, wishing the scarlet veil could be pulled aside so that he might see her face. But the veil could not be removed until she was in her husband's home, and so she stood mutely before him.

Aquila stooped and lifted her into his arms. He was so tall and she so small that there was an instant cry of delight from the guests and laughing remarks were made about how easy it would be for this groom to carry his bride over the threshold. But Aquila still seemed to be oblivious of everyone but the girl in his arms, and she felt the quick, hard strokes of his heart against her shoulder as he carried her inside. There, he put her down, so that she stood for the first time in Reuben's home, looking up into her husband's face.

"My lord," she whispered.

Quickly, before the invited guests could crowd in, he lifted her veil and bending, he lightly kissed her lips. "My love," he said.

The kiss was sweeter than anything she had expected, anything she had dared hope for. But before she had time even to look into Aquila's eyes, the guests had pushed through the door and were crowding about them. The women of Aquila's family clustered close to Priscilla, greeting her, making her welcome, and the men took Aquila with them into the peristyle where tables had been set up and food had been prepared.

The rest of the day fled by in a noisy blur. There was never a minute when Priscilla could be alone with her new husband, and she hardly had an opportunity to speak coherently to her mother-in-law, Sarah. But all this would come in time, she comforted herself. Today was a time for festivity.

Once, during the late afternoon, Priscilla sat wearily on a bench, grateful that for that moment she was alone, but almost at once, Marta appeared beside her.

"I only hope my wedding will be as beautiful as yours," Marta murmured. "Isn't it odd that they should be so close together? Who would ever have thought, when we were children and dreaming of what our lives would be, that we would be married only weeks apart."

"October is a good month," Priscilla answered. She patted the bench. "Here, sit down and talk to me a minute. Are you pleased with your parents' choice of men? Is this Cordelius nice?"

Marta shrugged. "How should I know? He's a Jehovite. He comes faithfully to the synagogue. He has a decent trade. What else can I say?"

"Nothing, I suppose," Priscilla said, but she felt her lips curve.

Marta looked at her curiously. "You look as though you already knew a great deal about your husband. Surely they didn't let you spend any time together?"

"Of course not. But—" She hesitated. Even to Marta, who had shared her childish griefs and joys, she could not speak of that brief kiss, those unexpected words of commitment.

"Well, tell me," Marta urged. "What has he done to make you look like that?"

"Don't be silly." Priscilla's voice was sharp. "It's just that my mother taught me that I must be a good wife, and so I plan to be."

"It's more than that," Marta insisted. "I'll wager it's more than that."

"What is Cordelius's trade?" Priscilla said.

Marta laughed. "All right, so I won't pry. But I hope I look like you do on my wedding day." She glanced across at a group of men and suddenly blushed. "He's looking at me," she whispered.

"Better than that he look at another girl," Priscilla said. "Answer me. What's his trade?"

"He's a tent maker. The same as the Justinius family. They're very close friends, did you know? Cordelius and Aquila. We'll be able to see as much of each other as we did before. It was one of the reasons I agreed to marry him."

Priscilla felt a quick rush of affection for the girl beside her. But before she could say anything, a group of women came up to them and any further chance to speak intimately was gone.

It was not long afterward that the guests began to leave, and almost before she realized it, Priscilla was alone, sitting in the atrium with Reuben, Sarah, and Aquila. She knew that Aquila's two sisters who still lived at home were out in the kitchen with the slaves, cleaning up after the feast.

"I should go out and help," Priscilla said, feeling shy. "It's not right that I sit here and rest while Tenia and Doria must work."

Sarah spoke gently. "Nonsense. You're exhausted, I know. There will be plenty of time for you to do household tasks. For now you are the guest of honor."

"But a guest of honor who really doesn't want to sit out here and talk to all of us," Reuben said stiffly. "I'm sure you are as anxious to get acquainted with my son as he is with you. It is permissible and proper for the two of you to go to your own room to talk if you wish."

Priscilla glanced swiftly at Aquila and saw the same blend

of shyness and eagerness that must be on her own face.

"If you will permit us, Father," Aquila murmured.

"I wouldn't suggest it if I didn't permit it," Reuben said.

Her father-in-law was very different from her own father and grandfather, Priscilla thought with a twinge of dismay. *I will have to get used to his brusque manner. I wonder if his son is like him.*

Aquila stood up. "Then come," he said to Priscilla and walked ahead of her toward the outside door. They stepped outside and turned to go up the steps that climbed the outside wall of the villa. The sky was still fairly light, but Aquila turned to take Priscilla's hand so that she would not stumble. At the top of the steps, Priscilla was breathless, but whether from the climb or the touch of Aquila's hand, she was not sure. He led her to a room on a balcony that looked down onto the peristyle, and pushed aside the leather curtain that hung at the door.

"This is to be our room," Aquila said. "And this is the wedding couch that your grandfather gave us. Had you seen it?"

"No. Oh, it's lovely." In the dim light of the oil lamp in the corner, Priscilla gazed with delight at the heavy, carved wooden couch, and the blaze of crimson cushions that were heaped on it.

"Yes," Aquila answered. "It's lovely. Almost lovely enough for you."

She smiled, but she was aware of a frightened pulsing in her throat.

"Sit down," Aquila said, pushing her gently toward the couch. "I'll sit here on this stool. We can talk a while."

But when she leaned back against the soft cushions, she was suddenly, ridiculously overwhelmed with fatigue, and there didn't seem to be anything in the world to talk about. Now was the time for her to be witty and warm and a little flirtatious. All of her mother's teachings stirred in her, but her weariness was greater than anything else.

Aquila looked at her with tenderness. "You're so tired," he whispered. "Lie back and rest a little while. I'll sit here so I won't disturb you."

She was going to protest, but when she looked at him, she saw that he was wholly sincere. Remembering her mother's injunction to be compliant and obedient, she allowed herself to relax into the pillows. She never imagined for one minute that she would actually fall asleep, and she was sure that in only a minute or two Aquila would take advantage of the privacy of the room and would join her among the cushions.

But, amazingly, Aquila sat quietly on his stool, and almost against her wishes, her eyes fluttered shut. In her dreams, the flutes played the wedding hymns, and the torchlight flickered on the faces of the merry guests.

When she awoke, no daylight filtered around the edge of the door curtain, and the room was almost wholly dark. Only the dim glow of the tiny oil lamp penetrated the blackness. For a second or two, she did not know where she was. Then Aquila moved, and she was instantly aware.

"I'm sorry," she said in distress, sitting erect. "Oh, my lord, I'm sorry to have fallen asleep. Forgive me. Please forgive me."

Aquila stood, and she saw that he moved stiffly, evidently weary from the long wait on the stool. "It's all right," he said. "You were tired, and I've had the joy of watching you sleep."

"Did I snore?" she asked, honest anxiety in her voice.

He laughed. "You slept like an angel, but I don't see how you could, with all those ribbons in your hair."

"They *are* a little lumpy," she admitted and lifted her hands. "I could undo them, I guess."

"Let me," he begged.

"Of course," she answered, and moved so that he could sit beside her.

His hands were gentle, untying the ribbons and smoothing her hair. "If you knew," he breathed at last, "how I have longed to touch your hair. It's so beautiful and is as soft as I had imagined it would be."

Her breath caught in her throat, but she managed to say bravely, "I wondered if you thought about it."

"Did you? But I thought about you all the time. All my relatives have been teasing me for months, telling me that I am lovesick."

She dared to look directly into his face. "And are you?" she asked softly.

"Yes," he answered simply and bent to her lips.

His hands, when they untied the Knot of Hercules at her waist, were very gentle and skilled. *From the use of needle and awl,* Priscilla thought. Her next thought was that he was not silly at all and there was no laughter in him.

And so my prayer was answered truly, she thought gratefully, and turned her face to Aquila's.

She felt his arms come around her, and unexpectedly she lifted her own to go about his neck.

There was no need for words, she thought in astonishment. For this moment there was no need for words at all.

= 7 =

The early morning held a hint of spring, and Aquila, walking briskly along the road that led from his father's villa to the shop, drew in deep breaths of the mild air. Winter mornings were often so damp and foggy and cold that the morning walk to the shop could be decidedly unpleasant. But this pale, luminous sky above the hills of Rome held a promise of something better, and Aquila was glad that he had left early so that he could walk alone without having to make conversation with his father.

He kicked a pebble boyishly along the road, feeling an absurd inclination to run from door to door shouting out his incredible news.

"My wife is with child," he wanted to shout. "Out of the great joy I have found in her, a child is to be born."

He laughed aloud, imagining the look on the faces of strangers—who would surely think him mad, who would call for the civil guard and demand that this capering, ridiculous young man be put away with other lunatics. "What's so wonderful about that?" they would probably snort. "Any woman can bear a child."

But Priscilla is not just "any woman," Aquila told his imaginary detractors. *Priscilla is merry and warm and funny. Priscilla is my wife!*

They had known of the coming child for only a few weeks, but the thought of it still ran through Aquila like fire. It would be a son, of course, a priest of the tribe of Levi. Or if, by some remote chance, it might be a girl, perhaps she would have Priscilla's beauty and charm.

The pebble flew awkwardly, bouncing from his bare toe instead of the sole of his sandal, and he yelped sharply with pain. Looking around quickly to see that he hadn't been observed, he drew his mouth into a straight line instead of the ridiculous grin that had been curving it ever since he left home. He was no longer a boy; he was a man with a man's responsibilities and obligations, and he must start acting like one. It was foolish of him to continue to think so often and so dotingly of his wife. Even though no one knew (not even Priscilla) how his thoughts hovered around her, he felt it was wrong of him. A man should be concerned with weightier things than love.

A quick hail stopped him. Turning, he saw Cordelius hurrying toward him.

"Spring is coming," Aquila announced as soon as his friend came close enough for conversation. "Can you smell it?"

"And about time," Cordelius answered. "I've had my fill of wet, cold days. A solid week of sunshine would be to my liking."

"I'll remind you of that in midsummer," Aquila said, grinning. "Although to tell you the truth, I agree with you."

"I wish you agreed with me about some other things," Cordelius said earnestly. "Much as I urge you, you won't come with me to the meetings where they talk of Jesus the Christ."

"I went once," Aquila defended himself. "I heard a great deal about him."

"And you didn't believe it?"

"I won't say that." Aquila's tone was cautious. "I was much moved by some of the stories. Even more by the conviction on the part of those who told the stories. I can't say I disbelieved."

"Then what holds you back?" Cordelius's voice was eager. "The promise of the ages has been fulfilled in this man, this Messiah. He overcame death! People saw Him and talked to Him—even ate with Him—after He had died on the cross. How can you just put that out of your mind?"

"My father—" Aquila began, but Cordelius broke in, impatiently.

"Oh, I know all about the traditions and the conservatism of the older ones. You don't have to tell me. But my own father is coming around. Slowly but surely, he's coming to believe as I do."

"You really believe?" Aquila countered. "I mean, you would stake your very life on it?"

"My life!" Cordelius insisted.

"But you have only heard stories," Aquila began.

"No, not stories. Accounts. From people who have talked personally to Jesus's disciples. One of the disciples, Peter, was a personal friend of Phineas. You know Phineas —the one who came from Jerusalem late last summer. Phineas and Peter were fishermen in the same village. Phineas is younger, of course, and never spoke with Jesus personally. But Peter shared many of his experiences."

"A secondhand account," Aquila argued.

"And did you stand beside Moses on the Mount of Sinai when he received the tablets of the Law? Or do you believe it happened simply because you received a secondhand account of it?"

The words stopped Aquila, and he stood for a few seconds staring at the ground. Then he said slowly, "That's true. I never thought of it that way."

"Then during the siesta today," Cordelius said eagerly. "Come with me to hear what Phineas has to say."

"I always go home during the siesta," Aquila demurred.

"You are still smitten with that pretty little wife of yours," Cordelius observed. "Has she wrapped you around her finger, then? Do you think she will object if you come to believe that Jesus is the Messiah?"

Aquila looked at his friend in honest amazement. "I

wouldn't discuss anything like that with her," he protested. "One does not speak to a woman of such heavy matters."

"Well, certainly *I* wouldn't," Cordelius said, "but you seem so smitten that I thought perhaps you shared your every thought with her."

Aquila strode on, and Cordelius had to hurry to keep up. "Wives are for delight and comfort," Aquila said. "We laugh together, and she—" He hesitated, certain that he could not make his friend understand that in the privacy of their room Priscilla was sweet or flirtatious or merry, as his mood demanded. And he never had to tell her what he needed; she seemed to know. "We are going to have a child," he confided abruptly. "I don't want to upset her."

"Congratulations!" Cordelius's hand came down warmly on Aquila's shoulder. "Perhaps there is also hope for me. After all, you've been married longer than I."

"Don't be impatient. You'll know the same joy soon," Aquila said comfortingly.

Cordelius's face sobered. "All the more reason, though, for you to come hear Phineas. If you are to have a son, you should teach him from his earliest days that the Messiah has come and has died for our sins."

Once again, Aquila spoke the words that held him back. "My father would be distressed," he said.

"Possibly," Cordelius admitted. "But perhaps even he would come to accept the truth. Your Uncle Joshua is a believer, I'm sure, but he is cautious about confessing it."

"Naturally. Such a step could cause trouble in his family, in his business. You know that the synagogue could be split in two."

"Jesus Himself never stopped going to the synagogue."

Aquila shook his head. "I would hate to see any trouble come about. The emperor has been generous about our religion. I wouldn't want to give him any cause to get angry with the Hebrews."

Cordelius looked around and then spoke softly. "The

Emperor Claudius is too easily influenced, perhaps. Almost anyone can sway him. I can't allow his reaction to dictate my actions."

"Be careful," Aquila warned. "The stones in the street have a way of hearing what is said about Claudius."

"Well, anyway, will you come to hear Phineas?"

"Not today," Aquila answered. "Priscilla expects me home today. Perhaps tomorrow. Perhaps."

"Tomorrow, then. And no perhaps. I shall expect you. Now, here's my shop, so I'll leave you. But tomorrow at noon, I'll come by to get you. My guess is that your Uncle Joshua will join us. Please, my friend, it is out of love for you that I beg you to come to hear the good news."

Cordelius's face was so intense, so serious, and yet so serene that Aquila could not deny him. "All right," he said slowly. "You can count on me. I'll come."

The following day, Priscilla went to her mother-in-law just before the hour of siesta.

"Mother, would it offend you if I went to see my grandparents today? Since my husband is not coming home during the siesta, I thought this would be a good day to visit them. I'll go directly from their villa to the baths and meet you there, if you'd like."

Sarah looked up from the weaving that seemed to occupy most of her time. Although there were several household slaves, she had none of the usual Roman matron's love for gossip or game playing. It was evidently impossible for her to set aside the training of her youth, even though it was no longer necessary for her to work all the time.

"Why isn't he coming home today? What will he do for his midday meal?" Sarah asked.

"Doria fixed bread and cheese and fruit for him, and he took it folded in a napkin. I'm not sure why he isn't coming home. He said something about being with Cordelius."

Sarah smiled at her daughter-in-law. "It's about time for

him to seek out the company of men. He's been home so much I was beginning to worry."

Priscilla flushed, even though she knew her mother-in-law was not displeased. Both of Aquila's parents had made it clear to her that they were delighted that their son found such joy in his marriage.

"I, too," she admitted bravely to Sarah. "I was afraid the men he works with would tease him. It's better that he occasionally stay with his friends."

Sarah nodded. "Occasionally, yes. Not every day. A man can become a stranger to his home."

"I know. Marta's father was like that. But I don't think Aquila—"

"Well, certainly not at this time," Sarah agreed, her hands busy with her weaving again. "I've never seen a husband so excited at the thought of a child."

"I know," Priscilla said again. "But are you willing? That I should go to my grandparents?"

"Of course. You should go as often as you can now before you get too large. Your grandparents are no longer young."

The words distressed Priscilla. Before her marriage, she had never thought of Marcus and Linia as old. Perhaps it was because she had seen them nearly every day, and when she was with them she had been completely caught up in study and in conversation. But it was true that she was suddenly aware of their age now that she saw them less often.

"I haven't told them yet about the child," Priscilla confided. "And I asked my parents not to tell. Today I want to tell them."

"Wonderful. Go right away so you'll have plenty of time with them. Tell Teris to walk with you. He can do the errands I outlined earlier and then come back for you and walk with you to the baths."

"Then who will walk with you?"

"Tenia and Doria and I will walk together. It's just not fitting for you to be alone on the street."

"Thank you, Mother." Priscilla stooped to press her cheek against Sarah's. "You're so good to me."

Sarah shrugged. "Why not? You're a good girl."

Priscilla ran to the kitchen where the slaves spent any leisure time they had, and explained her plans to Teris. In only a few minutes she was hurrying along the street. She could hear Teris, who was heavy, puffing behind her, but her feet felt as though they had wings. The whole two-hour siesta was hers to spend as she pleased, and what better way to spend it than with Marcus and Linia?

A twinge of guilt nudged her. What kind of wife was she that she should be so pleased by the fact that her husband was not coming home? *A dutiful wife,* she assured herself. *He will never, never guess that I sometimes cherish time away from him.*

But I cherish the time with him, too, she reminded herself. *He is the kindest, dearest man I have ever known, and I am glad that I was obedient and married him, even though we never talk of anything important. We share only the—the—*(her mind sought the right word) *only the sweets of life. We never share the bread.*

She hardly even felt a sense of disappointment. This was the way she had expected it to be. She hadn't really hoped that Aquila would be like her grandfather. But even though she accepted Aquila as he was, she often ached and hungered for profound conversation. So she went to her grandfather, and when Marcus had fed that particular need, she could go back to her husband and be what he seemed to want and need—a wife who laughed with him and who found joy in love.

The distance to her grandmother's villa was not great. At the gate, she dismissed Teris after giving him instructions as to when he should return. Then, with deep pleasure, she turned from the gate, not even taking time to enjoy the view, as was her custom, and hurried to the door of the atrium.

Linia must have heard her talking to Teris, because she was already standing in the door.

"My dear," she called out. "I had no idea you were coming. And so early. Before the siesta."

"My husband is staying at the shop today, so I was free to come." Priscilla hugged her grandmother. "Is it all right?"

"Of course. Of course. Your grandfather has been irritated most of the morning. He misses you, and he'll be very happy to see you."

"And I to see both of you," Priscilla answered. "Come with me to find him. Is he in his work room? I want to talk to both of you."

"Yes. In here. Come. Is everything all right? Just see, my lord," she called out, "who has come to visit."

Marcus drew back the curtain that kept his small work room free of drafts, his face shining. "Welcome, my dear, welcome. Come in, come in. Sit here on this couch."

Priscilla drew her grandmother in with her. "I want to talk to both of you," she announced. "I have news for you."

They had already guessed, she suspected, but the words were too important to be left unsaid. "I'm going to have a child," she said breathlessly. "Not until early next winter or perhaps very late fall. But I wanted you to know."

"The Lord be praised," Marcus said, "for his blessings on us."

"Oh, my dear," Linia murmured. "Do you feel well? Is everything going well?"

"Everything's fine," Priscilla declared. "If I feel less than perfect in the morning, that's only to be expected. My husband is very solicitous and insists that I lie late in bed."

"And does his mother object to such coddling?" Marcus's eyes twinkled. "Does she say, 'Nonsense! Every woman goes through this'?"

Priscilla laughed. "My husband's mother is good to me. If she thinks those things, she says nothing."

"Good," Linia said. "You have brought us the best news in the world. But now let me go and prepare a bit of food. I was going to do it when you arrived."

"Let me help," Priscilla insisted.

"No, stay and talk to your grandfather. I'll only be a minute."

After she had left the room, Priscilla and Marcus sat smiling at each other.

"You look happy," he said.

"I am. I'm happy that I'm here with you, and that there will be a child, and that my husband is good to me."

Marcus's face sobered. "Speaking of your husband, I've heard that his best friend, Cordelius, has become one of those who believe the Messiah has come. Has Aquila talked to you about it?"

She shook her head. "My husband is good to me, but he would never talk to me about anything so serious. Like most men, he believes that women have no room in their heads for anything as profound as religion."

"The more fool he," Marcus said tersely. "I heard one day that Aquila accompanied Cordelius to one of these meetings. What would you do if Aquila became one of them?"

She shrugged. "What my husband believes or does not believe cannot concern me if he doesn't discuss it with me."

"They demand baptism," Marcus said. "I've heard that they demand baptism of the new convert and his family. That would mean that you, too, would have to submit to the ritual."

Her eyes darkened. "No," she said clearly. "No, Grandfather, not unless I understand and believe for myself. I will not submit, like some mindless object, to such an important act. I've been a good wife, an obedient wife, but there are limits to what I will do."

⊰ 8 ⊱

Aquila sat, quiet and reserved, among the men who had gathered to listen again to the young man, Phineas. Some of the listeners were eager and receptive; some of them, like Aquila, were withdrawn and uncommitted; and some were angry and critical. During the weeks that Aquila had attended the meetings, he had been distressed by the increasing division. He saw in the growing antagonism a forecast of the anger that would surely fill his family if he or his Uncle Joshua ever made the decision to submit to the baptism and statement of belief that Phineas demanded of new converts.

And yet Aquila could not stay away. Neither his desire to be with Priscilla, nor his apprehension over his father's reaction could keep him away from these gatherings. Phineas's stories about the young Galilean who had been executed by Roman soldiers caught at Aquila's heart and mind and could not be dismissed.

Phineas was repeating the story of the Crucifixion. Aquila, familiar with the sight of writhing, tortured bodies on wooden crosses, felt himself wincing with pity as Phineas wove his account.

"And then He looked down and said, 'Father, forgive them, for they know not what they do.'" Phineas's voice trembled with vibrancy and excitement. "He loved like that. Can you turn your backs on that kind of love?"

Aquila had not intended to speak out. From the very first, he had maintained silence as a shield against the controversial forces that permeated the crowd. But today the words came of their own volition.

"Wasn't he speaking only of the men who were crucifying him? What has that love got to do with us?"

Phineas looked directly at Aquila, and his smile warmed his dark face. "He is as alive today as He was then—more alive. The love He expressed to his torturers was a reflection of God's love. It's a love He feels for us today."

Embarrassment lowered Aquila's eyes, but he heard the words with a curious sense of shock. No matter how many times Phineas spoke of the Resurrection, the idea still came with an unexpected force. It wasn't easy to think of a man conquering death. It wasn't logical or sensible.

But Phineas's conviction was a strength that no argument or contradiction could batter or bend. Phineas's belief was a force to be reckoned with.

Still gazing at the ground, Aquila allowed his mind to go over and over the words about love, about forgiveness. A man who could speak so in the midst of a long and terrible dying was no ordinary man. The centurion that Phineas had told about had been right when he had said, "Surely this man was the Son of God." But many people down the centuries had thought of themselves as children of God. That didn't necessarily mean that Jesus was the Messiah, the anointed one of Israel.

Or did it? Aquila's mind went over the familiar words of Isaiah that he had learned as a boy, the words of prophecy and promise. So many of them fit the stories that Phineas told that it was impossible just to discredit them all.

An angry voice was raised in protest, and Aquila realized with a sinking feeling that his father had joined the group and was protesting.

"This is blasphemy," Reuben shouted. "Many of us are faithful Jehovites with centuries of faith behind us. And are we to be taken in by tales of a man you never even met?" The words, directed at Phineas, cut through the air like a sword.

"But I did meet men who knew Him, who lived with Him. I spent many hours listening to Peter, and no one

- 65 -

knew Jesus as Peter did. I stood at the gate and saw Stephen stoned to death, and I saw the glory on his face when he saw the Lord before he died. I tell you, I *know*." Phineas kept his voice calm and level but no less intense than Reuben's.

"You're an evil influence on our young men," Reuben sputtered. "You should be run out of town."

Joshua spoke in a soothing voice. "And since when, my brother, do we send one of our own away without a hearing? It has never been necessary for two Jehovites to agree on anything except the Law, and Phineas does not deny the truth of the Law."

"Jesus insisted that he did not come to destroy the Law but to fulfill it," Phineas said.

"Then he should have stayed in his father's house and listened to his elders and kept out of trouble," Reuben said in scorn. He turned away, and his eyes swept over the assembled men until they rested on Aquila. "Come," he snapped. "There is work to be done."

Feeling like a chastened child, Aquila stood to follow his father. Cordelius, sitting beside him, caught at his wrist. "Listen," he whispered, "your father can command your body, but he has no control over your soul. That's between you and God. Don't be afraid."

Aquila shook his head and said nothing. But the words were not lost on him. They were stored in Aquila's heart with all the other words that Cordelius and Phineas had said. Someday, if he were fortunate, there would be an opportunity for him to discuss some of these things with his Uncle Joshua. There had to be someone he could trust and in whom he could confide. Cordelius was not the one. Cordelius was already converted, baptized—he and Marta, who probably had no idea what the act had been all about —and a staunch disciple of Phineas. Aquila needed to talk to someone who was a Hebrew Jehovite, born in the faith, who would understand the questions that tormented Aquila but who would also feel the pull of Phineas's words.

"You realize, of course," Reuben said suddenly, "that your friend Phineas is mad. Not only mad but a troublemaker. If he starts a quarrel among the Hebrews, he could get us into serious trouble. The Emperor Claudius only tolerates us now. What will he do if he hears we are quarreling? He may refuse to let us meet for worship."

"Oh, I don't think so," Aquila began, but his father interrupted.

"You're a naive boy. What do you know of emperors and decrees? You think only of love—and this ridiculous notion that the Messiah has come. What do you know?"

I know a great deal, Aquila wanted to say. But years of discipline kept him silent. Well, maybe soon he'd have a chance to talk to Joshua. In the meantime, he would comfort himself with Priscilla's laughter and beauty.

Priscilla performed the ordinary tasks of preparing the evening meal with a sensation that could be defined only as irritation. There was something wrong with Aquila, and whatever it was had made Reuben angry and suspicious. Sarah was as kind as ever, but Reuben was silent and sullen, and when he did speak, it was with asperity.

If things were only different, thought Priscilla with exasperation. She slammed a bread tray on the table with such force that it might have broken had it been made of less flexible material than woven reeds. *I could just* demand *that Aquila talk to me about it. I could say, "What's troubling you? Why is your father angry?" And he could tell me. In plain words and in simple terms.*

But, no, men and women don't act like that. Women aren't supposed to know what's going on in their husbands' minds. Women are just supposed to be sweet and coy and make their husbands laugh. It's stupid!

The clay cup in her hand hit the table with such a sharp rap that she instantly picked it up again to see if she had cracked it. Fortunately, the sturdy clay had resisted her angry gesture, and the surface was smooth and unharmed.

It isn't good for the baby for me to be angry, Priscilla thought, and laid a protective hand on her abdomen. *All the women say that. They say the baby will be hurt by negative or bitter thoughts. But I just get so angry!*

The sound of voices at the outer door alerted her that the men had come home for their evening meal, and she hurried to finish putting the food on the table. The savory smell of hot lentil soup wreathed out of the clay pot that she set in the center of the table. Her stomach twisted once queasily and then settled down, and she felt the first pangs of healthy hunger. Maybe tonight she would be able to enjoy bread dipped in the good soup and even eat some of the goat cheese and drink a bit of milk.

The voices were louder now, and she heard Reuben's shouting overriding Aquila's quiet response. At first she could not hear any of the words, but finally she heard Reuben say, "I tell you, you will not go again. I forbid it."

Aquila's voice was only a murmur, but there was a stubborn note in it that oddly enough made Priscilla's heart skip a beat. Reuben's anger was suddenly less frightening than Aquila's quiet determination. Was her husband capable of anger? Of real stubbornness? Would he risk alienating his father unless it were a matter of life or death?

She didn't know. What did she really know of this man who shared her bed and so much of her life? She knew his laughter, his gentleness, his love. Her body had come to delight in his, and what they shared was good and sweet. But she didn't really know him.

The voices became muted again, but she was uneasily aware of an ugly tension in the house. Why was Reuben angry? And hard on the heels of the question came the answer. She heard her grandfather's voice saying, "I heard one day that Aquila went with Cordelius to one of these meetings." That was it. Of course. Aquila was meeting with the Jehovites who were talking about the Messiah. Or the false Messiah. And Reuben was angry. Well, there was nothing she could do about it.

Aquila appeared in the doorway, followed closely by his father. Had he been alone, he would have come to kiss her, she knew, but he was careful not to show his affection in front of his parents. She was grateful for his reticence. It made the private times in their room even sweeter, because no one else knew how tender Aquila could be.

"Is the food ready?"

Aquila was rarely so abrupt, but she knew better than to take notice of it or comment on it.

"Yes, my lord, ready. The soup is good and hot. Come and eat it before it gets cold. You'll feel less tired when you have eaten. You, too, Father."

Reuben didn't even acknowledge her words. He simply sat, intoned the blessing, and handed his bowl to her to be filled. She ladled soup into his bowl without even trying to meet his eyes. Then she did the same for Aquila, but when his bowl was full, she dared to look at him. To her dismay, he was staring at the table with as dark a look on his face as his father had.

Wordlessly, she slid out of the room and sat quietly in the peristyle, hugging her arms around her to keep out the chill of the spring afternoon. When they had finished eating, she would call Sarah and the girls and they would eat together. She would blot the anger out of her mind and eat the good soup so that the child she carried would be well.

Aquila came to their room early, but she had gone up even earlier. She sat passively in a corner on a heavy cushion, resting her back against the wall. The sullen anger in the kitchen all during the time the men were eating had pressed on Priscilla's heart like a stone. For the first time in her life, she was aware that something beyond her control was happening, something that threatened the very fabric of her life, tearing her security into shreds. And for once, she did not want to run to her grandfather with the problem. He was wise and knowledgeable, but he did not know what went on in Aquila's mind any more than she did.

When Aquila came in, she got up instantly, forcing herself to smile. "Are you weary, my lord?"

He came to her and took her into his arms. "Don't call me 'my lord' in our room," was all he said, but he held her for a long time.

Finally he lifted his head. "Yes, I'm tired," he admitted. "It has been a long day."

"How?" she wanted to ask. "In what way? Tell me what is causing this quarreling between you and your father. Tell me what you are learning at these meetings that is tearing you apart."

But of course she didn't say it. She merely held him as he held her.

"You are so little to be so strong," he murmured against her hair. "You can lift my heart up out of the pit."

He tried to laugh when he said it, but there was no laughter in him.

"If I can lift you out of sadness," she said, "then I can only be proud that you are willing to reach out to me."

He lifted his head then and drew her over to the cushions heaped on the floor. "Tell me about your day," he suggested. "Tell me what you've done and how you've felt."

"I've felt fine," she said, hiding the account of the nausea that had wretched her in the morning, the anger that had burned in her as she prepared the evening meal. Such deceit was not really deceit, Flavia had taught her daughter. A man has enough to bear without hearing of his wife's ills. "I went to see my grandparents."

"Did you? Did you tell them about the baby?"

"They are excited and happy. My grandmother looked like a girl, laughing and clapping her hands. To be a great-grandmother is a rare thing, you know."

"And your grandfather?"

She wasn't even sure he was interested, but she knew that

her voice, weaving soft pronouncements in the dusk, soothed and comforted him.

"My grandfather was as close to being fatuous as I have ever seen him. He was strict with me, you know. Always. But I can just imagine how he'll be with this baby."

"What do you and your grandfather talk about all the time?"

Aquila's voice was not really curious. He had never asked her before.

"We talk of many things," she answered slowly. "He tells me of his youth and what it was like in Gaul. He says that I would not be so odd-looking there. Many people have blue eyes, and there are quite a few with red hair."

He was usually quick to defend her coloring when she spoke disparagingly of it. He always ran his fingers over her small, straight nose and across her full lips, gently touching the small dimple that indented one corner of her mouth. "You're just right," he always said fiercely. "Who would want a girl with black eyes and hair when he could have you?"

But tonight he said nothing. He wasn't even listening to her, she knew. *Well,* she thought resolutely, *there is still love for his comfort.* She turned in his arms and began to kiss him, wooing him deliberately from his dark mood. As his lips responded to hers, she felt the desire begin to burn in her own blood. But even then, one corner of her mind remained cool and clear. In that clear portion of her mind, she made a simple resolution. Next day she would try to see Marta at the bath. She would find out what Marta knew about the meetings Aquila had been attending.

— 9 —

"How would I know about the meetings?" Marta asked. "Cordelius goes, it's true, but it's none of my business."

"My grandfather said that the families of converts have to be baptized." Priscilla held her towel around her, glad that the plunge into the frigidarium was finished for the day, grateful to be in the soft, warm air of the unctorium. Spring was coming but it had not yet come, and the day was chilly. She chose her words carefully so that Marta would not think she was prying. "And it's my understanding that Cordelius is a convert. That he has been a convert for some time."

Marta looked around at the other women who sat on benches in the unctorium. "It's not wise to talk too loudly of these things," she whispered. "Some of the Jehovites are getting very upset with Cordelius and Phineas and the others."

"But were you?" Priscilla persisted. "Baptized, I mean. Were you?"

Marta nodded. "Of course. My lord was already a believer when we were married. So I was baptized as soon as it could be arranged after the wedding."

"Do you believe?"

Marta shrugged. "My husband believes."

"But do *you?*"

Marta dropped her voice still lower. "I think I do. If everything Phineas says is true, then I have to believe. But I don't talk about it, and I try not to think about it too much. My parents are angry and can accept me only if I pretend to be—whatever they want me to be. They know I have to obey my husband, but they like it better if—well, I just try not to think about it."

But I would have to think about it, Priscilla thought. *I would have to know why I was being baptized. I would have to want to do it. As fond as I am of Aquila, I could not take such a step just because he told me to.*

Marta spoke eagerly, obviously trying to change the subject. "My husband told me that you are going to have a baby. Why hadn't you told me?"

Priscilla felt astonishment touch her. "How did your husband know?"

Marta giggled. "He said Aquila was capering down the road like a man who has had too much wine. Aquila boasted about the baby, my lord said, as though he were the only man to accomplish such a feat."

Priscilla laughed. "It's true, and I haven't told you because we've only been sure about it a few weeks. I hadn't even told my grandparents until yesterday."

"I'm envious," Marta admitted. "I wish it were me."

"It will be," Priscilla comforted her. "Just be patient."

This was the kind of conversation Marta relished, Priscilla realized. Her eyes were sparkling and her lips curved with eagerness. But the other—the heavy talk of religion and belief—was only distressing to her. It had always been that way. Marta had become a Jehovite because her father had; now she had become a follower of Jesus because her husband had. *It would be comfortable to be like that,* Priscilla thought. *Easy and comfortable. But for me it would be wrong.*

Aquila sat among the dozen or so men who listened to the teachings of Phineas. As usual, when he heard the incredible things about Jesus of Nazareth, he felt a stirring within his heart. Until now, he had kept the emotion in check, out of deference to his father. Even last night, when his father had been so angry, when it would have been easy to have flown into rebellion and to have hurried to the house of Phineas just to spite Reuben, he had controlled himself. That was no way to come to baptism. He had known that from the very beginning.

But—if he could not come to Jesus out of rebellion, then equally he could not turn his back on Him out of deference to his father. More than simple integrity was demanded of him. The courage of total commitment was required of anyone who believed that the Galilean was indeed the long-awaited Messiah.

And I have believed for a long time, Aquila admitted to himself. *It is no longer a question of whether or not I believe. When Phineas tells of things like Peter's denial and the Crucifixion and the Resurrection, then I have to believe. This is surely the truth I've been seeking all my life. This is what I was looking for when I talked to the followers of Mithras and when I asked questions of those who believe in the Roman gods. I don't have to search any longer.*

As these thoughts took shape, Aquila was filled with a great calmness. The aching unrest that had tormented him recently was gone. Somehow, in some strange fashion, his father's overt anger the night before had released Aquila from the filial loyalty that had, until now, prevented him from confessing his new faith.

But here, in the clear light of the spring sunshine, listening to Phineas's exhortations, Aquila was suddenly strong and sure. What did it matter if his father was angry? What did it matter if the whole world was angry? Aquila's own mind and heart were at peace within, and so all other angers could be endured.

"He turned to the woman," Phineas said clearly, "and He said, 'Your faith has made you whole.' And she was healed."

Aquila raised his hand, heedless of anyone. "I want to be baptized," he called. "I believe all that you have been telling us, and I want to be baptized."

Phineas's face shone. "To God be the glory," he cried and came to clasp Aquila's hand.

Almost immediately, Cordelius was at Aquila's side, his arm cast warmly across Aquila's shoulders, and other men crowded up with exclamations of approval. Almost dazed, Aquila looked from face to face, seeing an open affection he had never seen before. But, except for Cordelius, none of these men were close friends of his family. Well, so much the better, perhaps. There would be even greater opportunity for him to pursue this "new life" that Phineas kept talking about.

Then he turned and saw his uncle looking at him. Joshua's face held a strange blend of approval and apprehension.

"Your father will be very angry," he muttered.

"My father is already very angry," Aquila replied. "But I had to do it. I could no longer hide behind the fear of my father's anger."

"I must talk to you," Joshua said quickly. "Alone. Will you come with me now?"

Phineas stopped them as they turned away. "There will be a baptism at dawn on the day following the Sabbath. At the usual place on the riverbank. Will you meet us there? You and your household?"

My household, Aquila thought wryly. *I have no household of my own. Only Priscilla. And, of course, the child. Well, it's enough. We will be baptized together.*

Phineas spoke again quickly. "Don't hesitate, my friend. Once the decision is made, the act must follow."

Aquila nodded. "Of course. I agree. We'll be there, my wife and I, at the stated time. But I'd like to talk to you further, just you and I. Would it be possible?"

"Any time. I am available when you are."

"Well, not now." Aquila nodded toward Joshua. "Just now I must go with my uncle." How calm he was, he marveled, when he had just made a decision that would surely turn his life around. "Late this afternoon perhaps. I'll come by your place of business."

"Fine. Perfect." Phineas clasped Aquila's hand again. "He is risen, and He is Lord," he said warmly. "You are blessed indeed that you have come to believe."

Aquila nodded, his throat suddenly too full for speech so that he could make only a silent gesture of farewell before he turned to follow his uncle down a side street.

"Blessed or cursed," Joshua muttered. "Your father will never accept this. Why do you think I have held back from baptism?"

"You believe?" Aquila said, the words unsteady.

"I believe," Joshua said somberly. "I don't dance or sing in my belief, but I can't turn my back on this Jesus. He has gripped me by the throat, but I'm not sure I can face up to your father." He grinned wryly. "My older brother has never been an easy man to deal with."

"But if we believe," Aquila argued, "then Jesus demands our first loyalty. If He is the Messiah, then we must be willing to die for Him."

"And are you?" Joshua demanded.

"Yes," Aquila said. His voice was strangely soft and gentle. "Yes, I'm willing to die for Him."

"And your wife?" Joshua asked.

"Priscilla?" Aquila laughed with an indulgent sound. "She's my wife and wholly obedient, so of course she will do as I say."

Joshua shook his head. "I don't know," he said. "Kara will shout very loud and wail and carry on. She'll point out that my brother may refuse to let me work for him. She'll say that she can't stand to have her friendship with your mother destroyed. She'll make a lot of noise, and I can't stand it when she cries."

Aquila shook his head. "Are you daring to risk your salvation because of a woman's noise?"

Joshua nodded. "Just as you risked yours because of a

father's anger. Your fear of being sent away is as great as mine."

Aquila flushed. "My father can't run his business without us," he said. "He doesn't have anyone else who is trained to cure the hides or cut and sew the tents. No matter how angry he is, he won't make us leave the shop. His business means too much to him."

"He may continue to provide bread for our tables, but he may never speak to us again."

Aquila started to answer lightly and then stopped. He was suddenly remembering other times his father had been angry, other grudges that had been held for years.

"We can pray," Joshua agreed, "but we've got no guarantee that God will change him."

Aquila hunched his shoulders up to his ears. "We'll have to think about it and talk about it some more. If you think it's best, I won't tell him today. I'll wait and talk it over with Priscilla first. And then I'll talk to you again. We'll work something out."

"I'm not so sure." Joshua's voice was heavy. "But you're right to wait a day or two, until God gives you the wisdom and discretion you'll need. Now, come, we must hurry or we'll be late getting back to the shop. No use making Reuben irritated over anything else."

Aquila nodded. His uncle's words had dimmed a little of the glow he had felt when he had announced his intention to be baptized. But only a little. There was still a strong core of calmness in him, a quiet strength he had never known before.

Later that same afternoon, Priscilla heard a sudden commotion at the door of the atrium. She heard her name called in voices that were at once urgent and stricken. A sharp uneasiness clutched her throat. Something was wrong. Something was terribly wrong. Hadn't she been feeling an odd restlessness even as she had been weaving? She had tried to attribute it to her pregnancy, but it had been more than that. If she had been superstitious, she would have said she had been given an omen. Hadn't the bright thread kept breaking while the dark thread remained strong and taut?

As she stepped into the atrium, Sarah hurried toward her, her hands outstretched. Priscilla allowed her mother-in-law to hold her, and even found some comfort in the older woman's arms until she saw old Dena, her grandfather's slave, standing breathless and weeping inside the atrium door.

"What is it?" Priscilla begged. "What's wrong?"

"Remember the coming child," Sarah said sternly. "Try not to get too upset for the sake of the child."

"But what?" Priscilla cried. "It's Grandfather, isn't it? What's wrong?" She pulled away from Sarah's arms and went to Dena. Looking into the withered old face, the wet eyes and trembling lips, she felt her heart falter and contract painfully. "Please," she said, gripping Dena's hands, "please. Not Grandfather. Please tell me he's all right."

Dena shook her head, and her mouth worked as she drew her lips in over her toothless gums. "He's dead," the old woman said. "He's dead."

The walls and ceiling of the atrium swam in a lurching haze around Priscilla's head. Sunlight, striking the surface of the little pool, burst and exploded behind her eyes. She heard moaning and knew she was the one who was making the sounds, but she could not stop them.

Sarah led her to a couch and lowered her onto the cushions. "You should have told her more gently," Sarah snapped at Dena over her shoulder, and Dena's head nodded foolishly like the head of a broken doll.

"She couldn't help it," Priscilla gasped. "She—" Her voice suddenly rose. "Oh, not Grandfather! Oh, please, God, not him."

"There was no pain, no sickness," Sarah said quickly, soothingly. "One minute he was talking with your grandmother, and the next minute he was gone. You must find your comfort in that."

But Priscilla's mind had stopped with the words "talking with your grandmother." She struggled to her feet. "My grandmother," she said. "I must go to her. She'll need me."

"Your mother is already there," Sarah said. "The slave says your mother and father are both there by now. You should rest."

Priscilla shook her head. "No, please, let me go. I only want to see her, to be with her."

"Well, then, I'll get Teris to accompany you," Sarah said. "I don't know why anyone let this old woman come alone like this."

Dena spoke with a curious dignity. "No one saw me come. I knew my young mistress would want to know at once. They had thought to protect her for a while—because of the child."

Priscilla went over and put her arms around the old slave. "Oh, Dena," she said brokenly. "Oh, Dena, thank you for coming."

Sarah was gone for only a minute before she came back into the atrium, followed by the lumbering Teris, who cast a quick look of pity at Priscilla. Sarah's hands were filled with cloth.

"Here," Sarah said, "here's a scarf to pull over your head and face. White as befits someone in mourning. Do you want me to come with you?"

Priscilla pulled the scarf over her bright hair and then threw her arms around her mother-in-law, sobbing bitterly. "You are so good to me," she wept, "but will you be kind enough to let us go alone? Teris will take care of us, and I must—I must be alone with my grandmother and my parents. Can you understand?"

Sarah patted the girl's back. "Of course," she said. "I will get the message to your husband as soon as possible. Please don't worry about anything."

Priscilla clung to Sarah for another minute. She realized with a sense of shame and despair that there was absolutely no comfort for her in the promise to contact Aquila. What would she and Aquila have to say to each other in this time of grief? Her duty to Aquila was to be what he needed her to be. But now, hollowed out by sorrow, she was nothing but a shell, an empty husk! How could she possibly be anything to Aquila?

"Thank you," she whispered at last. "But do not trouble my lord. When he comes home tonight, it will be soon enough to tell him. In the meantime, I'll stay with my grandmother and my parents. I'll comfort them as much as I can. Perhaps my lord wouldn't mind if I stayed all night? They may need me."

"Stay as long as you're needed," Sarah said. "You're free to do whatever you wish to do. Just keep in mind that you are carrying a child. Don't do anything to bring harm to the baby."

Priscilla's tears started again. "My grandfather was so happy," she choked out. "He was so happy when I told him about the baby."

"Then comfort yourself with that," Sarah admonished. "Be grateful that you went and told him, and that he was happy. There is much comfort in all that."

Priscilla nodded woodenly. How could she explain to Aquila's mother—or to anyone in all the world—that the loss of her grandfather was a devastation from which she might never recover? Not only had he been a source of love, but he had also been the source of knowledge and understanding in her life. There was no one, no one anywhere, who knew her as Marcus Justinius had known her.

I can't bear it, Priscilla thought. Somehow she found courage to lift her head and move away from Sarah's sheltering arms. Reaching out, she took Dena's hand, and Teris fell into step behind the two women as they began their dreary walk to the place where Priscilla had once found her greatest fulfillment and joy.

= 10 =

Grandfather is dead. The words shaped themselves dirgelike in Priscilla's head each morning at the instant of her waking. It had been five days since the funeral, and now it was the Sabbath, but the edge of her grief was still as sharp and cutting as it had been at the moment when Dena had made her terrible announcement.

Priscilla's heart ached for her grandmother, for her father, for everyone who had loved and depended on Marcus Justinius. But the real source of her anguish was her own enormous sense of loss. All day long, questions hammered in her mind, questions that only her grandfather could answer. There was no one else to whom she could talk. She felt as though she had entered some desolate country where no one even spoke the same language that she spoke.

Aquila stirred beside her, and she turned her head quickly so that he would not see her tears. She had hidden her grief from him as much as she could, although it had been physically impossible for her to smile or laugh in her usual fashion. She had stayed for several days with her grandmother—a privilege she had hardly dared hope for— and when she had come home, Aquila had greeted her with gentleness and silence. She had assumed that his reticence had stemmed from respect for her grief, and her appreciation had been great.

She moved to get out of bed, but Aquila's hand caught at her arm. Her heart sank. She was sure that she could not yet join in the joy of love making, but to refuse him would be a denial of the vow she had taken so solemnly on the day she had decided to marry him.

"Priscilla." Aquila's voice was hesitant. "I need to talk to you. I've waited as long as I could, knowing your grief, but it's necessary that I talk to you today. Will you listen?"

She wiped at her tears with her hands and turned back toward her husband. Talking might be bearable. But she couldn't imagine what he might want to talk about.

"Yes?" she said, and her breath caught in her throat.

His expression was tender as he wiped the rest of the tears from her face with the edge of the woven wool shawl that served as their cover.

"I hate to trouble you," he said with diffidence. "I know how you feel—or I can imagine, at any rate. But I can't wait any longer. Tomorrow morning I am to be baptized into the faith that believes that Jesus of Nazareth is the promised Messiah, to become one of those who are called Followers of the Way. It is, of course, necessary for my household to be baptized with me. You—you and the child you carry— are my household. So you must go with me to the riverbank at dawn. I want you to be ready."

She felt her body stiffen. "What do you mean?" she said in bewilderment.

"Haven't you heard anything about the new belief that is sweeping through our synagogue? I thought perhaps you would have heard."

"Of course I've heard a little." Her voice was impatient. "My grandfather spoke to me briefly about it, and I know that Marta and Cordelius are part of the new movement. But I certainly don't know enough to submit to the baptism."

Aquila looked shocked. "You don't have to know," he said. "I'm your husband and I understand what it's all about. That's all that's necessary."

Priscilla stared into Aquila's face. She knew every inch of it well; she knew the shape of his mouth and the way his eyes looked in laughter and in passion. But the man behind the face was a stranger still.

"You don't understand," she said at last. "I can't just do something out of blind obedience. I can't follow you into a rite like baptism unless I know what it's all about."

"Women don't think about those things—" Aquila began.

"Maybe not all women," Priscilla conceded, remembering Marta's easy acquiescence to Cordelius's request. "But I'm not just any woman. I'm me. You see, my grandfather—"

She could go no further. The tears overwhelmed her, and she turned away, ashamed. She had promised herself that she would be a perfect wife, and here she was pouring out her grief and revealing her old stubbornness to her husband.

Aquila pulled her back so that she faced him. He pushed her face against his shoulder and held her as though she were a child. "I wouldn't have spoken to you so soon," he murmured. "But tomorrow is the day chosen for baptism, and I couldn't wait."

When she could, she swallowed her tears and pulled back a little from the warm comfort of her husband's body.

"I just can't," she said helplessly. "I can't do it until I know something about this Jesus. Until I understand why you want to be baptized. I'm sorry, my lord, I would never disobey you in matters of less importance. But my grandfather taught me that I, too, have a mind and a heart and that my faith in God comes from within me—not from some outward source. All *his* belief, he used to say to me, could not create faith in *me.* I'm sorry, my lord."

Aquila was clearly irritated and bewildered. "It never occurred to me," he muttered. "It never occurred to me that you would question my decision."

"I don't question it for *you,* my lord. I only question it for me."

"But you're my wife," he protested.

"Yes, my lord, and grateful that I am. But your wife, not just an extension of you."

They lay staring at each other. Without deliberate intention, they had pulled apart until they were no longer touching.

"I could force you," he said finally.

"Yes, my lord." Her voice was sarcastic. "You could beat me, too."

His face flushed, and she knew that for the first time he was truly angry at her.

"I promised Phineas," he said. "You'll make a fool of me."

"Surely there will be another day, my lord? If it could be postponed, then I could have a chance to learn about it."

"Women don't come to the noon meetings."

"You could attend the meetings, my lord, and then come home and tell me everything. You could teach me, my lord."

"Don't call me 'my lord' in our room," he snapped.

"I'm sorry," she whispered, but there was no softness in her. She simply could not do what he had demanded of her. That day, in the synagogue, making her childish promise, she had not known that something like this could occur. And she could no longer go to her grandfather for advice. She could not go to anyone. She had to depend entirely on herself.

"I don't understand you," he said at last, and the torment in his eyes wrenched an admission from her.

"I know," she said. "I have deceived you a little, I think. I have never let you see the hard side of me."

"And now?"

She lay very still and chose her words carefully. "Now we are dealing with my salvation. Next to your salvation, it is the most important thing in my world."

"I hadn't thought of it that way," he admitted. He was

silent for a long time and then he said, "I'll tell you what I'll do. I'll ask Phineas this morning at the synagogue if we can come to baptism on another day—in several weeks, perhaps. He may laugh at me," he warned her.

She was aware of the enormity of his concession. "Don't tell him that I am so stubborn. Tell him it's because of my grandfather." Her voice broke. "In a way, you know, it is. And tell him it's because of the coming child. He'll just think that women are foolish and weak. He won't blame you."

"And what if he's willing to postpone it?" Aquila asked. "What if I teach you everything I know about Jesus, and then for some ridiculous reason, you still do not believe? What then?"

If he had not used the word *ridiculous,* she thought, her anger would not have flared quite so quick and so hot.

"Then, my lord," she said coldly, "you will probably have to divorce me."

The look on Aquila's face nearly brought a hasty apology from her. But not quite. The honesty that had made her take her independent stand hardened into obstinacy.

"Well, then, so be it," Aquila said and flung away the cover.

She felt her heart jolt in apprehension. "But before that," she said quickly, aware that she had gone too far, "I pray that you will teach me."

"But will you listen?" he flung over his shoulder.

"With an open mind," she promised. "You have my word on that."

He sat beside her again. "I shouldn't have become angry," he admitted. "Jesus preached constantly of love, of patience, of turning the other cheek."

"Turning the other cheek?" she asked, puzzled.

His mouth softened. "Teaching you will be challenging," he said. "I'll have to pray constantly for wisdom and understanding. But if Jesus will be with me—"

"You said he was dead," she interrupted. "How can he be with you?"

Aquila lowered his voice. "He isn't dead any more. He was raised from the dead."

She felt anger touch her. "Don't mock me," she said. "No one dies and then lives again. Didn't I feel my grandfather's cold hand? Don't you think I know what death is?"

The sudden sound of Reuben's voice carried through the house.

"Not now," Aquila said. "I can't tell you anything now. My father will be angry if I'm late for breakfast. And we must be ready to go to the synagogue. Later I'll talk to you."

She nodded, her emotions too chaotic to allow her to speak. Either Aquila's words had been total mockery, or they had held a truth too wonderful to be comprehended. The old hunger for knowledge filled her.

"And another thing," Aquila said, a warning note creeping into his voice. "Don't say anything about any of this to anyone else in this house. My father knows that I have been attending these meetings. He is very angry. He has forbidden me to go back."

"Forbidden you?" Priscilla's words were breathless with shock. "And still you do? Against your father's command?"

"This Jesus," Aquila said solemnly, "demands a commitment that is greater than obedience to an earthly father."

Excitement touched her for the first time. This was the kind of commitment she had been searching for all her life. She said nothing, however. She only got out of bed and said in a practical-sounding voice, "Come. We mustn't keep your father waiting."

The opportunity for Priscilla and Aquila to talk did not come at once. Before the Sabbath had ended, word came that Linia had fallen ill, devastated by her grief, and Priscilla had to go to care for her, because Flavia was still suffering from exhaustion herself.

Priscilla was torn by conflicting emotions. She was grateful to be the one on whom Linia leaned, but at the same time she regretted the fact that Aquila could not teach her as he had promised.

That the baptism had been postponed for several weeks, she knew, and that Aquila was defiantly attending Phineas's meetings, she knew. But beyond that, she knew nothing. It would not really be fitting for Aquila to come and stay with his wife's family, and yet she wished he would come. Linia was weak and listless, worn out by her weeping, and she went to bed very early each evening. *There would be time,* Priscilla thought, *for Aquila to sit with me in the atrium, and we could talk without being disturbed.*

Then, on the third day, Aquila appeared at the door.

"Did you come to take me home, my lord?" Priscilla asked.

Unexpectedly, she wanted nothing more than to fling herself in his arms, but her defiant remark about divorce stood between them like a wall.

"No," he said. "I have come to see if your grandmother would take me in."

She stood stupefied. "Take you in?"

"My father has told me to leave," Aquila said. The words were expressionless, but she felt certain that he was controlling his emotion with a tremendous effort. She realized that she was keeping him standing at the door, and at her gesture of invitation, he stepped inside and closed the door behind him.

"Why, my lord?" she begged. "Is it because of the new faith?"

"Yes, of course. Nothing else would make me defy my father. He won't listen to anything I say, he won't listen to anything anyone says. He just keeps saying that I'm a heretic and a blasphemer and that I must leave his house."

"But your mother," Priscilla protested. "What does your mother say?"

"My mother is an obedient wife, so she says nothing," Aquila said, but at Priscilla's look, he added, "She'll miss you, of course. She has learned to love you very much."

"You're not even baptized yet," Priscilla said.

"He knows I intend to be. I know I will be."

With or without me, Priscilla thought. She pulled Aquila into the atrium. "Let me talk to Grandmother," she said. "I know it will be all right, but let me talk to her."

Once inside the atrium, Aquila looked so bewildered that she could not resist putting her arms around him. "Don't grieve," she whispered. "We'll work it out, my love. Somehow we will."

He groaned and drew her close to him. "Everything has been so wonderful since we were married," he said into her hair. "I thought that my life was perfect. You, the baby coming, and now everything has fallen apart."

"Is he worth it, this Galilean you have chosen?" she asked.

Aquila did not answer for a second, but when he did his voice was strong and steady. "Yes," he said. "He is worth it."

She felt the shock of his conviction. "Then," she said, "then you must tell me all about him. But first let me talk to my grandmother."

Linia Justinius opened her villa and her heart to the two who had been dispossessed. "It will give me a reason to live," she assured Priscilla. "Aquila can become the man of the house, and I will live for the coming of the child."

For the next few weeks, she continued to seek the comfort of her own room as soon as the evening meal was finished, and Priscilla and Aquila took advantage of their new privacy to sit in the atrium and talk.

Aquila told the story of Jesus over and over, each time emphasizing a new aspect of his teachings. Several times he invited Phineas to come for discussion, and on those occasions, Priscilla was allowed to sit in a dim corner of the room to listen. During the time that Phineas was there, she was silent, but when she and Aquila were alone, she asked a hundred questions, and for the most part Aquila was willing to answer.

"Jesus had an unusual respect for women, didn't he?" Priscilla asked once. "I mean, He healed them and talked to them, and it was women who first claimed that the tomb was empty."

"I suppose so." Aquila was impatient. "That doesn't really matter. What matters is that He died for us and was raised again from the dead. What matters is that we, too, can look forward to eternal life. With Him."

She nodded. "Oh, I know, I know. I understand that. To think I might see my grandfather again—" Her voice trailed off. "Don't tell me that he had never been baptized," she begged. "He would have believed if he had been given the chance."

"He might have believed," Aquila conceded. "He asked me many questions and was never scornful."

Priscilla's mind churned. *If all that Aquila said is true, then surely Jesus would never have forced a son to leave home,* she thought with certainty. Jesus would never have ordered Sarah not to speak to her daughter-in-law again. Jesus would only have reached out in love. She turned to Aquila in sudden certainty.

"I'm ready, my lord," she said. "When you go to be baptized, I'll go with you."

Aquila face shone with joy. "Even with my poor teaching, you're willing?"

A new thought struck her. "My poor teaching," he had said. But it hadn't been poor teaching. It had been comprehensive and strong and moving. Her husband possessed at least a little of what her grandfather had possessed. She felt a wave of emotion that was stronger than any physical warmth she had ever known.

"If I had realized how wise you are," she admitted, "I might not have quarreled with your decision to be baptized."

"And I," he said, "if I had known all that I know now, I would never have been so angry."

They sat smiling at each other, and Priscilla was grateful for this moment of understanding. *For how do we know,* she thought, *what troubles lie ahead for us after we have been baptized? Maybe the entire Jehovite community will turn against us, and then what will we do?*

Aquila sat motionless in the synagogue. This Sabbath meeting had always been the high point of his week, the hour that had given meaning and substance to all the other hours. He wanted it to remain that way. Phineas had assured him that Jesus had gone to the synagogue every Sabbath, that he had come not to break the Law but to fulfill it. Aquila wanted to remain a faithful Jehovite as sincerely as he wanted to become a Follower of the Way.

But he was beginning to suspect that this would probably not be possible. It was obvious that those who believed what Phineas told them were sitting together on one side of the room while the rest, Reuben among them, were deliberately keeping themselves apart. There were no greetings between the two groups, no communication, no warmth.

It shouldn't be this way, Aquila thought with despair. *We should somehow love each other enough to be able to surmount this difference.* He glanced over at his father, willing the older man to look at him, but Reuben was facing away from his son. The back of his neck was stiff and rigid, and Aquila wondered if there could ever be warmth between them again.

True, Aquila was still permitted to work with his father. The prediction he had made to Joshua had been accurate enough. Reuben needed their help to keep his business going, but he never spoke a word to his son during the day. And necessary messages were delivered by Joshua.

"If I throw in my lot with the Galilean," Joshua had whispered one day, "your father will have to hire a boy just to carry messages."

Although Aquila had laughed, as Joshua had obviously intended he should, nothing eased the pain of his father's rejection.

I wonder, he thought now, staring at the back of his father's neck, *if he would have sent me away from his house if I had not had somewhere to go. He must have guessed that Priscilla's grandmother would take us in. How much of his anger is real, and how much of it is an act to convince himself?* Aquila wondered.

His glance moved away from his father and rested on Joshua, who seemed to be uneasy, sitting between the two groups of men. *He can't stay in the middle forever,* Aquila thought with a sense of compassion. *He'll have to decide one way or another.*

The time had come for the reading of the Scripture, and Cordelius stood to go to the front of the room.

Reuben pushed himself to his feet. "I refuse to sit and listen to a heretic read the Holy Scripture."

His voice was not loud but the intense silence that followed his words made it seem loud.

"My son is a believer in the Law. He is—" Cordelius's father began.

But Reuben interrupted: "Have you listened to the things your son has been listening to? Have you heard the claims that are being made? They are saying that this Jesus of Nazareth—a common criminal, if one is to judge from the manner of his death—is the Son of God."

His voice sank until the last words were almost a hiss. It was as though he were spitting out an obscenity.

A wave of protest came from the men who had been sitting with Cordelius, but Reuben ignored them.

"This is a place where those who follow the Law can come to worship. And we say this Jesus is a fraud and a blasphemer. Those who do not agree with us should leave.

Now!" Reuben's voice held such contempt and authority that no one answered him.

Aquila was the first one to stand and start toward the door. He looked in Priscilla's direction, and she stood up at once. She cast one quick, anguished glance at Sarah and Flavia, and then followed her husband from the room. One by one, the friends of Cordelius and Phineas followed.

"We can meet in my house," Phineas said as soon as they were outside. "We can hold our Sabbath worship there. Are there ten of us? If there are ten, there will be enough."

Aquila counted quickly. There were only nine men. He turned to report his count to Phineas when Joshua suddenly came out of the door.

"Are you with us?" Phineas asked.

Joshua nodded, his face wrinkled with distress. "I'm with you."

He looked back toward the room he had left, and Aquila knew that he was looking for his wife. Would she come out? And if she did not, what would Joshua do?

Kara was suddenly with them, but her eyes were angry. "What do you think you're doing?" she snapped at Joshua.

The wrinkles smoothed themselves out of his face, and a look of quiet relief replaced them. "I'll tell you soon enough," he said, and Aquila watched them fall into place with the others.

The ten men, with their wives and children, walked in silence to Phineas's home to begin again the reading of the Scripture. Following it there was a silence. This was the time for the rabbi to sit before the people and interpret some element of the Law. But they had no rabbi. After only a few seconds, Phineas pulled a stool so that he could sit facing his friends.

"He is risen," Phineas said.

"He is risen *indeed,*" the men exclaimed.

Immediately, any awkwardness or discomfort they had felt was gone, and they leaned forward eagerly to hear

Phineas tell once again the stories that the apostle Peter had told him.

"Well, it happened peacefully enough," Aquila said when he and Priscilla were alone that evening. "There was no angry shouting, no fighting."

"They wouldn't act like that on the Sabbath," Priscilla said.

"No, but they'd send their sons and their friends away without a blessing or a smile." His voice was heavy.

"Perhaps someday they'll come to understand. Perhaps they'll come to believe that the Messiah has really come. Just as Isaiah said he would. We can hope for that."

Aquila could not get used to the fact that they could talk of the sort of things he had previously spoken about only to other men, and for a second he looked at the floor, not wanting to meet her eyes. But when he looked up, she was smiling, the dimple flashing at the corner of her mouth, and Aquila felt his heart melt. He had thought, in his anger at her when she had defied him, that he might never feel about her again as he had felt when they were first married. He had been afraid that the softness and warmth and laughter might be erased forever, but he had been wrong.

In spite of the heavy talk they had shared, in spite of the hours they had spent in conversation, not touching, not smiling, she was as desirable as she had ever been.

He reached out his hand to her. "You're so lovely," he said. "You're the loveliest thing I know."

She came into his arms as lightly as down. He bent to her lips and for a few seconds, he permitted himself the sweetness of her kiss. Then he withdrew gently.

"We must prepare ourselves for the baptism," he said. "With prayer and abstinence. Are you willing?"

Her lips were parted, but it seemed she was in complete agreement with what he said.

The thought crossed Aquila's mind that Priscilla could be persuaded but she could not be forced. It was something he had not known before. Certainly his father had never suggested anything like that when he had spoken of the responsibilities of a husband. But perhaps Priscilla was nothing like Sarah. Perhaps women were as different from each other as men were. Not just in looks but in weaknesses and strengths. It was a new idea, and he would think of it further when he had time. For now, there was only prayer to be considered.

"Come," he said, and without a word, Priscilla followed him to their room and then knelt beside him as he lifted his heart to God.

The next morning was cloudy and a little chilly, but Priscilla was filled with such a fervor that she felt nothing but the flame in her heart. She had not even tried to make it clear to Aquila how moved she had been by the things that he and Phineas had taught her. Her first mild interest had grown and hardened into a solid conviction that filled her heart.

It's easier for me, she decided with honesty, *than for Aquila's parents. My family came later to a belief in God and the traditions, and so I am more open to the things I have heard about Jesus.*

For me, she thought, *there is no question at all. He has to be the only, true Son of God or He could not have healed as He did, He could not have said what He did. And then—the Resurrection. How can anyone hear of the many times His followers saw Him, spoke to Him, ate with Him—and not believe? Belief is easier than doubt.*

These thoughts and others like them winged through her mind as she stood on the riverbank waiting her turn to go into the water. The river was swift and muddy from spring rains, but Phineas had chosen a small cove for the baptism where the water was quiet and safe. New grass greened the riverbank, but Priscilla was aware only of the men who would lead the new converts into the water.

Aquila went first, and she watched him with eyes suddenly blurred with tears. *He has earned my respect during these recent weeks,* she thought. *He is not just a boy who can be gentle or loving or kind. He is a man with a mind and much courage. He may never really talk to me in quite the same way my grandfather did, but I am proud to be his wife.*

Aquila stood up, dripping, his eyes closed in prayer. It was not until he stepped onto the bank that he opened his eyes to look at Priscilla. And even then, his eyes were dazed and unfocused. *If he sees me at all,* Priscilla thought, *it is not as his wife.* His absorption impressed her far more than a look of personal affection would have done.

Then firm hands took Priscilla's arms and led her into the water. She heard the words spoken—the words that promised death to old sins and birth to new hope—and then the water closed over her head.

She was aware of nothing but a sort of singing in her head, and then she found herself standing on the bank, soaked, with Marta wrapping a warm, wool shawl about her.

"You mustn't get chilled," Marta whispered. "And don't let yourself get carried away by this thing. Religious fervor is all very well for men, but women have more important things to think about. You have to consider your baby."

Priscilla nodded, knowing that in a sense Marta was right. Women did have to touch solid earth and prepare meals and care for children. Only men could reach up to touch the stars.

But at the same time, she wondered if even Aquila could possibly have the same sense of conviction burning in his heart that she had. Certainly they could never discuss it, comparing their emotion as though it had substance and weight. Nevertheless, it was impossible for her to accept Marta's statement completely.

Of course the baby is important, Priscilla thought, *and already part of my life. But what has just happened to me is important, too.* She tried to smile reassuringly at Marta before she turned her head to look for Aquila. His eyes were clearer now, more focused, more familiar. His smile, sudden and warm, enfolded her like the comfort of Marta's shawl.

We have done this together, Priscilla exulted in her heart. *It's almost as though we were equals, companions. I'll never forget this moment,* she promised herself, *never, as long as I live.*

Some weeks after the baptism, Priscilla wandered slowly through the market, Dena at her heels, studying the displays of fruits and vegetables. It was the wrong time of year for grapes, and sometimes she thought she would give almost anything for a bunch of sweet, purple grapes with the bloom on them like a fine dust. There were a few berries and some early apples, and she supposed they would have to do. Among the vegetables, she found early onions and last year's beans. She would be glad when late summer brought a more abundant harvest, she thought dreamily, and rounded a corner of one of the stalls.

She found herself looking directly into Sarah's eyes.

"Mother," Priscilla gasped.

Sarah's eyes filled with instant tears and her glance went involuntarily to Priscilla's body, which was beginning to thicken slightly with a gentle swelling.

"Mother, how are you?" Priscilla begged.

But Sarah only shook her head and the tears fell across her cheeks. She turned as though to move away, but Priscilla spoke quickly.

"No, don't go," Priscilla said. "Listen, you don't have to talk to me. You can be obedient to your husband. But *my* husband has not forbidden me to speak to you. So, listen, and I'll tell you about your son and about—about the baby."

Sarah stood silently, and her tears flowed unchecked. Priscilla saw the frightened look on the faces of Doria and Tenia, who stood behind their mother, but she only glanced at them once and then looked back to her mother-in-law.

"He's fine," she said breathlessly. "Your son is fine. My grandmother has turned over her household accounts to him, and he serves her well. He grieves over his father's decision, of course, as do I, but he is well. And so is the child."

Sarah put out her hand and then drew it sharply back.

"When he's born," Priscilla went on, "I'll tell him about his grandmother and her goodness. Truly I will."

She wanted to say more, she wanted desperately for Sarah to have the courage to speak to her, but she realized soon enough that she was only making things harder for her mother-in-law.

Impulsively, she leaned forward and kissed Sarah's cheek. At once, Sarah's hand came up as though to scrub away the touch, but then her hand slowed and stopped and her fingers touched her cheek gently.

"Someday," Priscilla said fervently. "Someday we'll be able to be friends again. I feel it."

Sarah didn't smile, but the look she gave Priscilla was one of hope. She turned then and, followed by the silent girls, made her way across the market, away from Priscilla.

Dena, her rheumy eyes a little bewildered, looked at Priscilla.

"I know," Priscilla said. "I know how strange it must seem when you can remember how good she was to me that night you came to tell me about Grandfather. But terrible things happen to people when unfair decrees are passed."

Several hours later, staring at Aquila in horror, Priscilla remembered her words as though they had been prophecy. "Terrible things happen to people when unfair decrees are passed." But she had only been talking about a broken relationship between two women. What Aquila had just said would mean tragedy to hundreds of people. Surely he was wrong.

"Are you sure?" Distress tightened her voice. "Are you absolutely sure?"

"The decree was hung right by our shop. There are hundreds of them plastered all over the city. Anyone who can read knows what the decree says. And there's one thing to be said about us Hebrews, most of us can read." His voice was suddenly bitter.

"But to have to leave Rome," she cried, seeing anguish on her grandmother's face that must match her own. "For how long?"

"For as long as the Emperor Claudius decrees. For all I know, it could be forever."

She started to sob. "All Jehovites?" she asked brokenly.

"Probably not. Only Hebrew Jehovites."

"But why? Why?"

"Because of quarreling among ourselves, the decree said."

Anger touched her. "Who would have reported it? Who would have spied on us and gone to the emperor?"

Aquila shrugged, his eyes bleak and defeated. "It could have been anyone. The quarrel certainly wasn't private. And ours wasn't the only synagogue to be split by the new faith. It has happened all over Rome."

"It means I'll have to leave my parents. My grandmother." Priscilla ran to Linia and held her close. "It does mean that, doesn't it?"

"It means more than that," Aquila said. She had never heard his voice so grim. "It means that we will have to travel with my family—Hebrews traditionally travel in families. And I don't know which will be harder—to leave parents who love you, or to travel with parents who have come to hate you."

= 12 =

The summer sun beat down pitilessly on the column of people who made their way down the leg of the Via Appia that led from Capua to the port of Tarentum on the Mediterranean Sea. It was a fine road, paved with enormous, heavy cobbles, and there were always people walking or riding along it—merchants, pilgrims, soldiers, travelers, thieves. And outcasts. Claudius, and other emperors before him, had sent many groups of people from their cities, banishing them to other lands. It had happened so often that few curious glances were wasted on the company of Hebrews who made their way along the road. Some of them walked, a few—the very old or the very frail—rode in carriages pulled by horses. There had, after all, been money in the Hebrew community, and very little of it had been confiscated.

Priscilla walked listlessly, heavily, beside Marta. In the first refreshing coolness of early morning, they had talked eagerly, comparing their dreams for the children they carried, for Marta, too, was pregnant. But the sun was high now, and their conversation had dried up in the heat. It took all the energy they had just to place one foot in front of the other. They would ride later in the day if they got too weary, but both of them found the jolting of the carriages more distressing than the fatigue of walking.

Priscilla cast a swift look at Marta from under her lashes. The girl had admitted frankly that she felt none of the fervor that Priscilla felt for the teachings of Phineas, and yet she had come on this tragic journey without too much complaint. And she didn't have to come, Priscilla thought. Neither she nor Cordelius was obligated to leave home. Cordelius had chosen to be with his friends who shared his new faith, and Marta had seemed willing enough to accompany him.

If only, Priscilla thought with a wave of longing that was almost like physical pain, *if only my parents had felt the same. But my father has not really become a Follower of the Way. Not yet. He doesn't reject the idea, not the way Aquila's father does, but neither is he a true believer. And so it would have been foolish, I know, for him to even think of leaving Rome. I know that. Or my head knows it, but my heart breaks from loneliness.*

She remembered how she used to wake in the night when she was very small, crying out for her mother, and how Flavia had always come running, soothing the frightened little girl with her cool hands and her soft voice. *I wish I could call for her now,* Priscilla thought. *Sometimes I think I can't stand it.*

Marta spoke unexpectedly. "I should have studied the way you did. I should have learned history and languages, and how to write really well."

Priscilla made a sound of astonishment. "What an odd thing to say. Whatever made you think of it?"

Marta gestured at the land on either side of the road. "I was just thinking that I know absolutely nothing about this land we're going through, and I know practically no Greek. What am I going to do when we get to Athens? How am I going to talk to people? I don't even feel I can write a letter to my parents explaining what we're seeing, what we're doing, how we feel. I just feel—feel so stupid."

Priscilla smiled. "I've been thinking about many things as we've been walking along, but I certainly wasn't thinking about that. And yet—" Her voice slowed a little. "I understand what you mean. I have already written home, and my husband saw that the letter was put into the hands of traders traveling north. I just hadn't thought to be grateful for it."

"Of course," Marta said in self-defense, "everyone didn't have a grandfather who was able to teach them."

"No," Priscilla agreed, feeling the stab of loss she always felt when she thought of Marcus, "no, not everyone was so blessed."

"Is your grandmother alone? Did she stay on in her villa?"

"No, of course not. Not after we left. She and Dena went to my father's house. It was hard for her, but—"

"Did she sell the villa?"

Priscilla was grateful that Marta was willing to make the effort to keep up a conversation again. Time went by so much more swiftly if they talked as they walked. "No," she answered. "No, she didn't. She rented it, and my father will act as landlord. She—my grandmother—is hoping that someday Aquila and I will come back to Rome. That someday we will live in her house again."

Marta laughed, a short, rueful sound. "I hardly think it likely. By the time we get settled in Athens, by the time our husbands get a business established, it will be nearly time for our babies to be born. And, well, you know how it is. Dispersed people don't go home again."

"I know." Priscilla plodded slowly along, but her thoughts were suddenly firm and stubborn. "I'll go back some day," she said. "I will. Aquila and I will go back to Rome."

"Claudius doesn't have that short a memory," Marta argued.

"Shh!" Priscilla looked around. "Don't talk so loud. But sometimes he does change his mind. You know that. He says he's going to do one thing, and then he does exactly the opposite."

"Maybe." Marta's voice was gloomy. "But don't plan on it."

"Well, somehow it will happen," Priscilla promised. "Somehow, someday I will go back to Rome."

"You get so excited about things," Marta protested. "You take everything so hard."

Priscilla had the grace to laugh. "I suppose," she conceded. Her breath caught with a quick indrawn hiss.

"What is it?" Marta looked at her with concern.

"A pain," Priscilla said, stopping and touching her thickened body with anxious hands. "I had a pain."

"You should rest. Shall I signal for one of the carriages to stop?"

"No, I don't think I could stand the jolting. If I could just sit on the ground and rest." The pain had disappeared, but Priscilla was aware of a feeling of heaviness, of discomfort.

"Here," Marta took her arm and led her to a grassy place back from the edge of the road, away from the press of the people. "I'll find Aquila and tell him that you need him."

"Not Aquila," Priscilla said. "Men aren't supposed to—"

But Marta cut her off. "Don't be ridiculous. You're just having a pain in your side from so much walking. It has nothing to do with the baby. Wait here."

In a few minutes, Aquila was beside Priscilla, looking at her with anxiety in his eyes. "What is it?" he asked. "Are you all right?"

"Yes, it was Marta's idea to call you. I just had a pain. A sudden pain."

He squatted beside her so that he could see her face. "Is it the baby?" he asked.

"I don't think so. I don't—" But the pain came again, silencing her with its intensity.

Aquila said nothing. He only put his hand over hers and held her with comforting fingers. "I'll find someone," he said at last.

"You must go on," Priscilla said to Marta. "We're nearly to the harbor in Tarentum, and the ship is waiting. I heard them talking about it this morning. If we're not at the pier by late tomorrow, we won't be able to get on the ship

- *103* -

that is going to sail to Athens. You've got to go on."

Marta's face crumpled with distress. "I can't just leave you here," she protested.

"Don't be silly. There will be someone to take care of me."

But even as she said the words, Priscilla knew that Reuben would not allow his wife or daughters to stay with her. Nothing that had happened—the heartache, the frustration, the breaking up of the business—nothing had made him compassionate toward his son. Sarah and Priscilla were able to exchange glances of love when they happened to meet, but that was all.

Who then? Who would delay their journey for the sake of Aquila's wife? Was there no one?

As though her questions had conjured up the persons, Joshua and Kara were suddenly at Priscilla's side.

"What is it? What?" Joshua's voice was warm and anxious.

"I don't know," Priscilla gasped as pain wrenched her again. "I don't know."

Kara stared down at the girl and then knelt beside her to ask several questions in a soft tone of voice. When she heard Priscilla's answers, she stood up.

"This may be serious," she announced to Joshua. "Find your father," she commanded Aquila. "They are only a short distance in front of us. Tell him you need some of the supplies from his wagon. We need a tent, some skins for a bed, some bowls, some salt. Hurry. At once."

Aquila asked no questions; he only sped away, racing past the people who were trudging toward the sea.

"She needs privacy," Kara said to Joshua. "The wagons are coming now. If you recognize your brother's, halt it and take what we need. Don't wait for his permission."

"But—" Joshua began.

"Don't argue. Do as I say."

Priscilla listened with astonishment. She had never really had the chance to get acquainted with Kara. Things had moved too fast and too chaotically since that Sabbath when Joshua had chosen to join the Followers of the Way. The few brief encounters the women had had left Priscilla with the impression that Kara was angry and harsh, with no softness in her. But while her commands to Joshua were given with an air of authority that few women would dare to imitate, her hands on Priscilla's forehead were cool and light and gentle.

The next hour fled by in a blur of pain and confusion. Priscilla knew that Aquila came back, his face white with anger. She could not hear everything he said to his uncle but she caught enough to understand that Reuben had agreed to their taking the provisions but he had refused to let Sarah come back to help her daughter-in-law in spite of Sarah's tears and pleas.

Many people stopped to inquire if they could help, but when they heard that the problem was one that might delay their arrival at the ship they planned to take, they apologized and hurried down the road. Only Kara and Joshua stayed on, stubbornly ignoring Priscilla's and Aquila's urging to think of themselves.

"Here," Joshua said to Aquila. "Help me get this tent up. The women need to be inside. In case—" He did not finish the words. He merely bent his back to the task of erecting a tent.

Kara sat down and pillowed Priscilla's head on her lap. "Don't cry," she said, wiping Priscilla's tears with the end of her shawl. "The pains might stop. The baby may be all right. Don't cry."

But the tears would not stop. She was weeping for everything, Priscilla thought. She was weeping because her grandfather had died, and because she had been forced to leave her family and her home. She was weeping because Marta and the others were going to get on a ship tomorrow and head for Athens, and she had no idea in the world what would happen to Aquila and her. She was crying because Kara and Joshua had stayed with her, and because Reuben and Sarah had not. She was weeping because she might lose the baby.

"Oh, God, please, please," she whispered and gritted her teeth against a fresh onslaught of pain.

"The tent is ready," Joshua announced. "Come. It may be hot, but it will be private. And we've set it up in what little bit of shade there is."

"Can you walk?" Aquila asked, his face strained and pale.

"Of course she can walk," Kara said. "I've only kept her lying still to try to prevent the child from coming. But since the pains won't stop, we must get ready." She turned to Priscilla and her voice gentled. "Come, my dear. Here, lean on me. We'll put your feet up—bring something for a cushion, Aquila, and maybe—just maybe—"

Leaning heavily on Kara's arm, Priscilla went into the tent and gave herself up to pain and despair. What did God require of her? Hadn't she suffered enough? Was there no respite for her?

The hours passed by, and there was no longer the sound of people walking or wagons rumbling along the road.

"Is it getting dark?" she asked at last.

"Yes, dark," Kara answered. "But your husband even thought of a lamp when he was plundering the supplies." She laughed at her own choice of words. "Who would ever have thought that mild boy would become so fierce—grabbing everything he thought you might need or want, never even thinking of his father's anger or his mother's needs?"

"He shouldn't have," Priscilla whispered.

"Nonsense. Of course he should have. He should have kept the whole wagon."

Priscilla clutched Kara's hands. "I'm so frightened," she said. "I know I'm going to lose the baby. I know it."

"Yes. Probably." Kara's voice was very calm. "Women do lose their children. Sometimes before it is time for them to be born. Sometimes at birth. Sometimes when the children are grown. And every time the heart breaks."

"I thought if we accepted the truth about Jesus that He would take care of us. I thought—"

She stopped with a breathless sound and waited for the pain to pass.

Kara spoke slowly. "I don't know as much about Jesus as you do or as the men do. I'm only learning. But He also knew much pain, didn't He? I mean, He was rejected and beaten and crucified, and nothing could be worse than that. I don't think He promised anything easy. He only said He would be with us. Isn't that what He said? His spirit or something like that?"

Priscilla couldn't answer. The pain was suddenly grinding her into a mindless thing, gasping, reaching out in terror, feeling for Kara's hands. But Kara's words remained, cool and clear, in the middle of the pain. They were true.

"Oh, please!" Priscilla cried out.

It was all over. The child, bloody and much too small for life, had been delivered. Kara mercifully wrapped it in cloth and took it away to be buried. A boy, Kara said. It would have been a boy.

And she had nothing for her pain, Priscilla thought dully. No child to hold, no hope for the future. Her past had been ripped away from her, and now her future had been torn away, too. She was left alone and desolate.

Someone stood at the door of the tent. "May I come in?" Aquila said.

"I don't think it's proper," Priscilla managed to say.

Aquila came closer. "Nonsense. You are my wife and you've—" His voice broke. "You've had to suffer and now —oh, Priscilla, my love, please need me."

He was on his knees beside her, his face buried in his hands. His sobbing was ragged and bitter.

Until that minute, Priscilla had not thought of Aquila's grief. She had thought only of her own. But the lost child had been Aquila's son, too. And it was Aquila's father who had turned his back on them, so that Aquila was more rejected than she.

She lifted her heavy arms and drew Aquila's face down until his head rested on her shoulder.

"Oh, my dear," she whispered, "of course, I need you. I need you more than I have ever needed anyone in my whole life."

It was true, she thought. They needed each other. Neither of them had parents or sisters or brothers. They had only each other. And Joshua and Kara, she remembered gratefully.

When she could talk, she began to say a few words of comfort. "There will be other babies," she assured the weeping man beside her. "God will grant us other children. And we have Kara and Joshua, so we are not entirely without a family. It will work out."

"But the ship to Athens will be gone," Aquila said. "Kara says you can't be moved for some days. Fortunately, we have a tent, so we can live with some degree of privacy and comfort. But I don't know how we'll get to Athens."

The words were given to her. "Then we won't go to Athens," she said, making her voice strong. "We'll go somewhere else if necessary. We'll take passage on some other boat. We'll get along, we four. We will."

He sat back and his eyes were brighter. "You're so little to be so strong, so wise," he marveled. His voice slowed. "And I love you," he said.

He had never said the words before. He had said words of sweetness and passion but never those words.

Her eyes filled with tears. "And I," she whispered, shocked at her own daring, "I love you, my lord."

Their faces were stained with tears. They were young and frightened and bereaved. But their joined hands gave them a strength they had not expected to have.

We're not as alone as I had feared, Priscilla thought, remembering Kara's words. *We're not alone.*

⸗ 13 ⸗

Aquila stood on the pier in the harbor of Tarentum and stared about him with distaste. During the years he had been in Rome, he had forgotten the smell and chaos of a busy seaport. Now, the stink of the rotting refuse along the edges of the wharves, the sight of rats scurrying feverishly from ship to shore along the planks that served as walkways, and the sound of whips and cursing carried him back to the misery of the journey from Pontus to Rome. How could he have forgotten how terrified he had been, even though he had been nearly grown and his father had been there to stand between him and the horrors of the seafaring world?

How could he possibly bring Priscilla to this place? The thought of her was like a rawness in his heart. She was too small, too young, he thought, to have to have endured all that had happened to her lately. He could not even bear to name the losses. They overwhelmed him. It was true that he, too, had lost his home, his parents' love, his son. But he was a man, and men had been created for endurance. But Priscilla—

Deliberately, he pulled his mind away from her. He would only be undone by pity if he continued to think about her. He would think, instead, of the discussion that he and Joshua had had the day before when they had made the decision that Aquila should come to Tarentum to make arrangements for reaching Athens.

"Better you should go," Joshua had said. "You can walk faster than I and with less weariness. There are advantages in being young."

"But I hate to leave, to go so far and—"

"She'll be fine," Joshua said. "No one will harm her while I'm here to guard her and take care of her. Besides, no one would dare cross Kara. She could flatten an army with the whip of her tongue."

Aquila grinned. Joshua's sense of humor had already lightened the load of their misery. Reuben's shrewdness and strength could not buoy one up as Joshua's wit could, Aquila thought. Then, his face sobered.

"There may not be a ship to Athens for many days. We may not be able to catch up with the others."

Joshua shrugged. "Then we'll go somewhere else. We are a complete family, we four. You and I know enough about tent making to set ourselves up in business."

"We don't have enough tools. We don't have any hides or wool cloth."

"Don't be so sure." A wicked glint shone in Joshua's eyes. "When we were taking things from your father's wagon, I made sure your tools and mine were among them. We took enough skins for your wife's shelter and bed to make several small tents. When we get money for the first tents we sell, we can buy more skins and wool. The women can weave good strong cloth. We'll get along. You'll see."

"You didn't rob my father?" Aquila spoke slowly.

Joshua was indignant. "Would I do such a thing? Would I steal from my own brother? I took only what was mine, what was yours. I've given as many years to the business as Reuben has. I'm entitled to what I took."

"Then should I book passage on a ship that goes just anywhere?"

Joshua spoke judiciously. "Not just anywhere. It's better to go into Macedonia or Achaia. Don't you remember Phineas and the others saying that there were more Followers of the Way in Macedonia and Achaia than anywhere else yet? Try to find a ship that is sailing to one or the other, and then perhaps we can get on to Athens later. We may yet meet up with your father."

Aquila spoke bitterly. "And when we do he'll have one more reason to hate us. He'll say we took what belonged to him."

"We'll worry about that when the time comes. After all, we may not get to Athens for a long while. He may have forgotten by then."

Aquila suddenly took his uncle's arms in his hands. "You'll never know . . ." His voice broke and he had to clear his throat. "You'll never know how grateful I am that you and Kara stayed with us. I don't know what I would have done. I don't know what Priscilla would have done."

Joshua smiled. "My son is dead, and you and I share our faith. I could never have left you. And, besides, Kara wouldn't have permitted it."

Aquila had never decided whether or not his uncle was joking when he spoke of Kara's control over him. And yet it was true that when Kara spoke, most people paid attention. Aquila could remember how furious Reuben used to become when Sarah, after too much time around her sister-in-law, became too authoritative to suit her husband. Joshua, on the other hand, seemed to feel that anything Kara did was all right.

"Well, whether it was your idea or your wife's," Aquila said at last, "we're grateful, Priscilla and I."

"Never mind," Joshua answered. "Just go to Tarentum and book passage on a ship going to Macedonia or Achaia. We don't dare waste any more time. Priscilla is better, and the summer is passing all too swiftly. The only safe time to travel by sea is during the summer, so we must go soon."

"Yes, I know. Fortunately, the money for passage is still safe in the pouch I wear next to my skin. You have yours, too?"

Joshua nodded. "Safe. But in a pouch Kara wears next to *her* skin. Don't pay anything down to a stranger. Tell them you left the money with your family and you'll pay in full when we board the ship."

"I'll leave early in the morning," Aquila promised. "I

should be gone only two days. Three at the most. While I'm gone, you might investigate the possibility of getting a wagon for Priscilla to travel in. When you see one of the farmers going by with goods for market, ask if he goes to Tarentum regularly."

"Of course. I had already decided to do that. Everything will be ready when you return."

And now Aquila stood on the wharf, uncertain and miserable. Where should he turn? What should he do?

He suddenly remembered something Priscilla had said. "I'll be praying for you," she had promised. "I'll ask that the spirit of Jesus and the mercy of God will be with you." To his surprise, just the memory of the words brought a sense of comfort to him. For the first time, he could look around without feeling overwhelmed by panic.

His attention fastened on the movement of a man who strode along the wharf toward him. Tall and incredibly thin, the man wore only a dirty loincloth, but the expression on his face was certainly not that of the usual worker on the docks. There was none of the stupidity, cruelty, or cunning that Aquila associated with most sailors. This man's face was serene and kind, and his wide mouth was spread in a great grin above his straggly beard. His eyes were as blue as Priscilla's, and his hair and beard were a dirty shade of red. Aquila warmed toward the stranger.

The man stopped. "Can I help you? Are you looking for someone or something? I'm one of the hands on the *Fair Wind.* My name's Rufus."

Aquila grinned back. "I'm Aquila, from—" He nearly said "Rome," but bit it off and supplied "Pontus" instead.

Rufus raised his eyebrows. "A long way from home," was his only comment.

"I'm seeking to book passage on a ship," Aquila explained.

"Going where?"

"I had planned to go to Athens," Aquila said. "But we were delayed. My wife was—ill."

The blue eyes facing him softened with perceptible pity. It was almost as though the sailor sensed the loss, the pain. The two men moved to the edge of the wharf and sat together so that their legs hung over the edge.

Rufus spoke with regret. "I wish I could say we were going to Athens, but we're not going that far. We're only going as far as Corinth."

Aquila brightened. "But Corinth, that's in Macedonia, isn't it?"

"Not quite. It's in Achaia, south of Macedonia, on the neck of land that juts out into the sea. It might be possible for you to reach Athens at a later date, either by land or by sea, although the sea voyage is always risky."

Aquila was amazed at the fellow's knowledge. He was dressed like a common laborer and yet he spoke as though he had been educated and his face held that marvelous blend of warmth and serenity. Aquila knew he must be staring, but he realized that Rufus was also staring, probably trying to determine Aquila's background.

"And is your ship seaworthy?" Aquila pulled himself back to the subject at hand.

"Most of the time," Rufus said and grinned again. "Right now she's being repaired for a minor defect suffered when the captain brought her too close to one of the pilings in the harbor."

"How minor?"

"Minor," Rufus assured him. "She'll be ready to sail in a day or two. Are you in a hurry?"

As he was speaking, he leaned forward and appeared to be scribbling with his finger in the heavy dust that covered the planking of the wharves. He seemed to write aimlessly, then smooth the dust with his hands to make a sort of slate and write again. At first, Aquila paid no attention. Suddenly, he realized with a jolt of his heart that Rufus was drawing the same thing over and over, never looking at it, never drawing attention to it with any action. He was drawing the simple shape of a fish.

It would be a normal thing for a sailor to draw, Aquila thought. And yet, what had Phineas said, that the followers of Jesus were beginning to identify themselves with this drawing? But could this dirty sailor in a ragged loincloth be a believer?

Casually, Aquila smoothed the dust under his own hand and cautiously, almost carelessly, he, too, drew the stylized outline of a fish.

Rufus did not appear to take his eyes from Aquila's face, but no sooner had the small drawing been completed by Aquila's fingers than Rufus's face lit up.

"You're a Follower of the Way, then?" Rufus said without raising or changing his voice. "And a Hebrew, I'll wager. Banished from Rome."

"Yes," Aquila admitted, wondering if he were being foolish.

Rufus smiled. "He is risen," was all he said.

"He is risen indeed," Aquila answered and the two men clasped hands. Almost instantly, Rufus withdrew his hand, laced his fingers around his knees, and rocked back in a comfortable position. "Are there just you and your wife who want passage?"

"No, my uncle and his wife are also with us. We have money for passage. Not with me," he added hastily.

Rufus's eyes twinkled. "You're right not to trust anyone," he said. "When could you be ready to sail?"

"Are you sure there's room for us on the ship?"

This time Rufus laughed out loud. "I may look like a ruffian, but it's the only way a man can stand the heat of this place and escape from thieves at the same time. Nobody bothers a man who looks as I do. The captain of the *Fair Wind* is my brother. I'm the mate. There's room. And you'll be safe with us. You and your family."

"Your brother also believes?" Aquila asked.

Rufus nodded. "He believes. We were in the port of

Caesarea and heard the good news there. Could you be ready to sail the day after tomorrow?"

Aquila hesitated. "I could get back to my family by tonight if I am able to hire a horse. Then we could get here by noon of the day after tomorrow. If my uncle has been able to hire a wagon. My wife—my wife just lost a child. Born too soon."

Rufus's instant sympathy warmed his eyes. "May God grant you more sons," he said. "That's good enough—your plans, I mean. And don't worry if you're delayed. We could wait another day if necessary."

"Then I had better hurry," Aquila said and stood up.

"Wait," Rufus said. "Don't go until you've met my brother and seen the ship. Can you imagine what your uncle would say if you went back and reported that you had only talked to a sailor on one of the piers?"

Aquila felt his face grow warm. "I was so impressed when you said you were also a believer that nothing else seemed to matter."

"I can understand that, but your uncle might have trouble accepting it. Come, the *Fair Wind* lies down at the end of this wharf."

The little ship was no dirtier, no cleaner than any of the others that were docked at Tarentum, but the men who were working on her hull seemed less brutalized than other workers. Some of them whistled as they clung to the hull and struggled to repair the damaged area. And the captain, Rufus's brother Trolas, was warm and hospitable when Aquila came on board.

Furthermore, Trolas told Aquila where a horse could be obtained, and when Aquila finally found himself riding out of Tarentum back to the place he had left Priscilla and the others, he was filled with confidence and relief.

Aquila sat on the horse awkwardly, but he had been assured that it was gentle and biddable, and he had ridden several times before so he was not afraid. If Joshua had not found a wagon, he thought, perhaps they could load some of their goods on the horse and there might even be room for Priscilla to ride.

In a sort of euphoria, Aquila named his blessings. If they had been potters instead of tent makers, they would not have had shelter and privacy these painful days. If he had not met Rufus, who knows what might have happened to him at Tarentum. As it was, he had secured passage to Achaia, and he had learned that there might even be the possibility of meeting with the others in Athens in the future.

If, indeed, they wanted to, Aquila mused. After all, they had handled everything without Reuben. He and Joshua could continue handling everything. They were dependent on no one. Except God, Aquila added hastily. Except God and the spirit of His son. For it was God who had protected him and led him to the one man in Tarentum who was also a believer in Jesus, in the Messiah. Of this, Aquila had absolutely no doubt at all.

He was whistling when he caught his first glimpse of the tent that sheltered Priscilla and Kara. And his whistling soared in glad astonishment when he saw that a wagon had been pulled in close to the tent, and a burly farmer sat talking to Joshua.

"Ho, nephew," Joshua called at once. "You're back just in time. Our friend here had agreed to wait until dawn tomorrow but no longer."

At Joshua's words, Priscilla and Kara came hurrying from behind the tent where they had evidently been resting in the shade.

Priscilla stood decorously, properly, a few steps behind Kara, but Aquila saw the gladness in her eyes.

"Everything is taken care of," Aquila announced. "We have passage booked to Corinth. If we still want to go to Athens, we may be able to get there later."

"But guaranteed passage to Corinth?" Joshua asked.

"Guaranteed. On a ship called the *Fair Wind.*" His eyes

met his wife's. "We'll take it as an omen—the name of the ship. We have had very rough sailing for a long time now. Perhaps a *Fair Wind* will augur a brighter future."

Kara frowned. "Such fancy talk," she said.

But Priscilla turned to put her arms around the older woman and hug her. Aquila knew, without being told, that Priscilla simply had to hug someone. Since she could not reach out to her husband in front of everyone, she had to turn to Kara. He knew, without words, what Priscilla was feeling, and he gloated to himself as he climbed stiffly from his mount. He and Priscilla were sharing something without words or even a gesture. It was a heady feeling.

"But good fancy talk," Priscilla was saying, her voice trembling with laughter and relief. "Admit it, Kara. Admit it."

Aquila looked at them in time to see the softening of Kara's eyes as she returned Priscilla's hug. So—Priscilla had won another heart. *She is a persuader,* Aquila thought with pride, *a winner of hearts. And she's mine.*

He tried to hide his fondness with heartiness. "Well, then," he said. "Let's get everything ready so that we can leave at the first hint of dawn. Can the women sleep in the wagon tonight?" he asked the farmer, and at the man's nod he turned to Priscilla. "See, little one," he said. "Everything will be fine."

She nodded smilingly. "I'm glad you booked passage to Corinth," she said, her voice still breathless. "I have always loved the sound of the name. I have a feeling—I don't know why—that we will do well in Corinth. You have done everything exactly right, my lord."

He had never expected to be truly happy again. During these past weeks of loss and pain, Aquila had thought that misery would be a permanent part of his life. But now, smiling at his wife in the late afternoon light, he knew he had been wrong. Contentment was still possible for them. He turned to tether the horse to a tree, and his clear, bird-like whistle wove a pattern of hope in the sunlit afternoon.

= 14 =

Priscilla was completely exhausted by the time the small wagon reached the harbor of Tarentum. Although Aquila had spoken frankly to all of them about the odors and filth of the seaport, she was still shocked at what she saw and smelled and heard. Standing on the pier as the men unloaded the wagon, she thought longingly of the swept yard around her grandmother's villa, of the wide vista of hills pushing against the sky over Rome. Would she ever see anything like that again, she thought achingly, or would there be only dirty seaports and strange towns with their stranger people?

For example, the man Rufus, who stood talking to her husband, was not at all what she had expected. Aquila had been so enthusiastic about him that she had expected a man of elegance and culture. Here, instead, was only a lanky, dirty laborer dressed in a ragged loincloth. Trolas looked a little better but not much, and she could only hope that their disreputable appearance was no indication of their competence as seamen.

Aquila hurried up to her. "Good news!" he announced. "Rufus says that the Etesian wind has started to blow, so we will be able to leave at once. I was afraid we might have to wait a day or even two. I'll pay the farmer, and then I can get you settled on board the *Fair Wind.*"

Priscilla longed to retort that as far as she could see the only thing "fair" about the ship was the name, but she bit back the words. *I'm tired,* she told herself, *and everything seems worse than it really is. Somehow I must keep myself from becoming a whining, complaining woman.*

Kara evidently had no such qualms. She stood beside Priscilla and stared in horror at the little ship and at the dock area around them. "A pig sty," she declared, and the tone of her voice indicated how strong her condemnation was. "What's more, I know I'll be seasick. Every minute of the trip."

Priscilla did not have the energy to contradict her, and besides it was not necessary to pretend to be courageous in front of Kara. "I, too," she agreed. "I've never sailed but I've heard what it can be like and considering how I've been feeling lately, well—" She turned to Kara in despair. "What will we do?" she cried.

"Well, we probably won't die," Kara answered. "More's the pity. Here comes your husband now. I hope he didn't give that farmer too much money."

"Only what the trip was worth," Priscilla said. "You know I would never have got here if we hadn't found the farmer."

"Oh, I know, I know," Kara grumbled. "Are we to go aboard now?"

"Yes, my husband says the ship will set sail at once. I don't know whether to applaud or weep," Priscilla admitted.

They turned to see Aquila approaching them, but before he could reach them, one of the men hailed him and he stopped for a moment. Kara took advantage of the interruption to speak in suddenly urgent tones.

"One thing I want to say before we leave," she said. "I am not as knowledgeable as the men, nor, for that matter, as you are. But when I believe something, I believe it with all my heart. I didn't become a Follower of the Way because my husband insisted on it. I listened to what was said about this Jesus, and I know that what is being said is true. He *is* Lord."

Priscilla waited, not saying anything, but her heart was beating faster. She had never expected to hear anything like this from Kara.

"So," Kara went on, "if He is truly Lord, and if we have chosen to follow Him, then we must be in His care. Doesn't that make sense?"

Priscilla nodded but continued to remain silent. It was important to know what Kara was leading up to.

"So we can trust Him," Kara finished. "We can believe that he led your husband to this particular ship for a reason. We may not know the reason, and we may not like this journey or where it leads. But we can trust Him."

Priscilla only had time to whisper, "Oh, thank you, Kara. I needed desperately to hear that," before Aquila spoke at her shoulder.

"Come," he said, "the men are ready to cast off. See, there at the far end of the deck is a shelter built of wool cloth. It has been prepared for you two, Rufus tells me. Unless, of course, a storm should come up and you'd have to go below deck."

Priscilla shuddered. "If we can be out in the air," she said, "it will be better."

"Joshua and I will be close by," Aquila said, "so you'll be safe."

"Then we won't be afraid," Priscilla promised him and, putting her hand under Kara's elbow, helped the older woman climb the steep walkway to the deck of the ship.

Almost instantly, she heard the shouts to cast off, and in only a few minutes, the ship began to nose its way out through the harbor and away from the pier. With a heart that ached in spite of Kara's words of faith and Aquila's promise of protection, Priscilla watched the land diminish and disappear. *I will come back,* she said fiercely to herself. *No matter what happens, someday I will see this land again. Someday I will go back to Rome! Until then—well, until then I will simply do what I have to do.* She deliberately turned her back to the disappearing shore and faced the unknown sea that stretched before her, grateful that she had been given the courage not to weep.

Kara's predictions that she would be seasick were all too accurate, and Priscilla gave what solace and help she could to the older woman. Amazingly enough, Priscilla discovered that she herself did not get seasick. The fresh Etesian wind that had started to blow the day they left Tarentum had stayed strong and steady, and she found the brush of it against her face invigorating and the movement of the ship exhilarating. When Kara slept, Priscilla went out onto the open deck, sat in a patch of shade cast by the little shelter, and lifted her face to the wind. She might have been restless, she admitted, if she were not still so tired and so weak. As it was, however, she welcomed the chance to sit quietly, to let her mind rove over all that had happened to her in recent months.

Sometimes she named her griefs like a litany, like dark beads on a chain of tears. Then, in spite of all the promises she had made to herself that she would not weep again, she would feel tears sliding down her cheeks. Once, feeling the wind dry her face, she told herself that it was God's hand wiping the tears away. She knew she was being whimsical, perhaps even childish, but the thought was a comforting one anyhow.

But sometimes she was able to put grief behind her and to name her blessings. She always began with Aquila. How providential that she had been given the wisdom to marry him! Once the treacherous thought came that none of the things she was going through now would have happened to her if she had married a Roman. But the thought had no substance, and she banished it in an instant. There were other blessings, too. Kara and Joshua, of course, and the slow return to health, the beauty of the wind-swept, sun-spangled sea, and the memories that thronged her mind. She had only to conjure up a picture of her grandfather's face and she could instantly remember things he had taught her. Not only technical things like Greek and history, but lines of poetry that he had made her memorize. In recent

- *121* -

years he had insisted that she commit to memory many portions of the Jehovite Scripture. The two of them had delighted in the majestic, sonorous rhythm of the songs of King David, and her grandfather had said that no one had ever penned his praise of God in more beautiful words.

She sat one morning, after seeing Kara fall into an exhausted sleep, and felt the wind caress her face while she thought of portions of Scripture that might speak to her heart. She thought of her grandfather's scrolls, which they had managed to bring from Rome, and marveled anew that even in the panic of her going unexpectedly into labor, Aquila had rescued them from his father's wagon of goods. They were safely wrapped and stowed away in the hold of the ship, but someday they would be available for reading again. In the meantime, there were the memorized words. She whispered the first ones that came to mind:

I will bless the Lord at all times;
His praise shall continually be in my mouth.
My soul shall make its boast in the Lord;
The humble shall hear it and rejoice.
Oh magnify the Lord with me,
And let us exalt His name together.

Odd words to come to one sitting alone, she thought. Her grandfather and she had always said the words together. Some parts of worship should be done in the company of someone else. But that was certainly not a new thought. Wasn't that the basis for people gathering together to think about God?

Her mind delighted in this sort of thinking, and yet she needed another ear to hear, another mouth to answer, she thought with a sudden sense of aloneness. She had hardly formulated the thought when she heard a sandal scraping on the deck directly behind her. None of the sailors on the ship ever approached the area where she and Kara stayed, so she knew it must be either Aquila or Joshua. She turned with a slight quickening of her heart and saw Aquila smiling at her.

"Good morning," he said. "Are you well? Have you had anything to eat? Joshua and I have been watching some men catching fish, and I'm late coming to check on you."

She smiled in return. "I'm fine, and I've had some bread and water. Poor Kara finds it impossible to eat anything, and I feel so sorry for her. I always eat out of her sight so I won't distress her."

He sat down on the edge of the mat beside her and yet not too close to her. His face was ruddy from the sun, and his eyes were clear and warm. The pain and distress that had been on his face for so many weeks had been temporarily banished by the pleasure of seeing the men bring in fish from the sea.

"Are the fish fit to eat?" she asked.

"Indeed. We'll have fresh fish for our next meal."

They sat for a few minutes just smiling at each other. Such a silly little thing to be happy about, Priscilla thought. Fresh fish. Then she remembered the words of Scripture she had been quoting and her wish for a companion. Now here was Aquila. She had never thought of a husband as a companion, a friend. Only as a husband. But Aquila was more welcome, she thought, than Marta would have been.

Something must have shown in her eyes, because Aquila spoke softly. "You are so lovely. What have you been thinking as you sat here?"

She almost said, "I've been thinking about you," but instead she said, "I've been quoting some Scripture my grandfather made me memorize once."

She rarely ever mentioned anything she had learned from her grandfather, and for a minute she expected him to say, "Why would a woman do that?" but evidently the thought never even crossed his mind because he said, "What portion of Scripture?"

"One of King David's songs," she answered, and she began to say the words again.

He looked away from her, but he recited the words with her and their voices wove a tapestry of sound in the morning air. They sat silently together, then, and she felt a closeness to him that was as complete, as sweet in its own way as any touch of love.

Finally Aquila spoke. "Oh, I have good news for you. At least I hope you will think it good news. Trolas says that since the wind has continued fair, we will be in Corinth sooner than he had anticipated. We should be there tomorrow."

Her heart jolted with the unexpectedness of it. "Tomorrow?" she asked. "So soon?"

"I thought you'd be happy to get off this ship."

"Oh, I am. For Kara's sake especially. I said what I did because—well, because I guess I'm frightened. I've never been in a foreign country before, and I'm not sure I'll know what to do."

He nodded. "I understand. I remember how frightened I was when we went to Rome from Pontus. Everything was strange—the food, the customs, the buildings. But the strangeness passes. Truly."

She only shook her head, not much comforted by his words. "But what will we do?" she asked. "I mean, when we get off the ship, what will we do?"

"Rufus tells me that there is a fairly large group of Followers of the Way in Corinth. Maybe fifty or more, he says. So he has suggested that we seek them out first and get acquainted. Then, unless there is already a tent-making establishment, Joshua and I will set ourselves up in business. Rufus doesn't remember any tent makers, but I suppose he could be mistaken."

"You have a lot of respect for him, don't you?" she asked, thinking of the man's scruffy appearance.

"A great deal of respect," Aquila answered. "He's intelligent and wise, and he has a faith that I'd do well to achieve."

"I've been wondering," she said slowly, not sure she dared ask the question that had been bothering her. She glanced at Aquila and seeing the kindness on his face, she decided to risk it. "You've spent hours talking to this man and to his brother. They heard about Jesus in Caesarea, you say. And you heard about him in Rome. Neither of you heard the story from one of Jesus's apostles. Were there discrepancies?"

"Minor differences," Aquila conceded. "Such as would occur when any two men reported on an incident they'd seen. But in the major points, there is the most remarkable similarity. It's odd that you should bring this up." He stopped and grinned at her. "I still find it difficult to believe that I can talk to a girl as I am talking to you."

"Think of me as a man, then," she suggested.

His laugh was quick and hearty. "Believe me, little one, it's a lot harder to think of you as a man."

He touched her cheek lightly, but she felt the touch shiver through her body. She had wondered after the devastation of losing the baby if she could ever feel desire for her husband again. His touch answered her question eloquently.

"Well, then, just think of me as an unusual woman," she said, but she felt the warmth in her cheeks and she knew perfectly well that her eyes were as bright as his.

"I'll try," he said and then paused. "What were we talking about?"

"About the similarities or differences in the stories you and Rufus shared."

"Oh, yes. Well, as I said, it's odd that you should bring that up. We were talking of it only yesterday. About the need for some kind of authority. Either some teacher who could be utterly trusted or some written account that no one could doubt."

"I think," she began and then hesitated. "Is it all right, my lord, if I tell you what I really think?"

"Don't call me 'my lord' in our room," he said out of habit and then laughed a little. "It isn't our room exactly, is it?"

"Will we ever have a room again?" she asked wistfully.

"Not right away," he said. "We'll be very poor. It's very likely that we'll have to live in a tent until we get established. Could you stand that, do you think?"

She met his eyes bravely. "All of us, you mean? Joshua and Kara and you and I? In one tent?"

"Never," he said. "That's one reason I'm willing to settle for a tent. As tent makers, surely we can have our own room. Our own tent."

"Then," she said and looked away, "then I'll be able to endure living in a tent."

He reached out as though to touch her again and then dropped his hand as one of the sailors walked by. "You were going to tell me what you really thought," Aquila said, his voice a little rough.

She, too, had trouble keeping her voice steady and she had to force her mind back to the subject they had been discussing.

"About an authority," he reminded her.

"Oh, yes. Well, I believe as Kara does that we are in the Lord's care. That's not to say we won't have trouble, but we will be led in some way. Maybe that's why the stories are so much alike. Maybe God protects us, somehow, from false accounts. Oh, maybe there will be false accounts, but if we pray, we may never be tempted to believe them."

"That's more or less what Rufus believes," Aquila said. "He says that if Jesus is indeed the Messiah, God will prevent the truth from being lost."

She nodded without speaking and after a few seconds Aquila spoke again.

"Kara, you said? Kara has a belief like that? I would never have thought Kara—"

"You would never have thought any woman had such a faith," she said, but there was no criticism in her voice. "You are forced into a situation, my lord, where you either have to change some of the ideas that have been planted in you all your life or you will be miserable. I mean, you are stuck with a wife who, well, who is different."

Aquila didn't answer for a few seconds, and she knew he was taking her words seriously. When he spoke at last, his words were deliberate and strong. "Then I will change my ideas. Or some of them at least. But you mustn't expect me to do it all at once or ever admit to my friends that I have done it."

"It doesn't matter to me what you say to your friends or how you act around them," she said. "I will be more than satisfied to have your confidence and your approval when we are alone together."

A retching sound from the shelter brought Priscilla to her feet. "It's Kara," she said. "She needs me."

"Tell her it's only one more day," Aquila said. "Only one more day until she can put her feet on dry land." His voice dropped lower. "One more day, my love, until you and I can set up our tent and be alone."

She only nodded, but as she hurried past him to enter the shelter, she allowed her hand to brush against his face. His beard was rough and crisp under her fingers, and when he turned his head she felt his lips against her hand.

Her heart was almost buoyant as she went in to help Kara. Even the thought of Corinth was not as terrifying as it had been. Together, she and Aquila would manage to survive.

= 15 =

Aquila sat cross-legged on a woolen mat in the small dirt yard that served as the working area for the business he and Joshua had established in Corinth. He had pegged a goat skin to a sort of rude frame that kept it taut, and he was scraping it carefully to remove hair and imperfections. He used the sharp scraper with a skill and economy of motion that spoke of long practice. As a result, his mind was free to wander over the months since the day they had stepped, frightened and confused, off the *Fair Wind.* It was hard to believe that a fall, a winter, and a spring had gone by since that day, and yet so much had happened that it sometimes seemed that several years should have passed. *Does Joshua feel the same?* Aquila wondered and looked across the yard to where his uncle was sitting with several skins in his lap. Joshua's exasperated exhalations of breath as he tried to force the curved needle through several thicknesses of skins formed a sort of background to the regular thump of the thrown shuttle on the looms inside the building, where Kara and Priscilla were weaving lengths of heavy wool for tent material.

At least, Aquila reflected with a shade of complacency, *we are no longer living in tents at the mercy of the weather. At least my uncle and I were able to rent a few rooms to serve as a shop and to provide a home for our women. And we have made a few friends. How else,* he admitted, glancing behind him at the square, heavy, stone building that held a dozen apartments and as many shops, *would we have been able to find this place to rent? If Rufus hadn't introduced us to Titius, who had a little influence—*

Joshua got awkwardly to his feet and came closer to his nephew. "The needle broke," he said. "We need metal ones for this work on skins. The bone ones are all very well for the wool cloth, but they are not strong enough for what I'm doing."

"I know," Aquila said. "I've been meaning to go into the market place to look for them. But they're hard to find and so expensive. Besides, the last time Rufus and Trolas were here, we asked them to get us some. They should be arriving any day now, and I had hoped we could wait till they came."

"Well, there are several more bone needles," Joshua said. "I guess I'll have to try to make do." He lowered himself gingerly until he was sitting beside Aquila. "I've been wanting to talk to you," he confided. "I don't know, we never seem to have any time together, just the two of us. There are either the women—it isn't like it was in Rome, when they had other interests and other family members to occupy their time—or customers or men from the synagogue. Never just the two of us."

Aquila smiled. "Seems incredible, since we live together in a small place, but I know what you mean. Did you have something particular troubling you?"

"I'm troubled about a great many things," Joshua admitted. "I'm not at all sure that we've chosen the right place to settle." He looked around him and lowered his voice still more. "This is a wicked city, this Corinth. Oh, it's beautiful and rich and has as many marvels, in its way, as Rome does. But Rome didn't have the evils Corinth has. Or at least I wasn't aware of them if it did."

Aquila nodded and his face was as somber as his uncle's. "I understand what you mean. Priscilla gets very bitter over the fact that all women have to go veiled in the streets if they want to appear virtuous. It wasn't like that in Rome. She reminds me frequently."

Joshua gave a little snort of laughter. "Priscilla! You should hear Kara when we are alone in our room at night.

I tell you, my boy, it's fortunate that this place we found to live in has three rooms so each of us can be alone at night. If Kara couldn't pour out her irritation and frustration on me, I think she'd burst!"

Aquila raised his eyebrows. "I'm surprised that our presence would prevent her from saying what she wanted to say. That is, I mean—" He stopped, embarrassed.

But Joshua was not offended. "Don't worry, I know what you're trying to say. Discretion is not Kara's strongest virtue. But you have to understand how she feels about Priscilla. I don't think she even loved our own son the way she loves Priscilla. So she doesn't want to say anything that will upset her. Now that there is another child on the way—"

Aquila nodded. He remembered the way he had capered down the street in Rome so many months before, carefree, careless, unaware of sorrow or tragedy, wanting to knock on doors and announce that he was going to be a father. He didn't feel that way this time. Now he was all too knowledgeable about loss and loneliness and the fragility of hope.

"I know," Aquila said. "I guess I feel the same. I am afraid to talk to Priscilla about anything grievous or even too serious for fear I will cause her distress. She complains about that, too," he added gloomily. "She reminds me that once we talked of heavy things and shared many thoughts. Women are strange. They don't understand their own weaknesses or how a man feels."

"I don't suppose they were created to be understanding," Joshua said. "On the other hand, they weren't really created to be the way Kara is either—or Priscilla for that matter. We were unusually blessed, my boy, to have married such—well, such extraordinary women."

He was whispering so that the sound of his words would not carry into the room where Kara and Priscilla were sitting, and although his words were somber, his eyes were twinkling. "But this doesn't change the fact that maybe we ought to think of going somewhere else," Joshua went on after a few seconds of silence.

"Where? How?" Aquila asked, looking up from the skin he was scraping.

Joshua shrugged. "I don't know how. By ship, I suppose, since summer is safer for sailing. Certainly the land is too rough for the women to ever cross. Kara could never get up over some of these mountains."

Aquila swallowed the quick irritation he felt and did not answer until he was sure his voice was level and calm. "Come, Uncle," he said at last, "we've discussed this before, you and I. And now, surely you must know that I can't take Priscilla away from here until after the child is born. I couldn't take that risk. Not for her, not for me."

"Oh, I know, I know. I knew what you'd say before you said it. It's just that I have to be able to tell Kara at night that I've discussed it with you. Then she'll know I'm not ignoring her complaints."

"You mean, Kara wants to leave?"

"Hardly. She is as concerned about Priscilla as you are. But she just has to complain, and she has to know that I listen to her complaints and try to do something about it. To tell the truth, I think what she really wants me to do is to change Corinth. To make it a city of saints. To force them to stop selling meat that's been used for pagan sacrifice, so the market will have only decent products to sell. To abolish prostitution and wild drinking. I think she believes that she could do it if I would only give her the permission to try."

"Maybe she could," Aquila said and joined his uncle's laughter. Then his face sobered. "Nevertheless, it's what we should be doing. All of us. We Jehovites who understand decency and morality, and we Followers of the Way, who have the Holy Spirit to guide and direct us."

"What could we do?" Joshua asked. "We are so few in a city that is so big. How could we change anything?"

"I don't know," Aquila said. "But I know we should be doing it. Somehow we should."

Joshua laughed and lumbered to his feet. "Oh, I agree. I couldn't agree more. We should probably be turning the world upside down. But in the meantime I have to go and find another needle."

Joshua disappeared through the doorway, and Aquila turned back to his work. But before he could begin the task of scraping, he let his eyes lift to the high, rocky hills that reared against the blazing summer sky. A temple to Aphrodite topped the stark, stony heights, and even strangers in the city knew of the wicked orgies that took place within those walls. Joshua was right. Corinth was indeed a wicked city, but how could they even think of leaving? Their business was going well, they were secure in their small rooms, they had friends in the synagogue, and there was a baby coming. With so much that was good, a man had no right to complain.

"Ho, Aquila, my friend!" The hail came in a well-remembered voice, and Aquila looked toward the street in quick excitement.

"Rufus! We've been looking for you but hardly dared hope you would arrive so soon."

"The winds were fair. After five or six journeys when I thought we would never put foot on land again, we came this time with as much ease and pleasure as the time we brought you from Tarentum."

The two men met in the middle of the yard, clasping hands warmly and grinning at each other with affection.

"Will you be here a few days?" Aquila asked. "Are we going to have the pleasure of your presence for a while?"

"Not for long," Rufus said. "My brother has a load of goods due in Athens, and the journey around the southern tip of Achaia is never a pleasant one, even now in midsummer. But listen, my friend, I have something I must discuss with you."

"Even before you greet the family?"

"Well, I suppose that would be a little foolish. Only, before we go in, let me say quickly that if it's possible for you to walk down toward the ship with me later, just the two of us, I'd like to discuss something with you."

"That can easily be arranged. But, come in, come in, my friend. It's good to have you here again."

They stepped inside the long, narrow room that fronted on the street. There were two looms in the room, and Kara and Priscilla each sat before one, weaving heavy, grayish yarn into thick, solid cloth for tent making. Both women looked up and, seeing Rufus behind Aquila, dropped their shuttles and stood up to greet him.

"So you are safely in harbor again?" Kara said. "I bid you welcome to the land and to our home. Were the seas as horrible as they were when I sailed with you?"

Rufus grinned. "I thank you for your welcome, and I answer your question as I have each time I have come. If the seas were always as mild as they were when you were with us, I would never worry about reaching port. In fact, Mistress, I sometimes think we should carry you with us on every journey, trusting that you would bring calm seas and good winds with you."

Kara only laughed. "I would sooner die," she said.

Priscilla smiled. "I, too, bid you welcome and hope as I always do that you might have brought word from some of our family or friends who sailed to Athens. Have you been there recently?"

"We go there next," Rufus said. "But I do bring you a letter, Mistress. I have carried it next to my skin for weeks now, lest it get lost."

He reached into the front of his tunic and brought out a flat package wrapped in oiled cloth. He held it out to Priscilla, and she reached for it with a glad cry.

"It carried her inscription," Rufus said with an apologetic look at Aquila. "From her father, I think."

He still thinks it strange that all letters are not for me or Joshua, Aquila thought. *And I can't admit to him that she is the writer of letters in this family, that neither Joshua nor I have her gift with words nor her desire to communicate. He would think that I spoiled her or that I was foolishly permissive. Well, it's probably true, but what I do is my own business, and as long as she is docile in other things—*

Priscilla held her letter close to her body, and Aquila saw that Rufus involuntarily glanced at the swollen abdomen that announced so clearly the coming of the child.

"As you have probably noticed," Aquila said casually, "my wife is with child. So she is easily excited. Suppose we leave her to her letter, and I'll walk along a way with you."

"Excellent," Rufus said, averting his eyes from Priscilla. "Will you tell your husband that I have new needles for him?" he added to Kara. "And other things he ordered. Perhaps he will come down to the ship. We'll be lying at the pier for a few days."

"Of course," Kara answered. "I'll tell him." Her voice was cordial enough, but it was obvious that her mind was not on the men or on the conversation. She was watching Priscilla, only concerned with the way the girl was reacting to the letter she was clutching against her.

"They'll never even notice that we're leaving," Aquila muttered to Rufus as they turned to leave.

"A good thing," Rufus answered. "Then you will be free to stay away as long as you like."

"I wish it were so," Aquila said. "It would be good just to sit and talk to you and your brother as we did when we sailed with you. But when a man has a business—" He let the words drop, knowing perfectly well that Rufus would understand. "But you said you had something to discuss with me. Is there something wrong? Some trouble?"

"No, nothing. But I met someone today when we landed. Someone we have met a time or two in our travels. A man who is—well, I don't quite know how to say it. A man of such faith, such fire, such—" He groped futilely for words.

"And you want me to meet him? To hear him? You speak of his faith. He is a Jehovite? A believer in Jesus?"

"He is a Jehovite, a Hebrew, and a believer in Jesus. But I want you to do more than just meet him or hear him. I want you to help him."

"Well, we owe a debt to you," Aquila said quickly. "But are you sure that we're the people who can help? We don't have very much room, or much influence. We can't do the sort of thing that Titius did for us, for instance."

Rufus smiled. "You have something this man needs. He's a tent maker, as you are. He needs to work with his hands. He's tired and discouraged to the point that he looks as though he is sick, but I think he needs the kind of healing a doctor can't give. He needs to work at a familiar craft."

Aquila's voice was guarded. "Ours is a small business. We certainly couldn't offer a very large wage."

"He doesn't need a large wage. He has a genius for taking care of himself. No, that's not true. God takes care of him."

"Who is he?" Aquila asked.

Rufus looked sideways at Aquila. "His name is Paul. Paul from Tarsus, and he considers himself an apostle of Jesus."

"An apostle? You mean he was one of those who followed Jesus? He has met the Lord face to face?" Aquila's excitement was evident in his voice.

"In a way. Paul says he met the Lord, but it was a long time after the Crucifixion."

"How long? You mean, longer than—well, you mean before the Ascension or—or after it?"

"After it."

The two men were quiet. They walked a little way without speaking, hardly aware of the people who jostled against them in the street, the shouting of vendors, the chanting of priests, the bells that called from the temples.

Only when a small, shaven priest pushed against them, whispering of the charms of the temple prostitutes, extending greedy palms for anticipated coins, did they pull themselves out of their silence.

"We're not interested in your filthy religious practices," Aquila snapped. "Get away from us."

Rufus grimaced. "It hasn't been so long," he said humbly, "since I would have paid dearly for his wares. That was before I heard the good news. And you see, this Paul I'm telling you about is a preacher, a spreader of this good news. He has changed hundreds of hearts. Corinth needs him. If I could tell him that I know a family who would take him in—"

"I would have to talk to my uncle," Aquila said. He had almost said "to my wife" and had caught himself just in time.

"But would you do it? Talk to him?"

"Yes, of course. Let me go back now, not even taking time to go all the way to the harbor. Let me go back and present the idea to my uncle. Let me find out what he thinks. I'm not exactly sure where we could have this Paul sleep. Joshua covets the privacy of his room because he and his wife talk a great deal. Or she does, at any rate. And my wife and I—"

Rufus interrupted. "You don't have to explain. Paul wouldn't have to sleep at your home. There are other apartments with more room. But you and Joshua are the only Followers of the Way who are also makers of tents. I think you are the only ones who could make it possible for Paul to stay in Corinth. At this time, I mean. He needs to have work to do that will let him recover his strength and his confidence after the miserable time he had in Athens."

Aquila was quiet a minute, remembering the healing that had come to him when he and Joshua could return to the work they had been trained since childhood to do. Maybe this Paul had the same need to have a needle, an awl in his hand.

Rufus spoke abruptly. "I'll come to your shop later this afternoon. If possible, I'll bring Paul along. I'll let you meet him, you and the others. Then you can decide."

Aquila nodded. "All right," he said. "We'll do it that way. I'll tell them everything you've said, and then when we've met your friend, we'll let you know."

"He isn't my friend, exactly," Rufus said. "He's a man of God. He is probably the most important man I have ever met in my life." He waved and turned away, then turned back. "By the way, I have something for your wife. I'll bring it when I come."

Aquila thanked him and started home but he wasn't even thinking of the promised gift. *What will Priscilla think about Paul?* he wondered. *What will she say about having a stranger around all the time when we have a dozen other things to worry about?*

⚊ 16 ⚊

After Aquila and Rufus left the shop, Priscilla opened her letter and began eagerly to read. In a few minutes she looked up with shining eyes to find Kara watching her.

"Everything must be well at home," Kara said with satisfaction. "You look as though someone had just given you a handful of gold."

"Something better than gold," Priscilla said. "The letter is from my father, and he says they are all well—my mother, my grandmother, my brother, even Dena. No one is sick or—well, no one is sick."

"What about the others? In the synagogue, I mean? Do they dare meet together at all? Or does the Emperor Claudius restrict them in every way?"

"Naturally my father writes with caution. You never know who might open a letter and read it. But he says things, subtle things that lead me to believe that a few of the Hebrews are coming back. Just a few, of course, only those who had not gone too far or those who have the money to return. He mentions a few names, not the real ones but sort of code names that I understand. If he had only wanted to be, my father could have been a scholar or a writer. It's a pity he chose shopkeeping instead."

"Well, what does he say about the Hebrews who have returned?"

"Only that they are there. That they meet at each other's houses on the Sabbath. He doesn't say "Sabbath"; he says they meet to celebrate. But I can understand what he means. Oh, and he asks a few questions that make me think that some of them, Hebrews and Jehovites, are becoming curious about the new faith, the Way. There are things he wants to know. Oh, I must write to them soon and try to explain some of the things I think he wants to hear. Do you think I could?"

"You fret yourself with unnatural things," Kara said sharply. "You will disturb the child with all this thinking. You should let your mind become passive and calm so that the child will not be upset. I tell you this for your own good."

Priscilla made herself smile at the older woman. "Don't frighten me, Kara. You know how important this baby is to me. But it seems impossible for me to stop the thoughts that go flashing through my mind. I just can't help the way I am."

Aquila strode suddenly through the doorway, and both women turned to him in surprise.

"You're back quickly, my lord," Priscilla said.

"I have something that must be discussed with you," Aquila said. "With both of you and Joshua, too. Where is he?"

"He went over to the metal workers. He found an old, bent brass needle, and he thought perhaps it could be straightened. Did Rufus say anything about bringing new needles? My lord would have waited if he had known Rufus would come so soon."

"We didn't have time to discuss needles," Aquila said. "And what we did discuss must be shared with Joshua, too." His eyes dropped to the letter in Priscilla's hands. "What of your family, my dear?"

Priscilla felt a quick rush of affection and appreciation. She was absolutely sure that no other man would have asked that question. Any other man would have demanded that the letter be given to him to read. In fact, most men would never have permitted her to read it first.

"They're fine," Priscilla said, smiling, "and they have even received my letter telling that a child is expected. They don't say a great deal—out of fear of hurting me if things were to go as they did before—but I can tell they're happy. Here, my lord, take the letter and read it."

For a few minutes there was silence in the shop while Aquila read the news from Rome. Priscilla watched his face, wondering if he, too, would recognize the code names, the oblique references to Sabbath meetings. If he did not, she must not feel too critical, she told herself. After all, perhaps the reason she had understood was because families say things in ways that outsiders might not understand.

But when Aquila looked up, his eyes were bright and his lips, under the mustache, were curved with delight. "It looks as though a few of us have gone back," he said. "And as though they are meeting together again."

Priscilla felt delight touch her. It was in moments such as this that she knew her greatest joy, moments in which she and Aquila shared an understanding. Unfortunately, she thought, such moments occurred all too rarely.

"You see it, too, my lord?" she cried. "Then I wasn't mistaken. And the questions. There are questions, aren't there? Questions about our faith. May I try to answer them, my lord, or would you prefer to be the one to write?"

He had just opened his mouth to answer when Joshua came hurrying through the door.

"The needle has been polished and sharpened and straightened," he announced. "Now I can get back to my task."

"And in the meantime Rufus has come," Kara said. "So you have wasted your time and any money you gave to the smith."

"Oh, not wasted it," Joshua said easily. "You can't have too many good needles. But Rufus and Trolas have really come?" He turned to Aquila. "They had a safe journey?"

"Safe," Aquila answered. "But when Rufus got to Corinth, he met up with a situation in which he feels we could help."

"Help?" Joshua asked. "We owe him an enormous debt of gratitude, of course, but what kind of help does he want?"

"There's a man named Paul," Aquila began. "An apostle of Jesus—"

Priscilla interrupted breathlessly. "An apostle? Someone who knew Jesus, who talked with Him, followed Him?"

Aquila held up his hands. "Not so fast. And no, this Paul did none of those things really. But he claims that Jesus appeared to him in person several years after the Crucifixion."

Joshua's lips curled with disbelief. "Oh, come, are we expected to believe that?"

"I don't know," Aquila admitted. "Rufus claims that Paul is a great teacher, perhaps the greatest teacher among those that follow the Way."

"Then what does he need from us?" Kara asked bluntly. "What do we have to offer to a great teacher?"

Priscilla's heart was pounding in her throat. She had said nothing since her one impulsive question, but every word had been burned in her heart. A great teacher. An apostle. Someone who had met Jesus. Oh, if only she could hear him tell about it. If only she could once again sit at the feet of a man of power and intellect. It would be, she thought longingly, a little like having her grandfather back again.

"Kara's right," Joshua said. "What do we have to offer?"

"The man is a maker of tents," Aquila said. "Rufus says he has just had a bad experience, and he needs a time of healing, a time of working with his hands and letting his soul rest. Rufus has asked us to let Paul work with us."

"Oh, please," Priscilla wanted to say. "Oh, please say yes. Let him come. Please."

But she knew that such a show of enthusiasm on her part would be unbecoming and possibly even open to misunderstanding. After all, what did she know of this Paul? But although she was silent, she was sure that some of her yearning must show in her eyes.

"Do we have enough work to keep a third person busy?" Joshua asked. "Could we pay him adequately? Would he expect to stay here with us? Where would he sleep?"

The cool logic of the questions made sense even to Priscilla, and yet she knew that such considerations should not enter into this thing. She waited breathlessly to hear what the others would say.

"There is no room for him to sleep here," Kara said flatly. "It is very important that Priscilla have privacy and quiet at this critical time. I suppose he could be kept busy —if I am to believe all the complaints that my lord makes about how busy and overworked he is. But I don't see how this stranger can stay here."

"Rufus says there are others who will take him in," Aquila explained. "But it may be necessary that we let him sleep here in the shop for a few nights until all arrangements can be made. Could you tolerate that?" He spoke courteously to Kara, but his eyes swung swiftly to Priscilla, to gauge her reaction.

"My privacy is not that critical," Priscilla said in a small, taut voice. She was so afraid that she would show too much enthusiasm that her words came out cold and stilted.

"I don't want anything to happen that will upset you," Aquila said, worry tightening his mouth. "I can tell Rufus that it won't be convenient—"

"Still," Joshua said, "we owe a great deal to Rufus. We owe a great deal to many people. I like to pay my debts."

"Even at the expense of your family," Kara muttered.

Priscilla spoke up. "No, now, I beg all of you to listen to Joshua. Everything he says is true. And I have all of you to take care of me. Another person in the shop won't bother me at all. Please, if you want to make me happy, tell Rufus we'll do it."

"He plans to come back this afternoon," Aquila said. "And I'm sure he plans to bring Paul with him so we can meet him. Then we can be more comfortable about making such a decision. I, for one, am very eager to meet the man."

"Then shall we leave it at that?" Joshua said. "Now, I don't know about the rest of you, but I have work to do."

"I, too," Kara said. "The first thing I need to do is to get some water." She picked up a jug and walked quickly out of the door.

For a minute Priscilla and Aquila were alone.

"Are you sure?" he asked. "Are you absolutely sure?"

She could not resist the words that poured out. "Oh, yes, I'm sure. It will be wonderful to have a great teacher in our house. It will be the most wonderful thing that could happen, my lord. Perhaps this Paul will be the authority Rufus once said we needed."

Aquila frowned. "I'm not sure it's good for you to even be thinking of teachers and learning and that sort of thing. I'm not sure that such things are good for the child you carry. If I thought anything would happen to the child, I would tell Rufus to keep Paul away from here."

Anger, disappointment, frustration surged through Priscilla's mind, and she actually bit her tongue to keep the hot, hasty words from spilling out. She completely forgot that only a short time ago she had been thinking that Aquila was more sensitive, more understanding than most husbands. Now she could only think that he was like all men.

And yet, some part of her insisted, perhaps he was right. Maybe the reason she had lost the first baby was because she thought too much, because she was impetuous and sometimes arrogant. Hot tears filled her eyes and before she could stop them, they had spilled over her cheeks. She scrubbed at them furiously with her hands. Tears could be seen as a weapon to be used against a man, and she would not be guilty of using them for that purpose.

"Forgive me," she said, keeping her voice very steady.

"I am crying only because I am very foolish. I assure you that I will do nothing willingly to hurt this child. You may do what you wish about this man Paul, my lord. I will accept any decision you make."

Aquila's voice was soft. "You know I am only thinking of you. We'll wait until Rufus comes and we meet him. Then we'll make our decision. Will that do?"

"Yes, my lord." But she would not meet his eyes.

He bent and laid his cheek against her hair. "Don't worry, my love," he whispered.

They heard Kara returning, and he stood away from Priscilla. "Don't get too tired," he said and strode from the room.

Rufus came at the end of the siesta period. As usual, he was shy and reserved toward the women, but his arms were full of bundles and his eyes were warm. With him was a small man dressed in the traditional robe of the Hebrews, his head covered by a shawl. Priscilla watched him greet Aquila and Joshua, and she could see only his profile—a high-domed forehead, a clipped beard. There was nothing unusual about him, she thought, and she felt a momentary disappointment. Surely a great teacher, a man who claimed to have met with Jesus, would have some unusual feature about him.

Then Paul turned to speak to the women, and Priscilla saw his eyes. They were large and dark, with heavy lids that gave them a hooded look. But there was a light, a luminosity in them that shone with such a brilliance that Priscilla felt as though she could scarcely bear to meet his glance.

"My lord," she said humbly in recognition of the introduction that Rufus was making. She bent her head and knew that if she did what she wanted to do, she would bend her knees. But that was being ridiculous, and she could only hope that her feelings did not show on her face.

Paul looked around, seeing, Priscilla was sure, the barrenness of the rooms, the lack of furniture, the obvious fact that they were strangers in a strange land. But when he finally spoke to Aquila, he was almost enthusiastic in spite of the obvious fatigue that made gray smudges under his eyes and slumped his shoulders.

"You have all the tools, I see. And a good location. I, too, have my tools with me—and if you could use my services—"

There was a momentary silence, and Priscilla felt as though all of her life were hanging in the balance. *Please, God, oh, please!* she prayed silently, and honestly did not know what she was praying for.

Aquila smiled, his face suddenly looking very young. "I would be honored to have you with us," he said. "Not only to work together but to speak of Him who has risen from the dead."

Paul also smiled and his face changed entirely. The strict rabbinical look was gone, and in its place was such warmth and charm that Priscilla felt her heart melt, and even Kara responded with a welcoming look.

"To speak of Jesus to those who believe," Paul said, "is the joy of my life." He looked around at all of them. "And it is possible that here in this house that joy will be intensified by friendship."

Oh, thank you, thank you, Priscilla thought. *This man will change our lives. I know it, I know it.* She felt the child move within her, and she told herself that perhaps even the unborn child was moving with joy.

= 17 =

Paul stayed with Aquila's family for only a few nights, because it was perfectly obvious that there was not enough room for him to live with them. Rufus made inquiries among other Followers of the Way, and Titius offered to provide a bed for Paul. The odd thing, Priscilla thought as the arrangements were going on, was that Paul accepted everything with a quiet humility that would seem to be the trait of a slave. And yet the man had a fire banked within him, she felt, a power that was only waiting to be unleashed. One had only to look in his eyes to see it.

She wondered if the others were as eager as she was for Paul to begin preaching. And yet, for the sake of the child, she restrained her curiosity and her desire to ask questions. While the child was still in her body, she vowed she would think only of the things that women ordinarily think of. Surely the child would be calmed and strengthened by the steady throwing of the shuttle, the preparation of food, the other quiet tasks that women were supposed to do.

But in spite of her resolution, she could not wholly suppress the longing to question Paul. When he sat with them at the midday meal or when he worked in one corner of the shop, she wanted to ask him about his conviction that he was an apostle. She wanted to know how it was that he had met Jesus face to face.

"He must have marvelous things to tell," she said wistfully to Aquila one night as they lay in bed. "Rufus said he is the greatest teacher in the world, and all he does is sit quietly and work with the skins."

"He needs to be quiet," Aquila answered, keeping his voice very soft. "It's plain that he is using this time of working with his hands to heal himself from some sorrow or trouble. But I confess I'm eager to hear him talk or preach. He hasn't even told us of his experience on the road to Damascus, when he claims he saw Jesus."

"How do you even know that much, then?" Priscilla asked.

"Rufus told me a little before he left," Aquila answered, then made a sharp exclamation of amazement. "Speaking of Rufus, he brought a gift for you that I have completely forgotten to give you. What with Paul here, it just slipped my mind."

"A gift?" she said in astonishment. "For me? Why in the world would he bring a gift to me? And why would you permit it?"

Aquila laughed. "It was such an odd gift and such an unusual one for a woman that I couldn't refuse to let him leave it. I hid it under a stack of hides until the right time to give it to you."

"What is it, my lord? And is this the right time?"

"Hardly. Can't you just see me trampling through the shop and scaring Joshua to death—he's convinced we're all going to be robbed or killed in this wicked city—and all for some papyrus."

She clutched at him with excitement. "Papyrus? Truly, my lord? How much papyrus?"

"Don't call me 'my lord' in our room," they said together, and she giggled.

"No, but tell me," she begged. "More than a sheet? And why did he bring it?"

"It was left on the ship by accident, and when they tried to deliver it at a later date, the man who ordered it had disappeared. Moved or died, they don't really know. So Trolas told Rufus he could have it, and Rufus thought of you. He knew how much letters mean to you and guessed that you also wrote them. So—"

- 147 -

In her eagerness, she struggled awkwardly to sit up. "But how much?" she asked again. "You didn't say how much."

"Twenty sheets. Maybe more."

She clasped her hands together in rapture. "So much," she said gratefully. "Who would ever have dreamed Rufus would do that? When may I have it? When is the right time?"

"After the child is safely born," Aquila said. "Don't think me harsh, my love. But I don't want you doing anything that might be harmful to the child. Or to you."

She lay down heavily. "I'll try to be patient," she said without resentment. Then she added wistfully, "I hope the child is born soon."

Aquila laughed again and reached over to lay his hand on the curve of her abdomen. "You are surely the only woman in the world who is eager for a child to be born so she can have a bundle of papyrus."

She laughed, too, and put her hand lightly on top of his. "But that's not the only reason. I'm tired of being big and awkward and weary all the time, and you know how eager I am to have this baby safely born and in my arms. Can you feel it move? I think the child is also eager to be born."

"And I," Aquila admitted. "I find the waiting long. I was frightened for a long time, but now that the time is near, I'm sure everything will be all right. But I'll be glad when it's over."

"Even if it means you have to give me my papyrus?" she asked in a teasing voice.

"Even so," he said and kissed her lightly. "Now, try to sleep. Morning will come early, and you know Paul arrives at the shop almost before it's light."

"I know," she said. "Good night, my lord. My love," she said quickly and tried to find a comfortable position.

But she was a long time falling asleep because no position she assumed was comfortable, and she didn't want to disturb Aquila by moving and turning. She thought of the man

Paul, who was still a stranger to her, working quietly while he waited for health and strength to return. And at the thought of his patience, Priscilla was suddenly quiet and at peace. *We are both waiting,* she thought, and was able at last to fall asleep.

She had slept only a short time when she was wakened by the first fleeting sense of pain. She lay, startled and a little frightened, wondering if she had dreamed it. *Aquila will think I did it deliberately just to get the papyrus,* she thought and felt an almost hysterical urge to laugh. Then, after an interval, she felt the pain again, low and dull, not yet like the pain that had torn at her on the road to Tarentum. But with the pain came a sense of certainty. The child was coming. The child was going to be born. She felt no need to call Kara or to wake Aquila. She wouldn't be fortunate enough, she thought wryly, to have the child quickly. She had plenty of time before she disturbed anyone else.

She allowed herself one moment of bitter longing for her mother, and then she resolutely put the thought from her mind. *At least,* she said to herself for comfort, *I will have plenty of papyrus to write a long letter and tell them everything. For now, I must think only of the task I have before me.*

Please, she prayed, *give me courage, and oh, please, my God, let the baby be all right. Let everything be all right.*

She lay in a half dreaming state, waiting the dawning of the new day and the coming of the child. When the pains came, she clutched the shawl that lay across the bed, and when the pains passed, she lay in a serenity she would never have thought possible.

Just before daybreak, she heard Kara moving around in the next room, speaking to Joshua to wake him.

"Paul is here," Priscilla heard Kara say. "I heard him come into the shop. At least I hope it's Paul and not a thief."

"All right, all right," Joshua said thickly. "I'm coming. I wonder if everyone in Titius's house gets up at this awful hour, or if it's only Paul who can't bear to waste the night in sleeping."

Priscilla nudged Aquila. "Your aunt and uncle are awake, my lord," she said. "And furthermore, the child is going to come today."

Aquila raised himself on his elbow. "Are you sure? Are you having pain?"

"Yes, I'm very sure, and yes, I'm having pain. You'll tell Kara to come, won't you? Not right away. There's no hurry, but when you and your uncle and Paul are fed, then she had better come."

Aquila bent and kissed her. "I will pray for a safe and easy delivery," he said, his mouth tender. "I will ask God to bless you and bring us a healthy child." He slipped his tunic over his head and left the room.

Priscilla got up and washed herself carefully in the basin of water that they kept on a small table. Then she began to walk slowly, methodically around the room. Hadn't her mother said once that it was easier if a woman walked?

Kara appeared in the doorway. "The child is really coming?"

Priscilla nodded. "Yes. Really."

"And you don't need me until after I have prepared food for the men?"

"No. But then you will come, won't you? I just need you to be with me. To hold my hand as you did the last time."

"Of course. How soon should we send for the midwife?"

Priscilla stopped and bent forward while a contraction clawed through her body. "Perhaps," she said at last, feeling sweat form on her forehead, "perhaps you should send for her right away. I may need her sooner than I had dared to hope."

The morning hours crawled slowly by, and Aquila had great difficulty keeping his mind on his work. He welcomed the arrival of customers because then it was necessary for him to talk about the quality of leather and the structure of tents and for a few moments he could try to forget what was going on in his bedroom. His and Priscilla's. He had gone to the synagogue before breakfast and had prostrated himself in prayer, but even now, working in the yard, prayer coursed through his mind like a flowing river, filling him so that he sat with quiet hands in his lap.

Paul glanced over at him more and more often. For a long time Paul said nothing, and then at last he spoke. "You are deeply troubled, my young friend. It is only a normal function, after all, for women to give birth. Why are you so worried?"

"She lost our first child," Aquila said. "It was born too soon, but even so, tiny as it was, she suffered horribly. She is very small, you know." He stopped. He couldn't tell a stranger how he felt about Priscilla. He couldn't tell him that just to look at her made his bones melt and run together, and the thought of her pain was like a knife twisting through his own body.

"Yes," Paul said, "she is very small. Almost like a child. But I suspect she is very strong. Perhaps even stubborn. And if she has faith, then you don't need to worry."

"She does indeed have faith," Aquila said. "She wouldn't accept baptism until she had learned truth about Jesus so that she would go to the act as a believer, not just the wife of a believer." He stopped, afraid he had said too much. Possibly Paul would think Priscilla insolent, with a husband who was too lenient.

But Paul only nodded his head as though Aquila's words had not surprised him at all. "I thought so," he said. "I have watched her, and I had a feeling she was not the child she appeared. I am learning that women can develop a faith that is absolutely astonishing. I had not thought it would be that way. But in Philippi—"

Before Paul could tell him about Philippi Priscilla's scream shattered the morning. The scream came again in a minute, and then Aquila heard a high, shrill wailing that filled him with joy.

"It's the child," Aquila said breathlessly, looking over at Paul and feeling his mouth stretch into a wide grin. "The child is born."

"God be praised," Paul said sincerely. "And here's your uncle to tell you if it's a boy or girl."

Aquila had not even noticed that Joshua had gone inside, but now he looked up eagerly to see his uncle coming toward him, his hands outstretched, his mouth smiling.

"You have a son," Joshua announced. "Kara says that the child is a boy and healthy. They are cleaning him now, and in only a few minutes Kara will bring him out."

"But Priscilla?" Aquila could not help saying. "Tell me how Priscilla is."

"She's fine. When the midwife has finished her tasks, you may go to the door and speak to her. You can tell her then that you are proud of her, that you are grateful for the gift of the child."

Paul chuckled. "This is one young man who probably doesn't need to be told what to say. I have a feeling that his concern for his wife stems not from duty but from love."

Aquila felt his face flushing. "She is very lovely," he said and knew his voice was defensive.

Joshua grinned. "A wife does not have to be lovely to be loved. Kara is no longer young and slender and beautiful, and she has a sharp tongue, but I am not ashamed that I love her still. You will think us too fond, my friend," he said to Paul, "but we have only each other, we four, so to be able to love is more important for us than for most."

Paul smiled. "I'm not married myself, so I have not always understood these things. I suspect I'm going to learn much about marriage and families while I work with you."

Kara stood at the door with a bundle in her arms. "Your son, my lord," she said to Aquila, and it was the first time she had ever addressed him that way.

Almost timidly, Aquila walked over to her. With hands that shook a little, he pulled the cover away and looked in astonishment at the baby. He didn't know what he had expected but certainly not this small, plump face with the peaks of dark, damp hair curling over the round head. The eyes were squinched tightly shut, and Aquila looked up at Kara.

"Are his eyes blue?" he asked.

Kara smiled. "No. This child is more like his father than his mother. But he is perfect, and God has blessed us richly."

"May I speak to Priscilla?" Aquila asked.

"Not yet. The midwife is not finished. Here, take the baby, my lord. Hold him in your arms. He is, after all, your son."

She placed the baby in Aquila's arms, and he felt the fragile weight with a sense of wonder. How could anything so tiny, so vulnerable hold his heart in such a firm grip? Was this how his father had felt the first time he had held his son in his arms? *And yet my father sent us away,* Aquila thought with sorrow, *and it is Kara who has the honor of bringing this boy to me, not my mother. And I know my mother would have cherished this moment.* For a few seconds his grief was larger than his joy.

Then Joshua and Paul came to look at the child. Joshua stooped to lay his lips against the baby's cheek, before he moved away, unashamedly wiping tears from his eyes.

"I'll get some wine," he said huskily. "We will drink to life."

Then Paul put his hand on the baby's forehead. "Just think," he said in a soft, wondering tone, "our Lord was sent to the world in just such helplessness. It shakes the mind, doesn't it?"

Aquila looked into the shining eyes opposite his own. "Yes," he conceded humbly. "It shakes the mind. There is so much I need to know."

"And so much I need to teach," Paul said. "There is a burden on my heart that must be shared. Tomorrow, my friend, on the Sabbath, you and I will go to the synagogue together, and I will start to preach again of Jesus the Christ."

Joshua came back into the shop to pour the wine and the three men drank, Aquila still holding the baby.

"To life," Joshua said.

"To life," Paul and Aquila echoed.

The midwife appeared in the doorway. "You may speak to your wife, my lord," she said to Aquila. "She is very weak, but you may stand in the door and speak to her."

With the baby in his arms, Aquila went to stand in the doorway of their room. Priscilla was pale, and her hair was matted with sweat, but the smile she gave Aquila was dazzling.

"I gave you a son, my lord," she whispered. "This time I gave you a son to hold."

"How can I tell you how grateful I am?" Aquila said. "Or how beautiful I think he is? And you."

She laughed and put her hand up to her damp hair. "I, my lord? I must look awful."

"Can a woman who has been blessed by the Lord look awful?"

Her face was serious. "No, my lord. I was acting like a woman. The truth is we have both been blessed."

He smiled, wishing that he could go closer and hold her in his arms. Words of love churned in his mind, but he was too shy to say them. "Thank you," he said at last and could only hope she would understand.

⊸ 18 ⊸

The first time Aquila heard Paul preach, he sat and listened in total astonishment. Phineas had been convincing and persuasive, but his preaching was as nothing compared to that of this small, slight man who sat in front of the assembled Jehovites and told of the man Jesus.

He began, as Aquila suspected was his custom, with his account of the meeting with Christ on the road to Damascus. He must have told the story a hundred times, Aquila thought, but the wonder and reverence were still in his voice as he recounted the blinding light, the voice of his Lord, the darkness that descended on him until that day when Ananias had come and touched his eyes with healing.

"And so you see," Paul concluded. "I, too, have met Jesus face to face. I, too, have heard His voice. I am as much an apostle as Peter or any of the others who were with Him in His earthly life. And so I speak to you with authority. You can believe me when I tell you that Jesus is the promised Messiah and that He was resurrected from the grave."

Aquila was sharply aware of the mixed reaction that Paul's words were getting. Those who were already Followers of the Way listened with joy. But many reacted with anger and disbelief, and Aquila could hear muttered whispers that held the words *blasphemy* and *heretic*. Was there no one, Aquila wondered, who heard the words for the first time with wonder and amazement? Was there no one who wanted to hear more?

Without being too obvious, Aquila let his eyes move

around the room. He had chosen a back seat for this very reason, as it enabled him to observe without being observed. Some of the faces of the listeners were shining with excitement, and some were dark with anger.

"So," Aquila said later to Paul as they walked home, "will you try to speak to the Hebrew Jehovites again? Seeing how they reacted, will you risk it again?"

Paul looked tired, drained of the enormous vitality he had poured into his message, but his eyes were bright. "Oh, I'll risk it again. And again and again, until I am absolutely sure that their ears are really deafened to anything I can say. The good news should be offered to the Hebrew Jehovites first. It's their right."

"But if they refuse to listen?" And Aquila was thinking of his father when he asked the question.

"Then I will go to the Gentiles," Paul said. "To men like Titius, who believe even though they are not Hebrew Jehovites."

"Like Priscilla," Aquila said. "And her family. They are all Jehovites."

"But not all of them Followers of the Way?"

"Not yet. Priscilla is trying to win them over in the letters she writes home."

He stopped abruptly. He had not intended to say so much.

Paul looked surprised, and Aquila thought he saw disapproval in the hooded eyes. "Priscilla writes letters to her family? Letters in which she actually tries to defend the faith?"

"Yes, sir," Aquila said humbly. "Perhaps I should not have permitted it—"

"Well, I'll admit it's unusual to give a woman so much freedom," Paul conceded. "On the other hand, as I started to tell you yesterday, I am discovering that women possess talents I had not suspected. In Philippi I baptized a woman named Lydia, who is now deeply involved in the church that teaches the truth about Jesus. And there have been others. It may be that when your wife is older and her children grown, that she, too, will be a force in this movement."

Aquila was sure that he should only nod in agreement and let it go at that, but some honesty in him made him go on with words he had not really planned to say.

"I'm not at all sure she'll be willing to wait so long. At the moment, of course, she is absorbed with the baby. But she has been given a pile of papyrus, and although she hasn't said anything for several weeks, I'm sure that it won't be long until she'll be writing again. And saying the things she is planning to say."

Paul frowned, and then his face cleared. "Well, there is no use quarreling with her until I know her better and learn more about her. If her belief is sound, if she is blessed with understanding, if she is gifted with words, then who am I to say it is wrong?"

"I think," Aquila said cautiously, "you will find that she is more knowledgeable than most women."

And even more knowledgeable than some men, he added to himself, shocking himself with the idea. He was too discreet to say the words aloud because he did not want to risk making a fool of himself in Paul's eyes. Or, for that matter, in his own. What had ever possessed him to have such an idea? Was it because his love for Priscilla addled his brain?

"I feel the need for food," Aquila said awkwardly. "Perhaps you won't mind hurrying a little?"

"Not at all," Paul said. "I had no breakfast this morning, preparing myself to speak. So I, too, am hungry."

They increased their pace, and in a few minutes Aquila's shop was in view. Aquila was careful to keep his face averted from Paul, so that the older man might not guess that it wasn't really the desire for food that motivated the hurrying but the desire to see his son again and perhaps even have a chance to talk to Priscilla. Although he could not go through the door into their room until the child was seven days old, he could at least listen to her voice and watch her smile, and that would have to be enough.

Everything was different this time, Priscilla thought, as the days slid by. When she lost the first baby, there had been only grief and pain, strangeness and even a temporary dispensing with tradition. Now, in the relative security of this new life, tradition was again the controlling force in their existence. On the eighth day, the baby was circumcized and a name was chosen. It was Aquila who suggested that the baby might bear his great-grandfather's name, and Priscilla had been deeply grateful. It would be one more thing, she thought with pleasure, to tell her parents about when she finally felt it was suitable for her to write home. In spite of the fact that Aquila had brought her the papyrus soon after Marcus's birth, she had not yet written the letter she had looked forward to writing.

She did not really understand herself, but in her unexpected tranquility after the baby was born, she did not need Kara to remind her not to do anything that was the slightest bit improper for a woman. Her own inclination was to concentrate on the child, on the amazing miracle of feeding him and watching him grow. She saw miniature bracelets of flesh form around his tiny wrists and knew an intense satisfaction that she was providing from her own body the food that nourished him.

During the early weeks of his life, then, she did not feel the need to use the precious papyrus, nor did she feel any resentment that until her time of uncleanness was over, she could not go to the synagogue. She was oddly content to stay quietly in the apartment, to talk softly and foolishly to the baby and to let the days drift by in a sort of dream.

Kara was more doting than Priscilla ever thought she would be. All of Kara's loneliness for the life in Rome, Priscilla thought, all her homesickness for other members of their family seemed to flow together and take on the shape of a great love that she lavished on the baby and his mother. So it was often Kara's hands that cleaned the baby and wrapped him in his swaddling clothes. It was often on her shoulder that he howled out his anger and frustration at a world that included pain and hunger.

"You have spoiled me, you know," Priscilla announced one day. "You have let me be lazy and useless, and unless I get back into the habit of working pretty soon, I will have forgotten how."

"Not much chance of that," Kara said comfortably. "In only two days we'll be going to the synagogue for the purification service and for the redemption of the baby. At home we might have made two services of it, because of the number of friends we would have to invite in to help us celebrate. But here, with only a few friends, it will be better to celebrate everything all at once."

"I agree," Priscilla said, content to even let Kara make all the decisions.

They smiled at each other, and then both turned to look down at the child at Priscilla's breast. His dark, curly hair contrasted with his mother's creamy skin, and although he was sucking with fierce concentration, his eyes were wide and alert, obviously watching Priscilla's face.

"Perhaps he'll be like my grandfather in more than just his name," Priscilla said. "See how broad his forehead is, how well shaped his head is. Perhaps he'll be intelligent and wise."

Kara made a noise of dissent. "Of course, your grandfather was a remarkable man, but this little one is exactly like his father was at that age. I remember seeing Sarah hold him, just as you're holding Marcus, and Aquila had the same shape to his face and head, the same look to his eyes."

Priscilla thought of Aquila, of his pride in his son, of the expression on his face when he looked at her across the room. It would be good, she thought honestly, to have the day of purification behind her, to be able once more to sleep beside her husband. She had known women who did not feel this way, and she was deeply grateful that Aquila's tenderness had made her feel the normal desire her mother had hoped she would feel.

She smiled tenderly down at the baby. "And will you be good when we share our room with your father again?" she asked softly. "Will you be quiet at night so that he can sleep without being disturbed?"

Kara snorted. "You needn't worry about that. Husbands have a way of sleeping through the sound of the hungriest child in the city."

Priscilla laughed, and to her astonishment, Marcus pulled his mouth away from the nipple and smiled. It was his first smile, lopsided and wavering, but the sweetness of it caught at her heart. "Look," she cried to Kara. "Look. He smiled."

"An event to be chronicled in history," Kara said with amused irony, but she came quickly to observe for herself, and Marcus obliged by smiling again.

"From the sound of contentment in here, I can only suppose that there are no problems in this part of the house," Aquila said at the doorway. "May I come in?"

Priscilla drew her robe across her breast. "Certainly, my lord. We are only exclaiming over the fact that your son smiled for the first time. And he is very young for it, isn't he, Kara?"

"Very young," Kara agreed. "If a smile is a sign of intelligence, then this child is certainly more blessed than most."

"I came to ask a question," Aquila said. "Is everything in readiness for the trip to the synagogue day after tomorrow? We will close the shop for the occasion."

"Will that be necessary, my lord?" Priscilla asked. "Won't there be enough time during the siesta hour to go to the synagogue for the rites and the paying of the fee to redeem the baby? Kara has made arrangements to buy a dove for the offering, and I think it can all be handled very quickly. Then a few guests will come late in the afternoon for some sweet cakes and a cup of wine. Will it be necessary to close the shop?"

"Not if one of us could stay here," Aquila said. "But even Paul wants to go to the synagogue for the ceremony. There's something a little odd in his insistence on going," he confided suddenly. "He was very disturbed last Sabbath, and I really thought at the time that he might refuse ever to go back again."

"You don't just stop going to the synagogue," Priscilla protested. "I mean, he's a Hebrew, and a deeply religious Jehovite. You don't just stop going."

Aquila shook his head. "I don't know. He insists on preaching first to the Hebrew Jehovites, but I don't know how much rejection he will endure. His preaching fell on deaf ears in Athens. I don't think he'll tolerate that here."

For the first time since the baby was born, Priscilla felt a rush of the old desire to listen and to learn. "And I have never even heard him preach," she cried. "When will I be able to hear him?"

"Soon. Next Sabbath, perhaps. Will the child be quiet enough, do you think?"

She had honestly felt that the placid contentment she had felt in recent weeks would last a long, long time. But the words of her husband ran through her with a blaze of excitement.

"I don't know," she admitted honestly. "He is not always quiet, and it is certainly not customary to take babies into the service. I'm afraid people would frown at me."

"I'll hold him," Kara said. "We'll sit back by the door and if he cries, I'll take him out. If he gets really hungry, of course, you'll have to come to him."

"Oh, Kara, you're so good to me," Priscilla cried, her eyes shining. She turned to Aquila. "You did very well, my lord, to provide me with such a loving aunt."

Aquila's face was suddenly very somber. "I certainly did

nothing to provide you with a loving father," he said. "And I couldn't keep a loving mother with you."

Priscilla spoke quickly. "No, my lord. You mustn't say things like that. After all, Joshua and Kara have been given to us for our comfort. We must be grateful for what we have."

"Well, there's no point in talking about it," Aquila announced. "What's done is done. But to get back to the reason I came in here, shall I tell Paul that the ceremonies will be held about midmorning at the synagogue?"

"Yes, and tell him to invite the family of Titius to come to the house later and help us rejoice. I'm sure Paul must feel about them as though they were his family."

Aquila smiled. "I believe Paul's family is made up of all those who accept Christ as the Messiah. He even speaks of Joshua and of me as brothers sometimes. I feel sorry for him, though, that he doesn't have what we have—a real family who belong to each other. I only wish—" His voice broke suddenly and he walked quickly from the room.

Priscilla felt pain fill her as she saw this admission of the grief that Aquila usually suppressed. *I've got to help him,* she thought. *I've got to do something. But how?*

An idea struck her with the suddenness of a bolt of lightning. Why hadn't she thought of it before? She turned to Kara. "I'm going to write a letter," she announced, her voice breathless with daring. "Just as soon as the purification rites are over, I'm going to try to contact Aquila's mother. I'm going to tell her about Marcus and that we love her and that her son misses her."

Kara frowned dubiously. "How could you possibly do that?"

"I could try to send a letter to Marta. They are surely still in Athens. The Jehovites would still be together, the ones who are Followers of the Way and the ones who aren't. I could send a message to Aquila's mother through Marta."

Kara continued to look dubious. "Do you really think

you should? Do you think it's proper for you to do such a thing? Now while Marcus is so small? Will your husband permit it?"

Priscilla put her baby up over her shoulder and patted his back. "I have tried to be content," she confided. "And I have been. For a long time it has been enough for me to be the vessel that carried the child, to be his source of food and love. But now I think there's more for me to do. And I probably won't ask my husband for his permission." The words seemed to shock her into silence, but then she added abruptly, "Do you think God speaks to women?"

"Of course God speaks to women," Kara said. "What about Hannah? What about Deborah?"

"Well, then," Priscilla said, "if He does speak to women then I feel almost as though He were telling me that He wants me to do more than what I have been doing. He wants me to be a bridge between people. Does that sound silly, Kara? Am I presumptuous?"

Kara put her fists on her hips and stood frowning at the girl. But her face was not angry, simply creased with concentration. "No," she said at last, "it does not sound silly. Even with a baby to care for and weaving to be done, we will see that you find time to write your letters. All the time you will need."

⚊ 19 ⚊

Once she had formulated a plan to try to contact Sarah, Priscilla found it difficult to wait until she could actually work things out. Constantly, as she took care of the baby, as she busied herself with weaving or sweeping or baking, she shaped words and sentences in her head, trying to form convincing statements of her love and concern for her mother-in-law.

But even as she made her plans, she worried about Aquila, sure that he would be angry if he knew that his wife was deliberately planning to do something of which he could hardly approve. How could he possibly approve of an act that would surely hurt his pride? He had told her more than once that although he loved his father, although he would always be a good son, he would never go crawling back.

"After all," he had said, "it was my father who sent me away, it was my father who went off and left us alone along the road with you in labor. You can't expect me to ever be the one to make a move toward any reconciliation."

But Priscilla knew that behind the proud, angry words there was a great, aching emptiness. And if she could bridge that gap, or even if she could just make Sarah aware of the fact that Marcus had been born, then she would have accomplished something.

She tried not to think about it until the day of redemption and purification arrived. On that morning, concentrating on the rituals and their significance in her life, Priscilla went with Aquila, Joshua, Kara, and Paul to the synagogue. She and Kara went first to the women's courtyard, and there they offered to the priest the pure white dove that Kara had purchased. The proper words and prayers were uttered, and then the women walked into the inner room where the men were waiting with the baby.

Marcus had decided that he had been without his mother long enough, and his howls were penetrating the morning air. When Aquila saw Priscilla coming, a look of relief crossed his face, and he held out his son to her.

"The purification rites are finished?" he asked.

"Yes, my lord, the priest has declared me clean again."

Aquila did not respond, but Priscilla knew what he was thinking and she felt a quick twinge of shame that during the rites she had not even thought of her husband. She had completely forgotten the joy that had filled her a few days ago at the thought of Aquila returning to her bed. As the priest had said the words that declared her clean again, she had thought only of the fact that now she could write her letters and listen to Paul's preaching. *Why can't I be like other women?* she grieved silently. *Why didn't I think only of my husband? Why am I tormented by these other desires?*

Deliberately, she forced herself to smile at Aquila, to meet his eyes, and to her astonishment and great relief, she felt her heart quicken in response to the warmth in his eyes. She was not so wicked after all, she thought gratefully. She would be glad to be able to be a wife again, to feel Aquila's arms around her at night. And if that emotion did not constitute the whole of her gratitude that this day had finally come, then she could only hope her husband would never know how she felt.

"Well, come," Joshua said suddenly. "There's the family that was ahead of us coming out. Here, here's the fee to be paid. Are we all ready to go in?"

They all nodded, and cuddling the baby against her shoulder, Priscilla fell into step with Kara to follow the men into a small room with a simple altar where such rituals were performed. There, Joshua paid the fee that would redeem Marcus and claim him as a child of Jehovah.

Aquila, with Joshua acting as sponsor, said the prescribed words after the priest. Marcus yelled lustily during most of the ceremony, and the five adults who had brought him to the synagogue were all grinning broadly by the time the ceremony was over and they could walk back out into the court. *Even during such a solemn occasion,* Priscilla thought with amusement, *no one could keep from smiling at such frank outrage from one so small.*

She suddenly realized that the priest had *not* smiled. He had looked at each of them with shrewd, disapproving glances, and then he had performed the simple rite with an expressionless face and voice. *It was unnatural,* she thought. *Even the sternest priest is usually amused by a baby.* She looked up to see the priest striding toward them.

He planted himself in front of Paul and spoke sharply. "Was there any particular reason you accompanied this family?" he asked without even the courtesy of an address.

"I'm a friend of the family," Paul said, his voice cold.

The priest swung toward Joshua. "Do you subscribe to this man's teaching?" he asked. "Do you admit to the same heresy that has filled this man's words Sabbath after Sabbath?"

Joshua nodded, but his eyes were anxious. "Yes, my lord, we do. We, too, believe that Jesus is the Messiah."

The priest's face flushed. "This is blasphemy! You have no right to influence this innocent child with such beliefs." He turned to Paul again. "And you're trying to poison the people in our congregation. It's an outrage."

"I have met the Lord face to face," Paul insisted. "If you've been listening to me on the Sabbath, you know with what authority I speak."

"*I* speak with authority," the priest cried out. "I am of the house of Levi, and I represent the Law."

"I, too, am of the house of Levi," Aquila said, "and I am convinced that what Paul teaches is correct."

The priest glared. "It's even worse for Levites to be led astray," he shouted. He turned to Paul. "You have much to answer for, you and your false teachings. You desecrate our synagogue."

Paul bowed slightly, and when he spoke, his voice was bitter. "Then I will desecrate it no longer. I will shake the dust of this place from my feet." He stooped and pulled his sandals from his feet. He shook them vigorously and then turned to walk out of the court. "What you have rejected," he flung over his shoulder, "I will take to the Gentiles."

"Go and good riddance," the priest shouted, and Priscilla half expected to see him spit after Paul. Her heart pounded with fear and apprehension as she and the others followed Paul out of the courtyard. She had never expected a confrontation such as this. True, Reuben and his friends had sent the Followers of the Way away from their synagogue in Rome, but it had been done without too much name calling. The priest who stood in the courtyard staring after them was angry enough to cause real trouble, she thought.

"I am not a bringer of peace," Paul said ruefully as they left the synagogue behind them. "I cause trouble wherever I go."

"Don't worry," Aquila said. "It was bound to happen, sooner or later."

"I know exactly how the priest feels," Paul said, talking to the men beside him, but Priscilla and Kara could hear every word. "I, too, was once a persecutor of those who followed Jesus."

Neither Aquila nor Joshua looked as though he felt any of the astonishment that surged through Priscilla.

"I had heard as much," Joshua admitted cautiously.

"And yet you welcomed me into your shop?" Paul's voice held surprise.

"I had also heard that you had been changed," Joshua said. "My nephew and I had both heard stories—we weren't sure how true they were—of what happened. You, yourself, at the synagogue, told of meeting the Lord on the road to Damascus. And so we felt sure that you were exactly what you claim to be—a missionary of Christ."

Gratitude and appreciation warmed Paul's eyes. "Not everyone," he said huskily, "has understood or accepted me so quickly. There are still some who remember the persecutions after all this time. It is, of course, no more than I deserve."

Priscilla heard the humility in his voice and saw the way his hands gripped the arms of the two men on either side of him. Unexpectedly, she felt her throat tighten with emotion, and for a few minutes she hid her face against the baby's head. There was a blessing, she thought, in being the family Paul had chosen to work with, even though he had angered the priest—which might be a problem for all of them some day.

Kara spoke urgently but in soft tones. "I hope they don't talk so intently that they forget how to walk. We have guests coming later, and there is still much for us to do."

Priscilla smiled. Kara had a way of bringing her face to face with reality, she thought, by reminding her that women had to keep in touch with the ordinary things of the world so that men could greet their guests at the door and talk of important things.

"Perhaps you and I could slip ahead," Priscilla said quietly.

Kara shook her head. "It wouldn't be fitting," she said. "If Paul weren't here, I'd just tell Joshua to move faster. But Paul is the first man I've ever met who really—well, intimidates me."

Priscilla was not surprised, because she understood all too well what Kara meant. Paul was small and sometimes very quiet, but there was an authority about him that could not be ignored.

Aquila spoke abruptly. "If you won't go to the synagogue on the Sabbath any more, what will you do? How will you preach? Has this sort of thing happened to you in other places?"

"Yes, of course. I have sometimes preached in homes or in courtyards of certain houses. In other towns where I've been, I've considered renting a hall for meetings, but that hasn't been feasible yet. And certainly wouldn't be here. Not now. We don't have enough money."

"Perhaps you could preach at our house," Joshua suggested. "There isn't much space inside but the yard is roomy. Perhaps during the siesta time—"

Paul's face lightened as he glanced up at Joshua. "A wonderful idea," he said. "If you wouldn't mind—"

"Why should we mind?" Aquila said. "It's a fine idea. If my uncle had not suggested it, I would have."

"We'll give it serious thought then," Paul said. "I wish that some of the men who have accompanied me in the past could be here. It goes better if there are two or three to preach, to counsel, to teach, to explain." He made a sound of apology. "I know you two would be willing to help, but—"

Aquila interrupted. "You don't have to explain. My uncle and I need to be taught more ourselves before we can teach. We need to listen to your words, my friend, before we can shape words of our own."

Priscilla felt excitement mounting in her with every word that was said. If Paul's preaching could take place in her own yard, then surely there would be nothing improper or unbecoming in her listening. She could even sit inside the room and listen through the door or the window. Without being anything but an obedient, exemplary wife, she could still be exposed to Paul's teaching. *If I had prayed and asked God to work a miracle for me,* Priscilla thought in awe, *He could have done nothing more wonderful than this.*

Gratitude, joy, and anticipation filled her until she wondered if she could hold it all without having some of it spill over in some kind of demonstration. She thought suddenly of the old, old story of the Exodus, of Miriam dancing with exultation on the shore of the Red Sea. *If this were a wilderness instead of a busy city,* Priscilla thought, glancing around at the crowded stalls, the hurrying people, *I'd be tempted to dance and sing myself!*

Aquila suddenly looked over his shoulder. "We're making you late," he said apologetically to Kara. "I'd completely forgotten that we have guests coming. We'll stop talking now and hurry."

"We would appreciate it," Kara responded, but Priscilla noted with amusement that her tone was not so tart as it might have been.

Aquila was as good as his promise, and the men stepped out with no further conversation. They moved so swiftly, in fact, that Kara and Priscilla nearly had to run to keep up. Kara puffed along, panting, but Priscilla barely felt the weight of the baby in her arms. She could almost float, she thought, if she really tried. Marcus, rocked by the motion of Priscilla's body, slept soundly, his small head bobbing against her neck.

"Look!" Kara said, aghast. "There are men in the yard already. It's too soon for either customers or guests to arrive. Who do you suppose it is?"

"I don't know," Priscilla answered. "Perhaps they were going to one of the other shops and got into our yard by mistake."

But Paul, looking up and seeing the strangers, let out a sudden cry of welcome and sprinted down the street like a boy. Priscilla saw the warm embraces and heard the excited exchange of greetings. Obviously, the men were friends of Paul, and she felt a disquieting thrust of apprehension. Could they have come to take him away? Was her dream to end before it even started?

"Come," Paul called. "Come and meet my dear friends and co-workers. This is Silas, and this Timothy. They have come from Berea, where they have been teaching. Silas,

Timothy, this is Joshua and his nephew, Aquila. And their wives, Kara and Priscilla."

The men greeted each other warmly, and Priscilla and Kara shyly acknowledged the introduction. Silas was a tall, powerful man who appeared to be about Paul's age, but Timothy was little more than a boy, Priscilla felt. He was slender and quick with a smile that blazed like sunshine after rain.

"We bid you welcome," Aquila cried, "and thank God for your arrival on this special day. Our son has just been redeemed, and we expect guests to help us rejoice. You are just in time."

"We won't be in the way?" Silas asked, but it was purely a perfunctory question. He was already smiling and comfortable.

"You will be a welcome addition to our gathering," Joshua said.

Timothy shyly approached Priscilla. "May I see the baby?" he asked.

She lifted Marcus from her shoulder so that the young man could see him. "Of course," she answered simply. "Here he is. Our first son. Marcus."

Timothy grinned and bent for a closer look. "A handsome boy," he announced. "And I'm somewhat of an authority. I have seven younger brothers and sisters."

"Then," Priscilla said, amazingly at ease, "when you get homesick for a little one to play with, you may borrow Marcus."

"Now?" Timothy asked. "While you and your aunt are preparing for your guests, may I hold him?"

Priscilla heard the words with astonishment. She had made her suggestion without ever guessing that Timothy would take her seriously. Wasn't he afraid that the other men would mock him? Apparently not, because his arms came out to take the baby.

"If he cries," Priscilla warned, "call me at once."

"If he cries," Paul said, suddenly looking relaxed and more at ease than she had ever seen him, "there won't be any need for Timothy to call you. Marcus has a voice loud enough to be heard across the city."

Priscilla laughed and watched with what skill young Timothy held the baby. Then she turned, without reluctance, and followed Kara into the house. Not even Paul's words to Silas and Timothy—"Come, now, tell me everything that has happened since I saw you last"—tempted her to stay out in the yard. There was a time for everything, she thought contentedly. Now was the time to help Kara prepare food. Tonight there would be the time to be with Aquila and rediscover the delights of love. Then later, as God opened the way, there would be a time to hear Paul preach and to write the letters that were clamoring to be written.

~ 20 ~

A few days after the arrival of Silas and Timothy, Priscilla found that she had a free hour during which she had nothing particular to do. Marcus was sleeping contentedly, and there were no tasks clamoring to be done. For a few minutes she thought longingly of the leisure and luxury of the baths she had shared with her mother in Rome, but she resolutely pushed aside the memories. They had neither time nor money for that sort of thing here. Suddenly her momentary despondency fled as she realized that this might be just the time that could be used for writing the letters she had been planning to write.

She walked a little hesitantly out into the yard, hoping against hope that Aquila would be alone, so she could make her request privately. However, all three men were sitting together, stretching some cured hides.

Aquila looked up. "My lord," she said slowly. "I'm very sorry to bother you, but I was wondering if you—if this might be the time when you would be willing to—to give me the papyrus you promised me."

Aquila looked genuinely astonished. "I'm sorry! I totally forgot. Your parents will be eager for news, and I have been sitting on the papyrus as though it were eggs waiting to be hatched."

Joshua grinned. "He will sound even more apologetic if the papyrus has been stained in any way by its long contact with the skins. He had told me that Rufus brought the treasure for you but I confess I had forgotten, too."

Paul looked up. "Your husband told me once that you

wrote letters to your family, that you even took the liberty of discussing things not usually found in women's letters. But I presume this letter will carry only the good news of the baby's birth?"

Priscilla felt her face flushing. Although she had been listening to Paul preach nearly every day, although she was beginning to feel that she understood a little of the man's theology, she still felt as though Paul himself were a stranger. She had found young Timothy almost like a brother, but she felt shy and tongue-tied around Paul and Silas.

"I plan to write of Marcus, of course," she said. "I will probably boast, in the way of all new mothers. But my father's last letter contained questions that I may try to answer."

She knew that the words had come out sounding stiff and defiant, but she couldn't help it. She was afraid to meet Aquila's eyes for fear she would discover that he was embarrassed by the conversation. It did not occur to her that she need answer for her actions only to her husband. Like Kara, she found Paul's air of authority one she could not resist.

"Questions concerning your new faith?" Paul asked.

"Yes, sir," was all she said.

"It would be a pity if false explanations got back to Rome," Paul said, but his voice was strangely mild.

"Yes, sir," she admitted, capitulating suddenly to the mildness as she would never have done had Paul been stern. "So, to avoid such a problem, would you be willing to read the letter when it is written and correct me if I am wrong?"

Paul's eyebrows shot up as though her sudden docility had surprised him. "I'll listen," he said. "If you read to me what you have written, I'm willing to listen."

"Thank you," she said with honest gratitude. She was only too aware of her limited knowledge, and as long as she was going to be allowed to write, she had no objections to Paul's help. In fact, she would find the extra time of instruction a blessing. "I would be honored to have your help, sir. Truly I would."

"Then," Paul said to Aquila, as though he had the right, "give her the papyrus and let her write."

It was not until Priscilla was back in the shop, sitting at a small table with the precious papyrus in front of her, that she faced honestly the fact that she had, to a certain extent, misled both Paul and Aquila. She had let them believe that the letter to Rome was the only one she intended to write. She had not indicated that the letter that was really burning to be written was the one to Marta. There was some comfort in the fact that Kara knew of her intentions, and she would help keep the secret. There was still the problem of how she would get the letter to Athens, and Priscilla wasn't at all sure she could handle that without Aquila's or Joshua's help. Well, she would get it written, and then she could only trust that God would open up a way for her to get her message delivered. *I am only a human being, after all,* Priscilla thought with unusual humility, *and unless God helps me, I will fail.*

Aquila leaned his back against the wall of the house and stared in astonishment at the men gathered in his yard. It had only been a few days since Paul had stalked away from the synagogue in anger, shaking the dust of the place from his sandals, and already this noon gathering had become an established thing. Each day, when men left their places of business to go home for lunch and the usual two-hour rest, a group of them gathered here instead, to listen to Paul's preaching. There were a few Hebrew Jehovites among them, but for the most part, the group was made up of all the incredible variety of races and nationalities that filled a city like Corinth. In his quick glance around, Aquila saw men who were surely Egyptians, Ethiopians, Phoenicians, Romans, and Greeks and Hebrews. *And to each,* he thought with a sense of exultation, *Paul speaks in a fashion that each can understand.*

Several men, walking along the street, turned to come into the yard, and Aquila saw, with a sharp jolt of his heart, that one of them was Crispus, the leader of the synagogue. *Has he been sent as a spy?* Aquila wondered. *Has he heard of Paul's insolence from the priest and come to see for himself what is going on?* Crispus, like Titius, was a man of strength and influence. But unlike Titius, Crispus was a Hebrew Jehovite, not a Gentile convert to Jehovah, and his influence in the synagogue and in the Hebrew Jehovite community in Corinth was one to be reckoned with.

Crispus seemed to melt into the group of men, and for a few minutes Aquila lost sight of him. His uneasiness twisted sharply into fear. There could be real danger for them in the presence of men such as Crispus.

Paul seemed totally oblivious of any problem, and his words rang out with clarity and power. He was telling again of the stoning of Stephen and of the nefarious part he, Paul, had played in that tragic drama at the gate in Jerusalem. He spoke of the glory on Stephen's face and of the first stirrings of guilt and remorse in his own heart, the first acknowledgment that he might have been wrong to denounce Jesus's claim to be the Messiah.

But Aquila could not get caught up in the emotion of the discourse; he was too concerned with the fact that Crispus was in the yard. Whom could he tell? He glanced around, and this time he caught Timothy's eye. Aquila made a slight gesture with his hand, and Timothy, instantly alerted to a problem, moved so that in a few seconds he was standing beside Aquila.

"Something wrong?" Timothy asked in a whisper.

"See that man?" Aquila answered. "The one standing there by the pile of skins. That's Crispus, the head of the synagogue. Why would he be here? Somehow, Paul ought to be warned."

Timothy looked worried. "But not now," he said. "He gets very angry if he is interrupted in the middle of his talking. We can tell him later to watch out for this man."

"But what if he says something really incriminating? What if he gives Crispus an opportunity to—well, to bring him to trial? The man could be dangerous."

Timothy smiled. "All men could be dangerous, my friend. Paul bears the marks on his body of the enmity of men. It's a chance we have to take."

The words shook Aquila. In spite of all he had gone through, in spite of the fact that he was living in a foreign city as a stranger, he had not, until this moment, thought of danger. He had thought of heartache, of loss, of loneliness, of severed family ties. But he had not thought of danger.

And if there is danger for Paul, Aquila thought, *then it follows that there is danger for me and for Priscilla and the child. For Kara and Joshua. For all four of the people for whom I feel completely responsible.* He felt coldness spread through his body in spite of the warmth of the sun, and for the first time he wondered what they would do if violence were ever directed against them. Where would they run? To whom could they turn?

Cordelius, he thought abruptly. *I wish I had Cordelius at my back.*

Impulsively, he moved away from Timothy and stepped into the shop. As he had expected, Priscilla was standing near the doorway, intent on every word that Paul was saying. Her lips were parted, her eyes shining, and Aquila felt an unreasonable and unexpected stab of jealousy. Other men's wives, he thought with resentment, had such a look only for their husbands. He knew that Priscilla had absolutely no feeling for Paul personally or for any of his followers, but she could be caught and held enthralled by words. *To the point,* Aquila thought sourly, *where even my touch might not influence her at all.*

But as he thought these things, Priscilla turned and saw him. "Are you all right, my lord? Is anything the matter?"

Her instant concern washed away most of his bitterness,

and he was able to think again of the matter that had brought him away from the preaching.

"I've just thought of something," he said in a low voice. "I saw Crispus out there in the yard, and you know he's head of the synagogue. He might very well be a danger to Paul—and so I decided that we ought to be making an effort to keep in contact with all who believe as we do. To form a patchwork of believers so that if we ever need to flee to another city—well, I just think it's a good idea."

She looked puzzled. "I don't understand, my lord."

"I was thinking of Cordelius," he replied. "I think I should be in touch with Cordelius."

Her voice was oddly breathless. "With Cordelius? You plan to write to him, my lord?"

He shrugged. "If I have time. It occurred to me that if I tell you what to write, you might be willing to do it. That way, you could even put in a word of greeting to your friend Marta."

She touched her tongue to her lips as though they were suddenly dry. "I'll do anything you'd like, of course. How could we get the letter to him, my lord?"

"Rufus should be back soon. And if the *Fair Wind* is not going back to Athens, he will surely know of a ship that is. Tonight, before we sleep, I'll tell you what I think should be written and then, when you can, you will write the letter. I have no difficulty at all in thinking of the words that should be said," he confided suddenly, "but I hate the process of writing. You can be my scribe. Just as Timothy acts sometimes as Paul's scribe."

"You don't think it would be unseemly, my lord?"

He felt amazement touch him. "I thought you'd be pleased at the idea."

Color stained her face, and for some reason he could not understand, she did not meet his eyes. "Of course I am," she said quickly. "Look, my lord, the men are leaving the yard. Ought you to go out to be with them?"

With another puzzled look in her direction, Aquila went back outside.

After he was gone, Priscilla turned to find Kara watching her.

"Well, it looks as though you have found a way to get your letter to Marta, doesn't it?" Kara said. "You have only to slip it inside the one for Cordelius."

Priscilla did not smile. "It makes me feel even more deceitful for some strange reason. I never intended to deceive my husband in any way, Kara. I promised myself—" She stopped, reluctant to go on. She had never confided to anyone the vows she had made to herself when she had decided to marry Aquila.

Kara only shrugged. "Sometimes it is necessary to be a little—well, perhaps not deceitful, but devious. Didn't your mother ever explain that women must be skillful in their handling of men?"

Priscilla could not help the laughter that bubbled out. "Such words from you, Kara! You are always blunt and honest and open to your husband, and he accepts you as you are."

"Ah," Kara answered without taking offense, "but it wasn't always so. In the beginning, I was subtle and sometimes sly. The honesty could come only after he had learned to love me."

Priscilla shook her head. "I don't know. Sometimes I think that no amount of love can create honesty and candor. Sometimes I think I will always have to be one thing to my husband and something else to the rest of the world. Do you know what he would say if he knew I am hoping to send a message to his mother?"

Kara grimaced. "He would say it was none of your business and that you should let him handle his own family in his own way."

"Just as Paul is probably going to say that I have explained everything wrong to my father," Priscilla said in discouragement. "Sometimes I think it really was easier right after Marcus was born and I was too absorbed in him to think of anything else."

"Yes, of course, easier. Your husband is suddenly aware of the physical danger to all of us in choosing to follow Jesus. And you are just as suddenly aware that you may meet criticism from not only your husband but also Paul. What do you plan to do about it?"

Priscilla was silent a moment. She was thinking of many things, of the way she had felt when she had the first desire to contact Sarah, the way Aquila had looked when he had sidled inside the door, frightened but determined, the way the words had flowed through her head when she had started to plan her letters. And then, finally, she remembered Aquila's promise that there would be a way to get a letter to Athens. She had known that God would have to provide a way, and a way had been provided. She simply had to believe that God intended her to send word to Sarah.

"I plan to obey my husband," she said sturdily. "I'll write the letter he dictates, and when it's finished I'll add a message to Marta as he suggested. Then I'll pray that God will grant it safe delivery in Athens."

She stopped a little breathless, and Kara smiled at her.

"You know," Kara said in a calm, ordinary voice, "that's just exactly what I thought you would do. Now, come and help me with the thread. I need help in stringing a new warp."

⚈ 21 ⚈

Priscilla wrote her letters with care. Papyrus was too precious to waste on unnecessary words, and so she shaped her sentences with as much skill as she could. When the letter to Cordelius was complete, she carried it out into the yard and offered to read it to Aquila.

"Did you tell him exactly what I said?" Aquila asked.

"Of course. Not always in your exact words, my lord, because you know how important it is to write subtly and to compress the meaning into as few words as possible."

"But the meaning?"

"As nearly yours as I could make it," she assured him. "Shall I read it to you?"

He shook his head. "I'll take your word for it," he answered and turned to ask Joshua to hand him an awl.

Paul, who had overheard, glanced up sharply. "Don't expect me to be quite so lenient," he warned her. "Perhaps your husband allows his fondness to affect his judgment. I will be a sterner taskmaster."

"I want you to be," was all she said.

She hurried back to the room and picked up the letter she had written to Marta. It was brief, but she had asked Marta to try to get news of the baby's birth to Sarah and, if possible, to give Priscilla's love to her mother-in-law. *"This is something just between women,"* she had written, hoping Marta would understand, *"and no man need know that the love was sent or received. But if, later, a message could be sent to my husband telling him that his parents are well, I would be very happy."* She had not been able to say all she wanted to say, but she could only hope it would be enough. She placed the note to Marta inside the letter to Cordelius and wrapped them both in the same oiled cloth that had been around her last letter from Rome.

Then she turned, with pleasure, to the letter to her parents. After a warm greeting to each member of the family, she wrote her news. *"Your grandson, Marcus,"* she wrote, *"was born safely six weeks ago. He looks like his father and it is my prayer that he will be as good and wise as both his father and his great-grandfather, whose name he bears."*

She stopped and thought for a long time. How could she tell of the arrival of Paul in their shop, and how could she tell of the problems that were facing them here in Corinth without frightening her mother and grandmother and upsetting her father?

"We are all well," she finally continued. *"The business has improved to the point that we have hired another tent maker, who is also a Follower of the Way and a fine preacher. We are all learning and growing, and I pray daily that God will touch your hearts with truth so that you, too, will learn the great joy that we have found."*

Just then Marcus woke, announcing his need for food and comfort, so she laid aside her pen. It would be good to have a little more time to think of what she would say next, she thought. Yet when she held the baby in her arms to nurse him, she found that her thoughts were all of the child and of the delight she found in taking care of him.

Oddly enough, then, when she returned to the letter, she discovered that the words she had been seeking were there, waiting to be penned. It was as though the little respite with Marcus had cleared her mind.

"You asked, Father, if we truly believed that this new faith is in accord with all we had learned when we became Jehovites and put aside old pagan beliefs. I wish I could tell you this face to face so that you could see the conviction in my eyes, but I assure you that

everything I learn from my Levite husband about the history of his people, every fact about Moses and Abraham and other great men who have followed the faith only bears out the truth about Jesus. All of the prophecies were fulfilled in the birth and life of Him whom we believe to be the Messiah."

She stopped again, staring at the words anxiously. Had she said too much or not enough? Had she been too blunt? Would she offend her father by such candor? And yet to say less would only deny the truth as she knew it. Well, she would finish the letter and then read it to Paul to see if he was offended. Scraping words off papyrus was a difficult and tedious task, but it could be done. And until she had actually written the words, she could not expect Paul to pass judgment. He could not know what was in her head until the words were written down.

The rest of the letter told of Kara's and Joshua's kindness, of the fact that Marcus was smiling and growing, of her homesickness for Rome and for all of them, but of her willingness to be wherever her husband was. She closed the letter with a few words of love, and then went to find Paul.

"I have finished the letter," she said.

"Then read it to me," he said. "I can scrape this skin and listen at the same time."

"Most of it is personal," she explained. "There is only a little bit about our faith."

"Read only that to me," Paul suggested. "It's none of my business what you have written of the baby and your family. But the other—that's my business."

"Yes, sir," she answered and obediently read the portion of the letter that dealt with her father's question.

When she had finished, Paul was silent a moment, his head still bent over his work. She sat waiting, her heart pounding in her throat. If Paul spoke with censure, what would she do?

But there was no censure on Paul's face when he finally looked up at her. "I am astonished," he admitted frankly.

"I am not only impressed with your ability to put words in proper sequence so that they are logical and clear—and not everyone can do that, you know—but I am even more impressed with your grasp of the truth. You have obviously had fine teachers."

Relief poured through her. "My grandfather taught me my grammar, my Greek, my basic philosophy," she said, "but my husband taught me about Jesus. Oh, I heard Phineas preach in Rome, and I have listened through the door as you preach, my lord, but it was my husband who truly taught me."

"Then I must consider using his skills," Paul answered simply. "If you reflect his teaching, then his gift for teaching must be used."

Pride warmed her. "And the letter is all right?" she asked. "You will not object if I try to get the letter sent to Rome?"

"The letter is fine," Paul said, a rare smile illuminating his face. "I can only hope that there will be other occasions when you can use your husband's teaching and your own obvious skill. Naturally, I think your first concerns should be for your son and your husband. But I can understand your desire to share your knowledge."

"Thank you," she murmured. "I'm grateful that you can approve of what I've done."

She turned to go back into the house and realized that Aquila was watching her. If he was feeling any pride, she thought with a prick of resentment, he was very careful to keep it hidden. When they were alone, he might tell her that he was pleased over what Paul had said, but here, in the company of other men, he kept his face impassive. Well, he had warned her, had he not, that he could not reveal his approval of her accomplishments to other men.

"I'll prepare the evening meal, my lord," she said to Aquila.

He nodded. "Fine," he said. "We'll be ready to eat in an hour." He turned back to his work without another look in her direction, and she hurried into the house. At least, she thought, she wouldn't have to scrape the words off the papyrus. She could be grateful for that much anyhow.

The weeks drifted by, and the letters were sent toward their destinations. Trolas and Rufus had come into port again only a few days after both letters had been finished, and since they were going back to Athens, they took the message to Cordelius and simply made arrangements to put the other one on a ship headed for Tarentum. The captain, a friend of Trolas, had assured them that he would find a trustworthy person traveling to Rome. These were better arrangements than Priscilla had dared hope for, so she tried to put the matter from her mind, knowing that even if all went well, it would be weeks and weeks before she could get any responses.

After the letters had been sent, Paul's preaching continued to be a daily blessing to Priscilla as she sat in the doorway of the shop. Although Aquila never forbade her to go outside, she sensed that he would not be happy if she actually went out into the yard and sat on the fringes of the crowd that gathered to hear Paul. There were a few women among the gathered people, but Priscilla did not know any of them. The number of men who attended the meetings increased all the time. Fortunately, several large fig trees grew at the edge of the yard and threw a welcome shade over the men, so that the midday heat could be endured. Aquila and Joshua had built a small canopy over the place where Paul sat, so he, too, was comfortably sheltered from the sun.

Priscilla never missed a meeting unless Marcus was fussy. It meant, of course, that she could not weave during that hour, as the throwing of the shuttle blotted out so many words. At first she had felt guilty, but even Kara, after only a day or two, had laid aside the shuttle and joined Priscilla on the mat by the door.

"My husband says the shuttle is annoying to the men

closest to the shop," Kara confided. "At first, I was angry and told him so. After all, I said, we, too, have a job that must be done. But now I'm glad. It provides a nice rest in the middle of the day."

Priscilla looked shocked. "You mean you don't enjoy hearing Paul?"

Kara's eyes twinkled. "Now don't get upset. Of course I appreciate hearing him. Although I must confess that sometimes he confuses me. Just a little. It was all so simple and straightforward when Phineas told about Jesus. Paul's oratory is not always easy to understand."

Priscilla laughed with sudden excitement. "Oh, but that's the best part of it. Paul is profound, and his ideas are wonderfully thought-provoking. Never, since my grandfather died, have I been able to listen to someone who stirred my mind in such an exciting way."

Kara looked suddenly disapproving. "I'm not at all sure it's good for a woman to think so much."

"Probably not," Priscilla said in a tone that seemed to indicate complete agreement. "I assure you, I would hear Marcus crying out no matter how caught up in Paul's words I might be."

"In that case," Kara conceded and turned her attention to the gathering in the yard. Paul had just started to speak, and both women were almost instantly absorbed in his words.

It was Priscilla who noticed Crispus coming into the yard. Ever since Aquila had confided his fear of the man, Priscilla was always frightened to see the leader of the synagogue arrive at their gate.

She nudged Kara. "Look," she whispered. "Crispus again."

Kara frowned. "That's the third time he has come. Always with a servant and always they sit back away from the others. I don't like it. Paul should be warned."

"Haven't either of our husbands spoken to Paul about

it?" Priscilla's voice had dropped to a conspiratorial whisper.

"I don't know. I'll ask Joshua tonight."

"Or maybe the opportunity will come that I can speak to Paul about it myself," Priscilla said, remembering the kindness in Paul's eyes when she had read her letter to him.

Kara looked suddenly forbidding, but before she could say anything, Marcus began to wail, and Priscilla hurried to quiet him so that his cries would not disturb the preacher or his listeners.

Later that afternoon, Paul appeared unexpectedly in the doorway of the shop. "Are you busy, Mistress Priscilla?" he demanded, paying no attention to Kara who sat in front of the other loom.

"I'm only weaving," Priscilla said. "Can I help you?"

"Silas and Timothy have gone to the other side of the city for some teaching and will be gone for a few days. I am in need of a scribe, and I don't like to trouble Aquila. He's working on a really difficult skin, and must do the scraping and stretching while the skin is moist and pliable. I would like you to take some dictation for a letter that must be written at once as I have found a messenger who is going to Berea, and I would like to send a note to the brethren there."

She gazed up at him in a state of shock. Her mind dealt with and discarded several facts before she could even answer. Paul's assumption that Aquila's work was the more important, and the fact that he did not even ask if she'd be willing to do what he wanted, did not disturb her too much. All men, she thought, would do the same. But she wondered if Aquila would approve of what Paul wanted her to do. For just a second, she toyed with the idea of asking Paul if he had consulted Aquila, but then she pushed the idea aside. Why should she say anything that might result in Paul's choosing someone else to act as his scribe? Why should she risk being kept at her loom when she had been given a chance to work with a quill?

"I've never taken dictation, my lord," she said.

"You can write. I speak clearly. You should be able to do it well."

She could see that Paul was already totally absorbed in what he wanted to say. He would have no patience with her apprehension.

"Well," she conceded, "I'll try. Unless the baby demands my attention, my lord."

Paul looked across the room at Kara. "Your aunt can take care of the baby," he said.

Kara's eyes flashed, and Priscilla feared for a minute that the older woman might flare up with her usual sharp retort. For a second, Paul's and Kara's eyes met and the tension was so great that Priscilla felt a crackling in the air. Then Kara's eyes lowered.

"Of course, my lord," she murmured with as nearly a docile tone as Kara ever used. "Unless he gets hungry. Then his mother will have to attend to him."

"Well, let's get started," Paul said, "while he's sleeping."

Priscilla sat at the table and drew one of the precious sheets of papyrus toward her. She half hoped that Paul would say something about replacing it someday, but his thoughts were only on the letter that had to be written.

She dipped her quill into the small container of ink and sat waiting.

"Are you ready?" Paul snapped. "Speak up if you're ready."

Anger flickered briefly in her as Paul began his letter.

"Paul, an apostle of Jesus Christ, called by God, to the church at Berea."

The little man strode briskly up and down the room, and the words tumbled out faster than Priscilla could possibly get them down. Words of love and comfort and admonition. Words of warning against the Hebrew Jehovites of

Thessalonica, who were seeking to undermine their faith. Words of wisdom and entreaty.

Priscilla's anger dissipated as she struggled to get the words down exactly as Paul said them. How could she stay angry at anyone in whom the spirit of God so obviously flowed? But her pen simply could not keep up.

"Please, my lord," she begged at last. "I'm sorry but I cannot get all the words, and I don't want to miss any."

Paul stopped and spoke with contrition that was as obviously real as his irritation had been. "I'm sorry," he muttered. "I do this all the time. I get carried away." A sudden smile appeared on his face. "You don't think, then, that you have words at your disposal as good as my words? You haven't decided that you could fill in anything you missed?"

She looked quickly to see if he were being sarcastic, but when she saw the smile, she relaxed and smiled in return. "No, my lord, I know that I couldn't possibly do that. Not until I have learned much, much more than I know now."

"And maybe not even then," Paul said. "You are only a woman, after all."

"Yes, I know," she answered and bent her head over the letter. "Go on, my lord."

Paul nodded and began to speak again, but Priscilla noticed that he made a real effort to speak more slowly. So intent were both of them that neither of them saw Aquila come to the door. Worry and irritation creased his face when he saw his wife's occupation, but he turned without a word and went out into the yard again.

= 22 =

The baby had been fed and settled securely in the small boxlike extension to his parents' bed. Aquila had listened to all the sounds of Marcus's nursing and Priscilla's soothing whispers but he had found none of his usual delight in the nighttime ritual. He was a man who was rarely angry, but tonight he was angry.

It was not just because Priscilla had acted as Paul's scribe without asking permission, he knew, or even because Paul had demanded her help without first consulting her husband, although both of these actions rankled in Aquila's heart. He was perfectly willing to concede that Paul was an unusual man and that Priscilla was more clever than most women. *But I'm still Priscilla's husband,* Aquila thought, *and I deserve more consideration than I've been getting.*

Aquila's anger, however, was due to more than the problem of the dictation. Priscilla had simply gone too far in two other directions, which he had found out about inadvertently. He meant to have it out with her before he slept.

She finished with Marcus and turned with her usual nestling movement to curl up to her husband, but Aquila did not put out his arms to gather her in as was his custom.

"Are you asleep?" she whispered.

"No, I am not asleep," he said coldly.

He knew he did not dare take her into his arms because his body would betray him. It was simply impossible for him to hold her without feeling the stirrings of desire. And tonight he wanted to talk to her without any treacherous intrusion of tenderness or affection.

"Is something the matter?" she asked. "Are you angry?"

"Yes, I'm angry."

She was not coy with him, acting innocent or bewildered. He was glad for that, at least.

"I should have asked your permission to write Paul's letter," she said at once. "I knew it then, and I know it now. I could say that Paul gave me no time to ask, but that wouldn't be true, my lord."

He failed to answer, and lay waiting for her to go on. He had no intention of making things easier for her.

"I was afraid if I asked you and you refused, Paul would get someone else. And I wanted to do it, my lord."

"That's obvious," Aquila said finally. "Neither you nor Paul seemed to care at all how I might feel. It's quite possible, you know, that I would have been pleased that my wife had been chosen to serve. Did you think of that at all?"

"No, my lord."

He could not tell, since they were speaking in whispers, if her voice was really sullen, but he chose to believe it was.

"I would appreciate it in the future," he said coldly, "if you gave me a chance to be either dictatorial or lenient. I would prefer that the decision be left up to me."

"Yes, my lord," she answered, and there was no doubt this time that her tone was sullen.

She turned onto her side with her back to Aquila, and he reached over to pull her back toward him. He knew his fingers were probably hurting her wrist, but he didn't care.

"I'm not finished," he said. "There are other things to discuss with you."

"What other things?" she asked.

"A letter you've written to Marta and something you've discussed with Paul."

She did not answer at once, but he still held her wrist in his hand so he could feel the way her pulse leaped and raced against his fingers. He loosened his grip at once, fearful that her terror might weaken his resolve.

"What letter, my lord?" she whispered, and he saw in the dim light of the tiny, flickering lamp how she had to wet her lips with her tongue before she could speak.

"I don't know what letter. I certainly don't know what was in it. I only guessed from something that Joshua said today—and tried to cover up at once—that you have written something to Marta. Not a word of greeting added to the letter to Cordelius but a letter of your own. With a message you could not trust your husband to read."

She drew in a quick breath, and Aquila spoke sharply before she could say words that might perjure her. *I can stand anything,* he thought, *except her lying. I will not be able to endure it if she lies to me.*

"Don't lie," he said sternly. "I won't tolerate it. And I'll know. I'll surely know."

Her voice came out in a shaky whisper. "How, my lord? How could you know if I lied?"

"Because I know you better than you realize," he answered. "Do you think I don't know when you are teasing and when you're serious?"

But do I really? he thought. *Do I really know her at all?*

"I wrote to Marta and asked her to contact your mother," Priscilla said in an expressionless voice. "I asked Marta to tell your mother about the baby, to tell her we're both well, to tell her that I still loved her." Her voice had grown more defiant as she went along.

"It's my place to contact my parents if they are ever contacted," Aquila snapped. "You had no right."

"Yes, my lord," she answered but he knew she was not speaking in obedience.

"Then why did you do it?" he demanded. "Why?"

"Just at this moment, I'm not sure," she responded. "But at the time I was writing it, I thought it was because of you. Because I couldn't stand it that you were so hurt. Because I thought she ought to know that we still think of her."

He felt conflicting emotions twist in him. He could remember with what pride he had said he would never go crawling back to his father, but Paul's recent talks of love and forgiveness had weakened that resolve. Still, Priscilla had no right—

"How could you still love her," he argued, "when she went off and left you alone with a baby coming too soon?" In spite of himself, his voice was gentler.

She began to cry. "I don't know," she said. "I can't help loving her, and it wasn't her fault that she left me. She was only being obedient to her husband. As you expect me to be, my lord."

He felt himself wincing inside. And yet, that letter should not have been sent without his permission.

"I don't think I mind so much that you wanted to contact my mother," he said at last. "What I mind is that you didn't trust me enough to tell me about it."

"What if I had told you? What would you have done?"

"I don't know," he admitted.

"You would have forbidden that I send it," she said. "If you are as honest as you expect me to be, you'll admit you would not have let me send the letter."

He wanted to tell her she was wrong, but he knew himself too well.

"Well," he said at last, "I can at least hope that she'll never receive it."

"I have prayed that she will," Priscilla responded, her voice defiant again.

"The problem is," Aquila blurted out, "how am I going to trust you in the future? How am I going to know you aren't deceiving me by doing things behind my back? How am I going to live with that?"

She was quiet a little while, and then she said, "I'm sorry. Truly I am. I hadn't thought of it as deceit. I won't do anything like that again, my lord. I was wrong."

He longed to gather her close to him. She was so seldom humble that he hated to let the moment pass, but there was still something else he had to discuss with her.

"And another thing," he said quickly before his resolve

failed him, "Paul told me that you had mentioned Crispus to him. That was my responsibility. Mine or Joshua's. Have you any idea how humiliated I was when Paul questioned me about it? It was as though I were hiding behind a woman's skirts. I don't think I have ever been more embarrassed."

Her voice held nothing but surprise. "I never thought, my lord. He was telling of the problems in Berea and of how dangerous some of the Hebrew Jehovites from Thessalonica had been. It just came out. I told him Crispus could cause trouble for us here, too. That's all."

Aquila felt something very close to despair. "What am I going to do with you?" he groaned. "How am I going to make you aware of the fact that you are a woman and my wife, and that you should act like other women and other wives?"

When she spoke, her words were jerky and widely spaced as though she were hunting for just the right words to say. "I've never told you, my lord, that my grandfather taught me as though I were a boy. He taught me to make decisions, to think clearly, to understand things most women never understand. My mother said it was wrong. She told me over and over that it was wrong."

He heard the way she swallowed to hold back the tears, and he had to keep his fists clenched to prevent his hands from reaching out to touch and comfort her.

"The day I decided to accept your marriage proposal, I promised myself that I would never let you see that side of me. But then when you wanted me to be baptized, I began to forget my promise. I began to act around you as though you were my grandfather. I let myself act naturally. I was wrong."

"Perhaps you let me see a little of your intelligence and your training," Aquila conceded, "but you didn't really trust me."

"How could I trust you? You're a man."

"Your grandfather was a man," Aquila said.

"But you're not my grandfather," she said. Almost at once, she turned and threw her arms around Aquila. "I didn't mean that the way it sounded," she cried. "You are wise and clever and good. I don't know why I do the things I do. I told you before that I am not like other women. I don't know what to say."

Her tears wet his face as she pressed against him. "I'm sorry," she wept. "I'm not a good wife, and I'm sorry."

He didn't know how to answer. In a way, she was right. She wasn't a good wife in the conventional sense, because she was too highly educated, too arrogant. But he would rather have her, with all her faults, he thought, than anyone else.

With a groan that was almost a sob, he gathered her against him and began to kiss her. He felt her ardor grow in response to his. *But we have solved nothing,* he realized. *Even though our anger has turned to love, we have solved nothing. And I am not sure that we ever will.*

When Paul came to the doorway of the shop the next morning, Aquila thought that he had never seen a man so filled with light. It was as though there was something blazing inside of him that emanated through his eyes and his smile.

"Good morning," Aquila said tentatively. "Are you well?"

Joshua also looked up, and Aquila could see that he, too, was aware that there was something different about Paul. He said nothing, however, but merely waited with Aquila to hear Paul's response to the greeting.

"I'm fine," Paul answered. "And I greet you both in the name of the Lord. But I warn you—I am not myself today. I have had a vision, and it seems as though I am not yet back on solid earth."

"You saw the Lord?" Joshua said in amazement.

- *195* -

"Not in the same way that I saw Him along the Damascus Road," Paul answered. "It was simply a light that shone around me and a voice that spoke in my ears. But the voice spoke with a clarity that I have never heard before. Every word was vividly etched on my heart."

Aquila felt Paul's conviction as though it were a tangible thing. "What did He say to you?" he asked.

"You know how worried I was about Crispus," Paul began, "even though the warning about him came from a woman, and women are usually given to exaggeration. Nevertheless, I recognized the danger and I have been deeply concerned."

"I had intended to speak to you about it personally," Aquila said, his voice stiff with embarrassment, "but my wife—"

Paul interrupted. "It doesn't make any difference. She told me because the dictation reminded her of it and the words came out without thought. She's an impulsive girl."

It was as though Paul were explaining Priscilla to her own husband, Aquila thought, and while he was relieved that Paul wasn't angry, he felt irritated that Paul thought he needed to make the explanation.

"If I had thought it had only been her idea, I wouldn't have been so worried," Paul assured Aquila. "It was because I knew she had heard of it from you. You confide a great deal in her, don't you?" he added as though his mind had suddenly veered away from the main topic of conversation.

"Too much, evidently," Aquila said and saw the amusement flash in his uncle's face.

"Well, no matter," Paul said. "The fact remains that I was worried. I prayed for a long time before I slept, but there was no sense of peace or confidence in me. Then, after a few hours of sleep, I woke and saw a brilliant light filling the room."

"Not a dream?" Joshua ventured.

"Not a dream. I was awake. And the voice spoke so clearly that I have not forgotten a word. The voice said, 'Do not be afraid any longer, but go on speaking and do not be silent; for I am with you, and no man will attack you in order to harm you, for I have many people in this city.'"

Aquila's mouth felt dry. "If that is true," he managed to say at last, "then why is Crispus coming to the meetings? Why does he sit in the back and watch us all with suspicious eyes?"

"I don't know," Paul admitted. "It will all be clear in time, I imagine. Perhaps he isn't suspicious. Perhaps he is just curious. Perhaps he, too, is eager to hear the truth."

Aquila gave a short laugh. "I can't imagine it. The head of the synagogue?"

"He wouldn't be the first," Paul said serenely. "In other places, the most prominent Hebrew Jehovites in the synagogue have chosen to follow Jesus. You must understand, my young friend, that all things are possible. You remember what the angel said to Abraham: 'Is anything too hard for the Lord?' It's still true today."

"I know you're right," Aquila said. "But I must confess that I find I still worry about many things."

"Something will happen," Paul promised. "Something will happen someday that will make you so certain of God's care that you will never worry again."

Aquila nodded politely, but his thoughts were not so agreeable. He was thinking that it was all very well for Paul. Paul was someone to whom the Lord appeared with words of comfort and assurance. Paul was not married to a girl who both bewitched and betrayed him.

Paul smiled his rare smile. "You're stuck with me, my friends. Because the Lord has spoken to me, I will stay in Corinth. I will preach and serve the Lord in this city. But it means that you will have me with you, possibly for a long time."

"You are very welcome," Joshua said quickly. "There is

no greater privilege than to have you here with us in our shop and in our house."

"In fact," Aquila added, "your work in the shop is not so important as your preaching. Let us do the work with the tents. You work with the winning of souls."

Paul's eyes glowed. "I am blessed," he said. "And I do not deserve it, because I have insulted you who are my host. In my sudden desire to write to some of my beloved people, I turned your wife into a temporary scribe. And I didn't even ask your permission. Can you forgive me?"

"There is nothing to forgive," Aquila said. "It was she who should have asked permission, not you."

"Then you must forgive both of us," Paul said. "She is an unusual woman, and I think this troubles you. Which I certainly understand. But she is your wife and the mother of your son, so you will have to work it out."

"I know," Aquila said. "I am not as lenient and forgiving as my uncle. There is pride in me."

"Then I will pray for you," Paul said.

Joshua spoke up suddenly. "There's someone coming in the yard. I think it's Crispus."

Aquila felt fear jolt through him, but Paul's face was utterly serene as he turned to greet the man coming toward them.

"Good morning, my friend," Paul said in a calm, clear voice. "You are really early for the meeting."

"I came early," Crispus answered, "because I want to talk to you alone. I want to know what I must do to accept Jesus and be saved."

"The Lord be praised," Paul cried out and ran to grip Crispus's hand. "Come, my friend, come and sit here with me in the shade and let me tell you what the Lord requires of you." He turned back to Aquila and Joshua only long enough to say, "You see, it is just as the Lord told me it would be."

Joshua let out a great sigh of relief and turned to his

work, but Aquila stood for a long time, looking dazedly around him. Paul's vision was a true one, and the proof of it had taken place in front of Aquila's eyes.

But what kind of a man am I, he thought, *that even after all my anger, my first inclination is to hurry in and tell Priscilla about what has happened.* He knew that he would not be able to settle down and work as he should until he had told her of the vision and of the confirmation of its truth. *Well, that's how I am,* he admitted to himself, *so I might as well get it over with.* Without even a glance in Joshua's direction, he turned to go into the room where Priscilla was.

⚊ 23 ⚊

The ship that brought the letter from Athens was not the *Fair Wind*. A friend of Trolas's came from the harbor to deliver the packet to Aquila at the shop.

"Trolas's ship was headed for Ephesus," the young man said. "He asked me to personally see that this letter was delivered to you. He told me to warn you that the letter contained bad news."

Aquila looked down at the packet in his hands, then up at the messenger. "Did Trolas give you this in Athens?"

"Yes. But I did not see any of the people you were sending messages to. I can't tell you any more than what I have already told you."

Aquila nodded. "I understand. Thank you for being good enough to come all the way to our shop to see that we got this safely. Is there anything I can do for you in return? May I offer you a cup of wine?"

The messenger grinned, revealing missing teeth. He lifted a grimy hand and touched his forehead in a sort of mock salute. "Thank you, no. I've got to get back to the harbor in a hurry. There's a fleet of ships coming in from Rome. Bringing some important officials, I understand. Such ships demand the best berths, and they don't stand on ceremony about how they get them. They're not above shoving a smaller ship aside, and if a bit of hull is broken in the process, it's no loss to Rome."

Although he spoke lightly, Aquila thought he saw anger and resentment in the fellow's face. If he was discreet enough to hide that anger from a stranger, Aquila decided, then he was clever enough to have earned Trolas's trust. No wonder he had been chosen to bring the letter from Athens.

"Then, if you won't stay, I'll thank you again for bringing the letter," Aquila said. "Did Trolas or Rufus indicate when they thought they might be in Corinth again?"

"Not for some months." The fellow turned as though to leave and then swung back. He seemed to be trying to make up his mind about something. "I have a small package for your wife," he blurted out. "I was told to put it in her hand."

"Trolas told you that?"

"Rufus did."

"Then, by all means, you must give it to her personally." Aquila felt sure the fellow was wondering why a husband would be so lenient, but he only turned and called Priscilla's name.

In a few seconds, she came out of the shop. She was wiping sweat from her forehead, and Aquila felt a thrust of guilt that they could not move the looms out into the yard where the women would get a bit of breeze. But the noon meetings filled the yard so completely that there was no room left over for looms.

"Did you call, my lord?" Priscilla asked.

"Yes. A messenger has come from Athens, and he says he has a package for you that is to be placed only in your hands."

"From Marta," she said at once. Her eyes were excited, but she waited discreetly until the messenger reached into his tunic and pulled out a small package. Carefully, so that he should not inadvertently touch her fingers, he handed the little bundle to her.

"Here, Mistress," he mumbled.

"Thank you," she said. Aquila could see her squeezing the package as though her fingers would recognize the contents.

"So, then, I'll be on my way," the messenger said quickly. "I have duties facing me."

Aquila put a coin in the fellow's hand and then stood quietly beside Priscilla until they were alone in the yard.

"He thinks I'm too doting," Aquila observed. "But Rufus had said you were to receive the package in your hands. Rufus would have had his reasons."

"Rufus would have thought that my attempt to contact your mother was still a secret," Priscilla responded. "He wouldn't know that I no longer have any secrets from you."

They smiled at each other, and Aquila felt his heart move in that ridiculous way that he never seemed to outgrow. He didn't know what pleased him more—that she was still so lovely, even though she was hot and sweaty and her hand had left a streak of dust on her face, or that he was beginning to believe that he really could trust her.

"Read your letter first, my lord," she suggested. "Whatever is in my package is not as important as what will be in your letter."

He pulled the outer wrapping away and then stood staring in perplexity down at the little scroll. He knew Cordelius's writing, and the inscription that he saw was not recognizable. A quick thrust of apprehension stabbed him. Had something happened to Cordelius? And if so, who had read the letter Aquila had sent so trustingly to Athens?

"It's not from Cordelius," he announced.

Priscilla moved a little closer to him. "Then who?" she asked.

He shook his head. "I don't know. I don't recognize the writing." He unrolled the small scroll and quickly scanned the first few lines. "It's from my sister, Doria," he said in astonishment. "Not written with my father's permission, I'm sure. Wait, let me read what she says."

The news from Doria hit him with a blow. He had intended to read the message aloud, but he discovered the words could not be pushed past the sudden constriction of his throat.

"Greetings to my brother Aquila from Doria," he read in silence. "I write to you with reluctance because I have bad news and because I have been forbidden to contact you. However, I have been assured that a message can be sent with safety. I can only trust the man who has told me this.

"Your friend Cordelius is dead. There was an accident that is not yet fully understood. At any rate, his body was found on the street one night, and that is all I can tell you. His widow, Marta, and his child are now with us. Marta has won our father's affection by agreeing to live as we do.

"I wish I could say more. I send you my love. Please tell your wife that I wish things were different."

Aquila handed the page to Priscilla and watched her face as she read the words it contained. He saw the color drain from her cheeks and wondered if he looked as stricken as she did. When she glanced up at him, compassion had softened her mouth and filled her eyes with tears.

"Oh, my lord," she said in a voice that shook.

Aquila swallowed and managed to get a few words out. "He was a good friend."

"And how brave of Doria to risk sending the letter. It must have taken much courage."

"Do you suppose it was Rufus who encouraged her to write?" His voice was a little more manageable. "How would Rufus have met her?"

"Rufus has contacts all over," Priscilla said. "In all sorts of groups. Hebrew Jehovites and Followers of the Way and even in pagan communities. I will never cease believing that God sent you to Rufus that day in Tarentum."

Aquila knew she was right. He had often felt the same way. But just now all he could take in was that Cordelius was dead and Marta was lost to the new faith. There had been much comfort in the thought that Cordelius was somewhere, even though it was far away, and that his strength and faith were available. Now he was gone. And what had Doria said? An accident that could not be explained. Could he have been killed because of his faith? If so, what did the future hold for him, for his family?

Priscilla spoke abruptly. "I know what you're thinking. I know because I'm thinking it, too. We are all in danger, or will be eventually. You mustn't worry about it. We've simply got to trust in God."

Paul came through the gate and, seeing the unusual sight of Priscilla and Aquila standing talking in the middle of the day, he paused in obvious surprise. "Is something the matter?" he asked.

Aquila handed over the letter. "We've had bad news," he answered. "My friend is—" His voice broke and he stood in silence as Paul read the brief message.

Paul handed back the letter. "So it goes on," he said softly. "Stephen was stoned—to my eternal shame—and others will die for the faith. It will be my own fate someday. I'm certain of that. But, as I heard Mistress Priscilla say when I came through the gate, we've simply got to trust in God."

"At least," Priscilla said, "I didn't go into baptism the way Marta did. At least I would have the promise of the Resurrection to comfort me if I were in her position."

"You would also have danger hanging over your head if you were to persist in being a Follower of the Way," Paul said.

Aquila saw both the surprise on Paul's face and the conviction on Priscilla's, but he was still too stunned to react to either of them.

Priscilla suddenly turned to her husband. "What do you suppose happened to the message I sent to your mother?"

"If you're lucky," Aquila answered slowly, "it was just destroyed. No doubt the letter was delivered to Marta, and she gave it to Doria. Didn't you tell me once that Marta was no scholar at all? Doria can at least write a clear letter."

"Maybe," Priscilla answered. She looked down at her

hands as though she had just suddenly remembered that she was holding something. "But wait," she added, her voice growing warm and eager. "Maybe there is some sort of an answer here."

"Your wife wrote a letter, too? With your permission?" Paul asked Aquila.

"Yes, she wrote," Aquila answered.

"With your permission?" Paul persisted. "A wife must be subject to her husband. This is especially important among those of us who follow Jesus. That we might set an example."

Aquila met Paul's eyes. "If she wrote it without my knowledge," he said, "it was only a temporary thing. I am fully aware of the message she sent, and I'm not angry."

Paul shook his head. "You are too lenient," he muttered.

"Someday we'll talk about it," Aquila said, stiffly.

Priscilla had been unwrapping the little package while the men talked, and her sudden cry made Aquila turn to her quickly.

"What is it?"

It was obvious that she could not answer him with words. Mutely, she held out her hand, and he saw the slender silver bracelet that lay on her palm, glistening in the sun. He recognized the bracelet immediately. He had never, since his earliest childhood, seen his mother without that circle of silver on her arm.

"It's my mother's," he said in amazement. "Is there a message with it?"

"No message, my lord," Priscilla managed to whisper. "But what do I need of words? This bracelet tells me all I need to know. It tells me that your mother got my message, and it tells me that she still loves us."

Completely unaware of Paul, Aquila took Priscilla's hand in his so that he might look more closely at the bracelet. The sun glittered against it, highlighting the tiny dents that marred its surface.

"Look," he said. "Those dents are where we bit it, my sisters and I, when we were teething."

Priscilla's breath came out in a sound that was half laughter, half sob. "And when Marcus begins to cut teeth, he can do the same," she said. "Your mother must have known it, my lord. Surely this is her way of saying that she knows she is a grandmother and that she cares about her grandchild. Don't you agree?"

"But how do you suppose she got your message? Would Marta have given it to her?"

Priscilla shook her head. "I don't think so. But Doria. Doria is a brave girl, and she might have—" Her breath caught and she said in a rush, "If she actually talked to Rufus, my lord, it's possible that she is beginning to believe as we are. Isn't that possible?"

Aquila, still holding her hand, gazed at her in wonder. She had a wisdom and a perception that constantly amazed him. But in spite of this, her touch was still able to delight him. Slowly he took his hand away, because it was important that he be able to think clearly, without distraction.

"I suppose it could be possible," he said.

"We'll find out when Trolas's ship comes into harbor next time," Paul said. "In the meantime—"

"In the meantime," Priscilla said, her attention so much on her husband that she did not appear to be aware that she had interrupted Paul. "In the meantime, we can pray. We can pray that God's spirit of truth and love will move among the family in Athens. And then, someday, who knows? We may even meet again. In love." Her fingers gently pushed the slender bracelet onto her arm, and her eyes were warm when she looked up.

Even the thought of Cordelius's death was bearable, Aquila thought, with Priscilla's comfort and strength available to him. He had married her out of desire; he had never dreamed that someday she would be a source of courage and hope. Perhaps it was wrong of him to feel so. Was it proper and right to turn to one's wife for such things? And who could he ask? Paul would surely say he was foolish, and his father would have laughed at him. There was Joshua, of course. He could talk to Joshua.

"In the meantime," Aquila said, forcing his voice to be practical and firm, "there is work to be done. Even grieving and praying must occasionally be put aside for work."

Priscilla bent her head in acquiescence. But Aquila knew that she understood his curtness. She would be willing, as he was, to wait until they could be alone to talk. Then they would be able to share the sorrow of Cordelius's death and the possible miracle of a new faith for Doria.

Unexpectedly, Paul spoke up in a humble voice. He had never seemed humble before. "Your faith and your confidence impress me greatly, Mistress Priscilla. It's time, I think, for me to begin to talk more seriously to you and to your husband. I had thought to use him as a teacher. I believe now that I must use both of you. Are you willing to serve?"

Aquila saw the excitement flame in Priscilla's eyes, saw the eager curve to her lips and knew instantly that she wanted to let words of willingness tumble out. Instead, she looked at her husband first as though to get his approval.

When she spoke, her voice was meek. "I'm grateful, my lord, that you think I'm worthy," she said to Paul. "But it all depends on my husband. If he consents, I will do anything you desire. But if he forbids it, then of course, I must do as he says."

She was wholly sincere, Aquila realized with a rush of joy. Her obedience was not a form to be observed out of duty but an act to be performed with love. He was as sure as though she had told him so. Again, his throat closed with emotion, but he forced himself to speak.

"If Paul thinks we can serve in the ministry," he said, "then I am completely willing."

"Thank you, my lord," she said, the simple words shining with happiness.

"Then," Paul said, "we'll plan on it. But for now we must begin to work on the new tent that has been ordered. And you, Mistress Priscilla, must get back to your weaving."

Neither Aquila nor Priscilla questioned his right to make decisions. This home was Paul's as much as it was Joshua's or Aquila's. And his authority was even greater.

⚊ 24 ⚊

Marcus was crawling everywhere and pulling himself to his feet, chuckling and crowing with pride at his accomplishments, when Priscilla discovered she was pregnant again. For a few days, she felt only a sense of resentment. It was too soon. She wasn't ready for the discomfort of another pregnancy. Besides, she would be so restricted with two small children that Paul would no doubt think her incapable of helping with the teaching or writing. He had continued to use her occasionally as a scribe, always carefully asking Aquila's permission first, and he had encouraged her to teach the few women who had come to the meetings. At first, he questioned her closely as to what she had said and what facts she had taught, but in only a short time, he had evidently come to trust her implicitly.

Now, with another baby on the way, he might think her unfit to do these things. As Aquila might. And she had to admit, she reflected honestly, that Marcus was a healthy, intelligent little boy. There was no denying the possibility that this had come about because she had neither studied nor written during her pregnancy and the early months of his life.

It's not fair, she thought rebelliously. *It's not fair.* But that same evening, searching her grandfather's scrolls for a portion of Scripture to comfort her, she found the section of Proverbs in which the scriptural writer had spoken of a virtuous woman. The words glowed with praise and appreciation, and Priscilla read them over and over.

Aquila found her sitting in the doorway, turning the scroll to the last bit of daylight.

"What are you reading?" he asked.

"The part of Proverbs about a virtuous woman. I had become so fond of being a teacher and a scribe that I felt unhappy about the fact that I am going to have another child so soon. It was wrong of me, and these words seem to help me."

Aquila sat down beside her. "I know how you must feel. I do. You have blossomed under Paul's tutelage, and I have watched your growth with amazement." He hesitated. "And pride," he added slowly.

"Truly, my lord?" She could not really believe that she had heard the words.

"Truly. But there is a season for everything, my love," he went on. "Perhaps during the slow growth of the new baby, you will be able to grow so much spiritually just by being obedient and quiet that you will be an even better teacher someday."

She smiled and watched with delight the way his lips curved under his beard in a slow, answering smile. "It's easy for you to say, my lord," she said demurely. "You don't have to be obedient to anyone."

"To my God," he said. "Sometimes to Joshua and sometimes to Paul. Many times to Kara and occasionally even to you."

They laughed together and then her face sobered. "It's not easy for me," she confessed. "I'm not naturally obedient. You will have to help me, my lord."

"I will tell you many things about our history and our faith," he said in a decided tone. "As a member of the tribe of Levi, I have been taught things that even many Hebrew Jehovites do not know. I wouldn't want you to study, exactly, and I certainly don't think you should compose your letters—other than a woman's note to your mother— but I see no harm in your listening to tales. Does that comfort you?"

She rolled the scroll carefully between her two hands. "You are better to me than I deserve," she said in a low voice. "Why do you suppose God chose to bless me so much by giving me to you?"

He grinned. "Probably because He knew that every other woman in the world would bore me—and nearly every other man in the world would beat you on a regular basis."

Once more their laughter blended together in the evening air. "I know you're happy about the coming child," she said at last. "So I'll try to be happy, too."

"Yes, I'm happy," Aquila said slowly. "But I'll never be happy the way I was the first time. Now I know that one can only pray for blessing on both you and the baby. I—" he hesitated and then blurted out the words. "I don't like it that you have to suffer. I don't like that part of it at all."

Daringly, she reached over to take his hand, not even caring that Joshua or Kara could come out and see her. "Thank you, my lord. Not many men could say that. In an odd sort of way, it makes the whole thing easier for me. To know you understand and care."

"You will never know," he said in a whisper, "how very much I care. Even when I am angry with you, I still love you."

He had said the words only once before, and the impact of them jolted her heart.

"And I love you," she answered. "I'll be able to wait now, my lord, until the baby is born. Then when he is old enough, you and I will begin again to do the Lord's work in Corinth."

A brisk, clean breeze, smelling of early autumn, blew across the water, topping small waves with foam and keeping most of the stench of the harbor away from the deck of the *Fair Wind*, where Aquila sat on the warm planking facing Rufus and Trolas.

"It has been many months since we've seen you and even

more months since you've been able to sit and talk like this," Rufus commented. "I wish it happened more often."

Aquila nodded, aware of the weariness that seemed to fill him so much of the time lately. There was never any time to just sit and relax and talk of the things that delight a man. He was constantly exposed to the worry of the business, to the intensity of Paul, to the problems and privileges of being a father and husband. He remembered the times when he and Cordelius had discussed politics and had made jokes together about a dozen things. Sometimes, he thought, a man needed to just be with other men for a little while, men who talked about things as casual as fishing or as serious as the Law.

He grinned at Rufus. "I wish it did, too. But the opportunity is rare. Fortunately Joshua thought I should come down to the ship and pick up the supplies you brought for us. I brought a small cart to haul them in, and I informed the family I'd be gone for a while. Paul and Joshua can handle things while I'm gone."

"Is everything well at your home? Your wife? The little one? Paul and Joshua?" Trolas seemed to understand exactly how Aquila was feeling, and he stretched out on the deck in a manner that suggested the entire day was at his disposal.

"Everything is fine," Aquila answered. "My wife expects another child any day, and little Marcus is already saying a few words and demanding more attention than any child should have."

Rufus grinned, locking his hands behind his head and stretching out in the same position his brother had assumed. "I know of no child who deserves it more," he said. "A fine little lad. May all go well when the second child is delivered."

Trolas nodded his agreement, and for a few seconds the three men were silent.

"What of Paul?" Rufus asked at last. "He's still with you?

Still preaching? Word of his power is spreading all over the world. Or at least every part of the world where the *Fair Wind* puts in. We keep hearing his name wherever we go."

"He's still with us and still preaching," Aquila answered. "But I must confess that I get more and more worried about him. It seems to me that he is gaining more and more enemies in the Hebrew community. I thought that when he left the synagogue they would ignore him and just leave him alone. But instead I keep hearing reports of slander against him and indications that the leading Hebrew Jehovites hate him."

"Really hate Paul, you mean?" Rufus asked. "Do you think they plan to make trouble for him?"

Aquila nodded, his face somber. This was the real cause for his fatigue, he realized. The constant burden of apprehension sat on his shoulders with the heaviness of a woman's water jar. "They keep seeking a way to silence him," he admitted. "I wish he would be a little more discreet, but nothing can make him stop preaching as he does. It's true that he wins souls, but he also wins enemies."

"What can the Hebrew Jehovites do?" Rufus asked. "They have their laws, which apply to their own people, but what can they do to someone who is outside their door?"

"They can do many things," Aquila answered somberly. "You surely heard what happened to Cordelius in Athens. Although I know nothing of the details, my sister indicated that his death was not a normal accident. My own guess is that he was killed."

Rufus and Trolas exchanged a look, and Aquila saw the confirmation of his suspicions in their faces.

"We don't know any details either," Rufus said. "But we heard many rumors. Your guess is undoubtedly correct."

"So, you see?" Aquila said. "It could happen here, too. Paul could meet with an 'accident' as easily as Cordelius did."

Trolas looked dubious. "It's risky, though," he argued.

"In a city where Roman rule is in effect—as it is here in Corinth—there is a risk in such activities. Especially to a Roman citizen, which Paul is."

"They mean to do something, though," Aquila insisted. "I'm sure they mean to hurt him in some way."

"Didn't I hear that there is a new proconsul in Corinth?" Rufus asked. "A Roman magistrate named Gallio?"

Aquila nodded. "Yes. A famous man, I understand. The brother of a great Roman poet. Seneca? Is the brother's name Seneca?"

Trolas grinned. "Even poor sailors have heard of people like Seneca and Gallio. Perhaps Gallio has absorbed some of his brother's gentle philosophy, in spite of his legal training, and he might bring a new atmosphere to Corinth."

Aquila's grin was rueful. "Corinth can stand any help it can get. But something has just occurred to me. Do you suppose the Jews would dare bring a legal suit against Paul? What if they would take him before Gallio?"

"Then you can only hope that Gallio will be fair and just and generous," Rufus said. His face had grown somber. "If Paul gets into that much trouble in Corinth, it's possible that his ministry here will be finished. To try to fight against organized opposition is a little like banging one's head against a stone wall."

Before either Aquila or Trolas could comment, the sound of running feet was heard, and they all turned to see a young boy bounding up the plank that led from the wharf to the deck.

"I bring a message to Aquila," the boy panted.

Aquila stood up. "Yes? What is it?"

"Your uncle told me to tell you that by the time you get home, your second child will have been born. He knew you would want to know."

Aquila felt the same fear that had filled him when Marcus had been born. Why had Priscilla let him come down to the harbor? Why hadn't she told him that her time had come? Surely, she must have known. She was too small to have a baby in only the several hours he had been gone.

He had a sudden memory of the way her face had looked that morning, white, strained, anxious. And he had not paid any attention. He had thought only of his own fatigue, his own need to get away and talk to his friends. It was very possible that she had been in labor most of the night. She had kept it from him when Marcus was born; she would be even more apt to do so now.

"I must go," he announced quickly. "I must be there to greet my new child when it arrives. I must be the one to tell my wife that she has been courageous and strong. It would never do—"

"Just hurry home," Rufus said. "Leave the little cart here, and I'll fill it with the items you ordered and deliver them to your shop later today. That way, we can hear the good news first hand."

"Would you do that?" Aquila said. "I would appreciate it very much."

"What are friends for?" Rufus answered. "And, listen, tell your wife, when she is safely delivered, that we have brought her another bundle of papyrus. Larger than the first. It came into our hands by accident. Or so pagans would say. We Followers believe that even the smallest events can be brought about by the hand of God."

Aquila laughed. "She'll begin to believe that papyrus comes to her automatically when she has a child. I'll let her thank you herself. But I can tell you now you could not bring her anything that could make her happier. She and Paul look on papyrus as though it were gold."

"Good. Now, go, my friend, so that you'll arrive in good time to welcome the new member of the family."

Aquila waved and sprinted down the plank and along the wharf. But as he ran, his every breath was a prayer that Priscilla would be safe, that the child would be safe, that in the future he would be more aware of Priscilla's needs and less aware of his own.

Joshua was waiting for him at the gate, his face bright with a smile.

"The child is born?" Aquila gasped, completely out of breath from his running.

"Only two minutes ago," Joshua cried. "Priscilla will never know you weren't here at the instant of birth. A girl this time, my son. Kara has announced that it is a girl."

"Should I pretend I'm disappointed that it's not another son?" Aquila asked, feeling his mouth stretch into a smile that he knew must be fatuous.

"My own conviction is that a strong man never needs to pretend to be anything he isn't," Joshua said. "There are men who believe I should be unhappy because I have a sharp-tongued wife. But what do they know of her goodness and her strength? If you are happy to have a daughter, then admit it."

Aquila put his hand on his uncle's shoulder. "I've been meaning to talk to you," he said. "This certainly is not the time, but one day soon, when we both have an hour to spare. I want your opinion on certain aspects of marriage."

Joshua shook his head in mock astonishment. "You are free to talk to me, of course. But what do I know about any marriage but my own? Have faith in yourself, my boy, in your own feelings. Ah, here's Kara with your daughter."

But before Aquila pulled the covers from the small, new face, he asked, "Is Priscilla all right?"

"She's tired and weak," Kara said. "She wanted you to leave, you know. She didn't want you to have to hear her this time."

"She's braver than I am," Aquila said and lifted the cover with a gentle hand.

The baby, even though she was so new, was obviously like Priscilla. Damp hair formed small whorls of reddish gold on the small head, and Aquila was sure the little eyes were blue.

"Lovely!" Aquila said. "God be praised! May I speak to my wife?"

"As soon as the midwife is finished," Kara said. "In the meantime, hold your daughter and let your uncle bring you a cup of wine."

It was easy to forget, Aquila thought, in this moment of fulfillment, that danger still lurked along the edges of their existence. But he did not dare forget. If anything, this small bundle of helplessness in his arms only made his responsibility greater. He bent his head. "My God, my God," he prayed, and did not have the words he needed to finish his request.

When he was finally allowed to stand by Priscilla's door and look in at her, he felt as though he could not bear to see how worn and tired she looked.

"And what will we name her, my love?" he asked after he had expressed his appreciation for the gift of the child. "Have you any ideas at all? We have talked only of boys' names—which was your idea, not mine."

Her voice was weak. "I knew all the time it would be a girl. Are you disappointed?"

"No. She's exactly what I want."

"Then may I name her Sarah? She's not very Roman at all, so Flavia wouldn't be suitable. I guess she doesn't look like a Sarah either, but the name would suit my heart."

"My mother would be honored," Aquila said, "as I am. She will be Sarah. And may she be as beautiful as her mother—"

"And as good as her grandmother," Priscilla finished.

"I have a surprise for you," Aquila said. "You won't believe me when I tell you that Rufus and Trolas have more papyrus for you."

Her face lit up. "How wonderful," she said. "When the time comes, I'll write more letters to my family. And some day, God may grant our prayers and bring them all to a belief in Christ."

What had Joshua said? Trust your own feelings? "If anyone can persuade them," Aquila said earnestly, "then it will be you. God has given you a special gift with words and understanding. I could never write as you do."

She had looked happy when he had thanked her for the baby, but now she looked radiant.

"I'll let you rest," Aquila said and turned to leave. *We have given each other a gift,* he thought. *She spared me the pain of hearing her scream, and I gave her the compliment I've been too cowardly to give her before. There has been more than a child born to us. We have experienced a growth in our love.*

= 25 =

For several months following the birth of her second child, Priscilla experienced the same dreamy contentment that had been the core of her life after Marcus was born. However, the tranquility was shorter-lived the second time. Almost imperceptibly, she began thinking of things that had nothing to do with her children, her weaving, or her household chores. Sitting at her loom or nursing her baby, she found herself thinking of the history of the Hebrews that Aquila had taught her during her pregnancy. Portions of Scripture, tag ends of old tales, prophecies, and poetry ran through her head. Paul's convictions that Jehovite prophecy had been fulfilled in the coming of Jesus blended so perfectly with the things she had learned from Aquila that she felt sometimes as though she simply had to write it all down. She was no longer satisfied with the brief references she made to her faith in the letters she wrote home. Someday she would have to write at length and in detail about the convictions she had.

Somehow she felt that the time to write was not yet. And it wasn't only because she was a new mother. For some reason, she was not ready yet to say the things she wanted to say. As knowledgeable as she was, as convinced of the truth as she was, something held her back. There was still some lack in her although she had no idea what it was.

So, although her mind writhed and twisted with constant thoughts, though she shaped sentence after sentence in her mind, she was content to wait.

As absorbed as she was in her thinking and her children, she was less aware of what was going on around her than usual. Even Aquila's growing apprehension and concern escaped her at first. Then one day Kara startled Priscilla out of her self-absorption.

"Are you at all aware of the strangers who have been coming to the noon meetings?" Kara asked abruptly. "I know you still sit at the doorway to listen, but I don't think you even look out into the yard. Joshua says there have been both Hebrews and Romans among the usual men. He's upset about it, I'll tell you. And no wonder. I don't like the looks of it myself."

"I don't know why I haven't noticed," Priscilla said with real distress. "I suppose it's because I've been so absorbed with the baby, and Marcus gets more active every day. Although," she added honestly, "you do so much for Marcus that I really can't use him as an excuse at all. What does Joshua say about these men? And why do you suppose Aquila hasn't said anything to me?"

"None of us have said anything until now," Kara said, "because we didn't want to trouble you. It was enough, we thought, that you take care of the baby. But I've seen the way you've been thinking. I can tell that you are anxious to get back to the teaching, the writing. I would have scolded you for it when Marcus was tiny. But now things are—different."

"Does Joshua recognize the Hebrew men?"

"Some of them. They're leaders in the synagogue. And the Romans who come may or may not be connected with them. It's hard to tell."

"Some Romans have accepted the fact that Jesus is the Christ," Priscilla said in a hopeful tone.

Kara threw her shuttle with vehemence. "Don't try to be too optimistic about this. I'm frightened."

Those were not words that Kara would ordinarily say, and Priscilla reached out to touch Marcus, who sat beside her playing contentedly with several small blocks of wood. There was comfort in the solid warmth of him, and fortified with this small solace, Priscilla was finally able to speak calmly to the older woman.

"Oh, come, Kara, you're not one to be frightened. I would have thought that was a word you didn't even know."

"I'm frightened more often than you know," Kara said, her mouth grim. "There's so much more to be frightened about. Marcus and the baby. You and Aquila. Even Paul. If anyone had ever told me that I would come to care for him so much that the thought of his being in danger would distress me so—"

"I know," Priscilla said quickly, "you wouldn't have believed it, would you? But there's something about him, some quality that catches and holds your heart. I feel the same way."

"He's definitely in danger," Kara said. "In more danger than we are. In fact, you and Aquila are in more danger than Joshua and I are. We don't teach or preach. All we do is offer some hospitality to the faithful. But Paul—and your husband—even you—though I can't believe that anyone would do anything to a young mother—"

"If Paul's in danger, we're all in danger," Priscilla said definitely. "I guess I've known it all along but just refused to accept it. What can we do?"

"Joshua says we can't do anything. He says that the only possibility is to move away from Corinth. To pack up and take our business and go. But we'd have to persuade Paul to go with us. And it would be as easy to persuade this loom to throw its own shuttle."

"Easier," Priscilla agreed. "Well, if we can't do anything about it, we can't. But, Kara, what if we did have to move away? Would you be willing to go?"

"I wish we could go back to Rome," Kara said.

Priscilla looked across at the older woman and saw, with

a stab of pity, the homesickness that etched lines of age on Kara's face.

"I wish so, too," Priscilla said gently. "But if we couldn't go to Rome?"

"Then," Kara replied, some of the old vigor coming back into her voice, "then we'd have to go where the Lord leads us. I told you once I thought we were in His care. I still do. But I never believed for one minute that being in His care meant we were safe from all danger. I'm not even sure that all my belief will make me any braver if terrible things start to happen."

Joshua spoke suddenly from the doorway. "Trouble," he said hoarsely. "We're in terrible trouble."

"So soon?" Kara said, dread weighing down her voice. "I knew it would happen. I had only hoped it would not happen so soon."

Priscilla was on her feet in an instant. "Aquila?" she cried. "Has anything happened to Aquila?"

Joshua's eyes swung from one woman to the other. "Not to Aquila exactly," he said. "But to Paul. And Aquila chose to go with him. As a witness, he said. As a friend."

Priscilla stood stricken. "What?" she whispered at last. "What exactly happened?"

Joshua shook his head from side to side, seeming to grope for the words he needed to say. Finally an explanation came out in jerky sentences. "The men who have been coming to the meetings. They must have been spies of a sort. They've come with Roman soldiers to arrest Paul. They've taken him away."

"And Aquila went along?" Priscilla seemed unable to take in anything except that Aquila was gone. "Didn't he know he couldn't do anything to help Paul? Didn't he know he'd be helpless around Roman soldiers?"

She started to shake, her teeth chattering as though she were very cold. Kara moved over to Priscilla and put her arms around her.

"I tried to tell him," Joshua said shakily. "I tried to tell him, and so did Paul. He wouldn't listen. He just kept saying that he was going along."

"And he didn't even say goodbye," Priscilla cried, the tears coming at last.

"He wanted to," Joshua assured her. "He would have come in if the soldiers had given anyone any time to do anything. But they didn't. They just tied Paul's hands behind him and marched him away. Aquila had to almost run to keep up."

"But we need him," Priscilla wept. Turning, she threw her arms around Kara's neck. "Oh, Kara, Kara, what will I do?"

For a few minutes, Kara held Priscilla's slim body, patting her gently. Then, firmly, she pushed the girl away. "I've heard you say again and again that we have only to trust God, only to pray. Are you unable to follow your own convictions then?"

Shame stopped Priscilla's weeping. Kara was right. It had been so easy to talk about trusting God when the problem concerned someone else. How simple it had seemed when they talked of the possibility of Doria's discovering the true faith to suggest that the whole thing be left up to God. And how impossible it was to speak so glibly now when Aquila had deliberately thrust himself into danger.

"I'm sorry," Priscilla said at last. "It's wrong to be so frightened, I know. You'll have to pray for me," she said to Joshua and Kara. "I just don't think I can stand it."

"Don't forget there are a few powerful men on our side," Joshua said. "I sent word to Titius immediately. He lives only a stone's throw from the proconsul's residence. If he can do anything, I know he will."

Joshua was obviously suppressing his own fear in order to offer comfort to Priscilla, and she was grateful.

"This is twice," she said softly, "when you two have

somehow given me enough courage to go on. I hope you both know how much I love you."

Kara looked embarrassed and Joshua cleared his throat as though he intended to speak, but he said nothing.

"You're overwrought," Kara said, her voice stern. "You'll have no milk for the baby tonight if you don't stop upsetting yourself. My advice to you is that you go to your loom and weave for a while. The motion of the weaving will soothe you. In the meantime, my lord, you go and see if you can learn anything about what's going on. Be careful, of course, but perhaps you can discover something."

It seemed perfectly natural for Kara to order everyone around, Priscilla thought, sitting down in front of the loom and seeing Joshua hurry out the door. Kara was the strong one. Priscilla picked up the shuttle, fitted it between the threads, and tossed it across with the motion that women had used for centuries.

It was true that the repetitious movements of her hands soothed some of the panic that filled her, but at the same time her mind was freed by the automation of what she was doing to move in a dozen different directions. Why had Aquila done what he had done? Hadn't he thought of her? Of the children?

Once more she felt shame touch her. She was being selfish. She should be feeling pride that her husband had risked so much for a friend, for what he believed. Hadn't they discussed it many times? Hadn't they honestly faced the fact that they had not chosen the safe way? Hadn't she been the one to say over and over that if they only trusted enough—

But that was when she had been lying safely in her bed, Priscilla admitted to herself, and her husband had been lying beside her. Now he was gone and she was alone.

And the thing that tore her apart, she realized, was not that she was physically afraid because of her aloneness. Joshua and Kara were with her, and there were a dozen friends to whom she could go for protection. It wasn't that at all. It was because Aquila was dearer to her than anyone else ever had been or ever could be. Dearer than her grandfather had been, dearer than her children could ever be.

I thought I knew how much he meant to me, she reflected in growing terror, *I thought I knew everything there was to know about love. But I didn't know anything until now. I didn't know that the heart can break with a pain that is worse than anything I ever felt in childbirth.*

The tears began again but she made no effort to wipe them away. *If it means I am weak and cowardly, then I will just have to accept that,* she thought. *Not everyone can be as strong as Kara is.*

She looked across the room and met Kara's eyes. To her astonishment, she saw that Kara's face, too, was wet with tears.

"You can cry all you want to," Kara said. "Just don't stop praying."

Mutely, Priscilla shook her head. Every breath she drew was a prayer, she thought. But was it enough? And treacherous and destructive, the question filled her: had Marta prayed that Cordelius would be safe? And if so, was it any wonder that she broke when her husband's body was found on the street of Athens?

Oh, God, oh, God, Priscilla thought, *keep such thoughts out of my heart. Give me the kind of faith I need to bear this pain and fear.*

Aquila sat, trembling with weariness, in the back of the large room where the proconsuls of Achaia held their public hearings. Thanks to Titius's quick thinking and wise discretion, Aquila had been rescued from the precarious position he had been in when Paul had first been arrested. Titius's calm logic and persuasiveness had finally convinced Aquila that he could not serve Paul if he angered the soldiers. It was better, Titius had assured him, to simply be a casual bystander, to blend himself in with the crowd of curious Jehovites who had come to see what was going to happen. There would be time enough later on, Titius had said, to take a stand if it became necessary. But perhaps it would not be necessary. Rumor had it, Titius had whispered in Aquila's ear, that Gallio was a man of compassion.

Aquila tried to hide his weariness, his fear. He kept his hands knotted in fists in his lap so that the trembling he could not control could not be seen. He remembered what Trolas and Rufus had said about Gallio, and he dared to hope that Titius was right, that the man who would try Paul would indeed be a man of justice and generosity.

He simply had to hope for that because he didn't know what they would do if Paul were condemned to death or even if he were sent to prison. If the Jehovites succeeded in getting rid of Paul, everyone who was a Follower of the Way would be in trouble. Paul's prestige and Roman citizenship might protect him a little, but not everyone had prestige—nor, for that matter, Roman citizenship.

At least I am a Roman citizen, Aquila thought with a sense of relief, *and so my family is protected a little.* It was the first he had allowed the thought of Priscilla or the children to even enter his mind. If he had thought of them, he would not have followed Paul. *That is the penalty of being a husband and a father,* Aquila thought. *Paul is responsible only for himself. I am responsible for three other people. No, five. Joshua and Kara are as much my responsibility as though they were my own parents. But in spite of all of this, I couldn't just stand there and let them take Paul away. Perhaps if Timothy or Silas had been there, but they were away again, preaching across the city. So there was only me.*

There was a sudden sharp announcement that rode clearly over the babble of voices that filled the room. The proconsul was coming in. Everyone immediately stopped talking, and heads swiveled to watch Rome's representative stride through the doorway and go to sit on the chair that had been placed on a small dais. Gallio was a tall man with military bearing, dark, piercing eyes, and a mouth that looked as though it could be grim and hard. Surrounded by soldiers, he exuded an aura of authority.

Here was the man who would decide Paul's fate, Aquila thought, and almost at once prayer filled him. He had been praying almost constantly since Paul had been arrested, but nothing had seemed to comfort him.

"The trial of Paul of Tarsus," announced the court crier. "The accusers are Simeon, Jacob, and Eliab. I call them all to hear my lord's pronouncements."

Almost immediately, Paul was hustled in from the side door, and a half dozen men, all of them known to Aquila, came to the front to take the position of the accusers. Paul, in spite of the fact that his hands were bound and that he had obviously had no rest, looked calmer than the men who had been responsible for bringing him to this place of trial.

"The accusation?" Gallio said quietly.

Eliab stepped forward. There had been a time, Aquila thought, when Paul had hoped that Eliab would join them. His attendance at the meetings had been regular, and he had never been one to call out angry or barbed questions. But the frank hatred in Eliab's eyes as he now looked at Paul was proof that the man had simply been a spy and a fine actor.

"This man, my lord," Eliab said in a loud, angry voice, "has been persuading men to worship God contrary to the Law."

Gallio's calm response seemed even more quiet in comparison to Eliab's blustering. "What law do you refer to, sir? Roman law? We have no rules as to how a man must worship his god."

"Not Roman law, my lord," Eliab cried. "Jehovite law. He is a Hebrew Jehovite, this Paul, and he has distorted our Law and twisted it to suit his own fancy. He—"

Gallio's voice rode over the angry sputtering of Eliab. "You have made your accusation. Let me speak."

Eliab stepped back, obviously irritated at the interruption. His voice was a muffled attempt at courtesy. "Yes, my lord, we await your verdict."

Gallio glanced at Paul, and Paul took a deep breath as though to speak in his own defense, but Gallio waved him to silence. Turning to the accusers, Gallio spoke firmly. "If you had accused this man of some wrong or some vicious crime, it would be reasonable to expect me to listen to your claim and to put up with your complaint.

"But such is obviously not the case. You are quibbling over the way you observe your own religious law, and this has nothing to do with me. Look after it yourselves. I will have absolutely nothing to do with the matter. You may leave the court."

"But, my lord," Eliab cried.

"You heard me!" Gallio's voice had not actually increased in volume, but the authority in it was so intense that none of the accusers dared to speak up again. "Leave the court at once. Untie this man," he added to one of the soldiers, "and clear the room of these people. I am ready to hear the next case."

Aquila watched the ropes being taken from Paul's wrists, but the gratitude he felt was tempered by a very real apprehension. The Jehovites had failed in their attempt to get rid of Paul in a legal fashion. What method would they try next?

Quietly, unobtrusively, Aquila got up to leave the court. He saw others leaving too, both men who were friends of Paul's and men who were enemies. His eyes met the eyes of Titius but they both immediately looked away again. There would be other, safer places where they could acknowledge their friendship and their mutual concern for Paul.

Once outside the judgment hall, Aquila strode rapidly toward home. He did not even wait to see what disturbance was going on among the angry Jehovites who had gathered just outside the door. He had seen Paul being escorted away from the building, and that was enough for him. If the Jehovites who hated Paul were fighting among themselves, that was nothing to concern him. He was free now to hurry home.

Aquila had no doubt at all that this trial, no matter how well it had turned out, would have serious repercussions that would affect him and his family. But for now, at least, the worst was over, and in a few minutes he could hold his children again and look at his wife. Perhaps, he thought, and quickened his pace, this might be a time when he could take her in his arms even though others were around. Didn't Scripture say that David had embraced his wives when he rescued them from the Amalekites? Well, then, this was almost the same. God had rescued them from the Romans and from the anger of Paul's accusers. By the time Aquila's thoughts were fully formed, he was running down the street, running like a boy, his weariness forgotten.

⇒ 26 ⇐

There had never been so many people crowded into this room before, Priscilla thought. Always the meetings had been held out in the yard. If the rain had been too heavy, the meetings had been postponed or canceled. But this gathering tonight was too important to be changed in any way and too private to be held in the yard. If it had been less important, Priscilla reflected, there would probably have been some fuss over the fact that two women were sitting among the men. But there was no room in the minds of those gathered together for anything but the critical question of whether or not Paul should leave Corinth.

Some days had passed since the hearing before Gallio and nothing more had happened to the Followers of the Way. Oh, it was true that Sosthenes had been brutally beaten in front of the proconsul's residence, but everyone knew that had just been a bid for Gallio's attention. And even that had failed. Gallio had not paid any more attention to Sosthenes's cries than he had to Paul's accusers. Titius and his friends had managed to rescue Sosthenes, and that had been the end of that.

But the rumors had not died down. And if there was any truth in the rumors, it was Paul alone who was in danger. The Jehovites who opposed him seemed to have no fear of the ordinary people who made up the congregation of believers in Corinth. They seemed to think that if Paul were driven from the city, the Followers of the Way would dissolve.

But it wasn't true, Priscilla thought, glancing around the dim, shadowed room. Crispus was totally established in the faith, and Sosthenes had shown no signs of weakening and returning to the synagogue, even though his body still bore bruises from the beating he had suffered. The church of Corinth was established, she was sure, whether Paul stayed or left.

"I am not persuaded," Paul said after listening to all the arguments for and against his leaving, "that God wants me to leave. Always before, when the time came for me to leave one place and go to another, God has spoken clearly and unmistakably. This time I'm not sure."

"Have you prayed specifically for instruction?" Timothy asked. "You know your mind has been absorbed in other things. And I think, if you'll forgive me for saying it, that you don't really want to go. So perhaps you have not asked God clearly what you are to do."

Anger flashed momentarily in Paul's eyes and was as quickly blotted out by the sudden humility that came to him only rarely—but when it did, his humbleness was totally sincere.

"You're right," Paul said. "I am so often guilty of pride and arrogance even though I crave the same qualities of love and humility that our Lord possessed. My own desire to stay in Corinth has kept me from seeking God's will in the matter." He paused and looked about him. "I have never been so reluctant to leave a place," he confessed. "I'm not sure I can bear to go away. I know you can continue as a church without me. That's not what grieves me. It's the thought of leaving you who have become my family."

He looked slowly around the room, his eyes resting longest on Aquila and Joshua. "You are like my son and my brother," he said gently. "I have great love for all of you, but these two who have shared their work and their lives with me—well, I dread the thought of leaving them. Just as

I could not bear leaving Timothy and Silas. But Timothy and Silas did not have families to tie them down, so they could come with me. I can't ask men with wives to tear up their roots no matter how great my need is."

Priscilla felt the words as though they were hands reaching out to pull her. She knew perfectly well that Paul was not trying to persuade anyone to do anything. He was speaking out of an honest conviction that Aquila and Joshua were unable to go with him. *But we're* not *unable,* Priscilla thought. *There is nothing to hold us here. We moved once, not even knowing how to conduct our own business or how to adjust to a new place. And we not only survived, we were successful. How much easier it would be for us to make a change now!*

But she dared not speak up. It was not her place nor her right. If any suggestion of a change came, it would have to come from Aquila or from Joshua.

"Nevertheless," Crispus said with determination, "you are not safe here, Paul. You have been commissioned by God to spread the good news of Christ, and you dare not stay in a place where you are in so much danger. You have no right to deliberately take a chance on cutting short your ministry and your life."

Paul nodded thoughtfully, but Priscilla could see that his eyes were misted with tears. "I will ask God for guidance," he said. "Tonight before I sleep."

"I'm satisfied with that," Crispus said. "Do you all agree?"

There was a sound of general approval, and then Silas spoke up. "If we did leave, where would we go?"

Paul shook his head. "At this moment," he admitted, "I haven't the least idea. But if God wants me to leave, He'll make it clear where we're to go. Either we'll get a message from someone, or a way to a certain city will be provided. There is no point in worrying about that."

"Is that how God speaks to you?" one of the men asked. "I thought that when you spoke of hearing God, you meant you literally heard His voice. In the same way you might hear mine."

"There have been times," Paul said slowly, "when I really have heard His voice. On the road to Damascus, in visions, in dreams. But for the most part, He speaks to me through the events and people in my life. Something is just made so obvious to me that it can't be ignored."

"In ways that the world would call *coincidence,*" Joshua said wisely.

Paul nodded. "Exactly."

Priscilla sat in a fever of impatience, wondering how men could talk so easily and glibly of other things when only a minute or two before, they had been discussing matters of life and death. She glanced at Kara, but Kara was looking down at Marcus who slept in her arms, and there was nothing on her face but tenderness for the child. From all appearances, Kara might not even have heard the discussion.

Am I the only one who feels the agony of this? Priscilla thought. *Am I the only one of our family who wants to run to Paul and say, "We'll go with you. We'll go with you to the ends of the earth"?*

She looked away from Kara, and her eyes met Aquila's. He was looking at her with such longing and anxiety that she knew exactly what he was thinking. He was remembering his willingness to follow Paul to Gallio's judgment hall. He was thinking that if it were not for his love and responsibility for his family, he could follow Paul anywhere. She knew in that instant that Aquila would never resent the claim of his family. He would never say to her, "If it had not been for you—"

But he wanted to go with Paul! The certainty of it exploded in her heart. Aquila felt exactly as she did. Happiness and excitement bloomed in her, and she was sure that her face must show her feeling. She willed Aquila to understand her. Silently, but with great intensity, she sent her thoughts winging to her husband. *Tell him we'll go, my love, tell him we'll go.* The words were so sharp in her mind that she was afraid for a few seconds that she had said them aloud.

Aquila continued to look at her, and she saw the way his face changed, the way the longing gave way to momentary confusion and then great certainty.

Quietly, as though there were no one else in the room, Aquila spoke to his wife. "Are you sure?" he asked.

Several people looked at him in astonishment, but Priscilla answered in the same quiet voice. "Very sure, my lord. Very, very sure."

Aquila turned to Paul. "You don't have to worry about going away from us, Paul. My family and I will go with you. I haven't discussed it with my uncle yet, but he has expressed his willingness to leave Corinth before this, so I'm sure he, too, will agree to go with you."

Paul looked bewildered. "That is surely too momentous a decision to make on an impulse without discussing it with your wife. It's true that I've often said a wife must be subject to her husband, but I'm also aware of a woman's needs and feelings. Surely Mistress Priscilla should have something to say about all this."

Priscilla was sure that Aquila would explain that he and his wife were so close, so aware of each other's feelings that a discussion had already been held between them. They had simply looked at each other and each had known what the other was thinking. Surely Aquila would say something like this.

But, instead, a faint color climbed into Aquila's cheeks, and he avoided meeting his wife's eyes. "You don't have to worry about that," he said. "My wife is in complete accord with me in all things. I know she will agree with my decision."

The excitement and joy that had filled Priscilla a few minutes before faded and died. In their place she felt only anger and a sort of dull despair. Would Aquila never reach the point where he dared confess his closeness to his wife to others? Would she never reach the place where she no longer desired his public approval?

There was so much in their marriage that was good and sweet, she thought achingly, and just when she had reached the place where she thought Aquila could never disappoint or fail her again, something happened that brought back some of the old resentment, the old anger.

"Then I accept your offer with more joy and appreciation than I can ever express," Paul said. His face was warm, but his eyes, when he glanced at Priscilla, were anxious.

"My nephew certainly expresses the desires of my heart," Joshua said, "but he is apparently more sure of his wife's reaction than I am of mine. I would have to discuss this with her."

The men laughed, but Priscilla saw that there was no embarrassment on Joshua's face. In fact, she was aware of the quick flash of tenderness that flew between Kara and Joshua in the instant between Kara's looking up and looking down again at the child in her arms.

"May I say something?" Priscilla said stiffly. "I don't mean about my lord's decisions, as I have no right to comment. I would only like to make a woman's practical suggestion. I don't think you should go out on the streets so late at night, Paul. It's a long way to Titius's house, and a group of men may be perfectly safe—especially since both Titius and Crispus brought slaves with them—but I don't think you would be safe. May I offer you the hospitality of this house for the night?"

"A wonderful idea," Joshua said heartily. "We can fix a mat for you here in the shop so you will be safe."

"I agree with Mistress Priscilla and Joshua," Titius said. "I think you should stay here."

Paul smiled. "You are all too worried about me, but I confess I am grateful for your concern. Thank you. I will be glad to stay here. I don't know how much I will sleep, but in this room, I can pray and thank God for the love of my friends and ask Him what I should do next."

The meeting broke up quickly after that, and Priscilla and Kara made a bed for Paul in the shop and then turned to go to their own rooms.

"Mistress Priscilla," Paul said, an odd hesitation in his voice, "were you resentful that your husband agreed to go with me without discussing it with you? I thought I saw resentment on your face."

Kara looked from Priscilla to Paul and then walked away to her bedroom, so Priscilla was left alone to try to answer Paul.

"Not resentful that he agreed to go with you," she said vehemently. "I want to go with you. There is nothing in all the world I want to do more than to accompany you and continue to serve as a teacher and a scribe. My husband knew how I felt."

"How could he have known? You'd had no chance to discuss it."

She hesitated, wondering if Aquila who had stepped out into the yard might come back and hear her. Then, deciding to risk it, she blurted out her true feelings. "He knew because he and I understand each other. We have only to look at each other and we know what the other is thinking. Only my husband is ashamed of this closeness. He thinks it's a sign of weakness. He—"

"It's obvious that he loves you," Paul said.

"Oh, of course," she cried. "There's no disgrace in loving your wife. That's not what he's ashamed of. He's ashamed of the fact that he and I talk like equals. He warned me once that he would never admit it to another man."

"Then why do you keep demanding it?" Paul asked, and there was no condemnation in his voice, only curiosity.

"I don't know," she wept. "Out of pride, I suppose, out of arrogance. I don't know."

Aquila spoke from the doorway. "Surely Paul has

enough to bear just now without the added burden of our problems."

"I'm sorry," Priscilla said. "I'm sorry." She turned and fled into the room she shared with Aquila. She heard the murmur of voices—Kara's and Joshua's, Paul's and Aquila's, but she could not understand anything that was being said. She had thought during the meeting when Aquila had offered to go with Paul that this was a wonderful evening, rich with understanding, bright with hope. Now she felt desolate and lost, angry and frustrated. She lay on the mat for a long time, half drowning in the confusion and grief that filled her. When Aquila came in, she decided, she would not let him see how much he had hurt her. She would pretend to be asleep so that nothing need be said between them. But Aquila did not come for so long that pretense was unnecessary when he finally joined her. She was sleeping so soundly that she never even heard him come into the room.

= 27 =

The autumn breeze that had been so crisp and refreshing in Corinth was more like a gale out here on the sea, Priscilla thought. She remembered the gentle winds that had carried them from Tarentum to Corinth, the sun sparkling on the water, and knew that the blessings of that pleasant voyage would not be theirs this time. But otherwise, she could almost believe she was reliving a slice of her life. Mentally, she named the similarities.

She was sitting on the same deck of the same ship, sheltered by the same rough curtains, weary, as she had been on the first voyage, from tending Kara, who was just as ill as she had been before. The major difference was that this time Priscilla was not alone, grieving over the loss of a baby. This time, Sarah slept beside her, tethered to her mother by a line so that no pitching of the boat could take her beyond Priscilla's reach, and Marcus, frightened and tired, slept huddled against Kara who, in spite of her illness, never weakened her hold on the little boy.

Priscilla leaned her back against the box that acted as a support and deliberately loosened her muscles so that she could relax. Her weariness seemed almost unbearable, and she knew that her fatigue stemmed from more than the work she had been doing ever since they had decided to leave Corinth and accompany Paul to Ephesus.

Everything that had occurred during the past several weeks had just happened too fast, Priscilla reflected, glancing up at the dark skies. She still wasn't able to take it all in. Only hours after Paul had announced that God had indeed told him to leave Corinth, Rufus had walked into the yard announcing that the *Fair Wind* was in the Corinthian harbor but would be sailing for Ephesus in a few weeks.

Paul had never doubted for a minute that this was God's way of telling them what their destination should be, and the others agreed with him. When a man put his life in God's hands and asked for a direction in which to go, it would be foolish to question the miraculous arrival of a ship manned by friends.

In all the confusion of packing, settling business affairs, making plans for travel, there had been no time for Priscilla and Aquila to discuss the anger she had felt the night of the meeting. Aquila had been so gentle, so considerate during the following days that it would have been pointless, anyhow, to even bring up the subject. But the hurt had not wholly dissipated, and Priscilla thought of it again as she sat on the tilting deck, watching the gray waves climb in front of the ship and then crash into the watery valleys behind them.

She knew, to her shame, that Aquila was not wholly to blame. But neither, she told herself, was she. Was it really so terrible for her to want Aquila to—well, to be like Joshua —to be proud of a wife who was not cut at all to the ordinary pattern? She remembered Joshua's frank admission that Kara was sharp-tongued, stubborn, opinionated, but the admission had always been made in a voice that held no apology. If Aquila could only be like *that.*

"May I join you, Mistress Priscilla?" Paul stood beside her, holding to the rail, balancing himself easily.

She was startled and was sure her face showed it. Paul had never sought her out unless he wanted to dictate to her and surely that could not be done on these rough seas. What could he possibly want?

"Of course, my lord. Can I serve you?"

"You can listen to me," Paul answered. "I have asked

your husband for permission to speak to you—perhaps admonish you. He has given his permission."

She felt a ridiculous nervous trembling in her body, as though she were a small child about to be punished. "Admonish me? Have I offended you then?"

Paul sat down on the other side of the mat so that he could face her. "You don't offend me," he said. "You are my dear daughter, and I find great satisfaction in your faithfulness and ability."

"Then what?" she questioned, somewhat comforted by Paul's words but still aware of a dryness in her mouth.

"Do you remember the night of the meeting in the shop?" Paul began. "You ran from the room weeping, because you were confused and angry. Aquila came in, and he and I talked. Do you remember?"

"Of course I remember. How could I forget?"

"That night Aquila and I talked about marriage. I'm not married myself but I've observed many marriages—good ones and bad ones and ordinary ones that are neither good nor bad. My parents were contented together, I think, but yours—and, oddly enough, Joshua's and Kara's although I can't begin to understand why—are the first truly good marriages that I've been intimately acquainted with since my childhood. I don't mean the first I've seen; I mean the first I've lived with."

He hesitated and she didn't know what to say, so she remained silent.

"You understand," Paul said somberly, "I don't need marriage myself, and I believe that those of us who can devote our entire selves to our mission are more blessed than people who have the responsibilities and burdens of a family. I could wish that no one had to marry."

"But children?" Priscilla began.

Paul brushed her interruption aside impatiently. "For us who wait the second coming of the Lord, there is no need for children. But I'm not here to discuss this aspect of marriage. The fact is that you are married, and your responsibility is to serve your husband."

"I know," she responded, eager to absolve herself of any guilt. "He's the finest man I know, and I do everything I can for him."

"Everything except permit him to retain his pride," Paul said in a firm voice.

"I don't think I—" Priscilla began, but Paul cut in sharply.

"You demand something from him that for some reason he is unable to give. He was not brought up to think of women as intelligent or able. It is not part of our culture to treat women as equals. Yet you demand it. Part of it is your Roman training, no doubt, and part of it stems from your grandfather's teaching."

"How do you know about my grandfather?" she asked. "I hadn't told you of that."

"Aquila told me."

"My husband must have told you a great deal about me that night," she said bitterly.

Paul's voice was unusually gentle. "He told me how much he loved you."

Her eyes burned with unexpected tears, but the bitterness was not flushed away. "And did you reprimand him for being very foolish?" she asked, wondering at her daring. It would be easy for Paul to get angry and walk away from her.

He sighed. "No, I didn't reprimand him, because I think he's a fine young man who is better to you than you often deserve. He loves you as he loves his own flesh, and so why would he do anything deliberately to hurt you? You create your own pain by refusing to accept things as they are."

For a few minutes she could not meet Paul's eyes. Shame, hot and dark, rose in her like the towering waves. Paul was right, and she knew it, but she also knew her own nature.

"I can't seem to help myself," she choked. "I don't know why I act as I do. I'm sorry—"

"You know what Jesus said about forgiveness," Paul said. "So you know that sins can be forgiven. What you don't know is—" Once more he hesitated, and when he spoke, his voice was as decided as she had ever heard it. "What you don't know is what it's like to really have the spirit of God in you."

Priscilla stared at the man who sat facing her. What could he possibly mean? He had been the one to tell her over and over that she understood the message of Jesus, that she understood prophecy and its fulfillment. What did he mean?

Paul's face was very tender. "You know so much, my child. Your mind is agile and clever, and intellectually you know as much about the message of Jesus as almost anyone. But it's only your mind that knows. Not your soul. You believe in Jesus, that He is the Messiah, but you have never truly *felt* Him in your heart."

"I don't understand you," she protested.

"You haven't ever truly put your trust in Him," Paul said. "You pray readily enough, but then you go about solving your own problems in your own way with your own efforts. I can't tell you what to do or how to go about opening yourself to this spirit that will fill you with such joy and assurance that you will be happier than you've ever been. You'll no longer need Aquila's praise and approval. You'll be content. Whatever the circumstances."

"Then you must surely be able to tell me what to do," Priscilla cried.

Paul shook his head. "No, not really. I told Aquila once that something would happen that would prevent him from ever worrying again. I don't know what it was—the news of Cordelius's death, or my arrest, or the discovery that no trouble is greater than God's love—whatever it was, it happened. He may not even know it, but he is as firm in the faith as a man can be."

"And you think I'm not?" Priscilla asked.

"Do you think you are?"

Sarah stirred and whimpered, and Priscilla's hand went out to comfort the child. "No," she said quietly, "I don't suppose I am. But I want to be."

"Of course you do. You're closer to it than most women, closer than some men. I can only advise you to pray without ceasing for God's spirit to bless and fill you. When that happens, all the rest will be easy."

"Why do you take so much time with me?" she asked abruptly. "I'm only a woman, after all."

Surprisingly, Paul smiled. "If you think I'm going to contradict that statement, you're wrong," he said. "Nor will I flatter you by saying you're different from other women. Everyone is different. Your major virtue at this moment is that you don't get seasick, so you can continue to take care of your children. Can you think of that as a blessing?"

Unexpectedly, a sense of lightness touched her, and she found herself laughing. "Yes," she said. "A blessing indeed. If poor Kara had to feed and clean the children—"

"You see?" Paul said. "God cares for you in ways you never think about." He looked up at the sky and out at the angry water. "You're going to need your sailor's ability, I'm afraid. This weather promises to get worse, and Trolas has warned us that we might have some very, very rough sailing."

"Then I'll have to tie both children to me," Priscilla said.

"If your husband comes to tell you to go below deck," Paul said, "don't argue with him. Obey him with the same love that he will be feeling in his fear for you."

She nodded. "I'll be wholly obedient," she promised. "And I will pray as you suggested. Will you pray for me?"

"I pray for you and your family every day. As I pray for all those I love and with whom I share the faith." He stood and let his hand rest briefly on her head. It was the first time he had ever touched her. "May God bless you richly and grant you His grace."

She watched him walk away, leaning against the movement of the ship. His words of admonition burned in her heart with a real pain, but she knew that she loved this man of God and that she and Aquila were blessed because he loved them. Sarah's whimpering turned to a lusty cry, and Priscilla picked her up to carry her to a more private place so that she could nurse her. And all the while the baby fed, Priscilla thought of Paul's words until finally her thoughts turned to prayer.

"Oh, God, fill me with your spirit," she whispered, hardly able to see the baby through her tears. She half expected some great exultation to fill her, but she was aware of nothing beyond the tenderness that always filled her when she held one of her children in her arms.

There was no exact moment when they could say later that the storm struck. The wind simply worsened and worsened, the sky turned darker and darker, and the waves grew to terrifying heights. Long before the water had reached its wildest force, Aquila had taken the women and children down into the hold. The hold was dark and evil smelling, but at least there was no danger of losing one of the children from the wildly pitching deck. Nor, for that matter, one of the adults.

Kara's illness seemed to lessen as her terror increased. For this, at least, Priscilla was grateful. Her hands were full, just protecting her children, and she honestly didn't know how she would have cared for Kara, too.

Aquila and Joshua and most of the sailors soon joined them in the hold, and they huddled together in the darkness, too frightened to do anything but pray. Aquila sat close to Priscilla and held her with one arm while he held Marcus with the other. Marcus, too terrified to cry, clung to his father with fingers that seemed to be frozen with fear.

"I can't even unfasten his hold," Aquila said to Priscilla. "Not that I want to, but it's unnatural the way he's clinging to me. And he doesn't answer when I try to comfort him.

He seems to be almost unconscious but in a frightening way."

Priscilla groped through the darkness until her fingers found the small, cold, rigid hands of her son. "Does he breathe?" she asked in terror.

"Yes. Can't you hear him? He's panting. I've never seen a child in this condition."

Priscilla curved her hand over the small clutching ones and began to pray as she had never prayed before. "Oh, merciful Father," she whispered, her face close to Aquila's, knowing that he would be praying, too, "I don't ask for safety for all of us. It may be your will that the sea swallow us. But for this little boy, I ask your mercy and your love. Take away his fear, grant him peace. Let him fall asleep in his father's arms. Oh, please, my Lord."

At that moment, there was an alarming crash, and for one second it seemed to Priscilla that the ship was surely going to capsize. The floor beneath them tilted so crazily that nothing, not Aquila's arms or her own frantic grasping for something to hold, could prevent her from sliding helplessly through the darkness until she slammed into something that at first she did not recognize. All she knew or even cared about was that it was not hard and that she had hit it with her shoulder and side so that Sarah had been protected from the impact.

Her free hand went out and began fumbling about as she tried to ascertain where she was. But nothing felt familiar and she could not hear anyone close to her. Men's voices came muffled and far away, which was ridiculous. The hold was not that large. Gradually, she realized that she was surrounded by sacks of grain—the roughness of the sacks and the dusty smell of the grain told her as much—but to her horror, she discovered that the bags seemed to enclose her. Not only on every side but above her as well. Somehow the sacks had become dislodged by the motion of the ship and she was buried beneath them.

Her mind seemed to move sluggishly so that it was several minutes before she took in the miraculous fact that she was not being crushed. The sacks had landed in such a way as to make a natural sort of cave for her. But would further movement of the ship bring them tumbling down, smothering her and Sarah?

Panic swept through her with such force that briefly she was a mindless thing, wanting only to claw and scream. Then sanity filled her again, clean, decent sanity, and she knew that the others were praying for her. She was still in God's hand.

She sat very still, cuddling Sarah against her, marveling that the child was still all right and only whimpering with discontent, not screaming in pain or terror.

"Thank you, Father," Priscilla prayed aloud. "Thank you for taking care of me and my baby. Thank you for being here."

The words were barely said when Priscilla was suddenly aware that she was not alone. Never in Aquila's arms or at her grandfather's knee or with her mother, had she been so aware that someone was with her. It never occurred to her to put out a hand to touch the other presence in her grain-sack cave. She knew instantly that the presence with her was God. Or perhaps this was what Paul meant by the spirit of God. It was something real and powerful enough to erase her fear and give her a sense of security.

Over the crashing of the sea, the lashing of the rain on the deck above her head, she finally heard words clearly. Aquila was shouting her name.

"In here, my lord," she called out, her voice calm. "The sacks of grain have slid around me but we're safe. They'll have to be removed carefully so they won't fall. But don't be afraid. There's nothing to fear. Not any more."

"If we could only light some kind of lamp," she heard Aquila groan.

"Too much danger of fire," a voice protested.

"How will we ever find her?" Kara cried.

"She'll keep calling us," Paul said, and Priscilla was sure that somehow he knew of the presence with her. "She'll show us where she is by calling us, and we can remove the sacks one at a time until we reach her."

"But if they collapse in on her?" someone asked.

"They won't collapse," Priscilla called. How could she ever make them understand how secure she felt?

At that moment, Sarah began to cry, a normal angry cry that told the world that she was tired of darkness, tired of loud noises, tired of being hungry.

"Listen," someone said in delight. "They're over in this direction. What could be easier to follow than a baby's cry? Here, the sacks are piled up here. Come on, if we're very careful—"

Before the sacks had all been removed, Rufus had removed the cover to the hatchway to call down that the storm was nearly blown out, that in a short time everyone could safely come above deck and breathe fresh air again. The opening let down enough light for the last sacks to be quickly removed so that Priscilla and Sarah were no longer in danger.

Aquila took her into his arms without embarrassment. "Oh, thank God, you're safe," he cried, his voice shaking. "I was so afraid—so afraid—"

She clung to her husband. "I was afraid, too," she confessed. "At first I was. But God was with me. As truly as you are this minute, my lord. As close as you are. As real."

"I know," Aquila said. "I felt Him, too. During the greatest danger, Marcus suddenly loosened his grip on me and fell asleep. Kara has him now. And you're safe, my love. You're safe."

She nodded. But she was more than safe. She was filled with a sense of God's goodness and power in a different way than she had ever been before. She turned in Aquila's arms and, in the pale light that filtered down from the deck opening, she saw Paul looking at her. She only smiled at him. There were, she knew, no words necessary.

She looked up at her husband. There were no words necessary for him either. Someday he would know, someday she would make it clear by her actions and her love, that she would never again feel cheated by anything he said or failed to say. It was enough that they loved each other. It would always be enough.

≠ 28 ≠

The Followers of the Way stood close together on the deck of the *Fair Winds* as the ship entered the port of Ephesus. Paul tightly grasped the railing and stared at the city. "Ephesus," he murmured. He had heard much about the great goddess Artemis, as had every traveler. Pilgrims came from all over the world to see her great temple or to lie in the embrace of her cult prostitutes.

Paul rubbed his eyes repeatedly. Then he saw it—the top of the temple, glistening in the bright afternoon sun.

"What are you looking at?" Aquila asked.

"There." Paul gestured. "Look closely . . . see the top of the temple."

"I thought you had never been here before. How did you know that was the temple?"

"I haven't but I have heard so much about this temple, built with the assistance of Alexander the Great."

"The temple of Artemis," Priscilla added.

"Yes," Paul said. "The ten-breasted goddess."

"Don't they say that Artemis fell from the heavens?" Joshua interrupted.

"More likely erupted from the bowels of hell," Paul snorted.

"It's an old city, is it not?" Aquila scratched his head.

"Old and sin-cursed," Paul nodded. Then he pointed. "What is that?" he asked, as he gestured toward a row of tall columns.

Rufus, who had been scanning the harbor rather than the

city, looked up. "That's their great avenue. It connects the harbor with the market. It's seventy feet wide, and is the place to see and be seen."

"This is the most important city in the Roman provinces," Rufus said, "and if you don't believe it, just ask the inhabitants! The Cayster River comes in this way"—he drew a rough map on the palm of his hand—"and the Koressos mountain ranges are here. So Ephesus is the end of the caravan routes and a natural loading point for goods bound for Rome."

At the mention of Rome, Priscilla stirred. Oh, would they ever go home? First Corinth, now Ephesus. Each destination farther from home rather than closer. She thought back to her first glimpse of Corinth; now she saw another "first" view: new customs, new traditions, new religions. She remembered an afternoon conversation with her grandfather.

"Grandfather?" she had asked intently. "Why do Hebrews prosper wherever they go?"

"Some Hebrews," he had promptly corrected her.

"Why do *some* Hebrews prosper wherever they go?"

"Ah," he had chuckled. "That's better. Always make your questions precise and accurate if you expect the right answer. It is far better to ask a correct question than to give a correct answer." Priscilla smiled at his admonition.

"But to answer your question," he said, "Jehovah wills it so. Jeremiah wrote, 'Build houses and settle down; plant gardens and eat what they produce. Marry and have sons; find wives for your sons and give your daughters in marriage. And seek the peace and prosperity of the city to which I have carried you into exile. Pray to the Lord for it, because as the city prospers, you too will prosper.' "

"Grandfather, how can you remember so much?" she had asked in astonishment.

"And how can you remember so little?" he laughed, nudging her with his finger. "It is because the Holy One wills it. Now, I want you to memorize this." She leaned over the scroll and read aloud as he slowly moved his finger across the markings. " 'For I know the plans I have for you,' declares the Lord, 'plans to prosper you and not to harm you, plans to give you hope and a future.' "

"Oh, Grandfather! What beautiful words."

"Not just *words,* Priscilla. A promise!" Then he took a deep breath and repeated himself. "A promise. And you must always remember that. *Always.*" She recalled the seriousness in his voice.

A generous splash of seawater brought her back to the moment. Priscilla wiped her face, and softly repeated the phrase "a future and a hope." Two words, two promises. "A future and a hope," she spoke into the wind.

"What did you say?" Aquila asked, turning to her.

"I was thinking about something my grandfather once told me," she answered and smiled up at him. She repeated the words of Jeremiah, and watched as Aquila's face glowed with understanding and response. "Yes," he said softly. "And also a great joy."

As the ship neared its berth, the travelers spotted groups of people crowding the dock waiting for first buy on the ship's goods.

"Well, this is Ephesus!" Rufus gestured broadly with a sweep of his hand.

"And who knows what surprises wait for us," Paul added.

"Or will come to us by way of this harbor," Joshua said.

"Well!" Kara snorted. "I'm just delighted to be so near land. I don't care where I am—just give me land!" They all laughed. Poor Kara had detested every moment of the voyage and had had to endure some teasing.

Rufus laughed. "And aren't you going to thank me for such an easy voyage, Mistress Kara?"

" 'Easy voyage?' " Kara scowled. "Ha!"

"How long will we be here, I wonder?" Priscilla said softly.

"As long as the Lord wills," Paul said firmly.

Kara said, shaking her head, "I cannot stand another voyage."

"Oh, Kara," Rufus grinned. "How you go on and on! And I was just about ready to offer you a permanent position on my crew. I thought there was hope for you."

"Watch your tongue!" snapped Kara. "Or you'll be swimming to the dock."

"I hope your reputation has not preceded you," said Aquila to Paul, quietly, so that Priscilla should not hear.

"I doubt it," Paul replied, too quickly. "They say there are over 300,000 inhabitants here; most worship Artemis."

"But they tolerate other religions," Rufus said, wrapping the rope around his hand, ready to toss the rope to the dock slaves to pull the ship into the berth. "These Ephesians are philosophers at heart. They amuse themselves with new ideas and new religions."

"Well, there is little of our faith that amuses anyone. We must find a synagogue. The Sabbath is swiftly approaching."

"Yeah, there should be enough time to get docked and then find a place to spend the night."

"So there are Jehovites here?" asked Joshua.

"There are Jehovites, and Hebrews, everywhere," Paul laughed.

"Thousands of Hebrews here," Rufus called out, "some of whom won't be amused with Paul's preaching."

"What about Followers of the Way?"

"I can't answer that. But Paul's preaching and your reputation as tent makers should change that."

"I think we should remember Jeremiah's words," Priscilla said.

"What?" asked Rufus as he tossed the rope to a muscle-bound black slave on the dock. "Pull us in!" he shouted.

"His words to the exiles in Babylon: 'Seek the peace and prosperity of the city to which I have called you into exile. Pray to the Lord for it, because as the city prospers, so you too will prosper.'"

Paul stared at her. "Priscilla," he said, slowly rubbing his head, "how can you remember so much Scripture?" Priscilla laughed and looked away.

"I once asked my grandfather that question."

"And what did he reply?"

"He said, 'The Lord wills it.' Besides, did not David the King say, 'Your word have I hid in my heart that I might not sin against you'?"

"He did say that." Paul smiled. But Aquila stared at the blue waters. Priscilla wondered if she had again embarrassed him.

" 'Seek the peace and prosperity of the city,' " Paul repeated the words deliberately. "Well, so far, we haven't found much prosperity—"

"But we have found peace in our hearts—" Priscilla added. Aquila cleared his throat, and Priscilla sensed his growing impatience.

"—that the world cannot take away," Paul concluded.

"Look!" Joshua pointed to the rows of white pillars lining the avenue; the marble glistened in the afternoon sunshine. Boats were packed against the harbor walls; crowds of slaves hastened to obey masters' orders and avoid the sharp sting of a whip. But hundreds of people milled around the dock: buying, selling, talking, bickering.

The boat touched the dock with a jolt. A big slave quickly wrapped the rope around the piling and pulled in the slack. Rufus shouted greetings and snapped orders. Kara said a prayer of gratitude as she pushed her way forward. "Please," she pleaded, "I want to be the first one off this thing."

Ephesus—another new home.

They found lodging and a synagogue quickly. Paul seemed preoccupied, distracted, when he returned. He had initially seemed so excited to be in Ephesus, to have a chance to preach to the Ephesians, yet over the meal he seemed subdued. As soon as Priscilla and

Aquila were alone, Priscilla asked if something were wrong.

"I don't know," Aquila said, lying back on the mat. "I thought that he had changed too, but then, you know Paul is sometimes moody."

"Well, Kara is certainly glad to be on land again."

"That she is!" Aquila laughed. "Joshua says he'll never get her away from here. She insists that three moves is too much to endure and that her next destination will be the grave."

"She will outlive us all," she answered quickly. She looked down, and frowned sadly at her feet.

"Priscilla?" Aquila prodded. "Is something wrong? Did I say something wrong? Priscilla?"

"The truth is, I don't want to feel too comfortable *here* or anywhere other than—" she couldn't complete her sentence.

"Rome?" She nodded. "Priscilla, I know what you're thinking—"

"And what is that?" she demanded, propping herself up on her elbows.

"You keep thinking we'll go back to Rome."

"No, Aquila! You won't talk me out of my hope. Someday we will return to Rome!"

"Priscilla—" he hesitated, struggling with his words. "That faith might have made sense when we were in Corinth, but not now. We're even further from Rome." His words, coupled with her fatigue, overwhelmed her, and she broke into sobs.

"Priscilla!" he said gently. "You must give up this silly notion that we're ever going back to Rome! That will never happen!"

For a long time she cried; he did not interfere. Long ago, he had abandoned any hope of ever seeing the Via Appia or his friends again.

Now Ephesus was their home, just as Corinth had formerly been. They must find a place to live and begin their trade.

He pulled her into his arms, and she lay against his chest, softly sobbing. Slowly he stroked her long red hair and wrapped the ends tightly around his fingers. As he pulled his fingers free, he thought, *Let go, Priscilla. Otherwise you'll get hurt.*

Meanwhile, Paul paced the small room. Tomorrow, he would go to the synagogue but a name kept ringing in his mind like a hammer on an anvil: *Caesarea.* In searching out the synagogue, he had stopped to admire a boat and had asked its destination.

"Caesarea," the deck slave had answered. "Want to go along?" Paul's mind stirred. The chance to go to Caesarea and on to Antioch! Certainly, the voyage would be long and risky, at this season, perhaps dangerous—but why not go? He could leave the tenters here; they were strong enough to defend themselves against the Artemis devotees. Besides, it would be a while before there was enough work to support all of them.

Yet, on the other hand, a solid church should be planted here. So many pilgrims came here, too many unmentionable acts took place, no doubt even now in Artemis's lust chambers. There was little difference between Ephesus and Corinth—the Ephesians were simply less ostentatious in satisfying their appetites.

The harbor at Ephesus beckoned sailors, merchants, and rogues from all ports of the world. A church here could become a flame that could not be hidden or extinguished.

Yet—Caesarea? "What should I do?" Paul prayed as he walked. The answer did not come until dawn.

That night, as he lay wrapped in a bit of discarded sailcloth from the *Fair Wind,* given him by Rufus, Paul slept fitfully. He dozed and woke; dozed and woke. Near dawn, he pulled the sailcloth tighter against the chill air and dozed again. He began to dream. And Paul, remembered flying, and sunlight through fog, and that unmistakable divine voice. He understood that the voice was that of Jesus of Nazareth, and that Caesarea—and wandering—were both penance *and* reward. For Paul, like the seagulls, was truly happy as God's messenger.

Whether it was the travel, the constant motion of the ship, or the water, or just being in a new place, morning dawned to find Priscilla hurrying back and forth among the sick tenters. Marcus was the worst, with severe diarrhea, but both Kara and Joshua were vomiting and had high fevers.

Paul looked in for a few minutes but realized no one could accompany him to the synagogue. He had to go alone. And one never knew what to expect from any group of Jehovites these days. Yet, Priscilla whispered, he would not be going alone: the Lord would be at his side. Yes, Paul nodded.

On the way to the synagogue, however, Paul again found himself staring at the *Blazing Sun.* What a beautiful ship; trustworthy. *Tomorrow,* he thought, *this ship will sail for Caesarea. And I will go, too.*

Paul shook his head as he looked around the small room. His people, all descendants of Abraham, tightly packed into this synagogue. Here, within the shadow of Artemis's temple—what so many thought to be the most beautiful structure in the world—Hebrews had gathered to worship Jehovah God. They had no ornate pillars like those which lined the avenue or supported the great arches of the city, but they had each other and a rich heritage.

Paul pleaded for over an hour, building his argument on Isaiah:

Who has believed our message
    and to whom has the arm of the Lord been revealed?

He grew up before him like a tender shoot
  and like a root out of dry ground.
He had no beauty or majesty that we should desire him.
He was despised and rejected by men,
  a man of sorrows and familiar with suffering.

The men had listened carefully as Paul recited the ancient words—the longing of every son of Abraham. He traced the work of John, and explained the life and death of Jesus. He quickly realized his words were both surprising and annoying to them. Yet he detected a longing, a hunger in a few who wanted to hear more. "Go on," someone called out, "continue."

Afterward Alexander was the first to approach Paul. "You must stay. We would hear more of you," he argued with a broad smile after Paul's statement that he was to sail to Caesarea. "We will not take no for your answer. You are like a man who serves only a small amount of the best wine, then snatches away the wineskin. We want to taste more of your wine, sir, to hear more of your words about this Jesus."

Paul now felt torn. They had been so receptive, so willing to listen. Perhaps he should stay, a while at least. Yet the whole time he had been speaking, he kept seeing the *Blazing Sun* and remembering his remarkable dream. By this time tomorrow he would be far from Ephesus.

"Alexander," Paul said, "I appreciate your hospitality and your gracious invitation but I have had a dream from God which compels me to move on."

"Whatever it takes to get you to remain with us, we are willing to do."

"It's not that. I am not trying to get you to promise more —I can make my own way, I assure you, as a tenter, but I *must* go to Caesarea." Obviously his dream meant little to these men.

"Why would anyone want to go to Caesarea when they

are already in the most beautiful city in the world?" huffed an old Hebrew Jehovite with a long, white beard. Paul looked at the old man and struggled for an answer he could accept.

"Perhaps he does not think our city so fair—" the old man's companion suggested.

Paul demurred, "Oh, no. Ephesus is beautiful. Splendid. It's just that—"

"It's what?" Alexander demanded impatiently. "What could be more beautiful than being here in our city, debating with us, enjoying our hospitality? A Hebrew and a Jehovite could only be happier in Jerusalem."

"I will come back," Paul answered calmly.

"Of course you will," the old Hebrew responded, "but some of us may lie in Sheol's grasp by that time. We want to hear you, now." Paul looked at the old man and touched his hand.

"I suspect that you are one step ahead of Sheol," he said, laughing. The old man grunted, and smiled.

"I will come back," Paul said, turning to Alexander, "*if* it is God's will. Just as now I must go because God's will was made clear to me in my vision."

"Then it shall be God's will. We will expect you to keep your word."

"But why would anyone want to risk his life to go to Caesarea this time of year? The chance of shipwreck—" the old man stopped.

"Yet I *must* go." Paul smiled at his new friends, and set off down the street.

The tenters were all too sick to try and dissuade Paul. He had returned from the synagogue and announced to Priscilla that he intended to sail the next morning. Aquila had tried to protest, but his stomach prevented too much argument.

When he fell asleep, Priscilla walked out to where Paul

dozed, grateful for a few minutes to escape the stench of the sick. As the breeze toyed with her hair, its redness dazzled in the sunshine. She thought she had never been so exhausted in her life.

"Do you have to go?" she asked. Paul sensed her concern.

"Yes."

"I am not going to ask why," she said, rubbing her hands wearily across her face. She took a deep breath.

"Priscilla, did your grandfather ever talk about Abraham?" Priscilla looked at Paul. What kind of question was that?

"Certainly!"

"Did he not say that Abraham was called to go to a place and obeyed, even though, at the time, he did not know his destination? By faith, Priscilla, *by faith,* he made his home in the promised land like a stranger in a foreign country— like you and Aquila. He lived in tents but he was looking for a city." Paul didn't give her a chance to interrupt.

"Abraham did not deny that he was a foreigner and a stranger. He didn't mourn for the country he had left. All that was *behind* him." Paul moved closer and took her hand in his. "They were looking and longing for a better country —a heavenly one. And God, as a result of their faith, their obedience, was not ashamed to be their God."

"What are you saying?" Priscilla demanded.

"I am saying that he is your God whether you are in Rome or Corinth or Ephesus—"

Priscilla's eyes flashed with temper. "So you agree with Aquila. You don't think we'll ever go back to Rome, do you? Oh, Paul, you know I chose to follow you, and I would follow Aquila anywhere. I am just so tired now, I feel childish and homesick."

"It doesn't matter what I think, but what God has destined. Priscilla, he has work for you to do *here.*" Paul patted her hand. "And not just in making or mending tents but in making disciples. Through this harbor travel the greatest minds in the world. The bravest men, the wealthiest, and the strongest. Perhaps God has brought you here, right in the shadow of Artemis's temple, for a purpose."

"And what would that be?"

"To be an outpost—just as these Romans are. An outpost. You are to represent the Lord's interests here in Ephesus, as they represent Rome's. I can sail tomorrow with confidence knowing that you are here."

Priscilla felt a glow inside; Paul was showing her his faith in her. Aquila's moan interrupted Priscilla.

"You'd better go. He sounds sick."

"But why aren't you sick?" Priscilla demanded, smiling at last.

"Because I am sailing in the morning," Paul answered, and his bright eyes shone at her, heartening her for the struggle to build the church in Ephesus.

Even though Alexander himself came by to try and talk him into staying, the next morning before dawn Paul made his way through the darkness to the harbor. As his friends slept fitfully, the *Blazing Sun* slipped from its berth and found the wind that would carry it toward Caesarea.

In the darkness, Paul stood on the deck, watching the receding city. Resolutely, he looked toward the east, where the horizon had begun to pale before the rising sun. He thought of Priscilla's flaming hair, and smiled; she would be as a torch for the Lord, a little sun of her own.

Priscilla strained to hear as the man read the Scripture. He definitely wasn't an Ephesian. His dark color, his clothes suggested Egypt, and he had a slight accent, too, softening his speech. Yet he had a Greek name—Apollos. She shifted forward on the hard bench, wanting to catch every word.

He eyed them. A silence, even greater than was common when a rabbi spoke, descended on the Sabbath congregation. It was as if his listeners had stopped breathing; no one coughed or shuffled or moved. Silence prevailed. Outside in the marketplace, a beggar sang a sad, monotonous plea for God's mercy, and for charity.

"A voice of one calling!" The force of the man's voice lent new life and meaning to the ancient words.

In the desert prepare the way of the Lord.
Make straight in the wilderness . . . a highway
for our God.

Highway! Priscilla's mind flashed back to Rome, to the Via Appia, the highway of their exodus from Rome. She pictured the roadside where she had buried her stillborn baby and had said goodbye to Marta and Cordelius as well as to Aquila's family.

Every valley shall be raised up,
every mountain and hill shall become level,

the rugged places plain
and—

Apollos paused. " 'And the *glory*—' " his voice rolled on
that phrase "the glory," he repeated in a whisper, "of the
Lord will be revealed and *all* mankind together will see it!
For the mouth of the Lord has spoken.' "

The man smiled broadly, his large white teeth gleaming
in his dark face. Sweat beaded his forehead. "Those are
Isaiah's words, of course. I need not remind you of that.
Your fathers and your fathers' fathers have read and have
memorized those words. And who has not longed for the
fulfillment of those precious words?"

"But what could it mean to *you?*" he pointed to one man
"or to *you?*" and he pointed to another. "if it were true? If
one had come through the desert to Ephesus crying?" His
listeners mumbled among themselves.

"Well, that voice has come!" His voice crackled with
energy. "That voice has come—and his name was John,
John the Baptist." But at that moment he lost control of his
audience; murmuring and sounds of amazement and protest
broke out among the men. The women looked at each
other, then to the men, trying to decipher their reactions.

"Who is this man?" Kara whispered.

"Apollos," Priscilla answered in a tone to discourage
more questions.

Since Paul had left for Caesarea, Priscilla had come to the
synagogue, Sabbath after Sabbath, and had endured the
dry, joyless, rote reading of the prophecies. She had listened to long, dull explanations of the passages, longing for
Paul's freshness and the power of his preaching. And she
had assumed that she would have to wait until Paul returned from his wanderings. But this tall, dark man spoke
with such authority, such insight!

"John was not a rich rabbi, that we should pay homage

to him. Nor was he a man born to wealthy parents. He wore a loincloth of camel's hair and a leather girdle like the prophet Elijah.

"This man did not coddle the rich or the Pharisees. He spoke like lightening, his words like goads that cut to the heart of those wicked men.

"Oh, he saw those Pharisees and Sadducees along the banks, snickering, disputing, mocking—but believe me, they never got close enough to the water to do them any good. John knew their hearts, their sins, their smugness, their contempt. 'You brood of vipers!' he shouted at them. 'Do not think you can say to yourselves, "We have Abraham as our Father." '

"That sounds familiar today. John looked at them and spoke with authority. 'So what if Abraham is your Father?' And today I say the same thing to you. Perhaps John knelt down and scooped up some pebbles from the riverbed and held them in his hand." Apollos stretched out his hand as if he held stones. 'Out of these stones God can raise up children for Abraham!' Oh, they didn't like that! Or perhaps John flung the rocks at their feet.

"John believed, John *knew*—one was coming mightier than he. In fact, he said that he was not even fit to untie that man's sandals. The one who is coming will be far greater than John!"

Priscilla thought she had missed something; she thought he had said, "the one who *is* coming."

"Although John baptized with water and called people to repent, the one coming will baptize with the Holy Spirit and with fire!" The Egyptian's words resonated through the room.

"John's message was simple: repent! Repent! REPENT!" Each repetition grew in intensity. No one dozed today, Priscilla thought. Even the deaf could hear this man's booming voice.

Priscilla's heart beat rapidly. *Yes, now continue,* she

thought to herself. *Lead the people to Jesus,* she urged in her heart. Apollos could reinforce what Paul had preached. Hearing it from a different source would make it easier for some to believe.

"Naturally," Apollos smiled, "the Pharisees had a few things to say to John. They were so used to their fine clothing, their fine meals, their fine houses. They were not about to stoop down and be baptized in the river Jordan any more than Naaman wanted to wash in it to be cleansed of his leprosy.

"But it wasn't only the Jews who were uncomfortable with John's preaching. Herod trembled, too. For John had confronted Herod because he was sleeping with Herodias, his sister-in-law, Philip's wife. 'It is not lawful to have her,' John said courageously.

"The Pharisees, although they agreed, decided to let Herod deal with him, to silence him, if you will.

"But John was faithful. He could have held his words or said what Herod and the Pharisees wanted to hear, what some of you would like to hear, but he was a prophet and like Amos or Joel or Isaiah, he spoke God's words, not his own. Repent! Repent! REPENT! The Kingdom of God is at hand!" Apollos's fist drove down on the table, which crackled under the force of the blows.

"And John was beheaded for his courageous stand," he said, after a pause. "Yet he who comes, still comes."

Apollos looked around, then wiped sweat from his forehead with the back of his hand. Priscilla was speechless. *Now!* she thought. *Tell them about the Messiah.* He took a deep breath, stood and slowly walked to a bench, and squeezed into an empty space between Aquila and Joshua. She realized he had concluded his words; he would say no more.

Quickly, other men crowded in around the stranger. A few disputed or politely questioned his words, others shook his hand and thanked him. Slowly the synagogue emptied.

In the women's seating area, the conversation focused on the power of the speaker. Kara finally nudged Priscilla, who had not moved since Apollos had finished. Her eyes were tightly closed.

"Priscilla?" she said, shaking her arm.

Priscilla swayed.

"Come, the service is over . . . we must go. The men will be hungry." Priscilla opened her eyes, stood, and walked to the doorway, just happening to look up and directly into the eyes of the speaker. She nodded politely and turned to walk toward the other women but stopped when Aquila spoke to Apollos.

"Sir, would you honor us by taking your meal in our home?" While Priscilla wanted to hear more of his preaching, apparently Apollos had not heard of Jesus. His preaching sounded so acceptable in this synagogue. Too acceptable, Priscilla decided. If only Paul were here to challenge him, to correct him.

As the men ate, Priscilla strained to hear every word spoken. Apollos spoke crisply and articulately, his word pictures stunning. Unfortunately, the women had to wait to eat; she could not eat with the men and participate in the conversation. Now she was painfully reminded of the void in her life made by Paul's departure. How she missed Paul's tutoring, his clear use of words. It was like closing off part of a villa, not using it. She felt as if a part of her had been sealed shut.

Later the men sat in the garden. How long would he stay? Joshua had asked. Not long; he wanted to go on to Achaia, soon. *Oh,* Priscilla thought. *If only I were a man. I could talk to him, reason with him. I could share the good news of Jesus. But why weren't the men doing that? Did Apollos intimidate them?*

She stood, then paced the room slowly. She froze. She heard her grandfather's voice, clearly, as if he were standing behind her. Yet she hesitated to turn around. She was too afraid to move to confirm or deny the voice. Yet she heard his words, his breathing, his intonation, as he recited Joel: "I will pour out my Spirit on *all* people. Your sons *and* daughters will prophesy . . . even on my servants, both men and women, I will pour out my Spirit."

Priscilla shivered. No! Her grandfather was dead; yet, the voice—he was here, speaking to her. She turned, excitedly, and her smile disappeared as quickly as it had been created. No one was there. As she waited, she heard Apollos's slightly accented, polished formal Latin, his perfect diction, the cadence of a gentleman. She stared. A Jehovite with the name of a Roman deity, a graduate of the greatest university in the world. This Egyptian was part of the "all people" her grandfather had mentioned. *If God has spoken to him, why could God not speak to me?* The words "all people" kept reechoing in Priscilla's mind. If Apollos had heard the good news of the Gospel in Egypt, why couldn't she speak to him? She took a deep breath, then walked through the doorway into the garden and approached Apollos.

"Sir," she asked in a clear voice, "how is it that a Jehovite should have a name derived from a Greek god, especially if we are to avoid idolatry?"

"Priscilla!" Aquila said sternly, jumping to his feet, embarrassed by her boldness. He was still getting used to the idea that Priscilla was so gifted, and sometimes it still caught him off guard.

"She simply had a question," Apollos answered with a generous smile, showing his gleaming white teeth. "And a good question at that!" Priscilla stood, confidently expecting Apollos's explanation.

"My parents were Gentiles who converted after my birth," he said.

"But how did you learn of John?" Priscilla asked.

"Another good question. I'm surprised that the men hadn't asked me." Apollos winked. "Do you always listen so intently?"

"When someone has something to say, yes." She nodded.

"I wish all women were as responsive. I learned about John, in a roundabout way, actually from merchants—Jehovites, of course—who had been in Jerusalem during the annual feasts. These particular men, graduates of the university, and merchants, think of themselves as philosophers."

"It is a vice of many men," Priscilla smiled.

"Yes, well, they had been students of Philo Judaeus, a great wise man who reconciled Hebrew and Greek thought." He directed his words at Aquila, who looked a little shocked at this bold exchange. "In fact, Jehovites have lived in Alexandria for at least three hundred years, as long as the university has existed. So new ideas always find their way to Alexandria, often first through the ears and mouths of our merchants."

"But certainly not through your women," Aquila questioned.

"No," Apollos admitted. "But the merchants told me about hearing John. His power, his message appealed to me. He now has many followers in Alexandria. But, enough of that—now I have a question. How is it that a woman asks such intelligent questions?"

Aquila broke the mood. "Perhaps I owe you an explanation. My wife was tutored by her grandfather."

"Really?" Apollos asked Priscilla, both astonished and interested. "Do you write?"

"Yes," Priscilla answered.

"Really? I don't know what to say! What a pleasure to have such an intelligent wife. To have a gracious wife, a good cook, a skilled tenter, devout in the faith, and yet who . . . writes?" He laughed appreciatively.

"I am afraid that I sometimes shock my husband, at times such as this."

"Ah, I doubt that," Apollos replied, too quickly. But he

turned to Aquila and recognized the truth of Priscilla's comment.

"This bothers you? Annoys you?"

"Yes," Aquila answered, "it does take some getting used to."

"But what about your prophet, Joel?"

"What about Joel?"

"Did he not say that *in the day of the Lord,* Jehovah would pour out his spirit on all people—even Egyptians like me or Romans like you?"

"So?"

"Well, the rest of Joel deals with *daughters* who prophesy."

Aquila looked at Apollos. "Meaning?"

"Meaning that the day of the Lord is upon us. It will soon come. Didn't you hear me this morning?"

"Of course I heard you this morning. You preached only John's baptism."

"Who else's would I preach?" Apollos replied, startled.

"That of Jesus." Aquila looked equally startled.

"The Messiah!" Priscilla added, fervently.

"Jesus?" Apollos asked. "The Messiah? I have not heard of this. What do you know about him?"

"Not 'about' Him," Priscilla answered joyfully. "We *know* Him!" She felt like a child revealing a wonderful secret.

"*Know* Him?" Apollos frowned; now they were surely teasing him. *First they entertain you, then they tease you,* he thought. *What's next?*

"The Messiah has already come!" Priscilla exulted. "And we are Followers of His Way. We have been baptized."

"We?"

"Women included," Priscilla answered. "The daughters, of Joel."

"In John's baptism?"

"No, in Jesus's. In Rome. And we were Followers of the

Way in Corinth, and thence came to Ephesus to spread the good news."

"Ah, Corinth," Apollos frowned. "I have heard much about the wickedness of Corinth."

"Well, someday you will hear more about the Christians in that place. There is quite a church there."

Apollos looked uncomfortable. Abruptly he stood. "I've lost track of time. I need to be on my way," he paused, "that is, today. But I would like to hear more about the Way. It is my nature to be curious about new ideas."

Priscilla said quickly, "Oh, sir, you preached so eloquently, but the one John said would come has come. He *has* come!" Her determination rang in her voice.

Apollos glanced at Aquila and Joshua.

"I would like to come back and hear more," he said smoothly.

"I'll walk with you part of the way," Joshua offered.

"Oh," Apollos grinned. "That's not necessary. I can find my way back. No one will bother me."

"Oh, but I need the exercise," Joshua said with an uneasy laugh and pat to his stomach.

Obviously, thought Priscilla, Joshua sensed the tension between her and Aquila and wanted to let them alone. But Aquila seemed to be struggling with his own inner conflicts and left before she could speak. They passed the night in silence.

≈ 30 ≈

Priscilla sat at her loom staring at the material she was weaving; she couldn't concentrate. She glared at her evident mistake; now all she needed was for Kara to see it. Kara could scold without saying a word; one lifted eyebrow could do it.

Priscilla could argue that it was Aquila's fault that she couldn't concentrate. She hated it when he acted this way toward her. He and Joshua had borrowed a wagon and had gone to deliver a new tent to Tvia, an asiarch or provincial official who supervised and promoted the emperor's cult worship. Tvia, actually, had served out his one-year term but had held on to the ceremonial title.

Slowly, their reputation as tenters was gaining more orders from such affluent clients. Many Ephesians, when they wanted a tent, first approached Aquila and Joshua.

The tenters had laboriously sewn Tvia's tent—every stitch had to be perfect. If Tvia liked their work, naturally his wealthy friends would want their craftsmanship. As Priscilla shifted on the hard seat, she wished Paul were here. He could help them resolve this tension. Yet Aquila might have rejected Paul's efforts as meddling; besides, men generally sided together.

"Kara," she cried out suddenly. "What am I going to do?"

" 'Do?' About what?" Kara answered without looking up from her work.

" 'About what,' she says—as if you didn't know."

" 'Know?' " Kara shrugged.

"This house is too small for you not to know that Aquila is still upset with me over Apollos."

"And he may have a right to be," Kara said. "Well, he does! A woman shouldn't be as bold as you were with Apollos. It just isn't done and, Priscilla, you know that. Why did you do it?"

"Because I have freedom in Jesus!"

"Oh, I don't know about that," Kara huffed. "Your freedom may go too far. A wife could find a way to support and encourage her husband in those situations. You didn't see me asking questions of that Egyptian, did you?"

"No," Priscilla responded, cautiously anticipating Kara's logic.

"Certainly not! If I had questions about him, I would have asked Joshua to ask him." Priscilla saw the briefest hint of a smile on Kara's face.

"But we have no idea Apollos will be back. It was my only opportunity."

" 'Opportunity?' That's the right word for it. I saw his eyes on you. He'll be back, one way or another. We haven't heard the last of him."

"And what does *that* mean?" Priscilla joked.

"Men, especially Egyptian men, are known for their ways with women. A woman *has* to keep a constant eye out for them and their hands." Before Priscilla could answer, however, a voice intruded.

"Hello? Is anyone here?" The women looked at each other, then toward the sound of the voice. Instantly both had recognized the cultured voice: Apollos.

"Hello?" Apollos called again. Priscilla started to answer but Kara silenced her with a finger to her lips.

"Hello? Is anyone here?"

"I'm going to—"

"Shh!" Kara ordered.

"Oh, this is foolish, Kara!" Priscilla stood. "Yes," she called out, "just a moment." Priscilla brushed her hand across her red hair and stepped to the doorway.

"Oh," Apollos said. "Priscilla. I wanted to speak to your husband."

"He isn't here right now," Priscilla reported, catching Kara's warning look. If this Egyptian had wicked intentions, he shouldn't learn that the men were gone.

"But they will be back soon," Kara said firmly. "I'm sure if you come back *later,* they will be here." Apollos turned back to Priscilla. He stared at her for a long moment.

"I have never seen such red hair! In my country they would say that you have been kissed by the gods."

Kara snorted, and Priscilla started to apologize, but Apollos only laughed.

"You remind me of my mother," he said to Kara with a chuckle.

"How so?" Kara wondered.

"Your charming disposition." He grinned, showing his white teeth. Kara snorted again, but with a smile on her lips. "Actually," Apollos said, and glanced around, "I wanted to talk to your husbands about yesterday. I haven't been able to sleep or think since our discussion."

"It's too important to be forgotten," Priscilla replied.

"Well, I think they should be back soon," Kara interrupted.

About that moment, Marcus emerged, crying loudly. He had been asleep and had wakened fussy, as was his habit. Apollos clapped his hands and beckoned Marcus to come. But Marcus ran to Priscilla, grabbing her robe and howling.

"Maybe I should come back later," Apollos said.

"No. Wait!" Priscilla said. "I'm sure they'll return any moment. They've been gone for quite some time." Apollos turned around, spotted a stool by a stack of hides, and walked over to it and sat down. He laughed. "I still cannot believe that a woman could ask such questions. And can write too. I was hoping your husband would be here. I have so many questions to ask about this Jesus."

"Perhaps I could answer them."

Apollos considered Priscilla's answer thoughtfully. She added, "After all, I wrote some of Paul's correspondence."

"Well, maybe you could answer some of the *simpler* ones, until your husband returns. You see, this Jesus intrigues me. I have heard about him and his miracles . . . but a lot of people have performed miracles. So, I wonder, what makes this Jesus different from the other miracle workers? Why, not long ago I met a man, a Hebrew Jehovite, who had seven sons who went about exorcising demons. Sceva was his name. Rather strange man."

"Many do signs and wonders, but there is only one Messiah," said Priscilla firmly.

"You really believe that he is the Messiah?"

"As firmly as I believe that my name is Priscilla or that my husband's name is Aquila and that God has sent us here to spread the good news of His Son."

"Why?" he asked. "What makes you so certain?"

"Because He said He was the promised one."

"Ah," Apollos dismissed her answer with a wave of his hand. "Many have claimed that."

"But no one ever resurrected from the dead to prove it."

"Resurrected from the dead?" Apollos scowled. "I cannot accept that."

"Why? It confirms the prophecies. He was born in Bethlehem as prophesied by Micah. He was born of the tribe of Judah. And the death of the babies after his birth confirms Isaiah's prophecy."

"Wait!" Apollos waved his hand impatiently. "The fact that babies were killed doesn't prove that he was the Messiah. There could have been another Messiah born, at the same time, even in Bethlehem. It only proves that he survived the slaughter."

"But it fits the weave. Look," Priscilla said, moving to one of the uncompleted tent cloths. She raised one of the seams. "This tent is made up of several pieces of material stitched together. One piece of material might not be large enough to be a tent, but when the whole thing is sewn together it will keep the rain out."

"So that is your logic? What if I do not believe that babies were killed?"

"Then you have to ignore Jeremiah's words, and I suspect that you would not be anxious to do that. Ask around. No one has been able to hide the massacre of the boy babies." Apollos stared unseeingly at Marcus, who was sitting in the dirt playing with a loom shuttle.

"Jesus was the heir to David's throne," said Priscilla, "and on the cross he announced his thirst, just as the prophecies said he would."

"But again, those are coincidental. How do you *know?*" Apollos leaned forward.

"How do you know that you are your father's son?"

Apollos smiled. "I know. There is no doubt about that."

"Ah," Priscilla beamed at his concession. "There is no doubt in the believer's heart, either. His spirit bears witness with our spirits."

"Well, I believe in John's baptism."

"But that is not enough. John's baptism is only for moral reform; good works. You must also confess that Jesus is the Messiah."

"I cannot do that," Apollos shook his head. "I do not *know* that he is the Messiah."

"But John *confirmed* that Jesus was the Messiah!" said Priscilla eagerly. "John said, 'I saw the Spirit come down from heaven as a dove and remain on him. The one who sent me told me.' John testified that Jesus was the son of God."

For a moment it was still in the dark little room; sun streamed in through the open door.

"I have heard a lot of things about this Jesus—" began Apollos.

Priscilla said, more slowly, "But you must make a decision for yourself. It does not matter what others believe, what your countrymen believe, but what *you* believe. Is he the Messiah, the Promised One—or is he an imposter?"

"I never said he was an imposter!" protested Apollos.

"But you haven't said that he was the Messiah, either. If he is not one, then he is the other."

"I was baptized by John. Doesn't that mean something?" Apollos looked flustered.

"Baptism in John's name was only a preparation. You must be baptized in the name of Jesus. You must be baptized in his death and resurrected to new life. John baptized a lot of people, but he didn't raise from the dead and reclaim his head from Herod."

"But Jesus resurrected?"

"Oh, yes . . . and he appeared to his disciples and to the women."

"Women?" Apollos's voice showed his skepticism.

"Yes, *to the women,*" Priscilla answered, firmly. "Jesus treated women differently. He didn't see us as animals to be kept or as vessels for men's passions."

Kara gasped. She pulled at Priscilla's sleeve, and the younger woman followed her to a corner of the room.

"Priscilla," Kara whispered. "You *must* listen to me. If Aquila comes home and finds you talking so candidly to a stranger he'll—" Unwittingly, her voice rose in concern.

"I'll *what?*" They all turned to the gateway. There stood Aquila and Joshua. Aquila lifted his eyebrows, then walked toward Apollos.

"Apollos," he said curtly, without offering his hand.

"I've been waiting for you."

"You wish to buy a tent?" Aquila asked.

"A tent?" Apollos looked puzzled; then he broke into a laugh. "No. What would I do with a tent? No, I came here because I wanted to—"

"Aquila," said Priscilla, flushing, "I have been answering some of his questions about Jesus."

"Questions? You wanted to hear more about Jesus? You should have waited for me."

"Your wife stated her faith so clearly, so firmly. She seemed so knowledgeable."

"Apollos, it isn't proper for a woman to speak to a stranger without her husband's permission," Aquila said forcefully.

Apollos looked puzzled. "Forgive me if I seem forward, but I thought women who follow Jesus were freer than most. Why, your wife just told me that Jesus didn't see women as kept animals!"

"She's not! I mean, they're not kept animals," stammered Aquila, glaring at Priscilla. "That's not the point!" He steadied his voice. "My wife knows better than to speak so. She is not herself," he said, low.

Priscilla turned her head, trying to hide the hot tears that had begun to run down her cheeks.

Apollos saw the tears, then said, rather formally, "Perhaps I should leave."

"Perhaps you should," Aquila answered coldly. Apollos took a few steps toward the gate, then stopped. He turned to face Aquila, started to ask another question, then shook his head and strode out the gateway.

Priscilla didn't see Aquila's hand come up, but she felt its impact when it struck her cheek, knocking her backwards. Kara gasped and reached out to Priscilla, but when she saw the look on Aquila's face she withdrew and ran out of the room. Marcus began to scream, and Priscilla burst into sobs.

Aquila stood frozen in place, stunned. He had hit her! Actually struck her! When she whirled to run from him, he reached out to stop her, but she flung off his hand.

An hour later, occasional muffled sobs still penetrated the silence of the household.

~ 31 ~

The men ate in silence. Finally, Aquila looked at Joshua. "I don't know what comes over me," he confessed.

Joshua didn't respond immediately. Actually, for some time he had wanted to talk to his nephew. Aquila pushed aside his bowl and hid his face in his hands. Joshua waited. If he had talked to Aquila, this tension would not have happened.

"I didn't mean to do it," Aquila admitted. "I really didn't mean to hit her. It just happened."

" 'It *just* happened?' No, Aquila," Joshua said firmly, "few things 'just happen.' You were angry at her. Very angry.' "

Aquila looked up, somewhat surprised by Joshua's candor. Then he dropped his eyes and nodded.

"Anger makes people do things they regret. Things that are never forgotten. Sometimes things that cannot be corrected.

"Aquila, you are so—" Joshua gestured with his hands. "Priscilla is a unique woman. A woman you love. I do not think she is rebelling or testing you, although it would not be so surprising if she were. But you know she loves you truly. There is something within her that just bubbles out. It's from all those years with her grandfather."

"Ah. There you have it. The man who's really to blame!" Aquila scowled, but then he gave a little laugh. "And he's dead, so I can't have it out with him!"

"And her ideas are there, and you are not going to eliminate them."

"Well, perhaps not, but I can help her understand that there will be consequences."

"Ha!" Joshua laughed. "Now you talk like your father! He loved to talk about *consequences.* Aquila," Joshua smiled tenderly at his nephew, "you can frighten her, but the thoughts will *still* be there. She will grow colder and colder to you. Are these walls so thick that I cannot hear the two of you in the night?" Aquila flushed. Joshua reached out and put his hand on Aquila's shoulder. "Hear me out, nephew. I know that you love her, more than most husbands would." He saw Aquila's anger slowly dissolve.

"But what if this outspokenness makes me look like a fool!" Aquila protested.

"Only *you* can make yourself look like a fool. She has not made you a fool by asking a few, probably harmless questions. Or by talking of Jesus, which is her right. No. Fools are made by rash acts, such as—"

"Joshua!" Aquila's voice quivered.

"No, listen to me! I should have talked to you a long time ago. I am far more worried about your brooding resentment than about Priscilla's questions."

"So you are taking her side?"

"No. I am not taking 'her side.' But your problem is that you think that everyone thinks Priscilla is smarter than you. That's what really shocks you."

"No!" Aquila pounded the table with his fist. "That's not true! I don't care what other men think or say."

"Oh, but you do," Joshua insisted. "If you didn't care what men thought, you wouldn't have slapped her. You're like the Emperor Claudius, thinking someone will overshadow him. You are afraid—"

"I am not afraid!"

"But she is smarter than any woman I've ever met or heard about. So what if some men tease you? Sometimes we become dissatisfied with what we love because of brooding or resentment. Jehovah has entrusted you with an intelligent wife. Ignore the teasing."

"It's not the teasing."

"Then what is it?" Joshua stood and walked a few feet from the table.

"It's not the way we have been taught. She is a Jehovite. She should be more discreet."

"When was she indiscreet?"

"On the Sabbath."

"Ah," Joshua scratched his beard. "Had you commanded her *not* to speak to Apollos, not to ask her questions? Had you said to her, 'Priscilla—' "

"Of course not!"

Joshua chose his words carefully. "Apollos was no ordinary guest. Why did you invite him home from the synagogue?"

"I wanted to talk to him."

"And you wanted to teach him about Jesus, the Messiah? You thought that you could teach this great orator the way of the Messiah, and impress the brothers and Priscilla with your intelligence and wit."

Aquila shook his head in vigorous denial.

"Are you envious of Priscilla?"

"No! Of course not!"

Joshua stared at Aquila for a long time. *What a replica of Reuben,* he thought. *The looks. The attitudes. That sulking anger. I suspect that much of Aquila's anger toward Priscilla is what he really wishes he could express against a father who rejected him in Rome and then abandoned him on the Via Appia.* Aquila dropped his eyes.

"I suppose that you're going to say that I should apologize to her," he asked.

"Why should I tell you that?" Joshua asked, his eyes teasing. "You are the one that must lie beside her tonight. But maybe you could make a tent and sleep out here—

although the night can be very long and very lonely."

Aquila was silent.

"Maybe the Lord used Priscilla because he saw her willingness to obey after he witnessed our reluctance."

"What?"

"Priscilla has a point. We had talked with him all afternoon. Either of us could have turned the conversation to Jesus. And what did we talk about? Grain shipments from Alexandria, tributes to Rome, tents. Were we leading up to mentioning Jesus?"

Joshua did not flinch under Aquila's long gaze.

"Sometimes, nephew, the reason we are so angry at others is that they point out our weaknesses. Weaknesses we wish we could hide. Sometimes the Holy Spirit uses the voice of a brother or a sister or a wife as his voice. You are a tent maker—a good one, if the coins in your girdle are any indication. And you are an intelligent man. It is no disgrace to you that your wife is an intelligent woman. Maybe this is part of God's design for us. Maybe God would use Priscilla to bring Apollos into the fold." He rose and stood for a moment, then walked tiredly into the next room, where Kara lay.

Aquila sat hunched over the bowls. *The women must have eaten some bread,* he thought. *We have talked nearly till midnight. And I am still so troubled. But Joshua has at least opened a door into my darkness.*

= 32 =

Aquila listened carefully; Priscilla was asleep. He felt awkward lying down beside her, careful not to awaken her. *Maybe I shouldn't sleep here tonight,* he thought. But he wanted to be there.

He took a deep breath and tucked his hands under his head and stared through the darkness. He shouldn't have slapped her. But what could he do about that, now? As a husband, could he ask her forgiveness? He would appear weak if he did so. But he turned slightly and watched the dim lamplight on her face. He wanted to touch the place where he had slapped her; to kiss it away, to kiss away the tear stains on her cheeks.

Priscilla should have sent Apollos away, or left him sitting in the courtyard. But perhaps she had tried. Aquila sighed. He desperately wanted to go to sleep, to awaken in the morning and find everything the way it had been before Apollos had arrived.

"Oh, Priscilla," he whispered when she turned and mumbled in her sleep. As he looked at her, he thought of the part of the Book of Proverbs that asks, "Who can find a virtuous woman?" The verses echoed in his mind:

Her husband has full confidence in her
    and lacks nothing of value.
She brings him good, not harm
    all the days of her life.
In her hand she holds the distaff

and grasps the spindle with her fingers.
She speaks with wisdom
    and faithful instruction is on her tongue.
She speaks with wisdom
She speaks with wis . . .
She speaks . . .
She . . .

Aquila slept the sleep of an exhausted, weary man.

Across the way, the other tenters were not asleep. Kara spoke softly to Joshua.

"I tried to get rid of him, Joshua. I've known Aquila and Priscilla have been having trouble." But I must say, Priscilla is not helping matters. She insists on speaking; and Aquila is trying to learn how to respond to her boldness. How are we going to help them?"

"Well," said Joshua thoughtfully, "maybe Priscilla does know her place. Remember the Sabbath reading from Joel."

"Do you mean Priscilla is *led* to speak so openly?" Kara asked. "That might explain things a bit."

"Listen," said Joshua. "Joel says God's words: 'I will pour out my Spirit on *all* people. Your sons *and daughters*—'" he tapped Kara's arm for emphasis. "She is a *daughter,* and the Spirit is moving among us . . . *all people* includes the Egyptian with a Roman name and John's baptism. What could be more strange than that? But the Spirit moves in his own way. Now Moses—"

"Moses? Joshua, you are getting old—how your mind wanders! What has Moses to do with this?"

"Give me time, woman. Moses protested his own election. Did he not protest, 'O Lord, I have never been eloquent . . . I am slow of speech and tongue . . . please choose someone else.' "

"But what has that got to do with Priscilla?"

"Maybe she isn't repeating Moses's words or saying, 'Choose someone else.' Maybe she is God's vessel."

"A woman?" Kara smiled.

"Like Deborah, perhaps, or Esther." Joshua grinned.

"Joshua, my love, you may be right. But take care—people who break with tradition should always beware. And Priscilla, too," she said.

"What a day!" Joshua suddenly yawned. "I'm ready to go to sleep."

"Really?" Kara mumbled, disappointed.

"Oh, Joshua," she said with a snort.

"Well, if you're not too sleepy—" his voice trailed off.

Aquila moaned in a dream. *Where was he? Who were all these people? Why was everyone so angry? yelling? ranting? screaming? And who were the bound people? What had they done to be treated so harshly?*

The two leaders ignored their captives to arouse the anger of the crowd.

"Stop teaching or speaking in the name of Jesus!" the older leader screamed, his face crimson with rage. "Do you understand? Jesus is an imposter. You must never again repeat his name. Never!" The accuser had moved face-to-face with the bound men. Aquila had never witnessed such rage.

Peter shook his head vigorously from left to right. Then someone punched him repeatedly in the face and screamed, "Never . . . never . . . never repeat that name!" The nevers *echoed like hammer blows on an anvil.*

"But how can I not speak of what I have seen and heard?" Peter protested, as blood spurted from his nose.

"I've warned you," the priest said and smacked Peter again. The wallop echoed across the room, even over the ruckus of the crowd. Other men might have resisted or fought back but Peter stood silently waiting the next blow.

Aquila looked away and saw Priscilla. Although he smiled, she did not return the smile. She too was bound. To her left was a high stack of papyrus sheets.

"Are these yours?" the priest snarled. Priscilla nodded. "What do you do with papyrus?"

"I write letters."

"Letters," the priest hooted hysterically, clapping his hands together. "Did you hear her?" he baited his audience. "She writes letters," he repeated in a whine. The crowd laughed. Aquila shouted at Priscilla but she couldn't hear him.

"What are in these letters that you write?"

"I write about the Way."

"The what?" he scowled.

"The Way."

"The way to what?" he demanded.

"Jesus," she said. The smile disappeared from the priest's face. He stepped forward and smacked her. Aquila tried to stand but couldn't. His mouth would not open. He must get to her before the priest hit her again. But he couldn't move.

"Don't mention that name again in my presence," the priest screamed. "Besides, what would a woman know about religion? A woman knows only about—" he snickered and the men laughed, a lewd, raunchy laugh. Priscilla held her head high.

"And how did you learn to write?"

"My grandfather taught me."

"Your grandfather taught you?" he repeated the words in such a way as to doubt the accuracy.

"And what does your husband say about your letters?" Priscilla didn't respond.

"I asked, 'What does your husband say about these letters?'" He angrily waved the papyrus in front of Priscilla.

"He doesn't want me to write."

"Ah, a good husband's response." Then a voice spoke from the crowd. "Maybe we are being too hard on her. Peter and John we have a right to be concerned about. But who would listen to a woman's babblings?" The voice mimicked her. "Only a fool would take her seriously."

"But there are plenty of fools around here," another voice answered; there was disagreement and laughter.

"She is a woman. No one will take her seriously. If her husband has money to waste on papyrus, let her amuse herself with 'her letters.' But we have more important business. No one will listen to a woman! No one will listen to a woman!"

Aquila squirmed. He agreed, but he also disagreed.

"But she will set a bad example for the other women," someone objected. The crowd erupted into mass confusion. "But she speaks about Jesus," the priest screamed, and the audience hushed.

"Maybe this Jesus is a woman's god!"

"Get rid of her!" a loud voice hollered out.

Others picked up the chant. "Get rid of her! Get rid of her!"

"No!" Aquila shouted, bolting up on the mat. Priscilla half-woke. "What's wrong?" she asked sleepily, but before Aquila answered she was asleep again.

Aquila stared at her for a long moment without answering. He tried to catch his breath; sweat dripped from his arms and forehead. "I had a dream," he said to himself, running his fingers through his hair, "I must have been dreaming." He dropped back onto the mat with a thud. His throat was so dry; he tried to swallow. That dream sounded or seemed so familiar. Then he remembered. Paul's account of John and Peter before the Sanhedrin. Paul had taken so much care in describing it that Aquila could repicture it in his mind as Paul had preached.

Aquila recalled Paul's question that Sabbath when he had shared the story: "What would you do if you were forbidden to speak about Jesus?"

But what did Priscilla have to do with Peter and John? Aquila wondered as he rolled onto his stomach. She clearly belonged there, though. And why was she bound? He fell asleep again wishing he had gotten a good look at the accuser's face; that had been impossible because of the dark shawl drawn down over his face. Soon he dreamed again.

"I tell you that I forbid you!" The priest paused, his voice menacing. *"I forbid you to do* anything, *anything at all in the name of Jesus . . . even a single letter,"* he taunted Priscilla, *shaking his fist in front of her face. "And you,"* he whirled to Peter, *"I forbid you to do* anything *in His name. Do you understand me?"*

When they shook their heads no, his anger exploded. Suddenly the shawl fell off. Aquila gasped: he saw himself. I am the accuser! No wonder I had not been able to go to Priscilla's defense!

"No! No! No!" he shouted, thrashing about.

"Aquila!" Priscilla shook him. "Aquila. Wake up. It's only a dream!" But Aquila pulled away from her, reached for his robe, and quickly pulled it over his head. He grabbed his sandals and ran out of the door. She could hear his feet running down the silent lane. Worried, she lay awake, but her own exhaustion gradually wooed her back to sleep.

Aquila walked for hours, aimlessly—one direction, then another. Finally, he found himself walking down the Great Avenue, still lit by the bright torches on top of the columns.

He was troubled. Why had he been Priscilla's accuser in the dream? There had to be a reason. He dropped onto a marble bench and buried his head in his hands. What a day! He had sold a tent for an incredible profit and he had never been so highly praised for his craftsmanship. But how quickly the day had become a nightmare.

Perhaps he *was* jealous of Priscilla.

For a long time, he sat on the bench, arguing with himself, swaying back and forth, chilled by the night air.

What if Apollos was God's servant—one of those "all people"? What if he was hungry to know Jesus? What if he left Ephesus before Paul returned and could teach him the Way?

Without instruction, he's no better off than my father, Aquila thought. *Who could teach him? I can't begin to answer his questions or to match his rhetoric or logic.* Only Paul was capable of instructing such a great scholar.

Then he remembered something Paul had said, one day at the baths. After Peter and John were released, they had returned "to their own people." That phrase struck a response. If Apollos learned of Jesus, he could take that word back to *his* own people—the Egyptians.

But if he left before Paul returned? The Egyptians would remain in the darkness. *Oh, I must convince him to stay until Paul returns. But how long will that be?*

Aquila tried to remember the Sabbath Paul had talked about the beating. He squeezed his eyes tightly shut and rubbed his forehead. Paul had repeated a prayer, "Now, Lord, consider their threats and enable your servants to speak your word with great boldness." He reheard Paul's emphasis, "with *great* boldness." The words burned in his mind. He remembered the smile on Paul's face as he spoke.

Boldness. Priscilla's boldness had offended him, just as Peter's boldness offended the Sanhedrin. Aquila smacked his forehead with his hand. No wonder he had been the accuser in the dream. Priscilla was not being willfully disobedient or challenging his authority. No, the Spirit was moving through her. Through her gifts, her intelligence, her courage. Aquila struggled to reject his conclusion but something stopped him.

Priscilla could teach—no, *must* teach—Apollos. It was as clear as if someone had stood directly behind him and whispered in his ear. Yes, Priscilla must teach Apollos what Paul had taught her. Why not? Paul had trusted her with his letters. Once Paul had chuckled, "If only you were a man —we could turn the world upside down." And Aquila knew that Priscilla had been on Paul's mind when he had written the Corinthians about the restraints of marriage and service.

What was that statement of Paul's? "But a married woman is concerned about the affairs of the world and how she can please her husband."

And for so long, I have thought that the way she should please me is to hide her gifts. Why, she can no more do that than she could hide that she is a woman!

But I can't ask her to forgive me. That wouldn't be right. She has offended me. Maybe in a day or two she'll forget all about— He shook his head. He knew she wouldn't forget. *But I cannot ask her to forgive me. A husband can't do that. I would be powerless in the future; such an act would only encourage her to flaunt herself. How would Priscilla ever submit to me again if I appear weak?*

"Forgive, as the Lord forgave you—" he seemed to hear Paul's familiar voice. He once had interrupted Paul's dictation to challenge that statement. But he remembered Paul's explanation: "We have no *alternative!*"

Next morning, breakfast was eaten in silence. They had just started working. The sounds of their work filled the room as hides were scraped and the shuttle banged against the loom. Priscilla kept her eyes down, fixed on the cloth she was weaving. Aquila put his hand on her shoulder and turned her toward him.

"I have something to say to you," Aquila said. Priscilla looked up, a little fearfully.

"Yes, my lord?" she said, softly.

"About yesterday—" he looked down, nervous. He felt as frightened to speak to her as he had been to tell Reuben of his desire to be baptized. He pushed his left sandal through the dirt.

Priscilla glanced quickly at Kara and at Joshua. Did they know what Aquila was going to say? Had he talked to them? Apparently not. Their expression showed that they didn't know what was happening, either.

"I have something to say to you," Aquila repeated.

"Yes, my lord," Priscilla again responded. Kara smiled at the gentle tone of Priscilla's voice. *Soon the household will be back to normal,* she thought. She beckoned to Joshua to leave the room with her. They stepped out into the yard.

"I am sorry that I—" Aquila bit his lip and dropped his head. For a long time, he stood staring at the ground. Then, his voice rough with unshed tears, he said, "Priscilla, I am sorry—I am *so* sorry—that I got angry with you over Apollos. It will never happen again."

"No, my lord. In the future I will be obedient to your wishes."

"No," he shook his head. "It is I who have been disobedient." He struggled to gain control of his voice. "I have been jealous—of your gifts."

Hesitantly, Priscilla stood. Aquila went on: "I have not been obedient to the Holy Spirit. I have been so jealous of your gifts, your writing. When I found a virtuous woman, who speaks with wisdom, I—" he stopped, "became jealous. Oh, Priscilla," he blurted, "will you forgive me?"

"Aquila," Priscilla said gently, "you are my husband. You are the man I love. How could I not forgive you? And you, can you forgive me?" She shifted her weight, hoping that he would give her some indication that he wanted to touch her or hold her.

"Oh, Priscilla," he cried, raising his arms to her. She ran to him and buried her head against his chest. He wrapped his arms around her in a fierce embrace.

They made no tents that day; not another stitch was completed. But deep within their hearts the invisible strength of love sutured the gaping wound that one moment of rage and years of jealousy had torn in Priscilla's heart.

Apollos blinked, then rubbed his eyes.

"It's too early," he said, yawning.

"Yes," Aquila answered. "I hope you will accept my apology for waking you."

"Certainly." Apollos shrugged. "But what do you want?"

For a moment—a brief moment—Aquila wanted to turn and bolt out of Apollos's room; to flee from what he must say. Yet he knew that was impossible. There were moments one had to do the right thing, however inconvenient or uncomfortable. After all his words to Priscilla about obedience, now he felt the pressure of obedience to the Lord.

"I have come to offer you an apology."

"Apology?" Apollos sputtered, puzzlement spreading across his face. "How have you offended me? Maybe I should ask your forgiveness!"

"No!" Aquila answered strongly. Apollos blinked. He detected the subtle tone, the struggle in Aquila's voice. Aquila looked down, then glanced away and finally allowed his eyes to meet Apollos's. "I have been . . ." he looked down again, "jealous of you, and I have wronged you."

"Wronged me? How?"

"I find myself in a predicament. My wife is wise, very wise."

"That she is," Apollos agreed.

"And that is my problem—my burden. She is a good wife, but I have tried to put her in her place, to ignore her talents, to dismiss her questions." Apollos waited. "And now I must ask your forgiveness. When I came home and found you talking to her, I was jealous."

"Well, I have good news for you."

"What?" Aquila frowned.

"I'm leaving, soon, perhaps tomorrow or the next day."

"No!"

Apollos laughed, shaking his head. "Your response strikes me odd. I should think that would be delightful news to a jealous husband—although there was never anything to be jealous about. I'm going on to Achaia."

"But there is much for you to learn. You can't leave yet. That's why I am here. The Lord has sent me. He has burdened me about you."

"How so?" Apollos did not hide his skepticism.

"You are a great man, you speak with great fervor and teach accurately, you are well educated, you speak boldly," he paused. "But you know only John's baptism. That's not enough. You must know Jesus's baptism, the empowering of the Holy Spirit."

"I know Jesus lived."

"But it is more than that. Jesus *lives.* In our hearts. John's baptism was for repentance, but Jesus offers the Resurrection, the life everlasting."

"I have longed to meet someone who could teach me about Jesus," said Apollos eagerly. "Someone who could answer my questions."

"Then come to our shop. Priscilla can answer many of them. I am sure of that."

"But that would take her away from her work," Apollos protested.

"Hardly. *This* is her work!" Aquila smiled at Apollos, and the two men clasped hands to confirm their friendship.

And so an apology opened the door to the days Apollos spent with the tenters who sewed tents and sowed the Gospel at the same time. Priscilla had been surprised to look up from her work and see Aquila and Apollos walking through the gate. She had been speechless when Aquila announced, "Here is your pupil."

The days passed quickly yet productively. Apollos asked hundreds of questions, some of which stumped Priscilla. A few could not have been fully explained even by Paul.

Two weeks later (Apollos had gone to the countryside for a visit) Aquila walked over and stood behind Priscilla, protectively laying his hands on her shoulders and stroking gently. "He's close; so close," he whispered.

"Yes," Priscilla answered. "Very close. If only Paul were here."

"Why?"

"He could lead Apollos into the Kingdom."

"Maybe it is God's design that Paul be away. Remember what Paul said about the foolishness of preaching. To the Jehovites it is an offense, but to those who belong to the Lord, it is the glory. Maybe it is God's design that such a brilliant mind should enter the Kingdom of God as a child, learning from tent makers."

"Oh, Aquila!" Priscilla laughed. "That's what Jesus said! That one must become like a child to inherit the kingdom of God." She looked into his eyes; his face had grown so strong, cleansed of sullenness, lit and made radiant by the work of teaching the Gospel.

Two days passed before Apollos returned. He sat on the ground, eating bread and cheese, as Priscilla questioned him closely. She had been citing prophecies, and Apollos was explaining the fulfullment, in a sort of catechism.

"Micah promises what?" she asked, without looking up from her weaving.

" 'But out of you, Bethlehem Ephraim, though you are small among the clans, one will come who will be ruler over Israel.' "

"And what was Isaiah's prophecy?"

" 'For unto us a child is born, to us a son is given and the government shall be on his shoulders.' "

"And what shall he be called?"

" 'Wonderful Counselor, Mighty God, Everlasting Father, Prince of Peace.' "

"And upon whose throne will he sit?"

"David's."

"So, Apollos, what keeps you from saying, 'I believe'?" asked Priscilla. Apollos was silent. Joshua and Aquila looked at him—he had given such quick answers, why was he delaying?

"I *do* believe," Apollos said. "I *do* believe!"

"What do you believe?" Priscilla touched him, smiling.

"I *do* believe that Jesus is the Messiah!"

Priscilla burst into joyful tears. Aquila ran to Apollos and hugged him tightly. Apollos returned the hug. Joshua shuffled to both of them and waited to embrace his new brother. After much squeezing and back-pounding, Aquila let go and Joshua stepped up to Apollos.

"Brother Apollos," Joshua said, his eyes sparkling.

"Brother Joshua!" At that Joshua grabbed Apollos and wept. Aquila turned and beckoned Priscilla to join them. He pulled her into his arms and kissed her lightly on the cheek. "You have brought him into the Kingdom," he whispered.

So they had their first convert—and an impressive one, at that. The days of questioning and answering, guided by the Holy Spirit, had caused her to be gentle, firm, accurate, precise, yet effective.

Just before sundown that same day, they all stood along the riverbank. Aquila waded out a few feet and, once convinced of the safety of the stream, he turned to face Apollos, Kara, and Joshua. When he called Apollos by name, Joshua escorted the new convert into the water to Aquila. Aquila turned him to face the east and then asked him to fold his hands. As Aquila prayed, he raised one hand high over Apollos's head. Then he placed his left hand over Apollos's hands and slipped his other arm under his back.

"I baptize you in the name of Jesus the Christ," he intoned, pushed Apollos down into the water, and steadied him as Apollos stood up again, dripping wet.

Apollos grinned as he wiped water from his face. His smile was infectious. Aquila gripped Apollos's shoulder. "Brother Apollos," he said with great conviction.

Apollos laughed as he walked out of the water. He stopped in front of Priscilla, and said gravely, "If it had not been for you, I might never have known Jesus!"

Priscilla was overcome by the remark. She tried looking into the fiery-red sunset to slow the tears, but finally gave up. She had a right to cry; her courage, her bold question had brought this man into Christ's Kingdom. And who knew how many converts he might make! Truly she was blessed, in herself and her family, and in the work God had given her. She clasped Aquila's hand lovingly as they followed the others through the long path among the willows, back to their quarters.

⚍ 34 ⚎

Paul looked up at the sun and wiped the sweat from his forehead. He joined Priscilla and Kara under the old fig tree.

"They wait for me in the lecture hall," he said, almost to himself.

"It's nearly time for you to leave," Priscilla said gently, reluctant to disturb him from his reverie.

He glanced at the hot sun again. "I was just thinking how the sun was like this, turning the earth to dust, on the day I arrived back here in Corinth. Can that day really have been two years ago?" he mused.

Priscilla smiled. "They've been two blessed years."

Paul's eyes searched her face, and Priscilla saw their characteristic intensity return.

"Well, I had no idea I would be here this long. But as long as people keep coming to Tyrannus's lecture hall, and the Jehovites behave themselves, what can I do? I will continue to sew tents in the morning—and sow the Gospel in the afternoon. And I will trust God to bless both endeavors."

"While other men are resting!" Kara remarked sharply.

"Napping, more likely. Ephesians need their sleep."

"Not only the Ephesians, my lord," Priscilla scolded. Her voice and use of the term "my lord" raised Paul's suspicion.

"And what is that supposed to mean?" he asked.

"It means that I, well," Priscilla began, glancing around at Kara for support, "both of us are concerned about you.

At first, your schedule didn't bother us. But you are here every morning before daylight. Then, with only a little lunch and *no* rest you are off to the lecture hall until four!"

"I would preach longer, but I lose my crowd when the shops reopen—"

"But Paul, you *need* more rest. Every day working, every day teaching, then back here until sundown."

"The Lord gives me strength. Should I deny these Ephesians the greatness of my knowledge? I must work as long as it is day." Paul had meant it jokingly, but Kara seized the opportunity.

"Huh! You need a wife. You'd be in better health. You need someone—"

"Yes?" Paul said, impatiently, lifting his bushy eyebrows.

"Well," she fumbled with her hands, "to keep an eye on you."

"As you keep an eye on Joshua? No, thank you! I have everything I need." Paul shook his head and laughed. "Besides, what would I do with a wife? She would be about as useful to me as one of those silver statues of Artemis."

Paul stopped when a young woman entered the garden, a strikingly beautiful woman with dark eyes and long black hair. Priscilla clapped her hands.

"Ah, Neti! You found us!"

"It was not difficult to find. Everyone knows where the Orator lives and works." The bright blue robe, trimmed in silver braid, dazzled in the sunshine and set off Neti's dark features. Paul recognized that she had a wealthy husband; the large silver medallion around her neck as well as the two male servants who accompanied her proved that conclusion.

"Neti, this is Paul," Priscilla said, gently nudging Neti closer to Paul. "I met Neti at the baths. I have always looked for someone to talk to. And we had a long talk about many important matters. But Neti had some questions that I thought you might be able to answer for her. By the way, Neti's husband is a silversmith."

"Obviously, a prosperous one," Paul said curtly. Neti blushed and looked away. Priscilla directed her to a small stool near Paul's worktable.

"She does have some questions for you," Priscilla said, with a warning tone in her voice.

"That you can't answer?" Paul smiled. "Why do I always get the hard ones?" Under Paul's tutoring, Priscilla had matured; these days, few questions were referred to Paul.

"Maybe I should wait until another time," Neti apologized, looking to the two servants. "I am interrupting your work."

"I can stitch as I talk. No," Paul said, playfully smacking his forehead. "As you talk, I will listen and sew. Then maybe I will talk."

"Would you like something cool to drink?" Kara asked. Neti nodded and Kara walked inside the house.

"So, you have questions. Well, they must be good ones, because Priscilla is an excellent teacher—one of the best. If she were a man, she'd have taught all over Asia by now. So, if she can't answer the question, I am not certain that I can." Priscilla blushed at the compliment. How Paul had changed, she thought, recalling his fears that her letters would contain errors. But he had moderated to grudging acceptance and now to open praise.

"Oh, sir, word of your teaching is everywhere. They say you are a great thinker. A wise man. A philosopher."

"Ah, now you flatter me. But do great 'philosophers' spend their time with a hide? Sewing? stitching? But possibly you've heard other remarks as well." She looked down. "I thought so. 'Paul is mad' or 'Paul ignores the truth' or 'Paul is a libertine.' You've heard such things, yes?"

Slowly Neti shook her head to answer his questions. "But sir, I do not believe them. I believe what Priscilla told me." Paul scratched his head, then pulled on the seam to test his stitches.

"She has questions about the cloths," Priscilla said.

"Cloths?" Paul repeated, without looking up. "So ask!" he shrugged.

"I have a young servant girl who has been sick for years. On an errand, apparently near your lecture hall, she overheard your teaching."

Paul laughed. "My opponents say that I am loud enough to be heard blocks away; they accuse me of interrupting their naps."

"She became so ill," Neti continued, ignoring his self-effacement, "that I thought she would die. Then another servant laid one of your handkerchiefs on her forehead. I thought to cover her eyes, anticipating her death." She paused. Paul looked up and motioned, "Go on . . ."

"Well, she served me breakfast the next morning."

"The one who had put the handkerchief on her face?"

"No! The sick girl! She looked perfectly well. Her face was bright as if she had been in the sun. Her fingers were warm . . . there was a glow about her."

"And today?" Priscilla demanded.

"She has not been sick since."

"How long has that been?"

"Several months."

"Girls have a way of outgrowing illnesses," Kara said as she placed a pitcher and some cups on the table. "It's the way of women; they get used to it." She poured some mint tea into the cups.

"No!" Neti shot back. "This girl had always been sickly; we had never been able to expect much out of her. And now she is a totally different person." Kara frowned thoughtfully. Slowly she walked back to her loom and picked up the spindle.

"So?" Paul asked as he sipped his tea.

"So are you a magician?" Neti asked.

" 'A magician?' " Paul sputtered. "A magician, did you say? No!" He held up the hide. "I am a tent maker."

"But you have power, extraordinary power. I have heard

- 298 -

other accounts about you at the baths, from my neighbors, in the markets. They say if someone has become ill to get a cloth that has been touched by you."

"Who says that?" Paul demanded.

"People—all over Ephesus." Paul studied Neti's face. His eyebrows drew together in concern.

"Is that true?" he asked Priscilla.

"Well, I *have* overheard stories about your power or alleged power." Paul half-laughed, and looked down at the ground. His shoulders suddenly seemed too bent and weary, even for a man of his years.

"So, I am now thought to be a magician? No wonder my aprons and handkerchiefs keep disappearing. I'd better keep a close eye on my robe at the baths, or that will disappear, too."

"Then you can be even better known. The naked philosopher!" Kara chuckled, trying to lighten the atmosphere.

"But sir, you have the power!" Neti exclaimed. "Everyone knows it."

"Neti," Paul sighed, tapping his chest. *"I* have no power! Look at me! Do I look like a magician? No, I am just a man. A tent maker."

"They say in Derbe that those who worship Zeus wanted to worship you. They called you Hermes."

"Derbe!" Paul smacked his hand onto the table, dismayed. "That priest had lost his wits. He had bulls everywhere, wanting to sacrifice them, build an altar—it took everything I could do to stop him."

"Stop him? Why did you want to stop him? You had just healed a man who had never walked, according to the stories."

"How did you know about that?" Paul shook his head in astonishment.

"Your reputation, sir, is well known. You can do miracles."

"Well, it should be equally well known that I cannot heal

him or anyone. God did. All I did was to look at the poor fellow. When I recognized his faith and how much he wanted to walk, I merely said, 'Stand up and walk!' "

"And he walked?" Kara asked breathlessly.

"He jumped up!" Paul gestured, jumping from the table, "and began to walk." Paul hobbled. "And the more he walked the better he walked."

"Lame since birth?" Kara repeated, her face lined with skepticism.

"So they told me."

"They also say that you could be a wealthy man." Neti looked intently at Paul.

"I *am* a wealthy man." Priscilla gasped at the statement. Paul quickly held up both hands to ward off her questioning. "Oh, not in the way Ephesians, or most Jehovites, think of wealth. But in the real ways. I have a craft. I have a mind. I have friends like Aquila and Joshua. What more could a man want?"

"A wife," Kara muttered under her breath.

"Why do you not accept money for your power?" Neti asked.

"There is no power to pay for!" Paul's tone indicated that he was becoming exasperated with Neti's questioning. "Whatever I do, it is in his strength, not in mine!"

"His strength?"

"Jesus of Nazareth lives in me," Paul replied firmly. Neti looked so confused that he added, "Here in my heart. He dwells in me through the Holy Spirit."

"The Holy Spirit?"

"You remember me talking to you about the Holy Spirit, Neti," Priscilla cut in. "Our god is not like Artemis. You Ephesians go to the temple, or rub a little silver idol or figurine like your husband's crafters make. But our God lives in our hearts."

"How could that be?" Neti shook her head defiantly. "But I do know my servant is well. Not just better—but well! And I want to be well." She dropped her head and voice; the tears and soft weeping revealed her pain. Paul glanced at Kara and Priscilla. "I have not been able to give my husband a child. That's why I have come to you," she said, brushing aside her tears. "If you could use your power on me—or give me a cloth—so that I could have a child."

"And why is a child so important?" Paul asked. Kara raised an eyebrow. *Men!* she fumed. *Everyone knows why a child is important. Her husband could tire of waiting and take another wife. The poor girl could be turned into the street, without anything; not even her family would intervene in such a case.* Kara shook her head.

"I *have* no power," Paul said firmly. "I am not a magician wandering from city to city. I am a tent maker wandering from city to city. But I do know someone who does have power."

"Oh, sir, my husband is a wealthy man. He would pay, any price—"

"The gift and power are not for sale."

"But you have helped other people," Neti pleaded.

"Neti, magicians have always associated supernatural power with cloths that are blood-soaked or sweat-stained. I do not have that power." Priscilla put a comforting hand on Neti's shoulder.

Neti turned to her. "Make him understand, Priscilla. I would do anything to have a baby. Anything."

"Neti—" Paul stopped to clear his throat. "The only power I know is Jesus Christ. Your real need is not for a child. It is to know Jesus. To know the deep peace that he brings."

"This is true, Neti," Priscilla added, putting her arm around the young woman. "Jesus gives a peace that the world cannot understand *or* take away. He is with us!"

"I do not understand this Jesus you talk about. But I know I must have a child *soon.* I've waited on Artemis, and she ignores me and my sacrifices. I have made wreaths of flowers to lay at her feet. I have laid beside those gifts, begging—"

"Neti! None of that will do you any good. A statue can't help you. Artemis has no ears—just breasts. How can she hear what you are saying? How can she feel your pain or see your tears? Artemis is nothing but a mound of silver!"

"But I can see her!"

"But *she* cannot see *you!*" Priscilla responded firmly. Paul, delighted, nodded for her to continue. "Our God," Priscilla said, "is like a shepherd with his sheep." Neti began to weep softly.

She tenderly embraced Neti. "He knows His sheep by name. He seeks them out and calls them."

Silently, Paul watched as Priscilla gently stroked Neti. Her tenderness, no less than her reasoning, had stirred him. The gentle shepherd spoken of by Isaiah. Intelligent, gifted, Priscilla contradicted everything he had ever learned or assumed about women. She continually surprised him: her letters were precise yet eloquent at times to read or hear. She had shaped Apollos into the Christian leader he now was. And Paul had to admit that many preferred Apollos's preaching to his. And who knew how many Jehovites and Gentiles had come to believe because of the power of Apollos's words and life—people who would have otherwise gone down into the darkness of Sheol without the Lord. And all this the Lord had begun through Priscilla's boldness.

So much could be accomplished by gentleness. Paul stuck the needle into the thick hide, his morning's work over. He had not really taught or emphasized this quality of Jesus in his lectures. Maybe the Ephesians could better understand this allegory of the shepherd than those other metaphors Paul had tried.

He stood, stretched his arms, then walked over to Priscilla and Neti. He laid his hand on the young girl's head and prayed, "May you find peace and joy in Jesus." Then he walked out of the garden and slowly wound his way to the lecture hall.

As he walked, he remembered with pain the heated arguments, the bitter accusations that had forced him to abandon the synagogue. The first three months had been overwhelming; the Jehovites had seemed so hungry for the Gospel. Then, slowly, one or two stubborn men had turned the others against him.

He might have gone next door with the Christian Jehovites, as at Corinth. But then he discovered that the lecture hall was vacant every afternoon. Tyrannus, who taught philosophy in the mornings, agreed to let Paul have the hall in the afternoons, although he joked that he couldn't imagine the devotees of Artemis giving up their afternoon naps to listen to Paul's strange teachings.

However, because of the setting, Gentiles came in droves to hear Paul. Many would never have entered a synagogue. Now they came freely, bringing friends, merchants, travelers. Amazingly, God could work through all things for His glory. Paul appropriated Joseph's words many times: "You meant it for evil, but God meant it for good." If he ran into Arvi, his chief Jehovite opponent, Paul thought, he would tell him that.

As he thought of Arvi, a shadow passed over Paul. He felt uneasy. These rumors about his power made his heart ache. Nothing must distract from the Gospel; nothing—not his personality, not miracles. People came for miracles like a thirsty man seeks water. Had not the Master realized that? The people's cry "Heal us!" had no doubt wearied Him.

"Give us miracles. Give us signs. Give us proofs." *Always "Give us! Give us!" If they would listen to what I preach,* Paul thought, *they wouldn't need miracles. Jesus Christ is miracle enough.* Slowly, wearily, Paul made his way through the drowsy, hot, sun-struck lanes to the lecture hall. *I am tired,* he thought. *I too have need of the Great Shepherd.*

Demetrius the silversmith smiled as he slowly turned the statue of Artemis in his hand. Exquisite. Yes, no other word could describe his craftsmanship. Beyond anything Ephesians had ever seen or dreamed. How many hours had he labored to create this masterpiece? It did not matter.

Here, as in most cities, for economy and mutual support, the more skilled silversmiths' shops were clustered together. Everyone knew everyone's business. However, Demetrius had lied and connived to keep this piece secret. He had struggled with the blowpipes to keep the fire's temperature at just the right level. His fellow craftsmen would ask questions about his technique—questions he would ignore. The secret for this process was his, to be shared with no one.

He smiled as he admired his craftsmanship. He remembered the afternoon he had first conceived creating such a statue. He had been lying with a prostitute in the temple, exhausted from his passion. Indeed, some of his best ideas came in those moments after the ecstasies of worship and passion.

He owed everything to Artemis. She had favored him, prospered him over the other silver merchants. She had bestowed on him the highest reputation in the city. Elsewhere one could find all sorts of cheap, crude figurines. The wealthy, the aspiring, the devout, however, all made their way to the shop of Demetrius and bought the best.

He sighed. To put this figurine on sale would be painful.

Perhaps, he would not be able to sell it. He wondered if he could, without regret, watch someone carry it from his shop. Initially he had thought to keep it, prominently displayed in his home—but that would do little to spread his reputation.

With the approaching equinox festival, thousands of Artemis devotees would swarm through Ephesus. They would enter through the triumphant arches, their mouths gaping at the beauty of the pillars that lined the avenue. They would ecstatically chant, "Great is Artemis!" They would cheer the athletes at the stadium, applaud the actors at the theatre, enjoy the musicians at the Odeon—and pay the silversmiths. They would make their offerings in the sacred grove where Artemis had been born, stuff themselves at the great banquets. Then they would browse the tiny shops and stalls, looking for charms and mementoes.

Once this piece was exhibited, the word would spread through the pilgrims like wildfire. Although few could afford the piece, they would all want to look on it, to covet its ownership. And if there were other, cheaper figurines with Demetrius's seal, with cheaper prices—

Devius coughed. Demetrius looked up, hating to be interrupted in his ecstasy and self-adolation. "Yes, what is it?" he said impatiently.

"I have taken another count, sir, as you ordered."

"And?" Demetrius demanded.

"The count is the same as before."

"What?" Demetrius shouted, jumping to his feet. The slave cowered in fear. He had often been beaten by Demetrius.

"Sir, what can I say?" he pleaded pitifully. "The figurines are not selling." He showed his owner the papyrus inventory.

Demetrius cursed as he ran his finger along the columns, examining the slave's scrawl.

"Impossible! There can't be this many figurines unsold!

Look at this," he pointed to one mark. "That's the cheapest one—we always sell far more than that by this point."

Quickly Demetrius's mind raced ahead. If he hadn't reduced his current supply—and he knew the orders he had placed for silver bullion for the upcoming festival—he'd be heavily overstocked. The prices would drop—he could be ruined or made a laughingstock by his peers. He angrily shook his head, then glared at the slave.

Fear swept the face of Devius, and Demetrius briefly enjoyed that pained expression.

"I'm certain that I counted correctly, sir," he stuttered. "Please come, look for yourself." Demetrius cursed and spat at the slave. But he followed him to the storeroom. Admittedly in the past few months he had been so occupied with this new figurine that he had ignored everything else. While that may have been bad business, it was part of his gratitude and devotion to Artemis. She would honor such devotion, he had thought. He would be rewarded with big profits, big sales, fame.

Demetrius gasped in unbelief at the rows of silver figurines that lined the racks and shelves. In corners, on tables, under tables, in baskets—everywhere he looked he saw figurines. Devius was right.

Slowly he rubbed his eyes as if that would change the count. He walked around the room—touching the figurines. People always bought this one of Artemis lounging with her lions; or the ones of the temple itself.

Without a word to Devius, he turned and angrily stalked out the door. He'd ask Trevius and Caius about their sales. Devius trembled so fiercely that he dropped to the floor and hugged his legs tightly; he had escaped the beating he had expected—at least for the moment.

Paul looked up from the skins he was sewing and smiled at the young man who sat across from him. Faltius was so close to becoming a believer. Any day. The intense questions, the longing in the voice convinced Paul. Yet the hesitancy remained. In some ways, Faltius reminded him of Timothy: so intense one moment, and at other times naive.

Without abandoning his work, Paul continued the explanation. The young man moved closer. *I'll never get this section finished,* Paul thought, *but before lunch I may have a candidate for baptism.*

"How do you really know this Jesus?" Faltius fidgeted. "How do you *really* know that he is 'with you'?"

Paul coughed. "Your father . . . does he not have ways to tell you, to remind you that he is your father? Does he have to tell you every moment, 'You are my son'?"

"No, of course not. I know that I am his son."

"Ah," Paul beamed, threading the bone needle. "But how do you *know?*" He winked at Priscilla and Marcus, who had entered the back of the room and sat listening. She had heard most of the conversation and had followed Paul's line of logic. Later they would discuss the approach, but his eyes turned back to the boy, demanding an answer. "Well?"

"Well, I live in my father's house, I eat at his table, I work for my father, I listen to him—"

"And—" Paul gestured with the needle.

"I obey."

"Ah. You obey. And that is how we know that we are God's sons. We obey. We follow Jesus's example."

Paul looked back to the hide and quickly ran his hand over its rough texture. He fingered his stitching. Having gained this concession from the boy, he would continue to press for a decision.

Demetrius rushed angrily along a street, trying to clear his head. Trevius and Caius agreed—no sales were taking place. What could they do? Suddenly he stopped. Tent! He snapped his fingers. He was supposed to have talked with some Jehovite named Aquila about a tent for the festival.

Oh, just a small one. He wanted to put up a tent along the harbor road, to get first chance at the pilgrims as they entered the city. He needed only a small tent, and Tvia had said that Aquila was both fast and reasonable. He was tempted to find Trevius, but he'd have time for that later. First things first. He needed to order the tent.

He looked around and blinked. He was lucky—his ramblings had taken him to the quarter of the tent makers. Aquila must be somewhere near. He asked a man lounging by a doorpost, and the beggar pointed to Aquila's gate. *Ah, how convenient,* Demetrius thought. He stopped at the doorway and began to announce his presence, but—at hearing a clear, firm, cultured voice—he stopped, puzzled.

"Faltius," the voice said sternly, "Artemis is no god, at all. She is but a statue. Man-made idols are not gods to be worshipped. You waste your time and money with those little silver figurines you buy."

"Yes, Faltius," Priscilla said gently, stepping from the shadow into the bright sunshine. "God is spirit. Those who worship the true God worship Him in their hearts." The sun shone through her cloud of red-gold curls.

Demetrius's heart pounded furiously; his temple throbbed. He raised his hands to his forehead and rubbed lightly. He couldn't believe what he had heard. The statement "Artemis is no god" racked through his mind as a pebble kicked by a child echoed down a lane. Anger seethed within him. But he realized that he needed to hear more before he took action, so he leaned against the gate and waited.

"So, you go buy your statue of the great god, Artemis, you spend your money on a chunk of silver—and what do you have?" Paul snorted. "Huh? Nothing!" he shouted, before the boy could answer. "You have a god made by human hands, worthless as dung. In fact, it might as well be made from dung. It would be just as worthy but cheaper. One is just as good as the other."

"You insult our god!" Faltius answered tremulously. *An understatement!* Demetrius thought.

"Artemis, my boy, is no god to be insulted. Artemis is a big hunk of silver that ought to be melted down and used to feed the poor and clothe the naked. Ah, but Jehovah," Paul paused, waving his hands in the air, "Jehovah cannot be contained in silver or gold or clay or wood or stone or anything man can touch. He is the God who created all things—who *knows* all things. He thus must be greater than all things." Paul smacked the hide. "To give His son to be a ransom, to redeem us from his sins and from his—"

"Idols?" Priscilla suggested.

"Especially from his idols. Because as long as a man worships an idol, he will not find the true God."

"I don't know about that," Faltius sadly said, shaking his head. "It sounds so clear when I am with you, but when I am with my father, Artemis sounds so right. I just don't know."

Demetrius's hands formed into tight fists. He would love to burst through the gate this instant and beat these blasphemers senseless. No, they were already senseless. The very idea of comparing Artemis to dung! He struggled to know what to do as rage pulsed through his veins.

"Can I help you?" a voice asked.

Demetrius looked startled. A man stood staring at him. "I'm Aquila. Perhaps you are looking for my shop." Demetrius glared at the man. If this was the shopkeeper, he thought, who were the demented voices inside? Demetrius had to know the identities of the blasphemers. They could not go unpunished. It was his duty to report them.

Aquila stood waiting. The man was clearly trying to make up his mind. Finally, Demetrius's face relaxed.

"Yes, ah, I am in need of a tent," he began. Anything to get inside the shop. "Only a small tent that may not be worth your time." Demetrius fumbled with his hands.

"How soon do you need this tent?"

"For the festival." Demetrius saw the pained look in Aquila's eyes.

"Well, come into my shop and we can discuss what you need. I'm not sure we can meet your request that quickly, but we could try. And our price would be fair."

Aquila gestured toward the gate. As Demetrius entered he found Paul bent over a skin, sewing rapidly; a young boy sat near him. He heard Paul say, "So, don't waste your time or money on silver gods. Seek the one, true God. Jehovah!" Paul beamed and then suddenly looked up, nodding in Demetrius's direction. Demetrius eyed him coldly, his jaw twitching as he tried to disguise his anger.

Two leaps, and he could reach this old man and pummel him onto the floor. "Seek out the true god!" he had said. He glanced to the boy. Wonder whose fool this was? The boy needed to be beaten, severely. Obviously he was full of foolishness; more so after listening to the ravings of this lunatic tenter.

"This is my associate, Paul," Aquila said politely. "And I didn't get your name?"

Demetrius didn't answer immediately. He was memorizing the face of this short, graying man who sat smiling up at him. When he realized Aquila was waiting, he turned back.

"Your name is—" Aquila repeated.

"Demetrius."

"Ah," Paul said, "the silversmith."

"How do you know about me?" Demetrius hastily asked.

"I don't," Paul shrugged, "but I've seen your work, your statuary. You're quite a craftsman." Demetrius frowned. This man was either a lunatic or a fool. Only moments before, he had been denouncing silver craftsmen; now he was commending him.

"I have a high reputation in this city," Demetrius said, nervously.

"Not just in this city, sir," Paul corrected him. "Everywhere."

"He's the best," Faltius interrupted. "My father has bought many figurines from you."

Demetrius studied the boy's face. Now he recognized him. *Before sunset,* he thought to himself, *I will have words with your father. My boy, you'll wish you'd never met this blasphemer.*

"Yes, well." Aquila cleared his throat. "Demetrius is interested in a tent."

"Well, he has come to the right place." Paul chuckled. "And what size tent do you need?" As Aquila showed samples of their work, Demetrius slowly explained what he wanted. But he hesitated; too many things were racing through his mind to concentrate on details of the tent. Besides, he had no intention of buying anything from a Jehovite and particularly from a blasphemer. But he needed information. How dare these Jehovites come into Ephesus and conduct a trade and dare to impute the goddess of the city! There would be people most interested to know about this!

So he stayed; he asked questions, he gathered information. Demetrius's true loyalty to Artemis was well known. There was nothing he wouldn't do for her. Just as he had labored to sculpt the crown on her head that revealed her role as protector and defender of Ephesus, so she was the protector of his business and his prosperity.

So Demetrius wanted to know more about this Paul and Aquila and—he had almost forgotten—the woman. He turned but didn't see her.

It was an odd, long afternoon. Elsewhere, a light rain had fallen on several aspiring orators in the amphitheater; merchants had restlessly dozed their afternoon naps, dreaming of profits to be made during the approaching festival; mothers had gone about preparing the evening meal or settling disputes among children busy being children. But in Tyrannus's lecture hall, the Spirit had descended and bathed the hearts of the Ephesian Followers of the Way and made them "brothers"—not just in name or affection but in a deep reality.

Many could not explain what had possessed them to stand and confess their sins to Paul and the other men; some had revealed old sins, others had disclosed perversions, demon worship, blood sacrifice, sexual straying and lust: the imaginable and the unimaginable—yet slowly, surely a peace had grown up among the men. That afternoon, unknown to passers-by in the streets as the meeting took place, the church at Ephesus was rebaptized, cleansed.

Now silence prevailed. What more could be said? Paul stood wiping his tears, raising his hands high above his head, and spoke.

Oh, Lord, open my lips
and my mouth will declare your praise.
The sacrifices of God are a broken spirit;
   a broken and a contrite heart,
O God, you will not despise.
Our God is compassionate and gracious,
   slow to anger, abounding in love.
He does not treat us as our sins deserve
   or repay us according to our iniquities.

"For as high," and Paul let his voice ascend to the ceiling of the hall, "as *high*," he gestured, "as the heavens are above the earth, so great is his love for those who fear him; as far as the east," he pointed eastward, then thrust his hand in the opposite direction, "is from the west, so far has he removed our transgressions from us.

"As a father pities his children," Paul's voice broke, "so the Lord has compassion on those who fear him; for he *knows*—" Paul glanced about, then pointed a finger toward the ceiling, *"he knows* how we are formed, he remembers that we are dust.

"My brothers—" Paul said through a great smile, "and you *are* my brothers, every last one of you—I have never experienced anything like this before.

"It is difficult to confess sin, especially to stand before our brothers and share some of the things you have shared. But it is no sign of weakness. Rather, it is a sign of courage." Paul looked around as if someone might challenge him.

"It is a sign of strength. Of manliness. Some of you are no longer Ephesians . . . you are brothers. And I salute you!" The sound of approval spread among the men. "And brothers deal gently with one another; we support the weaker brother.

"Some of us would never be tempted to worship Artemis. We *know*—" he paused dramatically, "—don't we? that Artemis is only a big chunk of silver. Worthless! But that is because some of us have never bowed our knees to her as others of you have, since childhood. It is the only thing you have known until now. It is more difficult for you to give up Artemis. So we must stand with you, encourage you; but my brothers," he stopped, "there must be *no* compromise! Artemis must not be worshipped in any way."

"Sir?" a man waved his hand in the back; Paul recognized him. "What should I do with my figurines and medallions? If I throw them away, someone will find them. If I give them away, I am still encouraging someone to use them. I cannot sell them and profit by the money."

Joshua cleared his throat. "We could melt them. Maybe that would be the encouragement the weaker brothers need."

"When?" someone asked.

"How about tomorrow afternoon?" Aquila suggested.

"How about tonight?" another man countered. "That way, others can see the light of our fires and our commitment to Jesus." The idea quickly gained acceptance by the men. Paul announced a time and a place and then dismissed the group. Slowly, he walked back to the shop with Aquila and Joshua.

"Well, this has been quite an afternoon," Paul said.

"Paul, will they bring their figurines tonight?" Aquila asked. Paul scratched his beard for a moment before he answered.

"Some will . . . some won't. Men are unpredictable. But the ones that obey, the Lord will bless."

After sundown, Paul paced by the large, crackling fire Joshua and Aquila had built. Slowly the Ephesian Christians had gathered—not just the men but women and children, slaves, servants, and no small number of curious Jehovites and Artemis worshippers. The garden was packed; people waited outside the gate, hoping to get in.

"When do we begin?" Aquila asked Paul.

Paul stood and walked to the fire. "Brothers," he shouted, "I am overwhelmed. I had no idea so many of you would come. Let us thank our God and pray that He will give courage tonight to the weakest brother among us."

Silence swept across the group as Paul prayed simply, yet forcefully. When he finished, a young Follower of the Way spontaneously broke into a hymn:

Praise to thee, Jesus!
Praise to the Son!
Praise to the Father!
Praise to the Spirit.

Slowly the song was picked up by the throng. When it faded inside the courtyard, it echoed from outside. The simple words and haunting tune brought tears to many eyes. One by one the men stepped forward to face the fire.

They took off their medallions of Artemis, tossing them into the flames. The hymn grew louder, the flames brighter. The red streaks leaped higher and higher; occasionally the fire spit sparks and flakes floated high into the night air. Men fed the fire with dry wood and even dry cow dung.

Firelight bathed Paul's face; tears streamed down his weathered face. At times the fire died down and only highlighted Paul's tears; at other moments, sweat drops from the heat mixed with his tears. He laughed, he patted backs, he embraced his brothers as they walked away from the fire.

Still the men came; still they paused before the fire. A few waited to watch the fire burn, others turned immediately and walked away, only to be hugged or have their hands shaken.

"Praise to the Father! Praise to the Son!" echoed still through the hot night. The non-Christian Ephesians stared in utter amazement at what they considered senseless destruction. Some tried, some pleaded frantically to buy the medallions.

Among the spectators, one man scowled contemptuously, his face locked on Paul. Dark thoughts flooded Demetrius's heart. He knew the nuances of fire; fire was essential for melting down the stockpiles of silver in order to form his well-known figurines. What fools! he thought. What would possess them to do such a thing? Such wealth was being consumed by the fire. Not to mention the blasphemy, the destruction of that which was dedicated to Artemis. He watched the small flakes that rose in the breeze high above the people's heads. This was unbelievable!

Then suddenly a roar went up. He craned his neck for a better view. A young man paused in front of the fire, then raised high above his head a silver statue of Artemis. "I have no medallions to melt," the man screamed, "but I have *this!*" The crowd roared their approval. Even at a distance, Demetrius recognized his workmanship. As the boy turned, slowly showing the object, he waited until he had made a complete circle, then flung the statue into the fire. The impact of the heavy silver figurine sent sparks flying in all directions. The crowd burst into cheers. Now it was clear that people had been holding back; now they brought out the heavier idols, pitching them into the fire.

Delight illumined Paul's face. *Enjoy it!* Demetrius swore under his breath. *You will regret you ever heard of Ephesus. I will crush you into pulp as an act of devotion to Artemis!*

Ephesus had been able to tolerate the Jehovites and, for that matter, the Followers of the Way. Paul had initially added real diversity to the thinking of the Ephesians, who enjoyed debating new ideas.

But Ephesus could not tolerate religious fanatics. Paul had to be stopped. Soon! Demetrius turned and slunk off into the shadowy lane with two of his burliest slaves.

= 36 =

 If Paul had not already had a
reputation in Ephesus, he certainly did after Demetrius
finished with him. Demetrius's efforts were masterful; he
was as fine a craftsman with words as with silver. Now he
smiled with satisfaction at the room packed with colleagues,
competitors, apprentices, and slaves. They murmured
among themselves, exchanging reports of diminished sales.

After Demetrius had left the fire spectacle, he had gone
to find two other silversmiths, Trevius and Caius. Both
grudgingly admitted their misery with sales: statues and
medallions were not selling. At other times these men were
cutthroat competitors bad-mouthing each other's work, un-
dercutting prices. The fire, however, forced Demetrius to
put the rivalry aside. The silversmiths had to be united if
they were going to rid Ephesus of this blasphemous—and
ruinous—Paul.

When Caius finally decided Demetrius's motive was as he
had stated, he led him into his storage rooms and showed
him pounds of unmelted silver and baskets of silver medallions, amulets, bracelets. Caius shook his head. "I'll be
ruined," he said, furiously. He listened with rage as Demetrius described his encounter with Paul and the fire.

"What are we going to do?" Caius asked.

"Do?" Demetrius replied. "We are going to fight back
and hit hard!"

And, almost overnight, word had spread across Ephesus
about this meeting of the silversmiths. Naturally, some
merchants were reluctant to attend; for if they admitted that

they had large stockpiles of unsold goods, that could trigger more competition. A few were reluctant to trust Demetrius. Yet all the craftsmen needed the great equinox festival to bring money to their coffers, or it would be a long, lean year.

Demetrius raised his hand to quiet the crowd. "My fellow craftsmen," he beamed as he looked around. The silversmiths, as other crafters, had formed guilds to regulate their trade and to prosper under Roman license. They shared insights with each other, particularly in learning granulation, filigree, or cloisonné inlay techniques. The guild allowed for some measure of specialization; not everyone did the same thing.

Clearly Demetrius was the chief of the Ephesian silversmiths. And while he was anxious to get on with the business of Paul, he did not want this moment to escape. Here, in one room, were all the silversmiths of Ephesus. What better time to display his new creation!

The statue had been placed on a table near Demetrius and had been covered with a dark cloth.

"My fellow silversmiths, I have called you here for a couple of reasons. There has been a rumor among us for a long time of a new figurine. A new statue of Artemis. And the rumor is true. I have seen it. And tonight I want you to see it!" Dramatically, Demetrius pulled the cloth from the statue. The audience gasped. Even those in the back of the room could immediately spot the superb craftsmanship. The silver glistened in the torchlight. Demetrius's smile was almost as brilliant. He chuckled to himself as he examined the faces of his competitors: from astonishment to unbridled jealousy.

Slowly applause broke out; then a fervent chant, "Great is Artemis! Great is Artemis!" Demetrius arrogantly allowed the chanting to increase and intensify. He raised his hand and gutturally screamed, "Great is Artemis!" The silversmiths echoed back, "GREAT IS ARTEMIS!" Abruptly Demetrius dropped his hands and frowned; the group gradually silenced. A man in the crowd spoke out.

"Why is such a fine craftsman as Demetrius sad? You should be rejoicing!"

Demetrius nodded at the planted question. He looked up, his face deliberately contorted. "Why am I sad, you ask? Because there are problems facing silversmiths, great problems. There have crept in among us, unnoticed, enemies of Artemis. Voices who say that Artemis is *not* great. That she is nothing to be praised, nothing to be exalted, nothing to be worshipped!"

Angry murmuring broke out among the men. Demetrius let it go on until he thought the moment was right. He again signaled for silence. He stared at the statue. "I must admit that for a while this season I stopped being a businessman, a merchant, and became a craftsman again. My fingers lovingly created every line." His fingertips hesitated within an inch of the statue as he traced its features. "I wanted something to show my love to Artemis. My devotion. And I conceived this figurine in my mind as my gift to her. I wanted to craft something of such exquisite beauty that no one would *ever* question my loyalty to her.

"I spent so much time on this one statue that I failed to watch my shop, my inventories. I didn't notice that figurines weren't selling as in previous years, that I was overstocked. But then I discovered it. And I began to ask questions of my servants, and of some of you. And I didn't like the answers. Perhaps Ephesians no longer love Artemis!"

"No!" a group loudly shouted back to him.

"Of course Ephesians love Artemis," an old man said, jumping to his feet. "The world comes to our city because we are known for our temple and our devotion to her."

Demetrius took a deep breath. "Paul," he said softly. He repeated the name with a scowl. The third time, he slurred the name. "A Jehovite is blaspheming our god." He let his eyes roll across the crowd evaluating the impact of his words.

"This Jehovite has come among us, supposedly as a tent

maker—along with Aquila and Joshua. This Paul sews tents in the morning, and every afternoon he advocates dissent and blasphemy at Tyrannus's lecture hall.

"At first I thought, 'What could one man do? One lunatic's babbling.' " Demetrius paused to stick out his tongue and growl guttural sounds, incoherently, gaining loud laughter from the audience. "He babbles on and on . . . so I thought, 'Who would pay attention to such a man?' But—" he stopped and stepped closer to the men in the front row. "Juli, do you have more or less figurines unsold than at this time a year ago?"

"More."

"Baius?"

Baius blinked and sheepishly answered, "More."

Methodically Demetrius went around the room gaining the same admissions from each silversmith: large stockpiles of unsold statues and jewelry. Demetrius walked to the front; then turned. "This Jehovite is not harmless. Oh, was I mistaken! Obviously Ephesians are not buying statues because this lunatic and his followers say that the statues are worthless. As worthless 'as dung.' That's what he said. I heard him. It was all I could do to keep from killing him."

Demetrius knew the power of exaggeration—and used it well.

"One scrawny Jehovite has come into Ephesus and singlehandedly wiped out our profits for the year. Some of us, even if we sell our goods during the festival, will have to mark them down, and even then there will be little gain for us. One man, one lunatic is leading our customers astray.

"And not just we are suffering. I have reports from all over Asia Minor. Everywhere this man goes, he blasphemes the city's gods. He actually said, 'No man-made god is a god!' Now you ask him where *his* god dwells, and he will say, 'In my heart.' Can you imagine such a thing? And people believe him!"

"He's a lunatic!" someone shouted. The crowd rumbled angrily.

"But lunatics can be dangerous," Demetrius snapped. "And especially this Paul. He has a way of twisting words. If he keeps up, he is not only a danger to our trade but the temple of Artemis could be discredited." The group stirred restlessly. "And Artemis, who is worshipped throughout Asia Minor, Artemis will be robbed of her divine majesty!" Demetrius had been screaming, and the group ignited under his pathos. Men jumped up angrily waving their fists, pulling their hair, pounding their heads.

"I tell you, this madman must be silenced!" Demetrius shouted. He caught his breath, sensing his effect. The craftsmen were seething with anger, like caged leopards.

"Paul has insulted Artemis. Now, I ask you, not just because you are silversmiths, but because you love her, you adore her, what are you going to do about his insults?"

The roar of the men drowned out his next words. If Paul had walked into the room at that moment, he would have been torn limb from limb and his attackers would have felt justified in doing so. But Demetrius had not finished.

"Great is Artemis!" an old silversmith cried.

"Great is Artemis!" Demetrius screamed, his hand formed into a fist. "GREAT IS ARTEMIS!"

"Paul's not going to get away with this!" Trevius shouted.

"He won't, not if I have anything to do with it," another man cried out.

Demetrius smiled, satisfied. However, in the back, one apprentice glared. He had not joined in the chanting; he had listened carefully to Demetrius and the men. Faltius knew Demetrius's skill as an agitator. Sensing the danger, he waited until he heard someone ask, "What should we do?"

"Beat him! Chase him out," Demetrius snarled.

Now, slowly, Faltius slipped toward the doorway, carefully, so that no one saw him leave. As soon as he reached the street, he tucked his robe into his girdle and broke into a run. Paul had to be warned! He knew these men: day in, day out for two years he had worked in the guild, and his father before him. Demetrius was an evil man! He would not be satisfied unless Paul were killed. Fear gave Faltius wings as he ran. He only hoped he could stay ahead of the mob. Every second counted.

His heart pounded furiously against his chest; he had never run so fast. But every minute ahead of the mob was a minute that favored Paul's escape. Faltius rounded a corner, slipped in a puddle of putrid water, and nearly lost his balance.

Faltius thought his chest would explode with pain. He kept glancing over his shoulders, expecting the mob to be at his heels. He had taken the fastest route he knew; *not much further,* he encouraged himself.

Oh, what a night! he thought. *If my master could see me now, he would kill me. But whatever the consequences to me, Paul has to be warned.* There were courts to hear legitimate complaints. This Demetrius was a tyrant, a madman, a lunatic. Faltius had heard of his pathetic treatment of his slaves, his torturing, his sexual excesses. Faltius burst through the gate, across the yard, and frantically pounded on the door. "Paul! Aquila! Open this door!"

The tenters looked at one another in amazement. The pounding on the door increased.

"Open the door before they break it down!" Joshua exclaimed. Priscilla and Kara exchanged alarmed glances.

Aquila opened the door, and Faltius shoved him out of the way. "Paul! Paul!" he repeated breathlessly. "They are coming to get you. You must hide. Before they get here."

"What?" Paul grimaced. "You aren't making sense." The boy grabbed his side and doubled over in pain.

"They are coming to get you," he said, gasping for every breath.

Paul grabbed him and shook him. "Who is?"

"Demetrius—the silversmiths—they had a meeting tonight—they are coming now—I got a little head start on them! Oh, hurry, sir. Hide!" he pleaded.

Paul gestured to Aquila. "Shut the door!" He bent down to the boy. "Demetrius? Why would Demetrius want to harm me? He's attended the lectures."

"He says—" the boy panted, coughing, "—he says that you have discredited Artemis. That you made people stop buying idols. That you—" he dropped to the floor.

"Quick, get him some water!" Aquila cried out. The boy continued gasping incoherently as Priscilla knelt beside him. When Kara brought the water pitcher, Priscilla dipped her shawl into the water and lightly dabbed the boy's face.

"Oh, please," the boy pleaded, tugging on Paul's robe. "You've got to hide. There isn't much time."

"From what?"

"They will kill you! I have never seen Demetrius so enraged. He cannot be controlled."

"How many men?" Aquila asked, quickly assessing what he could do to protect Paul.

"Fifty, at least; perhaps more. Almost every silversmith in the city was at the meeting." Paul and Joshua shuddered.

"I'm going," Paul said, determined to walk out the door. Aquila grabbed his sleeve.

"Let go of me!" Paul demanded.

"*Where* are you going, Paul? *Where?*"

"I can't risk Marcus or Sarah getting hurt. If I am not here, they will not hurt you."

"But where can you go, Paul?" Before Paul could answer they heard the commotion: yelling, screaming, angry taunting. "We want Paul! We want Paul!" Each repetition grew more intense. Aquila couldn't wait until they came closer. He slipped out of the door to face them. Perhaps he could reason with them. He doubted that, though, as soon as he realized how many there were.

Caius stepped to the front of the mob. He glared at Aquila. "Where is Paul?"

" 'Paul?' " Aquila asked, calmly.

"Yes, Paul—the lunatic. Don't play coy with us, or you'll get some of the same treatment."

"I do not know any lunatic!" Aquila said firmly.

"He stays in your household. He works for you," someone yelled.

"There is a Paul who works with me, yes, but he is not a lunatic. He is a teacher."

"He is a blasphemer!" Caius screamed furiously. The men took up the chant.

Caius stepped within inches of Aquila. "Make it easy on yourself. We don't have a quarrel with you. Where is Paul?"

"Paul is a grown man. He works for me in the mornings. In the afternoons you can find him at Tyrannus's lecture hall. In the evenings he is on his own. He is not a child that I should keep up with him."

"Ahhh!" Caius screamed and spit on Aquila.

Slowly, the door opened behind Aquila, and Priscilla and Faltius slipped out. Eyes riveted on them quickly.

"Where is he?" Caius again demanded. Aquila knew where Paul was—he wished he did not.

"Why do you want him?" He would play for time.

"Because he is a blasphemer! He has ruined our businesses."

"How—could—a tenter do that?" Aquila was deathly afraid, but for Paul and Priscilla and the children, and Joshua and Kara, not for himself. *This alone—and God—sustains me, he thought.*

"Go with him, Jesus!" Priscilla breathed in prayer. Slowly she nudged Faltius and he slipped from her, delicately, a step at a time, inching his way toward the open gate. But Caius kept his eyes on Aquila, trying to intimidate him.

"Are you going to tell me where Paul is?" he grabbed Aquila's robe.

"No!" Aquila said, so sternly that Priscilla half-turned. "No, I will not tell you! And I am ordering you out of my yard. Or shall I call the authorities?"

"Hah!" Caius laughed. "Maybe you would like to taste some of what we have planned for Paul?" He shook Aquila.

Aquila thrust out his chest and took a deep breath. "I didn't know the gymnasia was open this late—but if you would like to match wrestling skills with me, I suppose I could accommodate you!" Caius heard the laughter of the men behind him.

"Wrestling? No, this—" and he punched Aquila hard in the stomach; as Aquila fell forward, Caius brought his fist up hard against Aquila's nose. Priscilla heard the wind escape from her husband as he dropped to his knees. Caius kicked him in the ribs, and Aquila groaned. Now Caius stepped over Aquila, closer to the door, but Priscilla moved to block his approach.

"Get out of my way!" he screamed.

Ignoring her first inclination to kneel by Aquila, Priscilla now knew that only she stood in the way of Paul and the mob. At the same moment, Joshua had his hands full keeping Paul quiet.

"Let go of me!" Paul grumbled, trying to shake free of Joshua's hold.

"Sh!" Kara whispered. "They will hear you!"

Priscilla realized that she had never faced such an angry man. As she looked into his dark eyes, she sensed the hatred, the rage. If Caius shoved her aside, then he would be through the door and at Paul in seconds.

She looked at Faltius, who was almost at the gate. Suddenly, Caius's eyes followed hers and spotted the boy slinking toward the gate. "Faltius!" he shouted. "You little sneak!"

"Run!" Priscilla ordered Faltius. "Tell Paul not to come here." The boy bolted and ran through the gate. Now

Caius assumed the boy was going to warn Paul. *God save him,* begged Priscilla silently, *and reward him!*

"After him," Caius screamed, "he knows where Paul is—" The mob, raving, wheeled to follow Faltius, unfortunately clogging the gate with their bodies. Men swung at each other, pushed, shoved, cursed, and trampled. Priscilla dropped to her knees beside Aquila.

"Oh, Aquila! Are you badly hurt?" she cried.

Aquila groaned, and pulled himself to his knees as the last man made it through the gateway. He could hear the howling mob chasing Faltius.

"What will we do when they figure out they've been tricked?" Priscilla asked. "They'll be back here in a few minutes. Then what?"

"I don't know," Aquila groaned. The door creaked open.

"Oh my!" Kara exclaimed, seeing the blood all over Aquila's robe.

"I tell you that I am going, *now!*" Paul screamed from inside.

"No!" Joshua yelled back. "It's too risky!"

"Risky? The risk is if I stay here. The children or the women could be hurt. Now, let me go."

"Priscilla," Joshua called out. "Come and see if you can talk some sense into Paul. He is determined to get himself killed!"

Through the night air came furious chanting: "Great is Artemis! GREAT IS ARTEMIS!" Paul stepped through the doorway, cocking his head toward the sound. "I must go," he said wearily.

Priscilla seized him with both hands. "No," she said with determination. "You will stay here, at least until we know for sure what is going on!" Priscilla gestured with her head. "Go back inside." Paul wavered.

"I tell you," he said, "I am not afraid of them. I must go." Paul's face flushed with anger. "Woman, you are not my keeper!"

But Priscilla would not give way. Her teeth clenched, she held tight to him.

"I am not ashamed of the Gospel!" Paul pounded his fist against his hand. "I'd preach in Sheol if I thought they would listen."

"Well, that's about what you would be facing if you go!" Aquila stood, holding his side, blood dripping steadily from his nose. "There's a mob out there, some of whom would *kill* for the opportunity to kill you. Besides, they would never quiet down long enough for you to even be heard. Listen to them!"

"I could *make* them hear me. God would give me the power!" Paul stepped closer to Aquila. "Don't you see? This could be my greatest opportunity to preach the Gospel. Priscilla is acting like a woman. I would not be in any real danger—"

"Well," Kara said, drawing herself up to her full height. "Priscilla may be acting like a woman but at least she isn't acting like an ass!"

"Kara!" Joshua sputtered.

"Don't 'Kara!' me!" his wife retorted, not attempting to hide her irritation. "If Paul wants to go down and face that mob and be torn apart, we'll just wait here and try to nurse him back to health—provided, of course, they don't kill him outright."

Paul glared angrily at Kara, his dark eyes flashing.

"Paul," Aquila said, ignoring Kara's outburst. "Those men are not going to listen to you. They would only jeer, scream, hoot. You'd be helpless against so many!" In his frustration, Aquila hit the wall as hard as he could. The chanting rioters could be clearly heard.

"Great is Artemis! GREAT IS ARTEMIS!" The chant echoed across Ephesus like thunder. They chanted without pause, each chant louder than the previous one.

"Paul," Joshua began cautiously. "I think Aquila is right." He walked over to the old missionary and placed his hand on Paul's shoulder. "No one thinks that you are afraid. Anyone who has ever seen you at the baths knows your back is scarred from such battles—"

"I tell you this is my moment—my opportunity," Paul said, pushing aside Joshua's hand. "It's an opportunity to be seized—"

"The only person who will be seized is you, you old hard-head," Kara noted, "and your 'only opportunity' is death!" Joshua motioned for her to be silent. "No, Joshua. I won't hush. Priscilla is right. Paul, you have to listen to reason. We're thinking of what is best for you."

"And for the church," Priscilla added.

"And the church needs a coward for a leader?" Paul grunted.

Aquila slumped, defeated, at Paul's response. Maybe he should not have detained Paul. Maybe he should have allowed him to face the mob. Perhaps he could have silenced them—*perhaps!*

Priscilla wept softly. She had convinced Aquila not to let Paul go. *I should have ignored her,* Aquila thought to himself. *Women have a way of exaggerating danger.*

"They've heard and seen every sort of foul philosopher and pagan spectacle. They've sung and danced to their ten-breasted goddess; they've worshipped idols. How many times have I prayed for an opportunity like this?"

"Paul," Priscilla interrupted. "This is *no* opportunity," she said through her tears. "If God wanted you to speak he'd have given you a quiet audience, at least, not a bunch of wine-crazed fanatics, yelling and ranting—"

"But why, Priscilla?" Paul responded, taking several steps toward her. "Why do they carry on so? Because they are desperate. They do not know the Christ, who brings peace. And how will they ever know if I sit here, day after day, sewing stitches on tents?"

Aquila winced; Joshua shrugged his shoulders.

So they sat in silence; too much had already been said. The last weeks, the almost unbearable tension stirred up among the merchants and silver craftsmen by Demetrius had been too much to endure or ignore. Everywhere they went, they had been jeered, spit on, jostled, taunted. For weeks, Joshua had done all the shopping at the market. One of the men always stayed within eyesight of Priscilla and Kara and the children. Being cooped up with Kara's forthright commentary had not helped. It was like kindling that had been soaked just waiting for the fire.

Paul stiffened. "I have faced mobs before. In Thessalonica, in Corinth, in Pisidian Antioch." Paul broke into a smile. "Why, the whole city," Paul looked away, as if in a trance, "the whole city gathered to hear the Word of the Lord. Oh, how the Spirit came upon us that day! Even the Gentiles listened and believed."

"But, unless I am mistaken, you ended up shaking the dust from your feet and fleeing to Iconium," Joshua reminded him gently. Paul swallowed hard and turned away.

"Yes," he reluctantly admitted.

"And you fled Iconium for Lystra, and Derbe." Joshua continued. "Where will you flee now? Everywhere the Jehovites are looking for you. Now the Ephesians are agitated. Maybe Rufus can find some obscure port for you. Why can't you be content to be a tent maker?"

"Joshua!" Kara gasped. But she had not seen his smile. A twinkle in his eye revealed his intention. Paul turned ready to explode, but the wide smile on Joshua's face disarmed him. He raised his head and laughed heartily. Aquila joined him.

Paul walked a few feet to the doorway, then turned and faced his friends. "Why can't I be content to be a tenter, huh?" He stood for a long moment answering the question in his own mind, going back a long way, retracing his spiritual journey to this moment. "Oh, if only the Ephesians could know Jesus. If only they could taste of the depth of his mercy, the height of his grace, the width of his compassion. If they could only *know!*" Tears streamed down his face. "All their silver idols and figurines and medallions—" he stopped, slowly shaking his head, "never give them even a moment's joy or contentment. Nor will their ecstasies in the arms of some temple prostitute."

A knock at the door silenced Paul. A persistent tapping. Aquila's face turned pale. Someone looking for Paul? If he were found here, the messenger could race to bring back the mob. Priscilla, Kara would be in danger. The knocking intensified. Quickly he motioned to Paul. "Over there!" he gestured with his head. But Paul either didn't understand or did not want to comply. Priscilla reached out and pulled his sleeve. "Please? For Jesus, that you may long preach for Him?" she begged. Paul dropped down, exhausted, onto a sack of hides, and Priscilla pulled a large tent section over him.

Once convinced that Paul was adequately hidden, Aquila opened the door a crack and peered out into the darkness. "Yes?" he said.

"Aquila the tenter?" a soft voice demanded.

"Yes."

"A message for you from Tvia, the aristarch." Joshua pulled Kara close to him. Tvia had recently purchased another large tent from them—the most expensive and elaborate they had ever made.

"And the message?" Aquila asked cautiously, trying to disguise his fear, ready to throw his shoulder against the door if this was a trick.

Tvia had been fascinated by Paul. He had sat for hours, listening to Paul's accounts of his travels as well as the claims of the Gospel—Paul couldn't tell one without the other. These last days, Paul had believed Tvia was close to a commitment. He was so spiritually hungry—why else did he show up day after day? Of course, Tvia explained that he was merely checking on the progress of the tent, but Paul felt sure the man was a God seeker, and soon to become a Follower of the Way.

"My master warns, 'Don't allow Paul to come out. *No matter what!*' He says to keep him hidden and quiet for a few days until this blows over. But he must not further outrage or irritate the Ephesians."

"Is that all?" Aquila asked, puzzled.

"He also said to tell you to tell Paul that he likes both the tent and the tent makers." The messenger melted away into the night.

"Someone may have followed him," Priscilla said, frightened.

"I didn't see anyone," said Aquila, peering into the darkness.

Paul stood, rubbing his knees. "I'm getting too old for stooping and bending. I feel like a coward under those tents."

"But you heard the message?" Aquila asked. Paul nodded.

"Well, if anyone knows that crowd, it is Tvia," said Aquila decidedly. "Is his opinion enough to persuade you?"

"Yes," Paul answered meekly, exhausted from the tension.

In that moment they heard the silence.

"Listen," Priscilla urged them.

"I don't hear anything," Kara answered, thinking she meant someone outside the door.

"Nor I," Paul mumbled, twisting his head so that his good ear was toward the east. Because the shouting had gone on so long, the silence was now as alarming.

"What's happening?" Joshua said. Then a loud roar broke the silence. Furious sounds, screaming, yelling, followed. The earlier commotion had not been nearly as deafening. The chants resumed, more intensely than before. How could that be possible? Priscilla wondered. How long could their voices hold out? She bowed her head and prayed. She didn't realize she was praying aloud. "Oh, Jesus, whatever's happening, *please* protect Faltius."

"And protect us, too," Aquila concluded her prayer. The little band stood with their arms around each other in the heavy darkness, waiting. Waiting and praying for God to send His light, His dawn.

The morning brought news that Faltius had escaped the mob and that Roman authorities had finally dispersed them. Demetrius had been humiliated.

⹀ 37 ⹀

The others had slipped away; just Paul and Priscilla were left. Paul glanced at her, then away. She saw his lips quiver.

He was leaving again. And she suspected that she would never see him again.

The festival to Artemis had ended, as had the agitation of the silversmiths. Paul had agreed to visit Greece. True, Ephesians still talked about the riot. Eripo had persuaded the Roman authorities that it would not happen again. "Hotheaded fools," he had explained, openly pointing the finger of blame at Demetrius. The Romans, disgusted, had made clear that the next time Demetrius put on "a party," he would end up in a Roman salt mine. In chains.

Paul remained aloof. He had not returned to the lecture hall. Mornings he sewed; afternoons he prayed and dictated. Aquila couldn't complain about the dictation taking up too much of Priscilla's time—there was no tenting work to be done. The Ephesians were boycotting them. At night Paul played with Sarah and Marcus, spending time tossing Marcus into the air while the little boy squealed in delight. Sarah would tug his robe and plead, "Now me!"

"I want a strong church here," Paul informed Priscilla, one hot afternoon. "Someday no one will remember Artemis. But they will remember the Ephesian Christians."

"Not everyone would agree with you about that," she said, glancing up from the papyrus. Then she bent forward to blow on the wet ink.

"You saved my life," Paul said firmly.

Priscilla blushed. "Paul," she admonished him, "don't bring that up—"

"No! It is you who should be able to accept the truth. If you hadn't sent Faltius running, those ruffians would have broken through the door, and I would have—" he looked away without completing his statement.

"The angels would have protected you."

"Angels?" Paul scratched his beard as he pondered her response. "Angels."

"Did not angels blind the men who threatened to break into Lot's house? Did we not read that they wanted 'to break down the door to get at the men'?" Paul nodded. What a memory for Scripture she had!

"But in the time of the judges, that did not happen." Paul stood and stretched and rubbed his arms. "Remember the story of the Levite and his concubine. When the old man invited him to spend the night and the men of Gibeah surrounded the house, no angels appeared to save them. The concubine died—"

"I do not like that story," Priscilla said curtly. "It seems so unjust the way women were treated then." She fingered the stylus. "And even now."

"And how are women treated so badly?" Paul chuckled. "Do you not have food to eat? a roof over your head? a husband who loves you?"

"But who also wishes I would be quiet and submissive." Priscilla's tone revealed more than her words.

"Like Kara?" Paul chuckled again. "He's come a long way since I first met him in Corinth."

"But there are days he's still—" she shifted on the bench.

" 'Very much a man,' you were going to say." Paul looked into her eyes.

"Yes."

"Priscilla, you must be patient."

"I try. And, oh, I sometimes feel as if angels are here today, when I remember your words that you wrote to the

Galatians: 'There is neither Hebrew nor Greek, slave nor free, male nor female, for you are *all* one in Christ Jesus. Did you not mean that?"

Paul smiled gently at her. "Certainly, I did. You must see, Priscilla, that Aquila is like a son to me. It takes time to change the ways a man has been taught. And there are always new men coming to Christ, who bring their culture with them. For example, those pillars that line the great avenue. That avenue wasn't built overnight. And if it were destroyed, someone would rebuild it."

"So?" Priscilla asked impatiently.

"So, ideas in our minds are like that. They take a long time to build. And ideas take even longer to die. Ideas don't vanish overnight. Give Aquila time."

"But Paul, what if you were a woman?"

"I would probably be more outspoken than Kara!" Paul grinned. Priscilla laughed, delighted. He asked, "How can I possibly imagine what I would feel like if I were a woman? I have no idea!"

"That's why Peter and some of the others fought so hard over the circumcision issue, isn't it? I mean, what if they had been able to insist that all Christian men be circumcised?"

"The Way would have become just another sect following Jehovah, like the Sadducees or the Pharisees. Only the Way would not have survived." He cleared his throat. "Priscilla, the night Caius's mob came here, why were you not afraid? I mean, most women would have been. Yet you stood up to them, even ignoring Aquila's pain."

"The Lord gave me strength."

"Then He will give you strength in the days ahead to endure patiently those who think women ought to remain in the background with the children."

"And definitely not writing letters to the churches?" Priscilla's smile provoked an answering smile. She sighed, serious again. "Will there ever be a time, Paul, when people will accept letters written by women?" she asked.

"Perhaps. Remember, you were not accepted as a teacher for Apollos. Yet that teaching has spread Christ far past *your* reach, or even mine! In time, your letters also will be recognized. But it will take time."

"The Romans are asking about angels," Priscilla said, looking down at her bit of papyrus. "What shall I tell them?"

"You tell me!" Paul grinned.

"Angels are ministering spirits—" Paul nodded in agreement. "—sent to serve . . . those who will inherit salvation." Then Priscilla repeated her statement, without the hesitations.

"Precisely, Priscilla." Paul clapped his hands joyfully. "Remember, everything you accomplish will be aided by angels . . . sent by a Father who loves you deeply. And angels will preserve your letters as well as guide them to the right readers."

Paul stood. "And now, I am afraid it is time to say goodbye. At least I am alive to say it. You have become my family: you, Aquila, Joshua—and Kara, of course. What would I do without her mothering? And then Marcus and Sarah—"

"Hah," Kara laughed as she walked in. "You won't miss me five minutes, but I," She burst into tears, "will miss you!" She embraced him.

"And if I never see you again," he said, "I will wait for both of you in His presence." His voice trembled as he talked. Priscilla bit her lip and fought the tear flow; finally, all she could do was nod her head. Paul walked over to where Marcus and Sarah were napping. He bent over and kissed each one and stood quietly praying for a moment. He cleared his throat and wiped away his own tears.

Then he walked to the doorway where Aquila and Joshua waited. He lifted one finger toward the heavens and smiled. When he stepped through the doorway, the Ephesian elders of the church grouped around him to form an escort as they walked to the *Fair Wind.*

Paul was greatly loved here, and would be greatly missed; but somehow this young band of believers must grow, must make their own way even in the shadow of Artemis.

= 38 =

Priscilla looked up as Kara entered with a cup of minted fig juice and a piece of goat cheese. "I thought the writer might need a break," Kara said cheerfully. "How is it going?"

"I am almost finished."

"Good," Kara remarked, and Priscilla caught the hint of tension. Priscilla realized she had something she wanted to say.

"Is anything wrong?"

"Not wrong, exactly. But I do need to talk to you."

"About?"

"Well, the shop work. Now that Paul has gone, there is the work of catching up on those back orders. Aquila is out trying to get new business."

"But not being very successful. He was so sad last night. He would hardly talk."

"The same with Joshua," Kara lamented. "These Ephesians won't forget. We may be the best tent makers in the world, but our opposition to Artemis makes them feel righteous in boycotting us."

"But we can beat any other craftsman's price!" Priscilla protested.

"They are proud to pay more, to revenge themselves on us."

"Well, something will surely work out."

"That's easy for *you* to say," Kara snapped. When she started to walk away, Priscilla called her name.

Kara didn't answer immediately; finally, after a sigh, she

said angrily, "You're spending all your time writing or teaching the young converts. And . . ." she hesitated.

"And?" Priscilla encouraged her to go on.

"Well, it means more work for me. I know your letters are important, but I have to do all my work *and* all of yours *and* look after the children. Sarah's into everything, and I can't keep my eyes on her all the time—"

Priscilla lowered her head and stared at the markings on the papyrus. She had spent a lot of time on this letter, more than on previous ones. She wanted to be precise, accurate in writing the young believers in Rome. She wanted to encourage them to be faithful and patient.

"I'm sorry, Kara. I haven't meant to neglect my work or Sarah."

"It's just that you get so wrapped up in these letters."

"Sit down," Priscilla patted the space beside her on the bench. Kara resisted. "Just a moment or so, so that you can go rested back to your—I mean, *our* work. You're entitled to that!"

"Oh, all right," Kara said, reaching for a bit of cheese. "This will be my lunch."

"I have something I want you to hear."

"Now, what would I know about—"

"Just listen." Priscilla smiled lovingly at the older woman. Then she ran her finger along the papyrus until she found the place she wanted to begin reading. She cleared her throat.

" 'Keep on loving each other. Entertain strangers, for by so doing some people have entertained angels without knowing it.' "

"Paul?" Kara asked, wonderingly. "An angel?"

"What if we had turned him away when Rufus brought him by? Where would we be today without his influence on us? How blessed we've been!"

"Well," Kara said, "there certainly would not have been as much excitement in our lives. All that ruckus with Caius and Demetrius would never have happened, and we would probably still be in Corinth."

"But," Priscilla interrupted to reach out and pat Kara's knee, "think how dull, how boring it would have been!"

"How *safe!*" Kara laughed.

"Oh, Kara, we were never really in danger."

"Ha! 'Never in danger,' she says."

"We weren't," Priscilla protested.

"Priscilla, what are you talking about? We could all have been killed. You saved our lives!" Priscilla shook her head no. "No, it's true . . . if you hadn't kept your head . . ."

"Saving our lives is too strong. They wouldn't have killed us, just roughed us up."

"Priscilla! If you had not sent that boy running toward the amphitheater, those ruffians would have—" she looked away and sat quietly.

" 'Remember those in prison,' " Priscilla resumed reading, " 'as if they were fellow prisoners, and those who are mistreated as if you yourselves were suffering.

" 'Marriage should be honored by all, and the marriage bed kept pure, for God will judge the adulterer and all the sexually immoral.' "

Kara shook her head approvingly. "You need to read that to some of our neighbors. All that—" she shuddered. "To hear Neti describe those orgies, all in the name of a god. Young girls, boys," Kara's voice trailed off.

"Yes, Neti," Priscilla said gently. How she had prayed for the dark little girl, the wife of Demetrius. How odd that two women whose husbands were enemies should become friends. Although Neti was now forbidden to talk with her, there were those moments at the baths when the eyes spoke eloquently. Yet, now in Demetrius's household a Christian believer—Neti—nursed a baby son. Neti's prayers for a child had been answered. Would that son take his father or his mother's faith? Priscilla wondered.

When Priscilla had questioned Paul closely about this

turn of events, he had responded that children were part of the natural order. God wasn't rewarding Demetrius or ignoring his part in the rioting. But there had been a slight twinkle in Paul's eyes as he talked about the believers in "Caesar's household." He said to Priscilla, "Maybe the boy will grow up to be an Ephesian Moses!" Even the thought delighted the tenters.

Priscilla longed for time to be with Neti, to teach, to encourage, to talk. She realized that it must be difficult at times for Neti when she could not fill Demetrius's demands. But God would keep mother and son safe in the presence of evil.

Priscilla took a deep breath and resumed reading. " 'Keep yourselves free from the love of money and be content with what you have.' "

"Ah," Kara laughed, amused. "That's our men! Free from the love of money!"

" 'And be content with what you have because God has said, "No way will I leave you, never will I—' "

"Forsake you?" Kara asked. Priscilla nodded and continued. " 'So, we say with confidence, "the Lord is my helper. I will not be afraid. What can man do to me?' "

"Is that what you were thinking when you confronted Caius?" Kara asked.

"I don't know for sure what I was thinking. Just that Paul had to be saved. But Kara, it's true. If the Lord is my helper what *can* man do to me or to you?"

"Well, we may find out in the next few weeks." Kara stood quickly. "I'd love to listen to more but the men will be wanting their lunch so they can go hear Gaius at the lecture hall. Maybe later this afternoon you can read some more to me."

Priscilla nodded and then resumed her reading, pausing to scrutinize certain words and phrases.

" 'Remember our leaders who spoke the Word of God to you. Consider the outcome of their way of life and imitate their way. Jesus Christ is the same yesterday and forever.' "

Priscilla repeated the last "forever." Yes, that was what Paul had said but she felt uncomfortable with it. She admired the brilliant blue sky for a moment and tried to remember Paul's face as he spoke those words. Suddenly, the thought struck her: "yesterday, *today,* and forever."

She examined the papyrus. Yes, she could squeeze in the word *today.* She picked up the stylus and carefully wrote in the word. " 'Jesus Christ is the same yesterday, today, and forever!' " she read with conviction. Yes, her heart echoed.

Priscilla rubbed her eyes. Paul had repeatedly taught that Jesus never changes—whatever our circumstances, Jesus remained changeless. *If that is true and if one considers the way Jesus treated women, then I can be confident in my teaching.* She looked back at the papyrus.

" 'Do not be carried away by all kinds of strange new teachings.' " Her finger slowly followed the line of words. " 'It is good for our hearts to be strengthened by grace, and not by ceremonial foods, which are of no value to those who eat them.' "

She quickly scanned the section on the high priest, nodding at word choices, and then stopped—struck by the words.

" 'For here we do not have an enduring city, but we are looking for a city that is to come.' " *Oh, how true,* Priscilla mused. *How true!* Rome, Corinth, Ephesus—and if the boycott held, they would have to move again. If only they could return to Rome! Nostalgia swept over her. Again she felt the waves slapping against the sides of the *Fair Wind.* She could smell the sea breezes, and she saw her grandfather's villa and her family. *Rome, oh, Rome!* she cried out in her heart. *To be home. To see Junius and his babies; my mother.* Priscilla's heart throbbed with memories.

Ever since Paul had left, Priscilla had been overwhelmed by a longing for Rome. She had shared the feelings one night with Aquila, but he had laughed at her until he realized how serious she was. He had pulled her tightly against him, and felt her tears splash onto his chest. He had kissed her eyelids, Priscilla remembered with a smile, "to drive away the tears."

I will always cry for Rome, Priscilla thought, feeling her eyes blur with tears. *How can I forgive these Ephesians? How can I sleep comfortably, trustingly, even with Aquila lying beside me? I will never feel safe again in Ephesus. Never!* Priscilla sighed. *But I must be content.* For a long time she let her mind drift, like the great clouds that billowed across the Ephesian sky that afternoon. *We will survive by His leading and protection.*

When she finally looked at the last line of the letter, she smiled. " 'We are sure that we have a clear conscience and desire to live honorably in every way.' "

"It's not right having a woman teach!" she could hear Aquis's angry voice and see him as he thrust his finger at her, angrily arguing the issue with Paul. Aquis, though a Follower, had such strong feelings against women—and how his poor little wife cowered in his presence! Priscilla smiled as she remembered how staunchly Paul had defended her gifts.

"Oh, my brother," Paul had insisted. "There are no males or females in Christ Jesus. Perhaps *you* would like to be my scribe? Perhaps *you* are so well trained with the stylus —" but Paul's words had only angered Aquis. She remembered the way he had glared at her and the way he had needled Aquila on so many occasions. Years before, Aquila might have reacted childishly, and would have forbidden her to write. But not now.

I speak to my own people. Not just the Ephesians, but also those within the household of faith. Maybe if I had such a clear experience as Paul had on the road to Damascus, maybe that would have exhausted the objections to my fitness to teach. True, there had been that moment below deck on the *Fair Wind* when all the grain had shifted and she and Marcus had been trapped. *But I need something now,* she thought. *Some new path to follow.*

The thought struck her. *I* do *have something. I have a clear conscience, void of offense.* She looked down at the space that remained. She always struggled with closing the letters, wanting to get in every word, yet anxious not to launch a new idea that she could not develop. She stood and stretched. Words began tingling in her heart, then phrases. She paced as she considered their order. Then she sat down and began to write. *"May the God of peace—oh, yes, peace, who through the blood of the covenant . . ."* She stopped. Better make that *"eternal covenant brought back from the death of our Lord Jesus."* She sighed. *If only I could write more quickly.* She wanted something to praise Jesus, a title the Roman readers could appreciate. She tapped the stylus nervously against the edge of the table. Then she heard a sheep baa. She had an answer! *Shepherd. "That great Shepherd."* She looked back at the sentence.

"Our Lord Jesus, that great Shepherd of the sheep," she wrote, *"equip you with everything for doing his will and—"* That's what my grandfather did, all those afternoons of studying and drilling and reciting, while other girls were playing, he prepared me for this.

"And may He work in us what is pleasing to Him, through Jesus Christ." She stopped. Yes, that said what she wanted to say. *If we do the works that are really pleasing to Him, He will abide with us.* She reread the words rapidly, smiling. Finally, she added, *"to whom be glory and honor forever! Amen!"* She put down the stylus and smiled. Yes. Yes. Yes.

The words were precise; accurate; helpful. The letter was finished. Now she could enjoy a few moments of quiet before she joined Kara to prepare the evening meal. But as soon as she shut her eyes to listen to the wind in the olive tree, she heard Aquila calling from the gateway.

"Priscilla!" he called impatiently, banging the gate. "Priscilla!"

"In here," she answered. Now what was wrong? His voice resonated with excitement.

"News! I've got news!" he shouted happily. As he rushed into the yard, his face beamed. He must have a tent order, she thought. She had not seen him so happy in weeks. Maybe the boycott was over!

"What news?" she asked, holding out her arms to him.

"We're going home!" exulted Aquila, embracing her.

Priscilla began to tremble. She pushed her cloud of red-gold hair back and stared at his jubilant face.

"We're going home!"

"Rome!" she whispered. "Truly, Rome?" He kissed her, and swung her around playfully.

"Rome! To build the church, to build a life," he answered joyfully.